Overcoming his initial shock, Charlie finally asked of the woman, "I'm sorry, you said something about the ground?"

"I said you are standing on hallowed ground."

"What's that supposed to mean?" Charlie responded, with just a touch of an edge to his voice. He wasn't thrilled about being startled by anyone, even if it was Carol Harmon, the good-looking superstar. *No, extremely fine looking superstar*, he quickly corrected himself. Begrudgingly, he admitted that she was even better looking up close, which was unusual, in and of itself, and she looked very alluring in her faded jeans.

Taking a step closer to Charlie, Carol continued, waving her left arm toward the burned out hulk. "That's a church, or was a church, thirty-five years ago. It was burned to the ground with a hundred people inside of it. No one survived. This place is hallowed ground now."

Charlie twisted up his face into a partial grimace, looked around the cleared area and said, "From the looks of the place, the litter and all, you are the only one who considers it hallowed anything. Looks to me like everyone else just uses it as a dumping ground."

Looking deeply into his eyes—*blue*, she thought, *maybe gray*—Carol persisted, "Just the same, it's hallowed ground. Any place Christian people die in faith is hallowed. I can't account for the other people in the area. How they treat the place or what they think of it. Take my word for it, this is a sacred place."

What They Are Saying About
The Preacher

The Preacher is a complexly woven mystery with a civil rights twist. From the very first page of this book, the reader is drawn into the racially motivated church fire and murders. Immediately, the reader wants to know the how and why of this horrible event and see justice served. Soon, however, the reader finds him or herself completely and deeply involved in a complex web of characters and coincidental events. This book is page turner from start to finish.

—Tracy Farnsworth
Roundtable Reviews

...a story that involves murder, mystery, love and hatred, unbelievable hidden secrets buried deep within this community, and intervention of a higher being to bring to light a truth that was buried so long ago. I will have to tell you, the ending totally surprised and shocked me. It was well worth waiting for. I could never tell you the storyline of this work as it is so complex and carefully woven together that I am unable to give you just bits and pieces of it, and do it justice, but I can tell you the author did an excellent job and his writing skills are superior to many that I have reviewed. To me, this was a story that showed no matter how long it takes, justice will prevail and the truth will be brought to light. Very highly recommended, a story you will not soon forget.

—Shirley Johnson
Senior Reviewer
MidWest Book Review

Other Works From The Pen Of

Robert James Allison

The First Suitor

A computer nerd from rural Indiana, newly hired by the National Security Agency, finds unexpected romance with the daughter of the President of the United States, but the President and the Secret Service aren't feeling romantic.

Scholarly Pursuit Coming July 2005

Mary Benton is an Army MP stationed in Germany and assigned to nursemaid a geeky General's son, but she soon becomes more than his nursemaid; and when terrorists kidnap him she is his only hope.

Wings

The Preacher

by

Robert James Allison

A Wings ePress, Inc.

Mystery/Detective Novel

Wings ePress, Inc.

Edited by: Lorraine Stephens
Copy Edited by: Elizabeth Struble
Senior Editor: Lorraine Stephens
Executive Editor: Lorraine Stephens
Cover Artist: mpmann

All rights reserved

Names, characters and incidents depicted in this book are products of the author's imagination or are used fictitiously. Any resemblance to actual events, locales, organizations, or persons, living or dead, is entirely coincidental and beyond the intent of the author or the publisher.

No part of this book may be reproduced or transmitted in any form or by any means, electronic or mechanical, including photocopying, recording, or by any information storage and retrieval system, without permission in writing from the publisher.

Wings ePress Books
http://www.wings-press.com

Copyright © 2004 by Robert James Allison
ISBN 1-59088-716-6

Published In the United States Of America

December 2004

Wings ePress Inc.
403 Wallace Court
Richmond, KY 40475

Dedication

To all the Preachers of the world,

ordained or not.

One

May 1962

    Inside a little wooden church, high up on a ridge and nestled in a forest of tall pine trees, a preacher mopped his brow with a multi-colored handkerchief and took his stance behind the pulpit. Gazing out over his flock, he declared to himself that he was satisfied with the Wednesday evening attendance. It was cooler in the evenings and with this unusually early heat wave, Wednesday evening services were working out quite well. So although it was eight p.m. and already dark outside, attendance was very good.

    Every window in the church was wide open in an attempt to catch a breeze, any breeze. The solitary floor fan, located below and to the right of the preacher, was clicking and rattling as it strained to grant the faintest of respite from the stifling heat within the sanctuary.

    The preacher waited patiently for the congregation to settle down so that he could begin his announcements. While he waited, he let his eyes wander around the inside walls of the church. It didn't take long for his eyes to completely traverse the meager furnishings; there wasn't much to see. This was a poor congregation and the building reflected that poverty. There were ten rows of pews divided in half by a center aisle. Aside from the pews, the church was bare of other furnishings, save only the necessities, a small organ, a freestanding altar and a pulpit. When he wasn't engaged in leading the worship, the preacher occupied the only other furnishing, a small chair off to the side of the pulpit.

The Preacher
Robert James Allison

Glancing at his watch, he realized that it was time to get on with the announcements and, speaking with his easy southern drawl, he said, "Good evening and welcome to the house of the Lord. I have some announcements, most of which appear in the bulletin, but bear repeating. First of all, don't forget that next Sunday marks the one hundredth anniversary of our church.

"One hundred years ago, a small handful of determined men and women began work on the very building we sit in today. It wasn't much then and it isn't much now, but it always has been the house of the Lord. So mark your calendars, we will hold a special service next Sunday evening at seven p.m. to thank God for His blessings. I hope all of you can attend the service and the picnic that afternoon..."

Smiles abounded and the chatter began anew, as many of the members confirmed to each other that they would be attending the picnic. Over in the 'amen' corner, plans were already being made for next Sunday's festivities. Thinking to himself that he had lost the control he had just gained, the preacher was smiling and nodding, waiting for the right time to resume his leadership position.

While the congregation basked in the glow of the milestone they were about to attain, outside, another glow was forming, an ominous glow, not yet seen by those inside the church. The glow outside was not figurative; it was real. This glow was being spread by shadowy, fleeting figures, as well as by the gentle breeze stirring the tops of the great pine trees surrounding the old church. The breeze aided the shadowy figures unknowingly, it knew nothing of the motives and intentions of men, it neither plotted nor acted in furtherance of a plot, it merely blew.

The figures that dashed around the outside of the church, just below the windows and out of the view of the congregation, did plot and they plotted in the most perverse ways. In furtherance of their plot, they were now engaged in its execution. The ominous spreading glow had its origin from a ring of fire. A liberal application of kerosene ignited by well-placed torches had caused the ring of fire to spring to life. That breeze, the floor fan was trying so hard to catch, was stirring more than the tree tops, it was also stirring the now rapidly spreading flames and breathing more life into the ever growing ring of fire.

By the time the congregation became aware of the flames, it was already too late. This nearly one hundred-year-old wooden church contained well-seasoned wood. That seasoned wood was covered with a liberal coat of oil based paint applied every three years without fail.

Inside the church, the construction contributed to the disaster, almost as much as the seasoned wood and the paint. In order to save costs, but still seat as many people as possible, there were no side aisles provided. Since no side aisles existed, all the members had to enter and exit the pews from the center aisle, in an orderly process supervised by the two ushers who were always in attendance. No one had ever thought about what might happen during a fire, when the ushers weren't likely to be supervising the exit and when the members weren't likely to be amenable to supervision, but were in chaos.

Such was the case now. By the time the flames were clearly visible above the windows, the gentle breeze, coupled with the noble effort of the floor fan, coaxed them inside. As a result, even the few people having the presence of mind to make a dash to safety through nearby windows, were trapped. The heat was so intense just moments after the first torch touched the kerosene that the paint on the inside walls was bubbling. Even before realizing the danger, there was nothing the congregation could do; their collective fates were sealed. They would all see Jesus this very evening, in a matter of moments, if not seconds. Some could already see Him.

Outside, a half dozen men, having consummated their perverse plot, gathered in a loose knot under a not so nearby pine tree. The heat was overbearing and building steadily as they watched the result of their deed. A few screams were faintly audible over the roaring of the flames, as they leapt higher and higher, until not one portion of the church was visible. It was clear to the men, without a word spoken among them, that their goal was accomplished. They knew without a doubt that not one small part of the church, or one small person, would escape the fire, save a small out building made of brick, sitting well into the trees south of the church.

The men weren't forgetting the out building, it hadn't been overlooked, it just wasn't important to their plot. The little building was for storage of lawn care tools and occasionally, albeit surreptitiously, to house some vagabond for a night. It was not worth the effort to try to burn. Besides, its destruction wouldn't make any statement and these men were here to make a statement.

Backing steadily away now, the men continued to gaze at the church, fascinated by the completeness of their handiwork. As they backed away, they passed a bottle between themselves and bantered with each other in a drunken chatter. These were young and rebellious men, who often felt the need to exercise their freedom by oppressing others. Tonight was such a night and the liquid courage made them all the more rebellious.

For a few more minutes they watched the fire burn uncontrollably and saw it engulf two cars that were parked close to the church. There weren't many cars here, mostly trucks and not that many of them. Most of the people who attended this church walked to the services and those who lived too far away to walk, rode with someone else. Not many of the members could afford a vehicle and those who could, shared their good fortune. All the cars and trucks now sat abandoned, those that weren't eventually consumed by the fire would be collected later, by someone, a relative, the sheriff's office, someone. The cars, like the little out building, were just inconsequential items not germane to the statement.

"Better get out of here before someone shows up. The place is done for anyway," one of the men said, while backing away from the heat.

With a drunken slur another man put in, "I want to see the finish. I want to see the whole place fry with everyone in it."

"We all do, but we talked about that already. We can't stand here and take the chance that someone will show up."

Passing his bottle to another, the slurring drunk said, "Okay, but we can come back. No one will know we was here at the start if we come back," laughing now, he continued, "it'll look like we was trying to help. Ain't that choice? Like we was trying to help."

Nodding in unison, without saying a word, the six men agreed that the plan to return sounded good. They would do that now. They faded as one into the trees and outlying brush. Soundlessly, the men rushed across the soft layer of pine needles and reached the safety of their own cars, sitting unattended, some two hundred yards from the church. Compared to the heat they had been subject to only minutes earlier, the hot May air felt cool and they quickly climbed into their cars. The noise of six car engines turning over almost as one, broke the silence of the forest.

The men were in a hurry now, but despite their concerns, it was unlikely anyone would respond in force to a fire this far out. Possibly some local resident would come to investigate the blaze, after all, not all the locals attended this church and each man knew he didn't want to be seen. At least not until it looked like they were only trying to help.

As it turned out, the men needn't have bothered planning their approach by car so carefully. No one responded. The few locals who were still at home, stayed at home, and though they knew something catastrophic was happening, they did not venture outside. It wasn't that they didn't care, it was that they couldn't care, not now. Later they would go to investigate, but not now. These were tumultuous times in the South, not times to stick your nose in where, even if it belonged, it might get broken. There were violent men roaming the towns and surrounding hills, men who would stop at nothing to make their point and impose their will on others. Such was evident by the large conflagration glowing in the distance this night. Everyone who had eyes could see what was happening in the distance, they didn't need to get any closer. They knew what was located beneath the glow, or rather, what used to be there.

When they were back in the parking lot of the church, the men gathered in front of their cars a respectable distance from the fire, still passing their bottle back and forth. They were joking, laughing, yelling and hollering as if this were a New Year's Eve celebration.

"Wow! Look at that baby burn!" one man exclaimed and the others hooted in satisfaction.

"Man, it's still getting hotter. I didn't think it could get any hotter. Hey look! There she blows!"

Every one of them looked up to see the roof falling in and the walls collapsing upon themselves. A giant ball of showering sparks spiraled in the rising heat, leaping several hundred feet into the air and spreading hot embers all over the surrounding forest.

"Uh oh. Watch out for the trees. Oh man, I hope it don't catch the forest," one of the men almost whimpered and the looks on the faces of the others showed ready agreement.

Nervously, the men glanced at each other, as none had reckoned on the severity of the fire. That they had just destroyed a quaint little church that would in other times be considered a historic building, concerned them not at all, not to mention the one hundred people who had been burned alive. No, it was the forest that concerned them. What if the forest caught fire? They hadn't considered that, the forest was valuable to them. They hunted in these hills and they cut the trees for firewood and lumber, lots of other people did too. The forest couldn't burn, the men knew they would be in serious trouble if any one found out that they had started a forest fire. Ironically, they could almost talk their way out of burning the church, but not the forest.

Some trees had already caught, but they were the few left in the broad expanse of the church lawn. Those trees weren't a part of the forest. Those isolated trees now burned like Roman candles as the pine needles burst into flames and the sap from the trunks ignited like hot oil poured on a campfire. The men were having no trouble imagining what the forest would look like if it caught fire. Each man silently prayed that the forest would not catch fire; the church and the people inside were their target, not the forest.

The irony of burning to death a church full of people, yet praying to God that trees not be burned, was lost on them. Not that these men were stupid, it was a matter of perspective. The men only knew that the forest meant something to them and that the little church didn't. After all, the people in that church weren't like them, they weren't the same; they were less than real people, not quite human.

A gentle rain began to fall as the men held their breath and watched the sparks descend upon the nearby forest. The rain wouldn't put out a fire, not the church or the forest, if it had caught already, but it could prevent the forest from catching fire. Though it had been unseasonably hot this year, it had not been unseasonably dry and with this additional rain, it might be that their prayers would be answered.

As they continued to watch, the fire began to diminish perceptively and the heat they had noticed earlier was now less intense. Less prevalent also were the sparks, and instead of drifting toward the trees they were swirling in place over what was left of the church. There would be no spreading of the fire to the forest, the men now realized and, as if in agreement, the rain began to pelt them all the harder.

With satisfaction and relief evident on their faces, they all realized that the fire was definitely waning now and the sparks were subsiding as the rain continued to fall. The rain would cool the remains of the church, but even with the rain the fire would burn all night and smolder all the next day. The show was over. Turning now for their cars, their statement having been made, it was time to go home and wait to hear what the rest of the world would have to say about their statement. As they reached their respective cars, five of the men climbed in, started their engines and immediately spun around and down the gravel lane to the main road.

One man stopped just short of the driver's side door of his spanking brand new 1962 Ford Mustang and looked back with what seemed to almost be regret, but it wasn't, not really. The man was merely curious. His attention was drawn back to the fire by the hissing of the rain as it fell upon the hot coals of the meager remains of the church. A fleeting thought passed through his alcohol-fogged brain that God had sent the rain, not to save the forest, but to cleanse the little church and the charred remains of the bodies inside. Cleanse them of what and for what he didn't know. Surely God didn't care about those people, why would He? After all, those people weren't chosen like he was, they were Negroes.

Two

August 1997

Mark Fribley liked Johnson City, it was small, but not too small and it had that country flavor. Plus the fact, that since it was a small town, it was as cheap to rent a small house than an apartment and a house was much less confining. In a bigger city he would have been stuck in some little one-bedroom apartment for the same amount of rent he was paying now. Having a house meant a garden, though he wasn't much of a gardener, it was fun to watch the meager plants he put in each spring grow, along with the weeds that he rarely got around to controlling. He had a yard to mow, too, that was good and bad, but once mowed, it was nice to sit on the expansive front porch of the little, one-story, white, clapboard house and smell the freshly cut grass.

The best part of all though was the room he had inside the house. Single and only twenty-five, he didn't need a lot of room. He had no kids, no wife, no live-in girlfriend, no girlfriend at all, but he did need to have a large work area for his computer equipment, of which he had plenty. He had always told himself he didn't need a girlfriend, so long as he had his computer equipment and his job working on computers at the Tieman Textile Mill, but he had not totally convinced himself of that. Especially now that he had seen Janet Longrade up at the mill. She was an executive secretary for a Mr. Willis up on the sixth floor of the headquarters building, single, blonde, blue eyes, five foot seven, one hundred thirty pounds and really hot looking, according to the photo in the file and his later observations. Mark knew, because he had hacked the personnel computer at work and read her file with great interest. All on the up and up, of course, he was in charge of setting up all the computers and installing all the software for TTM and he had to check for security breaches, so occasionally he hacked systems to see if the security could be breached. While performing his duties to the utmost of his abilities, he just accidentally, on purpose, happened to come across Janet's file, and it made very interesting reading. Not that he had any idea that a hot looking chick like her would have anything to do with a geek like him, but he could dream, and he did. From afar he watched her come gliding into the TTM parking lot in her cherry red Mustang and he told himself that the chance to see her made going to work even more appetizing, as if it was necessary to motivate Mark to work on computers.

Actually, Janet Longrade had been around the mill longer than Mark's three years, but he had, for some reason or other, not noticed her, as hard as that was for him to grasp. He guessed he just hadn't been lucky enough to be looking when she came to work, now that he knew when and what to look for, he saw her all the time. He was quite sure she had never seen him or at least never noticed him if she had. He was just a computer geek, with heavy glasses, who locked himself in the basement of the headquarters building, for eight or more hours a day, staring at computer screens. That's why he wore heavy glasses; he was near sighted from all those years of staring at computer screens. He could see the computer screens and the circuit boards, but across the room things got fuzzy, hence the glasses. No big deal, he wasn't a vain person anyway, computers didn't care what he looked like, and he was quite sure that Janet Longrade didn't even know he existed. She was just a dream, but a nice dream, very nice.

Standing up and stretching his tall frame, he bent toward the porch railing and tossed the remains of his coffee onto the lawn. *Time to get up to the mill,* he said to himself, *got to be there before Janet rolls in. She might have that short blue skirt on today, nice, very nice.* As he turned to enter the front door of his house, out of the corner of his eye he caught the whir of a car out on State Route three. *Cops*, he mused, *always in a big hurry.*

~ * ~

Rolling through the last stop sign in town and turning right on State Route three, Sergeant Todd Evans rapidly accelerated the Ford Town Car to seventy-five mph. Punching the cruise control 'on' button, he then hit 'set' in almost the same motion. A second later, he was pulling his right foot off the accelerator pedal and bringing it back toward the seat to flex his knee. He appreciated the size of the Town Car, but it still cramped his long frame and he took every opportunity to use the cruise control so that he could move his legs.

Sergeant Sam Pinehurst sat passively in the right front seat with his seat belt off. If Todd's driving bothered him, he didn't let on; he knew that cops were the worst drivers in the world. They came by it naturally, after all, as a practical matter they were immune from traffic arrests and they were always in a hurry to get to the scene of a crime or traffic accident, or a coffee break. Cops were generally too busy enforcing the law to live the law.

This time though, there should have been no hurry, they weren't on a call and Todd wasn't heading for their favorite coffee shop. Sam wasn't certain, but he had a good idea where Todd was heading. Still, as far as Todd's driving was concerned, it didn't matter where they were heading. Cops drove the same wherever they were going, besides, it was fun and they needed some fun once in a while. In their line of work, they encountered too many things that were down right depressing. Like where Sam was fairly sure they were going now.

Sam eased back in the seat, reached up with his right hand and adjusted the air conditioner vent to strike him precisely in the center of his chest. *Man it's hot*, he thought. He wasn't sure he'd get out when Todd stopped, wasn't anything to see anyway, if Todd were going where Sam suspected. Todd was a good partner and had been for years, but he had a hang up about one particular place that Sam would just as soon not visit.

"You headin' up to that there church again, Todd?"

No response was forthcoming and Sam wasn't surprised, Todd didn't talk much when he was in this mood, on his way to 'the church'. It was like he was somewhere else, doing something else, with someone else. He was a good partner though, a good man in a scrap, he never quit, he never ran and he never would. A man could do a lot worse in the way of partners and Sam wasn't about to trade Todd over a hang up about an old burned out church.

Turning off of the state road now, the car slid slightly until it caught the gravel road and once again Todd accelerated, climbing the long grade toward Burning Chapel Hill, although not to over forty mph. The old gravel road was narrow and washed out in some places, so it didn't pay to go too fast. This road only went to one place and was rarely used, excepting for the occasional lovers, hunters and sightseers.

With ease, the Town Car handled the steady incline until at last it topped out onto a slight plateau. Todd spun the wheel and made a sharp right-hand turn into what once was a gravel parking lot, but now was covered with grass and littered with trash, discarded by the occasional car full of sightseers or hunters. Todd stopped the car on the far side of the old parking lot and with a determined effort, climbed out. Despite the August heat, Sam got out too, after all, Todd was his partner; they rode together, through the good and the bad.

Sam walked over beside Todd and stared blankly at the burned out church. There wasn't much to see, as Sam had known there wouldn't be, just a few charred timbers from the roof and a few supports that used to form the walls. A few stones which had once comprised the foundation still stood together, but most of the foundation was widely scattered, some by the state fire investigators, some by vandals, some by kids just horsing around and some by Todd.

Todd was standing shoulder to shoulder with Sam, looking over the old church once again. The area was so badly overgrown with grass and weeds that all except a small part of the black hulk was invisible from more than fifty feet away. No brick chimney peeked up over the ruins like one could see when a burned out building was depicted on TV. This little church hadn't even had a chimney. There had been a small pot bellied stove that warmed the single room church on the coldest nights. The only things sticking up around here were a few blackened trunks from the burned pine trees that had once dotted the spacious church lawn. Those trees had died in place, just like the people in this church, never to live again.

Looking around the tree line now, Sam noted that the little brick outbuilding was still standing, but its roof was gone, or at least there wasn't enough left to matter. All of the glass in its solitary window was long ago broken out. Soon, the little brick building, the only building untouched by the fire, would also be destroyed, not in the spectacular manner that the church was, but destroyed just the same.

Eventually, even the burned out hulk of the church would disappear, claimed by nature, like everything and everyone else. *Would Todd come here then?* Sam wondered, and by way of answer to his own question, he said aloud, "You'll never stop coming here will you?"

"Yes, I'll stop one day," Todd responded, listlessly.

"When?"

Hesitating, to bring his mind back to the present, more than to form a reply, he finally said, "When I find the people who did this and why."

Disgustedly, Sam shot back, "The 'why' you know, but how are you going to find the 'who'? We've been all over this place with a fine-toothed comb and so have the fire guys, the lab techs and every arson expert you could find and convince to come up here. For what? We've got nothing Todd, a big fat zero. How are you gonna find who did this? It's been thirty-five years! Give it up!"

"I can't Sam. I can't," he spoke the words with the determination of one embarking on a solemn journey and as he spoke he set his jaw firmly, looking his partner level in the eyes.

"Yeah, I know how you feel. You're black and thirty-five years ago someone fried a hundred black people in this here church. No one investigated it and no one who was anyone back then even cared. I know that eats on ya, but it's going nowhere, Todd, nowhere."

Todd's reply was preceded by an inaudible sigh, "You don't understand Sam, you never have. This isn't about black and white, or the fact that no one even cared enough to investigate the fire for fifteen years. It's about crime. A crime was committed here, a long time ago, and we're cops, sheriff's investigators to be exact. There's no statute of limitations on murder, you know that, we can't quit no matter the odds." Motioning now with his right hand toward the ruins, he continued, "These people can't rest until we do our job, Sam, you just never understood that."

Almost pleading now, since he was so tired of coming to this forsaken and dismal place, Sam cajoled, "How we going to do our job on this one, Todd? The trail's too cold, there's nothing left to follow. Maybe if we could have started on this the day after the fire or if someone else had and left some records, but they didn't and you know why they didn't. To make matters even worse, whoever was in on this has had years to cover up anything that was here. This crime scene was never preserved; relatives even dug out the remains and hauled them off. There were no autopsies, nothing was done.

"You're asking the impossible. Look... I'm white and I know the guys who did this were white too, but I can't do a thing about it. I can't make up for all the things that whites did to blacks thirty or forty years ago. If I could, I would. You and me, we're buds, your color doesn't mean a thing to me. You know that."

"Who's asking you to make up for anything? This isn't about black and white, Sam! Can't you see that? It's about crime!" Todd blurted out, with frustration heavy in his voice.

Sam retorted, "So you say, but it can't help but be about black and white to a certain extent. I tell you it can't be helped. It was black and white, that was the motive and that's all we really know for sure. After all this time, that's all we know. Doesn't that tell you anything?"

Todd looked down, kicked a loose stone and said quietly, "Sam, I've been twenty years trying to get a line on this one and I'm no closer now than I was when I started. I started out a sheriff's deputy on patrol and right then and there I began working on this crime. Ten years now I've been a sheriff's investigator and I'm still no closer than I was as a patrolman. I think you're right, Sam. We have a motive and that's all. Who knows, maybe we'll never have anything else. We've got no more than the guy down the road had, the day after the fire. Even he knew the motive. Back then the motive was always the same, he figured that out and he didn't have the degrees we have."

Sam smiled now and said lightly, "Speak for yourself. All I have is two years at the junior college, no degree. You now, you're the really smart guy here. You got your bachelor's degree in law enforcement and your master's degree in social justice, so speak for yourself Mr. Joe College," he ended, with a broadening smile.

Todd loosened up at that. Sam had a way of loosening him up when he got too tight. Sam was good people, the best of partners; it made the job easier. Todd smiled back and said lightly, in an exaggerated southern drawl, "And don't y'all forget it neither, boy!"

They both roared with laughter and as quickly as that, the tension between them was gone. They turned as one for the car. Todd and Sam were partners and that made them closer than brothers, there were no holds barred between them. Black or white, right or wrong, they were of one mind; they were partners. Forging their bonds into steel was the fact that they were also cops. Cops were strange, often cynical people, who laughed when others cried and cried when others laughed. When they could remember how to cry that is, because more than anything else, cops were realists. It was an occupational hazard. The fact that they were realists, partners and cops, made Sam and Todd something special to each other.

They used words to communicate with each other, but neither ever took offense at what the other might say, nor the words he might use to say it. Someone else now, that was a different matter, but for them and between them, it was anything goes, any time. Both knew they had seen too much and done too much together to be surprised or shocked, especially by themselves. At least that's what they had convinced themselves of many years before. They had discovered that in their line of work, it made it easier to deal with the future if you convinced yourself you couldn't be shocked, that you had seen it all, just in case you hadn't.

~ * ~

His brown hair was speckled with gray and hung down over his ears, but it was clean. He was clean, though his clothes were worn and tattered. He walked slowly and deliberately, with eyes fixed straight ahead as he dragged his right leg ever so slightly. Years ago, when he was much younger, he had broken his leg and couldn't afford proper medical care; in fact, he couldn't afford any medical care, so now it was a little stiff. It was a bit of a nuisance, but it didn't hurt anymore, unless there was a dramatic change in the weather coming, and for him that knowledge had its good points. For one who lived on the streets, the fact that a storm was coming was a good thing to know.

Calling him a homeless person didn't really fit the bill, but he supposed he was the closest thing to one that Johnson City had. There were places for him to stay that weren't on the streets, from time to time he did sleep out, but that was more because he felt like it than because he had no place else. *It hadn't always been that way*, he bitterly recalled.

The man hadn't seen any people actually living on the streets in Johnson City and he was in a position to see them. For a city of almost fifteen thousand, he guessed that it was pretty good to only have one 'sort of' homeless person. Though there were those who wandered the streets in search of something, not even they knew what, but they didn't actually live on the streets.

He didn't think of himself as a street person, that's not what he started out to be anyway, but then he supposed no one started out to be that way. Yet he was enough of a philosopher to realize that no one started out to be anything less than great, but they didn't always reckon with what God had in mind.

"Believe in the Lord Jesus Christ and be saved!" he yelled, as a man and woman approached him. At the same time he stuck out his right hand, holding out a pamphlet for them to take. They didn't. Some people did, in fact most people took his pamphlets. It didn't occur to him that they just did it to be rid of him, but then as long as they took a pamphlet he didn't care. Figuring that if they took the pamphlet, they might read it and if they read it, the Holy Spirit might move them to accept Jesus Christ. That was his mission after all, it didn't matter to him that he had to wander the streets and sometimes live on the streets to accomplish his goal.

On he shuffled, and each time someone approached him he yelled one of many Bible verses he had long ago committed to memory, always holding out a pamphlet and always smiling, a genuine smile, after all, he was a genuine person.

~ * ~

With a stone face Shirley Becker watched the Preacher shuffle along. She knew him. He was a few years older than her, but he looked much older. She was sure he had no idea she was even alive, but that didn't stop her from watching him and wishing things were different. She loved him, but she was sure it was a one sided love, so she watched when she could and prayed for him always.

~ * ~

Sam was glad to be back in the car and heading down the hill to the city below, not that the old church bothered him that much anymore, but he was out of the heat. Sam was slightly over weight, no, he was fat and this August heat was more than his cooling system was capable of dealing with for any length of time.

Todd's mind was still at the church. He kept saying it didn't eat on him, but the old burned out church did bother him, more than he would admit. As long as he had been a cop and as much as he had seen, the realization that someone could calmly, or not so calmly, burn a hundred innocent people in a church, just because of the color of their skin, came hard to him.

He guessed what made it even worse was that if they were sure of anything; they were sure the motive of the people who did this was color. What bothered him even more was that he knew of white people who lived today, not far from this place, whom he was sure were quite capable of such a crime.

As Todd contemplated justice denied, Sam settled back in his seat and once again adjusted the air conditioner vents, listening distantly to the Johnson City dispatcher as he did so. The Meridian County sheriff's cars were equipped with multi-channel radios that scanned the county, city and state channels. Right now most of the activity seemed to be concentrated in Johnson City.

"One-oh-four, Central," the Johnson City dispatcher's calm voice drifted over the airwaves.

"One-oh-four," an officer responded in a deadpan voice, from as yet, an unknown location.

"One-oh-four, Central, Ten-twenty."

"Clark and Jackson, Central," the radio crackled with the crisp response.

Sam could hear the anticipation in the voice. One-oh-four, whoever that was, now located at the intersection of Clark and Jackson, knew he was about to get a detail and a detail was always awaited with eager anticipation by any patrol unit. Excitement is what attracted cops to the job; they thrived on it, but what they found instead was more often sadness and boredom. Ironically, the sadness was usually a result of the action that had created the excitement and the sadness is what eventually drove them away.

"One-oh-four, Central, report of a Dis Con at one thirty-one South Fourth," the dispatcher spat out, with no emotion. No more need be said. It was a given that one-oh-four was to proceed to the stated location and handle the situation. No excitement this time. Unless the report was wrong, unless it was more than a Disorderly Conduct and that's what made the job dangerous. Routine calls killed more cops than armed robberies in progress. Sam knew that, as did the dispatcher. And one-oh-four knew it, too.

"MSO ten, Meridian County."

Sam perked up, that was the Meridian County sheriff's dispatcher on a different frequency and MSO ten (Meridian County Sheriff's Office ten) was the call sign for sheriff's investigators Sam Pinehurst and Todd Evans. Now the blood in Sam's veins sped up a little. No matter how many times he heard his call sign come over the radio it always raised his blood pressure; it was the unknown, the excitement. He grabbed the 'mike' from its holder on the face of the dash, pressed the red button on its side and responded with practiced ease, "Ten."

"MSO ten, Meridian County, citizen reports a possible missing person at nineteen-oh-seven south two thousand East Road. Citizen will meet you."

"Ten-four Meridian, in route," Sam responded, hardly able to contain his disappointment. No excitement this time, just more paperwork and clear across the county, too.

"Central, one-oh-four." The scanner was back on the Johnson City frequency Sam noted and listened to hear what one-oh-four had really found at one thirty-one South Fourth.

"Go ahead, one-oh-four," came the matter of fact response.

"Central, one-oh-four, it's just the Preacher again. I'll give him a verbal and move him along."

There was only a second of hesitation before the curt response and Sam had the distinct impression that the shift commander was standing over the dispatcher. "Negative, one-oh-four, command directs that you are to bring him in and book him."

My sixth sense is dead on, Sam smugly thought to himself.

There was a long pause and just when Sam thought it was a sure bet that Central would ask for an acknowledgment, one-oh-four responded with clear distaste, "Ten-four Central."

Todd, who like any other cop, was always aware of the radio traffic on all frequencies, all the time, now said, "That's odd. Why pick on the Preacher after all these years? He's harmless. Wonder what's up?"

Sam shook his head in disbelief and answered, "Don't you read the papers? Johnson City has a brand-new mayor, or pretty brand-new. He said he was going to clean up the city. Guess the Preacher is an easy place to start. Sure beats taking on crime," he said with a laugh as he ended.

Todd began to roar with laughter too. Sam was right, why take on something hard like crime when you could look to be doing your job by picking off misguided homeless people, or what passed for a homeless person in the small town of Johnson City. Still, Todd didn't say out loud, the Preacher *was* harmless.

~ * ~

Gene Petrowski was finally able to relax. St. Louis was behind him now and all the crazy drivers that passed for sane in this area, seemed to have been left in the St. Louis suburbs. He was well into Missouri now and glad of it. His wife, Sarah, had been nodding off in the front passenger seat, but how, he couldn't imagine. All of the swerving in and out of traffic on the five-lane bypass should have kept her wide-awake.

This vacation was the first they had been able to take for too many years. Their two children were both firmly planted in college now and there was finally time for them. Not much time, but enough to get away for a couple of weeks. Deciding on a getaway in central Missouri, they had set out in their car two days ago and without pushing matters had easily made it this far. A few more hours and they would arrive at their final destination, for some just plain relaxing. No phone, no kids, no pets, just them. It had been too long, much too long. The trouble was, he already missed the kids. *Such was life*, he mused. Won't be too long the kids will be out on their own anyway, so he had better get used to them not being around. This vacation was an excellent beginning.

The traffic was much thinner now. It was suppertime and most people had made it home from work by now. Plus, they were entering a rural area where the most activity came from the occasional gravel and sandpit. The Mississippi River was still close enough that the sand and rock deposits were plentiful. Apparently the mainstay of this area was gravel and rock from the quarries.

Though it was past quitting time for the quarries, there were still some trucks on the road hauling rock. *Rush job maybe*, Gene decided, as the narrow two lane road swept to the left and dropped rapidly past just one more of many 'caution trucks entering the roadway' signs.

Just where the truck came from he wasn't sure and it didn't matter. The truck was in his path, having pulled onto the roadway before he even suspected the presence of a side road. Gene slammed on the brakes, but the pedal bottomed out against the floorboard and the car's speed seemed to increase rather than decrease. As the truck loomed in front of him, his brain seemed to speed up and everything except his car slowed. He had a second, which seemed like minutes, to realize that the car's brakes weren't working. The truck was not going to cross his lane before his car reached it and he was going to die.

Sarah had less time to realize anything. She came out of her state of half sleep to see a truck looming in their path. As she formed the thought to yell at Gene to look out for the truck, her time for thinking was over. The car slammed into the truck at over sixty miles per hour. The driver's side and passenger side air bags inflated within a millisecond, as they were designed, but they were of little effect. The truck was a fifteen-ton quarry vehicle and it was loaded to the maximum, if not just a shade over. It wasn't quite like a car slamming into a brick wall, but it was so close the difference made no difference.

The quarry truck was much higher than the Ford Taurus GL and as a result the bottom half of the car fit under the truck's bed. The same was not true for the top half, it stopped and the air bags that had inflated so properly were shredded along with Gene and Sarah Petrowski. The truck's left-hand fuel tank ruptured and sparks from the disintegrating car ignited the fuel. The fire didn't matter to the car's occupants, but the fireball was visible from the quarry office a quarter of a mile away.

At the quarry office, the supervisor whispered a prayer as he dashed out of the building to his waiting pickup truck. Not thirty seconds later, his worst fears were confirmed and he dialed nine-one-one on his cell phone while he bailed out of his truck and ran to the road to see if he could render any assistance. The quarry truck driver had climbed out of his truck on the passenger side, with his clothes smoldering and was wandering aimlessly around in the middle of the highway by the time the quarry supervisor reached him and helped him back to the side of the road. Turning back toward the scene of the collision, the supervisor dismally realized there was no helping the car's occupants and he closed his eyes, uttering a brief prayer for their souls, while making the sign of the cross upon his chest.

~ * ~

"X Forty-six, St. Charles," the state police dispatcher at district ten headquarters in St. Charles, Missouri barked.

"X Forty-six," Trooper John Greanias replied calmly into the microphone clipped to his uniform jacket.

"X Forty-six, ten-fifty BI at Simpson Quarry Road and Missouri highway AA."

"Ten-four St. Charles, in route," John replied and reached over to the middle section of his dashboard that resembled more the cockpit of an airplane. From amongst what seemed to the casual observer as a myriad of electronic switches and dials, he chose a switch and flipped it downward. Immediately the emergency light bar mounted to the top of his car was activated and in the early evening put out an eerie mix of red, blue and yellow light. Half a second later, he turned a dial two notches to the right and a high piercing wail sounded with a warble between high and low pitches that alternated every two seconds. His blood began to rush, as it had so many times before and he accelerated his patrol car to eighty-five, rapidly checking his mirrors for traffic that might not be yielding to his emergency equipment.

John knew exactly where he was heading and why. This wasn't the first time he had gotten such a call. People just didn't seem to take those signs about trucks entering the highway seriously. It seemed that once a month there was an accident along that same stretch of AA. This would be the fourth he had handled at the Simpson Quarry Road this year. It was especially bad because of the hill just short of quarry road that hid the road from cars approaching from the east. He would bet his last month's pay that this car had been heading west. The dispatcher had said BI, which meant bodily injury, but John hadn't handled an accident with a quarry truck yet that hadn't been a fatality and he was willing to bet this one would be no different. A whole night of paperwork and no supper was ahead of him. No matter, he never felt like supper after a quarry fatality anyway.

Three

"Mr. Chambers, I'm very close to finding you in contempt of court!" a gray-headed man in his late fifties, wearing a black robe, boomed from behind the large and intimidating judicial bench. Watching from his little desk across the room, the bailiff, a black man in his early sixties, with a white head of hair, fidgeted nervously with a sheet of paper.

"Why would you want to do that, Judge?" Charlie Chambers asked calmly.

"I would think that I wouldn't have to explain it to you, but I will. You are pushing to the limit the principle of a lawyer zealously representing his client. Your stubborn insistence on your client's rights, in contrast and in disregard of the ruling of this court is over the line," the judge responded, acidly and tersely.

"Yes, I disagree with you, Judge and I don't think you understand the issues and the law, but that doesn't make me contemptuous. Surely in this country a lawyer is free to disagree with a judge's decision, after all, isn't that why they make appellate courts?" Chambers let the words roll out of his mouth easily with plodding precision, as his large frame stood hovering over the counsel table.

Now the judge was livid and he responded with vehemence, "That's what I mean! You have no respect for my decision and you seem to be accusing the court of being stupid and ill informed."

The bailiff, who was watching intently and still fidgeting with the same piece of paper, could easily see that Chambers wasn't making much progress this day, not with this judge. The bailiff knew this judge and he knew that Chambers did not. Chambers was pushing and pushing hard, so hard that he appeared to be a complete fool, but the reputation that preceded him didn't say that.

Rapidly, Chambers interjected, "Not stupid, Judge, I never said that. Nor ill informed, but I do feel the court is improperly applying the facts of this case to the law. Now the facts are that my client has a right to proclaim his religious beliefs, on his own property, in any reasonable manner. Displaying a lighted cross between the hours of sunset and ten o'clock p.m. for two weeks out of the year is reasonable. I don't care if it is twenty-five feet tall and the city has a height ordinance that limits non-residential structures to fifteen feet. That ordinance is unconstitutional and you know it. I'm not being unreasonable, the city is, this court is, but I'm not!" Charlie was getting into his argument again; the tempo and pitch of his voice were rising.

Judge Ferrell broke in and shot back, "See, there you go again! You are contemptuous in your arguments and I'll not tolerate it. I find you in contempt and fine you one hundred dollars, pay the clerk or the bailiff will escort you to the sheriff's department where you will remain in his custody until you pay or apologize!"

Charlie, wagging his head back and forth in both disgust and amazement, responded calmly, "I guess the bailiff will have to take me away, Judge, because I don't have a hundred dollars cash, in fact, I can't remember the last time I had a hundred in cash. Would Your Honor direct the clerk to take my check?" he asked, without expectation.

"Not from an out of state attorney. The clerk may only take checks from local attorneys."

"I'm good for it, Judge," Charlie responded lightly, as he finished gathering up his papers, smiling at the bailiff.

"Are you going for two hundred, Mr. Chambers?" the judge shot back icily.

"No sir, like I said, I don't have the first hundred, no sir."

"Uhhhh... Judge. How about a check on my firm?" a slim man dressed in a neat gray pinstripe suit, ventured with a timid voice. Like the bailiff, Steve Barclay knew this judge and he didn't want to find himself in the slammer too, but Chambers was a guest of his firm and Steve had been designated local counsel to assist Chambers. Steve had been stuck with the task of holding his hand. No, he shouldn't say stuck, Steve had learned a lot from Chambers in the last two months, but he was at a loss to figure out the meaning of this move.

"Not for contempt, Mr. Barclay, not even if it was a local attorney, not for contempt, cash or go to jail, directly to jail and don't pass go," the judge finished flippantly.

Steve started to suggest that he be allowed to go elsewhere and cash a check, but the judge had other ideas.

Slamming his gavel down so hard that even the bailiff jumped, the judge spat out, "Case taken under advisement, court is in recess." Then he tossed the gavel roughly onto the bench and stormed out before the bailiff had time to react and tell everyone to rise. It didn't matter; just about everyone was already standing anyway. There were only a few people there, Charlie, Barclay, the bailiff, the clerk, the court reporter and opposing counsel, the judge was already gone.

The bailiff slowly made his way across the courtroom to take charge of Chambers, fiddling with the buttons on his bright red coat and nervously straightening his matching red tie. The bailiff's heart wasn't in his task, so he was moving very slowly. He had taken a liking to this fiery lawyer from Illinois. He hadn't been able to put his finger on why he liked Charlie so much, but he did.

Steve whispered to Charlie, "I'll get up the cash in a few minutes, no sweat."

Charlie whispered back, just as the bailiff reached them, "Take your time, Steve, tomorrow morning will be plenty soon enough."

"What! Are you nuts?"

"Walk with us, Steve." Then looking at the bailiff, he asked, "Is that okay?"

"Sure, Mr. Chambers, no problem. I'm sorry about this, but I gots my orders."

Charlie held up his hand to stifle more comment and said, "No hard feelings. I understand. I have a Christian heart."

The bailiff beamed back, saying, "Yes sir! I knew you was a Christian gentleman, I just knew it. When I hear you argue in court I can tell it. You got too much spirit when you argue, not to believe in what you is saying. Yes sir, I understand." He had just realized why he liked Charles Chambers.

"Well I'm glad somebody understands Charlie, because I don't," Steve said in puzzlement, as the trio headed across the courtroom to the main entrance.

"Maybe the bailiff and the sheriff will let you visit me after I'm booked and we can talk it over," Charlie said to Steve, but it was really a question to the bailiff. As they reached the ground floor of the courthouse, the bailiff responded, "Yes sir, I'm sure that can be arranged. I know the deputies over at the sheriff's office real good."

Charlie turned to Steve and winked, handed him his briefcase and said, "Take this on back to the office Steve, then if you've a mind to, drop over to see me a little later. Maybe an hour, that about right, Bailiff?"

"That'll do nicely, Mr. Chambers, lessen they are really swamped, but that don't happen too much."

As the trio exited the main floor of the courthouse and turned right, a swarm of reporters, some with cameramen following them, appeared from nowhere.

Seeing the reporters, Charlie commented to Steve, "Wow, folks move fast in this sleepy town. Why all the fuss over a lawyer getting a night in the slam for contempt?"

Chuckling, and before Steve could respond, the bailiff said, "Nawh, Mr. Chambers, these folks ain't for you. They is here to see Miss Harmon, she's get'n out of that there car over there," he ended, pointing to his right where a long limousine was parked. Exiting from the back door with the assistance of a tall, dark and well-built man, was a petite, but full-bodied young woman. Her jet-black hair, shaped neatly, hung well below the top of her shoulders. She wore a short-sleeved tan blouse and short black skirt, but not too short. Both the blouse and the skirt were just tight enough to accentuate her full body, but not so tight as to make that accentuation obvious. Charlie was having a hard time seeing much more with the crush of reporters rapidly closing in on the woman. He got the impression she was in her twenties, but early or late he couldn't say for sure and to his life, it made no difference anyway.

"Who is Miss Harmon?" Charlie asked with a certain amount of indifference to pass the time as they continued on toward the jail. The sheriff's department and jail were located in a two-story building just north of the courthouse. It was in the same block and only separated by about a hundred feet of lawn, but for some reason no one had seen the need to connect the two buildings. Charlie guessed that connecting the two buildings made too much sense for the government to do it.

Steve now put in, with a tone of disbelief in his voice, "Miss Harmon, Carol Harmon. She is one of the top country singers in the world, Charlie. She's got ten gold records and five albums out that I know of and there's a lot I don't know. Her latest single has been at the top of the country charts for ten weeks straight. Don't tell me you've never heard of her?"

Still with indifference, Charlie responded, "Can't say as I have, Steve. What's the big deal? I don't get out much."

"Get out much! Charlie, you have to live in a cave with no television and no radio not to know about Carol Harmon."

"Don't watch much television. I have a CD player. I usually listen to classical music."

Steve was dumbfounded and the bailiff just smiled, wagging his head back and forth in amazement. Even he had heard of Carol Harmon and he hated country music.

At the entrance to the sheriff's department, Steve left them and continued walking north to his office. *What am I going to say at the office?* he wondered. *A funny thing happened in court this morning. Judge Ferrell jailed Chambers for contempt. They're booking him now,* Steve grumbled to himself, as he contemplated telling the senior partners about this fiasco. After all, Chambers was basically in his care. Like a flash of light, the idea came to him. Chambers wanted to talk, so he would wait until after he talked to Chambers. *I hope he has a good reason for this apparent madness,* Steve reflected, then decided that he needed a cup of coffee anyway, so he headed for his favorite coffee shop. *Yes, that was the way to handle this,* he decided, as he turned for the parking lot of his office to stow the two briefcases in his car.

As Steve approached the parking lot, he noticed a city squad car pull up to the prisoner intake door of the sheriff's department—the county and the city shared a jail, cheaper that way. The officer got out of his vehicle and helped another man out of the back seat. Although Steve was across the street, he was pretty sure who the man was, but why were they hauling in the Preacher? The Preacher was a fixture on the streets of Johnson City, why hassle him? *Had he finally done something this time? Not likely,* Steve mused.

Officer Glen Cooley gingerly guided the Preacher to the prisoner intake door and pushed the intercom button located just below a speaker.

"Intake," came the deadpan voice, crackling over the speaker.

Glen replied, just as unenthused, "Johnson City P.D., Officer Cooley, one for intake." As he finished, he backed away from the door and looked up to his right, directly into the closed circuit TV camera mounted above the door.

The only response was a buzz as the electric lock released the door latch. Cooley grabbed the handle of the door, swung it open and guided the Preacher through. *The Preacher,* he mused, *don't know his name, but I guess I'll find out pretty soon.* Not that it mattered, the old man he guided would always be the Preacher to him, no matter what name he gave.

A door just to the right of a little glass fronted office opened and a correctional officer stepped out to take charge of the prisoner. Glen unholstered his side arm and opened the door on one of several small lockers provided for police officers to lock up their guns while in the jail. He slipped his gun into the open locker, slammed the little door, twisted the key, pulled it out and dropped it into his pocket. Finished, he took charge of his prisoner again and guided him through the door as the correctional officer held it open for them.

"Thanks, Hank," Cooley grunted on the way by the officer.

Hank Morris smiled and chuckled slightly as he replied, "We got the word you were bringing in a real desperado, Glen. What did he do, murder the mayor?"

Just inside the door, on the left, was a counter behind which two other correctional officers stood. Both officers were smiling broadly at Glen, as they continued with their task of booking someone else who was in the custody of a court bailiff.

With a sheepish look, Glen replied testily, "Cut it out, guys. I got nothing against the Preacher, but orders are orders."

The bailiff, looking at Chambers, said quietly, "I know the feeling."

Charlie stood watching the officer and his prisoner with marked indifference as the booking officer was preparing him for fingerprinting. This wasn't the first time Charlie had been fingerprinted. He'd been down this road before. It came with the territory he traveled.

"Cam, after Mr. Chambers is settled, would it be okay if Mr. Barclay came to see him? Say in about half an hour? I kind of already said as how I thought it would be okay with you guys," the bailiff said confidently from behind Charlie.

Cam, finished with Charlie's right hand, looked up and replied, "Sure, Smitty, whatever you want."

Smitty put on a broad smile and said, "Thanks, Cam, if you don't need me anymore, I'll be headin back on over to the house." That was Smitty's nickname for a place he seemed to spend more time in than his own home.

"Sure, see ya, Smitty. Come over for coffee in the morning, Sam's bringing in doughnuts."

"My pleasure, see ya," he tossed over his shoulder as he grabbed the inner intake door, waited for the buzz that meant the lock was released and passed out the door as easily as stepping onto an elevator. Easy for Smitty, but not just anyone could pass though that door, as he well knew—and a lot of them wanted to do just that.

Charlie was finishing cleaning the ink off his hands with some greasy hand cleaner and a paper towel as the booking officer started on the Preacher.

"Name?" Cam asked, with obvious boredom.

"Tommy Trenton," the Preacher replied, a little nervously.

"Is Tommy your given name or a nick name? I need your given name," the booking officer droned out as he leaned on the counter with his pen poised above the booking form.

The Preacher looked wistfully at Officer Cooley, Charlie and back to the booking officer, saying, "I don't know, it's all the name I ever had, I guess. Don't know of another 'cept maybe Preacher, but only the people around here call me that. I guess if I have a nick name it's Preacher."

"Good enough, Mr. Trenton. Now when were you born?"

"February 14, 1948 and my name *is* Tommy, not Thomas, just Tommy. I'm sorry, I'm a little nervous. I remember now though. I once saw my birth certificate and that's what it said. I used to have a copy, but I lost it. I haven't needed it for a long time. Most people know I'm of age now."

Cam looked up and wordlessly shook his head in the affirmative, as the Preacher looked over at Charlie and said, "Believe in the Lord Jesus Christ and be saved. I'd give you one of my pamphlets, but they already took them all."

Charlie, after wadding up the hand towel and dropping it in the wastebasket, smiled at the Preacher and responded, "Maybe next time."

"This way, Mr. Chambers. You need to change clothes, we'll keep yours until you are released," another correctional officer said, as he motioned Charlie into a side room.

~ * ~

There he is, same place, same time, Janet thought, as she strolled up to the entrance to the TTM headquarters building. Every day without fail, he was there at that basement window watching, without seeming to watch, as she came to work each morning. She didn't have to be at work until 9:30 a.m. and she figured he must get here much earlier, because he was always at that same window, even if she was a little early and today she was a little late. No matter. Mr. Willis was not too punctual and easy to get along with when she ran a little late. Today she had a good excuse, her car wouldn't start and an upstairs neighbor had to give her a jumpstart. That was one nice thing about being good looking, young and single, men liked to take every opportunity to help. It also had its disadvantages. A girl had to be careful. That's why she noticed Mark Fribley watching her from the basement window. A woman always notices when a man notices.

At first, she was alarmed, but after making some inquiries she became more intrigued than alarmed. They called him a 'computer geek' or 'four eyes' and sometimes 'nerd'. She was sure they were all wrong though. He was more than he appeared to be and she would rather have a bashful suitor than some of the leering fast handed men on the sixth floor. He watched from afar, but it wasn't a leering look. She knew the difference, good looking women learned the difference early on and his was a look of admiration and appreciation, not a leer.

Ever since she had first noticed him watching her, she had begun to be a little more choosy about her clothes. They were just a little more alluring than ordinary, a little more enticing, and she strolled to the door with just a little more of a swing than normal. He was obviously interested and she wanted to keep him that way. It wasn't that she was being a tease, that could be dangerous. No, she had checked out Mark Fribley.

He was a clean-cut guy with above average intelligence, single, twenty-five, six foot even, dark hair and a rugged face. He was just a little short on social skills and she intended to remedy that, somehow, someday, soon. All she had to do was figure out how to get him started on the right track.

At first, Janet figured she could accidentally run into him somewhere in the building, but that didn't seem to be working. Apparently he didn't eat in the cafeteria, so she quit going there. It seemed as though he never left that basement hideaway of his, he ate there, worked there and for all she knew, he slept there. She really had her work cut out for her in socializing this man, but she had a feeling he might just be worth the effort.

~ * ~

Meridian County Deputy Sheriff, Lieutenant Darin Ebbitt sat across from the sheriff's massive desk and explained, "I'll have another talk with them, Sheriff, but I don't think it's the jail personnel. I checked their paperwork myself and I tell you it looked straight to me. Someone may be dropping the ball, but not my people. I've hammered it into their heads any number of times that when someone bonds out they have to have the proper paperwork and it has to be properly maintained until the clerk says differently."

The sheriff wasn't impressed, but he wasn't stupid either. "Look, Darin. I'm not saying it is all our fault, but Judge Ferrell keeps harping on me because there isn't any paperwork in the court files and the clerk swears it isn't her fault. Personally, I think the clerk is dropping the ball, but I can't prove it yet. We aren't the only ones who take bail money around here. During business hours the clerk takes most of the bail money and some of that paperwork is missing, too.

"This new clerk has got the system so fouled up that she doesn't know half what she should know about where files are or should be. Most of the time the whole file is missing. If it weren't for the computer system linking the courts with the clerk's office, the whole system would come to a screeching halt. Bear with me, Darin. Stay on your people until I can nail this down. I want to be clean so that Judge Ferrell will get off my back, he can be a first class pain. Right now he thinks the Honorable little Miss Jeannie Rosmund, Meridian County Circuit Clerk can do no wrong. He says she's bringing us out of the dark ages and into the age of enlightenment. Personally I think we'll rue the day we ever let computers take over our lives. Okay?"

Nodding in the affirmative, Darin responded in the only way he could, this was his boss and he wanted something, so Darin obliged, "Okay, Sheriff, I'll stay on 'em. We'll be as clean as the mayor's new Cadillac."

Lightly, the sheriff now said, "He's got a new Cadillac? I knew I should have run for mayor. I went to school with Clayton, he's a first class clown and he gets a Cadillac while I drive around in a Chevy Caprice with more miles on it than Sputnik."

~ * ~

Charlie was sitting in the visitor's booth, reaching for the telephone, as a guard stood outside peering in through the glass door behind him. To his front he was watching Steve Barclay who was also lifting his phone's receiver. Charlie could see that Steve's booth was the same as his, except it had a regular door and no guard stood behind it. Then Steve began speaking.

"Give me something good to tell my bosses, Charlie. They aren't going to like me letting you get slammed, even by Judge Ferrell, who is noted for being a first class jerk," and then under his breath, he said nervously, "I hope these phones aren't tapped. They aren't supposed to be."

Charlie chuckled and Steve shot back, "Yeah, you can laugh, but I don't see the humor and I just can't see what you see about it that's so funny."

"Relax, Steve. Tell the partners I did it on purpose."
"Why?"
"You just said Ferrell is prone to be a jerk, right?"

"So?"

"So you tell me if he wasn't ready to pull the trigger on me in court, no matter what I argued. He had his mind made up and he had me tuned out. I had to get his attention."

"You did!" Steve exclaimed in amazement.

"Exactly, but I did more than that. If he had pulled the trigger in court, without more consideration, I would have lost, I could read it in his face and I could hear it in the tone of his voice. I've seen it before in other courtrooms and in other judges. I had to give him pause to think. He was so mad at me he didn't have the presence of mind to rule on the case, he had to go cool off and while he cools off, he'll be thinking. That's what I want. Maybe his decision will still be the same, but a night in jail is worth the chance that while he cools off he will think and maybe realize that I was right. Anyway, we'll see. Come tomorrow or the next day, we'll see."

In awe, Steve responded quietly, "I had heard there was no stopping you, Charlie, but until now I didn't believe it. Is there anything you won't do to win a case?"

"Lots of things," Charlie said simply and continued, "my methods are simple, I use the system against itself, but I don't abuse the system. I don't always win, but I always fight with one hundred percent of my ability."

Charlie tiredly rubbed his eyes with his left hand and leaned his right elbow on the metal shelf in front of the glass partition and continued, "So anyway, now you know what to tell the senior partners."

Steve eyed Charlie as he continued to rub his eyes, he could see that the day had taken its toll on him. Perhaps his lifestyle was taking its toll on him, too. Chambers jumped from state to state and courtroom to courtroom to champion the cause of any religious infringement. *How could you ever get any real rest that way?* he wondered and then said, "Okay, I'll let you get some rest. First thing in the morning I'll be over to pay your fine. We'll have a late breakfast, just you and me, I'll buy."

Lifting his head, Charlie nodded and with a smile said, "I'll take you up on that, Steve. Goodnight." With that he hung up the phone and stood so that the guard would know he was finished and ready to go back to his cell.

Steve continued to sit while watching Charlie leave the cubicle. It occurred to him that he would get up and leave with no guard and no bars, but Charlie could not. For his cause he had given up his freedom, at least for one night and that said volumes to Steve. A man, a fellow lawyer, had willingly given up his freedom for his cause and the cause of a client. Not many could say they had ever done that and even less would actually do it. *Could I?* The question remained unanswered as he left the room, yet he had the feeling that Chambers had done it before, perhaps many times. What didn't occur to him was that others had given up much more for what they believed in and had done it not so far away from Johnson City.

~ * ~

Evans and Pinehurst were working overtime on this one. Just as the call that unit one-oh-four took could have been more and turned out to be less, theirs had sounded like less and turned out to be more. The lab techs were just finishing and Todd was filling in Lieutenant Shore on what they had found.

"It looked like a missing person when we first arrived, Lieutenant. Several newspapers in the front yard, no mail picked up and the neighbor down the road not having seen him at the usual times, in the usual places. Then Sam noticed the car was in the garage and we started to suspect something might have happened to him. You know, a fall or an accident of some kind.

"We found the back door unlocked and I came in while Sam covered me. I know we should have called for a warrant, but we didn't suspect any criminal activity, just an accident.

"Anyway, I finally found him in the basement, he was hanging right about over here," Todd said, as he walked a few feet toward the north wall. "From this beam here and the chair was tipped over right there," he finished, motioning with his left hand toward the south.

"The Coroner figures he's been dead three, maybe four days. All indications are suicide, but no note and no indication from the neighbors that he was depressed.

"He didn't seem to have any family, but we'll check out his acquaintances. Used to work up at the textile mill. He had a pretty good job it seems. Retired not long ago. I make him fifty-five, or a little more."

"What was his name?" Shore asked.

Todd checked his notes and responded flatly, "Corey Merriman. Know him?"

"Nope."

~ * ~

"Who'd you have out there yesterday, John? A local?" Commander Pinkerton asked and John Greanias wondered if he was just passing the time of day or if he really didn't read the reports that came across his desk.

"Not a local, sir. Georgia plates. I just checked and they've identified the occupants already. Don't ask me how they did it so fast, I'd have bet it would have taken them a week to put enough together to nail this one down. Anyway, it was a couple out of Georgia. Meridian County. Fact is the guy was the Chief Deputy Circuit Clerk for Meridian County, Georgia. Two kids in college over in Atlanta. Tough."

Nodding solemnly, the commander agreed, "Yeah, tough. I'm ordering another traffic study on AA. Something has to be done. Slower speeds, traffic lights, something. Too many good people are dying out there."

"Yes, sir," John replied and decided that the commander might not read the reports, but his heart was in the right place.

Four

The Meridian County jail was divided into three cellblocks. All of the hardcore criminals were in cellblock 'H' and the less dangerous, but still serious offenders were in cellblock 'M' unless they became unruly and then they were transferred. The third cellblock known as 'A' handled the average miscreant who was afoul of the law, but not necessarily the system. It also contained those who were awaiting trial and until the trial no one knew if they would spend more time in the county jail or go into the state prison system.

Charlie Chambers and Tommy Trenton were in cellblock 'A' and would probably remain there for as long as they remained in the Meridian county jail. In Charlie's case that would be sometime tomorrow, but in Tommy's case the end was far from clear.

Tommy was sitting in his cell, looking pensively out through the steel bars of the door. He had never been in jail before, he had never been confined before, except for school and he hadn't minded that. It was beyond his understanding as to why they had arrested him today. After all, he was just preaching, that wasn't any different from anything he had done in the past. The police always waved at him and a couple even took his pamphlets. He didn't know much about rights, he only knew he wasn't free anymore. He had always been free.

Peering far to his left allowed him to watch a man in an orange jump suit make his way down the hall between the rows of cells. The man was mopping the floor and except for the occasional swish of his mop and muffled scraping of the bucket as he pushed it along, there wasn't a sound on the block. Tommy didn't have a watch, but he figured the time to be around nine p.m.

Once in a while Tommy could hear a hushed whisper from somewhere on the block, but he couldn't tell if it came from prisoners quietly talking, or guards. Though this was the first time Tommy had been in jail, he had talked to people who had been. According to the description those people had given, the time in Meridian County jail was dead time. At the time he didn't understand what they meant, but now he knew. There was nothing to do, nowhere to go and no reason to talk.

As Tommy watched, the man with mop and bucket came closer and closer. The front of his jump suit said 'Trustee' and Tommy knew that was why he was allowed freedom of movement within the block. The man was trusted and was allowed to work and move about, not bad Tommy figured, it beat sitting in a cell all day long doing nothing.

Tommy continued to watch, saying nothing, as the man drew nearer and finally dipped his mop in the bucket just outside Tommy's cell door. Tommy was alone in his cell so this was the first person to come within speaking distance since he had been jailed, excepting the guard who had brought his supper.

"Tommy Trenton?" the man asked quietly, as he peered into the cell.

Tommy was shocked that the man had spoken. He was someone to watch in order to pass the time, he didn't figure on the man actually speaking to him. Tommy didn't reply at first and the man continued, "You are Tommy Trenton, aren't you?"

"Yes," Tommy replied timidly.

"Thought so, you don't remember me do you?"

"No."

"We went to high school together for a while and I've seen you since, on the streets and here abouts. How did you wind up in here?"

"I'm not sure. I didn't do anything. I mean I didn't break any laws. I don't think. I haven't done anything different lately. How about you?"

"Shoplifting, second offense. I've only got a couple months to go now. Been here almost eight months."

"I don't remember you from high school. What's your name?"

"Perry Minton."

"Sorry, I still don't remember. I didn't stay in high school long."

"Yeah, I remember you dropped out our freshman year. I thought that was so neat that I almost dropped out myself. Must have been cool not to have to go to school and be able to just hang around?"

"No, not cool and not neat, just hard. When you're fourteen and out of school no one wants to hire you. Without a job you can't buy food and you have no place to sleep. It wasn't neat at all. I got used to living outside, in all kinds of weather and in all kinds of places."

"But you had a family, didn't you? I remember a sister, I think."

"Sure, I had a little sister. Like most people, I had a father and a mother, but it didn't do me any good. I was on my own at fourteen and miserable."

"They toss you out?"

"Nope, I left."

"What happened to your family?"

"I don't know for sure. Last I heard they moved out of town and I've never heard from any of them again. Before they moved I used to see my sister once in a while, but after they moved she never came around again. I didn't really want to know where they went. The old man and my mom, now they never caused me anything but pain. Sometimes I dream about them, especially my sister, but I don't really want to know where they went."

"No wonder you lived on the street. I always wondered why you had to do that."

"It wasn't easy, I lived mighty poor for a long time. Finally, I got a job at the grocery store on Fifth and Adams. I did the clean up in the meat department and everywhere else no one wanted to clean. It was bad, but it was work and it kept me fed.

"When I turned sixteen I tried to get my driver's license, but I couldn't. I hadn't had any driver training at school and I didn't have my parent's permission. Sixteen didn't mean as much to me as it did to the rest of the kids who were still in school. They were driving and I was still walking and cleaning up in the store. I tried to get me an apartment once, but no one would rent to a sixteen year old."

Perry pulled his bucket close to the cell door and sat on top of it asking, "Where did you live?"

Tommy shrugged and answered, "Where I could. An abandoned house sometimes. A shack in the hills, anywhere I could get in out of the weather, until someone ran me out."

Perry leaned forward, put his elbows on his knees and rested his chin on his hands saying, "That does sound rough. You still live on the streets?"

"Not really, only sometimes. The apartment I have across town isn't much, but it's something to call my own. I have a job up at the mill, cleaning up. At least I did, but I don't think they'll keep me when they find out I'm in jail or when I don't show up for work."

"Exactly what got you thrown in here?"

"Like I said, I don't know. I was just handing out my pamphlets and preaching, like I always do, when they arrested me. Disorderly conduct, I think they said. It doesn't make sense to me, because I wasn't doing anything different. Preaching the Word doesn't harm anyone. I mind my own business just like I always have. It doesn't pay to stick your nose in where it doesn't belong."

"How come they call you the Preacher?"

"I guess because I preach and pass out my pamphlets."

"How come?"

"I've seen things, living on the street, that made me the way I am. Another reason is that in the seventies there was a group of people here that everyone called the 'Jesus People' and I kind of threw in with them. They set up a big tent up around Burning Chapel Hill and I moved in with them. The 'Jesus People' had some good things to say and they lived a lot like me. We all seemed to be equally poor.

"They passed out pamphlets at their revival meetings. After a while the locals ran them off, but when they left, they left an old broken down station wagon filled with boxes of pamphlets about Christ and what it was like to be a Christian. I read them all and then I got the idea to continue the mission. I hauled the pamphlets off to my place and started passing them out when I preached. There are still a lot of the pamphlets left."

"So you're on a mission from God?" Perry stifled a snicker.

"Don't know about that. Almost every day I tell people about Christ and pass out pamphlets in my spare time. You see, I don't have anything else to do and I don't hurt anything or anybody. Can't say as I ever remember anyone caring what I did or what happened to me. So I just thought maybe if I cared about someone else it might make a difference. Can't say as it has, but like I said, I don't have anything else to do.

"You know Perry, you're the only person I can ever remember, who was even interested enough in me, to ask how I got to be what I am or why. I don't think I've talked to anyone, other than at work, without preaching to them, since I left the old man. Like I said, no one ever cared what I did or why. I got nothing and nobody on this earth."

Perry stood up now and gathered up his mop and bucket, saying, "Well, I think you got a raw deal. You ought to get a lawyer."

"Lawyers take money and I don't have money for a lawyer. Besides, maybe I'm better off in here, three squares a day and a warm bed."

Perry shrugged and over his right shoulder said, "See ya."

"Yeah," Tommy almost whispered as he watched Perry wander back down the hall with his mop and bucket. *Maybe I could get to be a trustee*, Tommy thought. *At least I could move around. I'm used to cleaning up.*

Across the corridor in the opposite cell, Charlie Chambers was sound asleep. Had he been awake he might have found Tommy's story interesting, but he hadn't been. He had been asleep for almost two hours, not peacefully, but asleep.

Tommy settled into his bunk just as the lights in the main hall went out, leaving only a small light at each end still burning. Bedtime he guessed. *Just as well*, he decided, he was tired anyway and there was nothing else to do. Before he dropped of to sleep, he thanked God for being alive and having a warm place to sleep, just like he had done every night since he was fourteen and on his own. He didn't always have a warm place to sleep, but he still thanked God for what he had. He knew there were others who were worse off than he was, he had seen them first hand.

~ * ~

"What time is it, Sam? My watch stopped," Todd said from behind a pile of papers on his desk.

Sam glanced up, looked at his watch and responded with a yawn, "Ten o'clock."

"Sure wish they'd get a clock in here. You'd think they could afford a clock for the investigators, huh, Sam?"

"I think you ought to buy a decent watch. That piece of junk you call a watch only runs about half the time."

Todd stood up and stretched, saying, "Let's knock off. We aren't getting anywhere tonight. The reports are done and the lab results won't be in for a couple of days. We've been on duty now for sixteen hours, what'd ya say?"

Sam tossed the papers he had been scanning onto his desk, and nodded tiredly saying, "Yeah. Coffee?"

"Okay, a quick cup over at Shirley's? Then I'm going home. I'm beat. Besides, my wife will kill me if I'm not home by midnight. She says she hardly sees me now and the kids never do."

"Yeah, my wife used to say that, too," Sam responded, with a faraway look in his eye.

Todd wished he hadn't said anything. He forgot sometimes that Sam's wife had died of cancer just a couple of years ago and Sam just couldn't let her go.

They walked out together and Todd killed the lights to the medium sized office they shared. Neither felt like talking as they left the building and approached their cars. Once in their cars it was only a matter of seconds that they were out of the lot and around the corner to Shirley's.

Shirley's was a little café on the main street where most of the cops stopped for breakfast, lunch and dinner, depending upon their shift. Shirley Becker was the owner, chief cook and bottle washer and she knew every cop in town by their first names and how many kids they had. She couldn't have gotten a traffic ticket in Johnson City or Meridian County if she had tried.

"Hi Todd, Sam. What'll it be?"

Todd rubbed his eyes tiredly with both hands as he leaned on the counter and said, "Just a coffee, Shirl."

"Me too, Shirl."

In seconds both had a hot cup of coffee in front of them and Shirley was again mopping the counter as she asked, "You guys got some work today huh? Suicide?"

Todd, who was never surprised at the information Shirley could pick up in this place, answered abruptly, "Looks that way. Lab boys aren't done yet. Nothing official."

"Suicide," Shirley stated adamantly and continued, "when was the last time there was a murder in Meridian County?"

Sam answered, "Oh, we've had some, Shirley, not many. Probably not half a dozen in twenty years, but we've had some."

"I suppose that's so, but not lately we haven't," she retorted, sticking to her guns.

"True, but we don't have your gift for intuition, Shirl. We have to investigate them all," Sam ended with a laugh.

"No statute of limitations on murder, Shirley. Just because we haven't had one lately, doesn't mean we can forget the ones we've had and haven't solved," Todd put in.

Shirley wrinkled up her nose and looked from Todd to Sam asking, "You been up to the old burned out church again haven't you?"

"So," Todd said defensively.

"So what's the use, Todd? You can't solve them all, especially not one as old as that one. Save your energy."

"It's my energy to waste," Todd shot out irritably.

"Humph," Shirley snorted and walked off down the counter.

Not ten seconds later she came back and said, "Hey, I heard the Preacher got pinched today, why?"

"Mayor's got a political promise to keep. We figure he's starting with the Preacher," Todd said, a little more congenially.

"That's not right. He never hurt anyone, he wouldn't hurt a flea," Shirley pouted.

Sam shrugged, as he responded callously, "Maybe, but he's a nobody and the mayor is a somebody. That's the way it works in this world, Shirl."

"But what about the law? Doesn't he have rights too?"

Todd put in now, "Funny thing about rights, Shirley, they aren't worth a hoot if you don't have the clout to preserve them. Kind of like the people in that little church up on the hill, they died exercising their rights too, but no one cared; then or now, except me."

"And me partner," Sam interjected.

With a slight smile Todd added, "Okay, me and Sam here, my partner."

Shirley twisted her face into a pout and pronounced, "The Preacher's got the same rights those people had, why aren't you two sticking up for his rights?"

It was Todd's turn to sound callous, as he responded, "The Preacher ain't dead yet. We're interested in violations of the right to live, not the right to live free, freedom isn't in our job description," then added, "what's the deal, Shirl? You got a thing for the Preacher?"

Shirley looked back and forth from Sam and Todd in disbelief, rolled her eyes into the back of her head and briskly walked to the other end of the counter. It was almost closing time and she had better things to do than argue civil rights with two stubborn cops or answer questions she didn't feel inclined to answer.

~ * ~

Leon Semple was a number cruncher. There was no other way to put what he did. His official title was an auditor for the state comptroller's office, but he was a number cruncher. Leon took a set of books apart and put them back together again. When he was done, the books either balanced or someone was in dire trouble. Especially since the only books he audited were public accounts and when someone misappropriated public money they were in for a long hard fall. That wasn't his concern though. He only checked the books and reported his findings to the comptroller. If there was something amiss, the comptroller notified the proper enforcement agencies and Leon only became a pawn in the evidence game.

Leon had been at this set of books for about seven days and he was almost finished. In reality this set of books didn't exist, at least not in the literal sense. There weren't any books; just data on a computer hard drive. A big computer hard drive, but still just electronic bits of data that couldn't be seen or touched without a computer screen. He liked the old way better. He longed for the days when he could sift through a pile of paper and hardbound books, making notes on a yellow pad of paper and burning up the keys of an electronic calculator. Those days were gone forever with the advent of the computer and the thousands of accounting software packages for sale across the country. No matter, Leon knew how to crunch numbers, it made no difference if the numbers were recorded in a hard bound ledger book or were just bits of electronic impulses etched on a computer hard drive.

The last screen went blank as he punched the escape key. He then exited the program. Glancing at his watch, he saw that it was past ten o'clock again. Leon had a habit of working very late when on an audit. Not that he wanted to get finished quickly for any particular reason; he just liked to finish an audit promptly. Had he been married with children it would have been a different story. Then he wouldn't feel right about working so late every night of an audit. The bottom line, which is all he ever worried about, was that there was no one waiting for him, so he worked as late as he wanted, when he wanted.

Stretching and glancing around at the barren office area, he started thinking about his report. He didn't like to judge people, he left that for others more suited to the task, but unless he missed his guess, someone around here was going to take a fall after this audit. These books didn't even come close to balancing. The documentation was all there, on the computer, but the figures didn't balance. The money taken in was much less than the money paid out. In any business that was not good, but in this particular business, it was nothing short of criminal.

Oh well, he thought to himself, as he closed up his laptop computer, *it isn't my problem*. He only reported to the comptroller that the accounts balanced or didn't balance. The comptroller made the judgment calls. He was content to do what he did. It was never his desire to have to sit in judgment over the actions of other people. That was something that happened in the real world and his work kept him insulated from that world. His world consisted of credits and debits and little else. Let the politicians play in the real world. It didn't suit him.

Leon picked up his computer case and left the office. Out in the corridor the guard rose when he saw Leon come out the office door. "All done for tonight, Mr. Semple?"

"All done for good," Leon commented dryly, as he made his way for the entrance door, followed closely by the guard.

The guard held the door open and Leon passed out the door, as the guard said, "Good-bye, Mr. Semple."

"Good-bye," Leon responded, distantly. He was already writing his report to the comptroller. He would be doing that all the rest of the night and tomorrow, in his head. In a couple of days he would put it on paper and submit it, then he would move on to the next assignment. That there would be another assignment was a certainty. The legislature had decided long ago that every set of public books would be audited every four years, without fail. There just weren't enough auditors to do that with any time to spare, but this audit wasn't over, at least the end wasn't known. Someone was in deep trouble in the Meridian County Circuit Clerk's Office.

~ * ~

The guard watched Leon walk away and as he did so, he thought to himself that he was glad to be seeing the last of this Semple character. He was a mousy looking guy and had a personality like a dead fish. Some kind of genius when it came to figures, according to what the guard had heard, but he didn't look like much. To the casual observer he was just a short, skinny little egghead with wide rimmed coke bottle glasses. *Doesn't even look dry behind the ears*, the guard mused.

Five

Jerry Bales pensively walked through the front door of the sheriff's department, staring nervously at the two cameras that tracked his approach to the information counter. The place was as quiet as a tomb and he felt as though he were dead. His footsteps sounded hollowly on the tile floor and as he approached the glass covered information booth, he could see light through a partially open door. Beyond the door there was movement from at least one person.

Once at the counter, he read a sign posted just above what looked like a doorbell button. The sign told him to push the button for assistance after ten o'clock. Glancing at his watch, he noted that it was eleven, so he pushed the button timidly and was rewarded by a harsh ringing in the room beyond the open door. *Got to get this over with*, he said to himself, *got to get out of here.*

~ * ~

Rattling keys and the clank of the steel door awoke him and when he heard the voice break the stillness of the night he sat up groggily. The voice drifted across the corridor to his cell, "Come on, Preacher, time to go."

Charlie looked at his watch and saw that the time was eleven thirty p.m. *Strange time to wake up a prisoner*, he thought and then he heard the guard continue, "Come on, Preacher, let's go. You made bond, we need the bed space."

"Bond? What do you mean bond?" a sleepy voice, which Charlie assumed belonged to the Preacher, responded.

An exasperated voice replied, "I mean someone put up the hundred bucks it takes to get you out of jail while you're waiting for your trial. Now come on, let's don't wake up the whole jail. Normally we would let you wait until morning, but we need the space."

The guard wasn't telling the truth. In reality they had plenty of space. Only a few of the sixty cells in the jail were double bunked. The jail had a capacity of one hundred twenty prisoners and right now they only had seventy-five. The truth was that the sheriff's personnel on duty liked the Preacher and when his bail was posted they were determined to get him out as soon as they could. They sensed that jailing the Preacher was like locking up a wild animal. A wild animal was born to be free and, so they figured, was the Preacher. None of them had any use for the new mayor anyway.

Charlie lay back down on his bunk and as soon as the noise from the Preacher's release had died down, he returned to a fitful sleep.

Out in the anteroom, the Preacher was still confused. "I still don't understand. Who'd put money up for me? I don't have anyone; no one cares about me. That jail cell was better than some places I've had to sleep, why would anyone care?"

"Look, Tommy, I don't know. All I know is that a Jerry Bales came in about an hour ago and put up a hundred bucks cash for you. You were arrested for disorderly conduct, which is a class A misdemeanor and the law says you can bond out with a hundred bucks cash, no judge or anything. Okay? That's all I know," the jailer said tiredly from behind the counter, where only hours before Tommy Trenton had been booked.

"Who's Jerry Bales?" Tommy persisted.

The jailer responded shortly, "The guy who posted your bail, now come on let's go; and stay out of trouble will ya?"

~ * ~

Herman Trenton scanned the article repeatedly, but he couldn't make the names appear. According to the report the names weren't being released until after the next of kin had been notified. He would have to keep watching the paper for the next few days to see if they printed another article with names.

Ordinarily he didn't care much about who got killed in a car wreck, Missouri or anywhere, but lately he had taken an interest in every death of a Meridian County resident or former Meridian County resident. Though he no longer lived in the county, he still had the Johnson City Gazette sent to his house, so that he could keep up. Not with the news, but with the deaths. Of late, the last few months at least, two prominent deaths had caught his attention. They weren't prominent in the manner that the people were especially well known in the community or were important by any stretch of the imagination. To Herman they were prominent in another way; their deaths meant something to him that would be lost on anyone else. Well, almost anyone else.

Herman wasn't scared. He didn't have any evidence that he should be scared, not yet. He was concerned though, enough to read the obituaries every day and to dissect the local news for the death of anyone who had any connection to Meridian County or Johnson City. He was an old man by most standards and had spent a fair portion of his life behind bars, so it took a lot to get under his skin. Being so old and having squandered almost every dime he had ever illegally or legally obtained, he had very little to lose, but he still didn't want to lose it. So until he was sure about what he suspected or was sure that what he suspected was false, he would continue to read the obituaries and glean any other bit of information he could from the Johnson City Gazette.

~ * ~

At nine o'clock the next morning, Steve Barclay appeared at the sheriff's office with a receipt showing that he had paid Charlie Chamber's fine and the wheels began to turn for his release. The wheels were moving a little slower this morning than they had last night for the Preacher, after all, they liked the Preacher. Chambers was just another lawyer that Judge Ferrell had bagged; he bagged about one a month.

By ten thirty Charlie had made it back to the booking counter to reverse the process and get out. A buzz caught his attention as the electric lock on the intake door released and the door was pulled open. In came the Preacher with a city policeman right behind him.

"Hey, the Preacher made bond last night," the booking officer said and continued, "what are you city boys hassling him for? He's out."

"He was out, but first thing this morning he was over at Fourth and Adams up to his old tricks. The mayor isn't happy with him. No one figured him to make bail in the first place, the mayor especially. He figured the Preacher was off the streets for a month at least, takes that long to get a trial in this here county."

The booking officer sighed in despair and said, "Okay, okay. Come on, Preacher. We got all the information last night. I'll just take you on through to the intake guard."

As the Preacher passed Charlie, he smiled and shrugged as if to say, *You can't change a tiger by setting him free, free or not, he'll still be a tiger.*

The booking officer passed Charlie a release form to sign and while he was signing, he didn't bother reading it, he asked, "Just what are his tricks?" He nodded toward the door though which the Preacher had just passed.

The city officer who had brought the Preacher in volunteered before the booking officer could respond, "Oh, he struts around out there on the streets passing out religious pamphlets, telling people to believe and be saved and the like. He's harmless, but annoying sometimes," the officer finished condescendingly.

Charlie raised his eyebrows and coolly asked the officer, "On public rights of way and other public property I suppose?"

With a smile the officer said, "Yeah sure, why else would we pick him up?"

"Why else indeed," Charlie said to no one in particular, as he passed through the intake door on his way out of the room.

Steve Barclay was waiting pensively as Charlie came out the jail door.

"Morning, Steve," Charlie said with a smile.

"It's morning, I'm not saying it's good and I'm not going to ask you how you slept," Steve responded.

"Why not? Actually I slept pretty well. I always do after a case is over, win or lose. The sudden release of tension just drains me. I could sleep on a bed of nails after a trial.

"Although I have to admit the strange surroundings disturbed me some. I'm not used to the sound of clanking steel doors in the middle of the night, but all in all, I've had worse nights, lots worse. Now how about that breakfast? The fare they put on in the slam isn't my cup of tea."

Steve looked at his watch and declared, "A little late for breakfast, but how about we go around the corner to Shirley's place for an early lunch. You remember it, the cop hangout, unless you've had your fill of cops?"

"Cops are okay, some good and some bad, just like lawyers and everyone else," Charlie replied dryly.

Rain was threatening as they made their way down the street and into the café. Charlie's mind was still on his latest case, he was wondering how Judge Ferrell would rule after his night of rest, or if maybe he had made up his mind before bed. Wrenching his thoughts back to his present surroundings, he noticed this little café was a might crowded for this time of day. Letting his gaze wander around the crowd, he soon realized why it was so crowded. From what he could see, through the crowd at the far end of the café, the focus of attention seemed to be on a young dark haired girl sitting with a tall, dark, well-built man. The same one who was assisting her from the car yesterday. It was Carol Harmon and she was drawing quite a crowd. *Still don't ever recall hearing of her*, Charlie mused to himself.

As they took seats at the far end of the counter Charlie asked, "Anything from Ferrell?"

Steve, drawing his gaze back from the area where Carol Harmon was seated, shrugged and answered, "Not that I know of, I nosed around this morning first thing and came up with nothing. His secretary is pretty closed mouth, but she likes me okay. She gave me the impression, without telling me expressly, that the judge hadn't ruled. At least he hadn't given her any orders to type and hadn't called for the court reporter. You know it's just possible he will sit on this a while. Maybe he wants to let you stew for a while before he hammers you."

"That doesn't sound encouraging, Steve," Charlie quipped.

"I don't think he's going to go our way. It just isn't his style. All the lawyers around here I've talked to can only remember him declaring one statute unconstitutional in his whole career and he was reversed on that," Steve rejoined in an even tone. He glanced over the menu, he had practically memorized over the years, then again looked up across the length of the counter to Carol Harmon. They were seated at the short end of an 'L' shaped counter. From where they were they had a clear view of Carol Harmon, or at least the part of her that wasn't covered up by the bodies of several men sitting in a semi-circle around her table and the on-lookers being kept at bay by the semi-circle of men.

But Charlie wasn't looking. "Yeah, I figure you're right. It's a shame we can't just take these cases right to the appellate courts. Very few state trial judges have the intestinal fortitude to declare a law unconstitutional." Charlie's response brought Steve back to the realization that he hadn't really heard Charlie or known he was speaking, he was trying to get a better look at Carol Harmon. It wasn't often that a star came to this little café. He was probably as star struck as the rest of the town.

A tall, dark haired woman in her early forties approached them from behind the counter and Steve greeted her warmly, "Hi, Shirl, how's business?"

She smiled and responded lightly, "If it was any better I couldn't stand it, Mr. Barclay, some days I think I ought to make the I.R.S. a full partner since I give them thirty-eight percent anyway. Now if I had her money, I wouldn't care," she ended, jerking her head toward where Carol Harmon sat.

Steve and Charlie chuckled and Steve made the introductions, "Charlie Chambers, Miss Shirley Becker, owner, cook and anything else you can think of that needs done."

Smiling Charlie responded formally, "It's very nice to meet you, Miss Becker, nice place."

Dryly, she said, "It's a living. I could use more help some days, but when I think about hiring help, business drops off and I realize I can't afford them." Again she jerked her head toward Carol Harmon and continued, "Don't get the likes of her in here often enough to do me any good. Most of that crowd ain't buying anyway, they're just looking, mostly at her. What'll ya have, gentlemen?" Small talk was over for Shirley, she had customers waiting and that translated to paid rent and power bills.

"Give me a burger with everything except cheese, an order of fries and black coffee," Steve shot out.

Shirley looked at him narrowly and decided she couldn't pass up the opportunity to zing a lawyer. "Mr. Barclay, a burger without cheese is a hamburger, a burger with cheese is a cheeseburger. A cheeseburger costs more and that's why it's on the menu separately. Okay?"

Charlie burst out laughing and Shirley smiled broadly as Steve turned slightly pink and coughed.

Charlie smiled impishly, as Shirley looked at him expectantly and he said dryly, "I'll have a plain hamburger with pickle, onion, mustard and ketchup. An order of fries and a coffee."

Shirley took a double take and said, "Mr. Chambers, a plain hamburger doesn't have pickle, onions, ketchup or mustard on it, it's just plain. You just ordered a hamburger with everything."

Charlie smiled broadly and fired back, "I didn't want any cheese."

Shirley threw her hands up in the air and walked off, as Steve and Charlie began laughing again. *Lawyers*, she thought, *they just try to be difficult.*

Charlie shrugged off his laugh and said, "Well, I guess this afternoon I'd better be making travel arrangements."

"You leaving?"

"Yes, nothing left to do here. I can handle the rest from Illinois, just as well as Georgia. I'll come back for oral argument in the appellate court, but the rest I can handle long distance, with your help. I've been gone too long now. I have things to take care of back in Illinois.

"Besides, The Fund doesn't pay me to just sit around waiting for a judge to rule after the case is tried. Any one can do that, I get paid to argue, not to wait."

"The Fund, why do you call it that?" Steve questioned.

"Truthfully, I tried to come up with something else, so did the rest of the team, but we couldn't agree on anything. There are already so many defense funds it's ridiculous and we figured one more would just get lost in the shuffle. The Christian Defense Fund was already taken and I just couldn't think of any other combination of words that said what I did, but still sounded good. What words can you use to say that you go where and when you have to defending people's rights to worship? I tried them all and none suited me, so I just called it The Fund and now it's almost too late to change it. People are continuously sending donations to The Fund. If I changed it now, it would be too confusing. After every high profile case we get more donations, it's really catching on and I don't want to upset the apple cart.

"It doesn't matter what we call it as long as people identify with it and know what it does and what I do. It doesn't need a catchy name to work.

"Take your firm as an example. I didn't ask them to help me on this case, they volunteered. Why? Because they know who I am and what I do and they like the image. They knew that associating themselves with me would help their image. I get a lot of help for that very reason. I don't promise anyone anything. That's why a night in jail doesn't bother me."

Steve now asked, "Earlier you said 'team' as if there were more than one, are there?"

"Yes, but I'm the only lawyer at present. Back in Illinois I have a secretary, a computer research assistant and some good friends who counsel me from time to time about what cases to take and what cases to pass."

"A talent like you could make some big bucks, Charlie. Why do you travel around the country beating your head against walls that local judges build over petty issues?" Steve asked innocently, he was a brand new lawyer who was still looking toward what the law could do for him financially.

Charlie took no offense. His skin was tough from banging against all those walls the local judges built in his path. "At one time I did, but I saw the error of my ways. In the end, I realized that there are much more important things in life than money. It was a hard lesson, but I learned it, now I have a second chance at life.

"Now I use the law, and my skill, to serve other people and preserve their civil rights. I always have enough money to pay the bills, more than enough and if I didn't, I'd still do what I do. I don't expect you to understand, it's enough that lawyers like you are willing to help me, if only to improve their own public image."

Steve was quiet a moment and then he said, "Now I know why you get so fired up in court. You take this personally, don't you? You aren't objective the way most lawyers are regarding clients and their cases. Each case is personal to you. That's dangerous for a lawyer."

Charlie smiled a disarming smile and responded easily, "Dangerous for the average type of lawyer. Lawyers like you, Steve, but I'm not the average lawyer. Not that I'm any better or worse, but I just don't do things for the same reasons you and the rest of my brethren do. Yes, each case is personal to me, I do a better job of preparing and arguing these cases because of that. My personal involvement doesn't cloud my thinking; it sharpens it. I take these cases more seriously than any other lawyer would. They really mean something to me, my clients aren't just fees, they're people. The issues aren't abstract principles of law; they are real life religious experiences. You don't get more personal in my book."

Steve just nodded with thoughtfulness. It was evident to him that Charlie Chambers was a form of zealot, but he wasn't about to condemn him for it without further thought. Zealot or not, Charlie was one whale of an advocate, in and out of court. Steve wasn't about to condemn that.

Nodding now toward Carol Harmon's table, Charlie asked, "What's the story on her, Steve? If she's as hot as you say, what's she doing in this berg?"

"Just like you, Charlie, a court case. Last year, she was through here and her chauffer took a little detour, more like a frolic, in the company limousine. He blew a stop sign and t-boned a car at fifty miles per hour. Luckily no one was killed, but it banged up a couple of kids and their mother real good. They sued and since it was the company car, and Carol Harmon was the deep pocket, they sued her.

They sued the chauffer too, but he doesn't have any money, they're after that Harmon money. The chauffer is history, she canned him, personally, the next day, but that didn't stop the inevitable lawsuit. I think there may be some question about the mother contributing to the accident. It was a four-way stop and there is an indication she may have been distracted by the kids and rolled through her sign. Anyway, there was enough to argue about, that Carol Harmon's lawyers advised her not to settle. Maybe they just wanted to make a few bucks, I don't know, they are from out of town, too. No matter, that's her story.

"Why do you ask? I didn't think you were interested. You haven't so much as glanced her way since we came in here."

Charlie responded easily, "I'm not I guess. Just passing the time. Idle curiosity is all."

~ * ~

Across the room, partially shielded by her ever present circle of bodyguards, Carol Harmon picked slowly at the food on her plate and let her gaze wander around the cozy little café. Carol was used to being gawked at wherever she was, whatever she did. The only thing that aroused her curiosity any more was when she noticed someone who did not notice her. She wasn't vain, she didn't have a big head, she didn't feel that her presence was so irresistible that everyone should look at her all the time and bow to her every whim, but it worked out that way most of the time. *No, all the time*, she mused, *except this time*.

Carol had been looking across the on-looker's heads to the end of the counter at the two men seated there in business suits. One in an expensive business suit, the other in a clearly moderately priced suit and not well pressed. The expensive suit had been watching her, without seeming to watch her, but Carol knew the look. However, the moderate suit had never even looked her way, at least she hadn't noticed him looking and Carol generally noticed everything. He was a nice looking man in a rugged sort of way. Probably in his mid-thirties, she guessed and about one hundred eighty pounds. She saw him come in and he looked to be about six feet tall or maybe just a touch under that. His hair was dark brown and neatly cropped, not short, but not too long. When he had entered the café and walked to the counter she had surreptitiously watched him and he moved smoothly, with sureness in every step.

She didn't know why, but there was something about his disinterest that interested her. It was refreshing to see someone who didn't want to gawk at her. She wanted to be normal, but she couldn't. Could there exist a man who didn't and wouldn't fall over himself in her presence? She had always hoped such a man existed, somewhere.

Aside from the band members and other entertainment types she was forced to associate with, she had yet to meet a man who didn't practically swoon in her presence. Not that she asked for them to do that, or wanted them to do that, it just seemed to happen. She knew she was good looking, a knock out to use the vernacular. Twenty-nine, dark haired, a hundred thirty pounds, well shaped and well endowed in all the right places. A good combination, she knew, but she didn't laud that over people. It was useful in her profession, but at the same time it was a hindrance. Her combination of good looks and fame generally attracted all the wrong kind of men and even those men had a hard time getting close to her. With fame came isolation, out of necessity and that definitely had its drawbacks. Could this man really be different? How could she think that? She knew nothing of him. He was probably just a weirdo. She had no reason or basis to think anything of him, let alone that he might be something special. Besides, she had no reason to believe she would ever have the opportunity to find out more about him. Undoubtedly he would be just like all of the rest of the people in her life, he would pass her way and when he was gone he would warrant no further thought.

That was what she hated most about her life; she never got the chance to get to know anybody, except those she worked with, then only professionally. She loved her work, loved singing and entertaining people. The money was good and the fame was neat, but that was only a part of life, there was much more to life than money, fame and security. She was missing life; it was passing her by. Her fans had lives; everyone had lives, but not Carol. Her life was slipping away and there was nothing she could do about it.

~ * ~

Shirley was at the far end of the counter getting set up for the lunch crowd and trying to ignore the tumult surrounding her uninvited celebrity, albeit not necessarily unwelcome. Her cook was getting organized in the kitchen and the lunch waitress was just coming on duty.

"Hi, Shirl," the deep voice drew her attention up the counter a few seats and she saw the familiar face of Officer John Lanter as he plopped down on his favorite stool.

"Hey, John, what's the good word?" she asked amiably.

"Not much, did you hear the Preacher got slammed?"

"That's old news, I heard that last night already."

"Nawh. He made bail late last night on that one, but they slammed him again this morning."

"What! How come!" Shirley almost howled.

"Same old samo. He was passing out his pamphlets and preaching again. Of course he's done that for years now, but just lately the city has taken a dim view of his activities. Glad I wasn't on that detail. I like the Preacher."

"Yeah," Shirley responded absently, then continued, "what do you know about the Preacher, John?"

"Huh? Oh, not much. Same as everyone else I guess. He's been around forever and a day. Never hurts anybody and never really causes any trouble. Likes to preach and so when he isn't working, he preaches. He works up at the mill sweeping and cleaning up. I don't know that he ever had any other job or wanted one, he just minds his own business. He's clean, I mean he doesn't let his hair grow long and stringy, he wears decent clothes, poor but decent. No bad habits that I know of, except preaching and I don't see that as bad. I think the world could use more preachers, not less, no matter what they look like."

"No, I mean where did he come from? Any family? Any friends? What makes him tick?"

John shrugged his shoulders, grimaced in thought and answered, "Guess I don't know, Shirl. Don't know as I ever heard. I can't say as I know his real name, he's just the Preacher. Why?"

Shirley shrugged and answered, "Oh, no reason, just curious I guess. Seems odd so little is known about a man who has been around Johnson City so long."

John smiled and said, "Well now, Shirley, I figured you'd know more about the people in this city than me. You got more contacts than an electric train. You tell me, Shirley, what makes the Preacher tick?"

"Guess I got the wrong kind of contacts for that one, John," she replied with a far away look in her eyes and then asked, "What'll you have?"

Six

Shirley was worn out, it was eleven thirty and she had just closed her café. Slowly and tiredly, she was walking the few blocks to her small apartment. As she passed by the sheriff's department, she was almost sleep walking, she didn't see the man until he had hit her.

"Oh, I'm sorry ma'am. I didn't see you there. I just came out the door and didn't look, I'm sorry, you okay?"

Shirley was stunned. Having been run into by a man while half asleep hadn't done much for the regularity of her heartbeat. She peered through the dim light at the man and saw that his face was familiar.

"Miss Becker, oh, I am sorry," the Preacher said.

"You know my name?" Shirley was shocked again.

"Oh, yes, ma'am. I know almost everybody in town. Yes, ma'am, you own Shirley's Place. I've been by there lots, but I never was inside. I figured it was too nice of a place for the likes of me, ma'am."

"Shirley."

"Huh?"

"Call me Shirley. Ma'am makes me feel older than I know I am."

"Yes ma'... sorry... Shirley, and you're not old, at least not to me... I mean... I... bye, ma'am," Tommy stammered and shot off into the darkness before Shirley could say another word.

~ * ~

Fred Malone opened the inner cellblock door and waddled through. It had been a long time since he had done anything other than waddle through any door. He was too big and too old for street duty, so the sheriff had assigned him to jail duty. Fred was just filling out the last of his thirty years to retirement. The sheriff was good that way, but then it didn't hurt that Fred was his cousin. Fred smiled to himself, he knew that anything was fair in Georgia politics, especially local politics.

"Hey, Fred," the booking officer greeted him and continued, "all quiet in Steel City?"

"Yeah, it's so quiet I was starting to go to sleep, so I thought I'd better walk around."

"Slow here, too. The Preacher was the last customer I had and he was going the other way."

Fred leaned his heavy frame against the counter and asked, "Who do you suppose is making his bail? Twice in twenty-four hours no less?"

"Beats me, but you can bet it ain't Jerry Bales. He's bringing the money I hear, but he never had more than two nickels to rub together in any twenty-four hour period, let alone two hundred bucks. So whoever it is, it's not Jerry. Though if Jerry's getting paid as a courier he ought to be doing pretty well. I expect to see the Preacher back in here tomorrow sometime. He's not going to stop preaching, no matter what, he..."

A loud buzzing interrupted his dissertation, much to the joy of Fred. Fred had heard these dissertations go on for hours and he wasn't in the mood. Walking the cellblock to stay awake was better.

The booking officer turned in his chair and punched a button on his control panel. "Intake," he said into the intercom.

"Shirley Becker. Is that you Leon?"

With a broad smile, Leon replied, "Yeah, Shirl, what's up?"

"Oh, nothing much. I had some rolls left over from dinner and I thought you guys might be interested. I brought a little butter and honey, too. Is Fred in there?"

With a broadening smile that almost cracked his face, Leon replied, "You bet. Just a minute, Shirl." Leon pushed the door release and out of habit glanced at the monitor to see that only Shirley passed through the door.

Fred opened the inner intake door and Shirley waltzed in with a basket of what smelled like freshly baked rolls. Fred was barely able to contain himself, his weakness for Shirley's rolls had been partly to blame for his jail assignment. *But what a way to go*, he thought wryly.

Leon was almost drooling as Shirley set the basket on the booking counter and set out the butter, honey and a butter knife. Shirley wasn't authorized to come into the intake area, but when she had rolls they made an exception.

"Shirley, you're a peach. Marry me," Leon said, still drooling over the rolls.

Shirley laughed and said, "Not on your life, Leon, I'm not marrying no cop. I know what they're like. They never come home, they're moody, grumpy and likely to die young."

All three laughed as Shirley began laying out rolls for the two to butter, spread thick with honey and consume in less time than it took to say 'help yourself'.

"All kidding aside boys, I heard the Preacher was in the slam."

"Was," Leon mumbled through the remnants of his second roll.

"Was?"

"Yeah, he made bail about an hour ago. Well, he didn't, but somebody put it up for him. Twice in twenty-four hours," Fred put in, just before he jammed an entire roll into his mouth.

"He must not be in much trouble then if you guys let him bail out every few hours," Shirley said with a chuckle.

Leon was poised to jam another roll into his mouth when he stopped to explain, "It ain't us, Shirl. We don't care. We like the Preacher. It's the judge. I don't expect Judge Ferrell is going to take kindly to the Preacher getting slammed for the same thing twice in less than twenty-four hours. Ferrell is kind of funny about stuff like that.

"Once is okay, he'd give the Preacher supervision, probably, but not twice in twenty-four hours. Old Ferrell is going to treat that like contempt of cop or worse, contempt of court maybe and he's going to slam the Preacher for a good long while. Up to a year on each offense, but probably just one full year with no early release. Too bad too, because we really like the Preacher," Leon ended and stuffed the whole roll into his mouth so as to get another one in his hand before Fred finished them all.

"I didn't realize it was that serious. He's just doing what he's always done," Shirley said wistfully.

Carefully eyeing Leon, who was grabbing the second from the last roll, Fred said, "It's always been illegal, Shirl, but no one cared to enforce it against the Preacher. The new mayor doesn't like him and the city is going to keep rousting him until he stops, which isn't going to happen. I'll bet he's back in here by tomorrow suppertime. He won't quit; he doesn't know anything else, except cleaning and sweeping at the mill.

"The problem is that if he gets popped too many times, on the same offense, old Judge Ferrell is likely to slam him for a felony. Now in here it's no sweat. We all like him. He'll get good treatment in here. Be the best year he's ever spent, probably, but the state pen, now that's different. Can't help him there," Fred finished as he snatched the last roll just as Leon's hand was moving toward the plate.

Shirley eyed the empty basket, the half empty honey jar and the last ounce of the quarter pound of butter with amazement. How could two guys consume a dozen rolls that fast? Amazing, just amazing. It was no wonder that Fred could barely fit through the cellblock door.

Gathering up her basket and the remains of the honey, she said, "Well, I have to be up early, guess I had better be going." Then, as if it were an after thought, she turned back and asked, "The Preacher, what's his name any how, nobody knows?"

"Tommy Trenton. I didn't know it either until I booked him yesterday morning." With pride the booking officer pulled out his register and read off, "Tommy Trenton, 211 N. Adams, Apt 3F, date of birth, is February 14, 1948. Now you know as much as we do, Shirl."

Shirley had known the name, but not the address and now she had that. Rolls loosened a cop's tongue better than alcohol on an empty stomach. Turning back toward the door, she said over her shoulder, "See ya guys," as Fred hurried to pull open the door for her.

"Thanks, Shirl," Leon and Fred said in unison.

Shirley just smiled as she passed on through to the outer intake door.

~ * ~

That next morning, Charlie crossed to the front window of his apartment. He had been in Johnson City for two months now, so long that he had taken an apartment just to avoid paying so much in motel bills. He supposed he technically could have gone home for two or three weeks during the time he was here, but he felt compelled to stay. He liked to get the feel of a place before arguing a case. Jumping back and forth between states was not a good way to maintain the continuity he needed in his thinking.

In each case he tried to become a part of the area and a part of the case. Like he had told Steve, these cases were personal to him and he liked it that way.

From his second story downtown apartment he had a good view of the street below. Far down on one end, by the corner, he could see people milling about. One person seemed to be directing his attention toward the others who were milling around him. *A peddler maybe*, Charlie thought, *not an accident or anything*. Everyone was standing up and the group was not knotted tightly like people do when they are crowding in to see an accident or someone down.

He continued to watch and after a few minutes he thought he had been wrong about there not being an injury, because a police car pulled up and stopped. He decided it must have been an accident or some sort of crime, but from this distance he couldn't see anything amiss. Moments later the crowd parted and Charlie saw the policeman escort the person in the center out and to his car. *A drunk maybe*, Charlie then decided. Some sort of criminal, since the policeman was very obviously arresting the man, or at the very least transporting him somewhere. *Curious*, he mused.

Since he was leaving soon, Charlie decided it was time to look about the country. He had never been to Georgia before and all he had done this trip was lock himself away in the firm's law library, study, write and go to court. This morning he was going to change that. Life was too short. He wanted to at least experience Georgia from somewhere other than a library or courtroom. So he was going to get into that little Geo Metro he had rented when he first arrived and hadn't needed except to get to Johnson City from the airport, and go for a drive in the hills.

The hills looked cool and inviting from the cramped Geo Metro, especially cool since the Geo didn't have any air-conditioning. Charlie hadn't been after comfort when he rented the car and he hadn't gotten it, but he didn't need much. Following State Route three out of town to the north he saw that a gravel road turned off and proceeded up into the hills. On impulse he took it and though the Geo had a tough time of it getting to the top of the hill, he finally made it. To his right he saw a partially cleared area and by the looks of the place it was a sort of park, so he whipped the car in and pulled to a stop under a shade tree.

After getting out of the car and looking carefully around, he realized this was not a park, but rather just a place where cars had parked and littered. Across the semi-cleared parking area he could just make out the remnants of a building of some sort. Out of curiosity he wandered over that way. *It is at least cool here*, he decided. A gentle breeze was blowing through the tall pines and, keeping in the shade, Charlie found the area quite comforting. He walked completely around the structure, trying to discern what it was, or had been. Not much was left. Obviously it had burned down. There were some charred timbers, some fire cracked bricks and part of a stone foundation. He was heavily pondering what it had been, lost in thought.

"You're on hallowed ground, you know," a voice from just behind Charlie said evenly and seriously.

Charlie nearly jumped out of his skin. He hadn't the foggiest idea anyone else was even near this place, let alone near him. His heart skipped three times before he gathered himself and turned around to see a strikingly lovely young woman dressed in tight fitting blue jeans and an equally tight fitting short sleeved denim top. Carol Harmon.

Seven

Overcoming his initial shock, Charlie finally asked of the woman, "I'm sorry, you said something about the ground?"

"I said you are standing on hallowed ground."

"What's that supposed to mean?" Charlie responded, with just a touch of an edge to his voice. He wasn't thrilled about being startled by anyone, even if it was Carol Harmon, the good-looking superstar. *No, extremely fine looking superstar*, he quickly corrected himself. Begrudgingly, he admitted that she was even better looking up close, which was unusual in and of itself and she looked very alluring in her faded jeans.

Taking a step closer to Charlie, Carol continued, waving her left arm toward the burned out hulk. "That's a church, or was a church, thirty-five years ago. It was burned to the ground with a hundred people inside of it. No one survived. This place is hallowed ground now."

Charlie twisted up his face into a partial grimace, looked around the cleared area and said, "From the looks of the place, the litter and all, you are the only one who considers it hallowed anything. Looks to me like everyone else just uses it as a dumping ground."

Looking deeply into his eyes—*blue*, she thought, *maybe gray*—Carol persisted, "Just the same, it's hallowed ground. Any place Christian people die in faith is hallowed. I can't account for the other people in the area. How they treat the place or what they think of it. Take my word for it, this is a sacred place."

"Okay, I'll bite, what's it to you? You say it happened over thirty-five years ago, long before you were born, I'll wager. Kinfolk of yours, not friends, not before you were born. What's the connection?"

"You're right. I wasn't born yet, but I have friends who had friends in there," she ended with another wave of her hand toward the rubble.

"Whatever," Charlie stated and continued, changing the subject, "how did you get out without your goon squad?"

Testily, she shot back, "I don't have a goon squad! I have bodyguards!"

"Purely semantics, Miss Harmon. To you they're bodyguards, to me they're goons."

"Anyone ever tell you how irritating you can be?" she responded.

Charlie laughed then and answered truthfully, "Yes, all the time, but you haven't answered my question. I wouldn't think a superstar would be allowed to walk around without protection."

"I do what I want, when I want! And just how did you know my name?"

Sarcastically, baiting her just a little, Charlie answered, "Why everyone knows the great Carol Harmon, superstar and country singing legend. Besides, someone pointed you out to me this morning and yesterday afternoon. Before that I didn't know you from any other singer. Never had heard of you. Never wanted to."

Fuming now, Carol said hotly, "I take back what I said earlier, you aren't irritating, you are rude and insulting!"

Charlie was stung by the retort. He realized she was right, he was being rude and insulting and she had given him no call to be that way. He admitted to himself that he had prejudged her based upon fleeting observations over the previous day and he had no right. He of all people should be disinclined to prejudge anyone. He often railed against others for doing just that. Mildly, and with a contrite look on his face, he responded sincerely, "Yes, you're right, I'm sorry Miss Harmon, I'll be on my way and leave you to your solitude." With that said he turned and walked away.

Carol watched his back intently as he walked back to his car. He was the same man she had seen in the café yesterday and figured never to see again. She had never met a man who could get under her skin like that man had just done. It was more than the fact that he had been intentionally irritating. It was something in his eyes, his face, his mannerisms—something there spoke to her, but she couldn't understand it. There was more to this man than an irritating attitude. When contrite, he looked mighty handsome she decided.

When the car had left the cleared area and turned onto the gravel road, Carol turned and walked back through the woods. She had been gone longer than she anticipated, and if they discovered she had taken a walk in the woods, without her bodyguards... what did he call them? *Goon squad*, she thought with a smile. Maybe he was closer to the truth than she cared to admit. At any rate, she would have to suffer a lecture from her manager if she were caught. Caught... she cringed at the word, but it seemed appropriate. *How did I get to this point?* she asked herself. Lately it seemed she got more and more of those lectures. She knew Dan Chase was good for her career, he had been a good business manager, but he was a little over-bearing at times, a little overly protective. Sometimes Carol felt as though she were ten years old and had to ask Daddy for permission to do everything.

~ * ~

Back on State Route three and heading for Johnson City, Charlie was still irritated with himself. He had been boorish, to say the least, to that woman and that was not his style. No matter that he thought she might be spoiled, or have a better than thou attitude, he should not have acted that way. It was like saying something to someone in the heat of the moment and immediately regretting you had said it and wishing with all your heart that you could take it back. Knowing you couldn't. The worst part was that he would not get a chance to let her see him in a better light. Sure he had apologized, but that wasn't the point. He was better than he had acted and for some reason he wanted her to know that.

~ * ~

The young man walked out of the First Bank of Georgia with a broad smile on his face and lightly fingered the crisp bills in his right-hand pants pocket. Not thirty minutes ago he had left courtroom three-A of the Meridian County courthouse a free man, his fine paid in full and a three hundred-dollar bond refund slip. He had promptly displayed the bond refund slip at the circuit clerk's office and obtained a check for the full three hundred. His next stop had been the First Bank of Georgia to turn his check into cash. After the deduction of a three-dollar check cashing fee and the payment of another one hundred fifty-dollar fee, he would still net one hundred and forty-seven dollars. On top of that, his five hundred-dollar fine was paid in full. *Almost worth getting slammed for*, he ruefully thought and continued to finger the money in his pocket, as he turned the corner for home.

~ * ~

Jeannie Rosmund was still in shock. *What would she do without Gene Petrowski?* Gene had been more than her right-hand man. He had done it all. Jeannie was a politician. She smiled at people and joked with them when they came into the circuit clerk's office, but she didn't do anything for them, not really. If they came in with a problem, she didn't solve it. It was always artfully given to Gene, who was a wizard at solving any problem, or to some other employee if Gene wasn't around. If Gene had a fault it was that he was too good, he could easily have taken her job. *No, she immediately decided, Gene was no politician and he never had wanted to be. He was what he was and he didn't want to be anything more.*

The people of Meridian County didn't know what they had lost, but Jeannie did and now she had a problem. For almost four years she had been the circuit clerk and no one had ever suspected, at least none of the general public, that she didn't know the first thing about the office. She either had to learn the office quickly or find someone else in the office to take Gene's place.

She had an election campaign to gear up for this fall and didn't have time to learn how the office should be run. The fact that she was running for an office and representing that she knew how to run it, when she didn't, didn't seem unnatural to her at all. After all, didn't all politicians do that? Politicians were politicians, they didn't really have to know how an office worked, just so long as they knew how politics worked.

~ * ~

Todd and Sam sat silently at their respective desks in the office. Each was busy with his own thoughts as they read the lab reports and the coroner's report. Todd was also reviewing the field notes he had made upon arrival at the scene of the suicide a couple of days ago.

For the longest time all that could be heard was an occasional cough, the slurp from a sip of coffee and the rustle of pages as they were turned. Sam finished reading his copies first and stacked them neatly, but quietly. He stared off in space, contemplating, as he waited for Todd to finish reading.

The morning was young yet and there was almost no noise from outside the room as Sam waited and contemplated. In an hour or so the noise level would increase as the administrative day shift arrived for work. The day shift patrol had already changed, although it only accounted for two deputy sheriffs in two patrol cars.

In the near silence, Sam enjoyed the peace and let his gaze rove around the small room, as he quietly sipped his coffee. The room wasn't much, but it was theirs. He and Todd were the only sheriff's investigators and in this small, normally quiet county, two were enough. Things were so slow that they usually worked the same hours or when one was called out the other got a call, too. Business for the investigators wasn't so brisk that they needed to hide from work. They both enjoyed what they did, for the most part, however, Todd was much more intense than Sam.

Todd was also several years younger than Sam and younger cops usually had more enthusiasm than the older ones. Todd had his 'causes', which were characteristic of younger policemen. Sam had been in the business long enough to have abandoned his 'causes' in favor of survival and no ulcers.

When Todd dropped his feet from the corner of the desk and onto the floor, Sam looked up expectantly and asked, "What do you make of it?"

Todd stacked his papers, less neatly than Sam and responded thoughtfully, "Sure looks like a suicide all right, almost too much."

"What does that mean?" Sam asked.

"What if someone is trying to make a murder look like suicide?"

Sam arched his eyebrows, narrowed his eyes and responded, "I suppose it's possible and I'm sure it's happened before, but never around here. We hardly get any murders, let alone any murders meant to look like suicides. You got something to base that guess on or are you just hoping?"

"One thing that doesn't fit as far as I see it. The note."

"What note?" Sam asked in a puzzled tone then continued, "There was no note. Was there?"

"That's just it Sam. Why wasn't there a note?"

Sam shrugged and continued to look puzzled. "I don't know! Who says there has to be a note! People do kill themselves without leaving a note, you know."

"Sure they do, but usually in those cases it's clear why they did it. They were in some deep trouble and everyone knew it, but here we have nothing. As near as I can see, this Merriman had absolutely no reason to kill himself and I think, until we find the reason, we can't rule out murder."

Sam scratched his chin thoughtfully, as he leaned back in his chair and finally said, "Okay, maybe you've got something and maybe you don't. How do we find out why he killed himself?"

"First we check with his doctor, if he had one. Then we check with his neighbors, friends and relatives. Let's see if he had any health problems. Then we'll check with his bank to see if he had any financial problems. Let's talk to anybody and everybody who knew anything about him, co-workers, friends, neighbors, ex-girl friends, anyone. Someone has to have some indication or some information pointing to the reason he killed himself. People don't do that without a reason. If there isn't a reason, then it wasn't suicide, it was murder."

Sam nodded thoughtfully and pronounced, "Okay, I like that. Maybe we can find something that will nail this down. If we can find a motive for suicide there will be little doubt this case should be closed. Besides, it'll give us something to do. It has been a little slow lately."

~ * ~

Unlike Todd and Sam, the morning was very old for Shirley Becker. Her morning started at four thirty a.m. The breakfast crowd was already easing off by the time Todd and Sam had finished reviewing their reports. As Charlie Chambers watched an unidentified man being arrested from his apartment window, Shirley watched the same arrest from a corner window of her café. She had stopped briefly to down a fast cup of coffee, her twelfth this morning.

Shirley was closer to the arrest than Charlie Chambers, she knew who was being arrested, he wasn't just some unidentified man to her. Even if she had been as far away as Charlie's apartment, she would have known the man's identity; she had watched him from afar for too many years not to recognize him at a distance or even at night. The Preacher was going down again. Dismayed, she turned from the window and surveyed her little café, it wasn't much, but it kept a roof over her head and that was more than the Preacher had. At least more than the Preacher had for the first twenty years of his life and he had little more now.

Nothing to be done for him, she supposed. What was it that the boys had said over at the jail? Three times and Judge Ferrell would likely elevate him to a felon—and that meant Statesville. She almost cried, and had she not been so toughened by years of making it on her own, she probably would have. She knew that crying wouldn't do any good, she had learned that lesson long ago, instead she prayed. There was nothing else that would do any good now, not for the Preacher and not for her. What the Preacher needed now, she couldn't give him.

Shirley worked on through the morning without more thought to anyone's troubles, but her own. Before she knew it, the lunch crowd had appeared and now was waning.

The front door opened for the one hundredth time this day and she looked up just as Charlie Chambers walked through the door. He had been in her café only a few times during his stay in Johnson City. The time he came in with Steve Barclay was the only time she saw him converse with anyone. Shirley had figured him for just another stuffed-shirt lawyer, but he hadn't come off that way when he was with Barclay the other morning. Maybe she was wrong, but she now figured him for a quiet, reserved and determined man, who rarely got the opportunity to laugh.

She had the distinct feeling that, over the years of his life, he had traveled some hard roads. Generally, Shirley had good instincts about people; she had met them all in her café at one time or another and categorizing them became her only pastime.

She saw that Charlie had found a stool about half way down the counter and she glided up to him, waving off the waitress who was making her way down from the other end of the counter.

"Morning, Mr. Chambers, still with us I see."

"Morning, Mrs. Becker, yes, for a few hours more."

"It's Miss Becker, never tied the knot," Shirley responded dryly.

"Oh, sorry, I figured someone who cooked as good as you would be married for sure."

"I'm sorry, too," she responded honestly and continued "my own fault mostly though. I'm too busy in here and with my church to have time for courting."

Charlie smiled and replied knowingly, "That's no excuse Miss Becker, there's always time for romance," he ended with a wink.

"Please call me Shirley, and at my age romance isn't what it used to be."

Charlie gave her an appraising look for the first time and confirmed that Shirley was far from over the hill. True, she was in her forties from all appearances, but her short hair was still black with no hint of gray. Her face was wrinkle free, except for some slight crows' feet at the corners of her eyes. She was far from being plain, and for someone who worked around food all day, she had very obviously resisted over-indulging. Her figure wasn't slight, but it was by no means too heavy. She was what most men would consider just about right, and a good cook, too. She also had a personality with just the right amount of humor.

Shirley sensed his appraisal and she flushed slightly from his frank stare. After another moment she asked lightly, "Well, Mr. Chambers, do I measure up?"

Charlie flushed slightly at that and chuckled, answering, "I'm sorry, Shirley. And yes, you do. I think your story about being too busy is a cover up. Church is as good a place to meet a good man as anywhere, in fact, it is better than most places. I don't buy your story.

I think you just haven't found him yet. When you do, you'll find the time. He won't let you not find the time. He'd be crazy if he did."

Shirley smiled broadly and responded with a laugh, "Mr. Chambers, I'm going to miss you. You're good for a woman's ego. Any woman ever told you that before?"

"Yes, but it's been a long time," he answered wistfully, with a far away look in his eyes.

Shirley watched him for a few seconds and then said, "You miss her a lot, don't you?"

Nodding affirmatively, he answered firmly, "I do and I think I'll add mind reading to your qualities, Shirley."

Shirley smiled, whirled to the rear of the counter and turned back with an empty cup and a pot of coffee in her hand. Without slowing perceptively, she set the cup down and filled it to the brim with piping hot coffee. As if she had never turned away, she continued the conversation, "Wife?"

"Huh?" Charlie's brain hadn't caught up with Shirley's movements.

She smiled mischievously, set the pot on the counter, leaned forward and whispered, "The woman you miss so much, your wife?"

Sadly, he responded, "Yes."

The way he said it gave Shirley the distinct impression that any conversation on this subject was over so she changed the subject, "Where's home?"

"Home is in Illinois."

"What exactly do you do? I know you're a lawyer, but I thought lawyers pretty much went where they wanted, whenever they wanted."

"Some do I guess, but not me, not all the time. I go where I'm needed and I stay as long as I'm needed."

Charlie had been glancing over the menu while they talked, but he didn't know why. He was planning to have a nice thick hamburger with everything and a side order of onion rings. His doctor told him that he shouldn't eat onions, but his motto had always been that everyone has to die of something and you might as well go with a smile on your face. Besides, no one said 'no' when God called and

Charlie figured God wouldn't call until He was ready for him, onions or not.

"So what'll ya have, Mr. Chambers?" Shirley finally asked.

"Call me Charlie, and I'll have a hamburger with everything and a side order of onion rings," as he said the latter, he smiled inwardly and thought, *take that Doc.*

Shirley didn't budge, she just turned sideways and yelled out the order as she grabbed up the coffeepot again. Spinning back to refill Charlie's coffee, she picked up their conversation again. "Charlie, what happens when you get arrested three time in two days for the same thing?"

Charlie raised his eyebrows; he thought there was a reason that Shirley was being so talkative this morning. He could usually see them coming. Those times when someone was going to tap him for some free legal advice, there was a loose pattern leading up to the question. A friendly, chatty time and then, bang. He really didn't mind, after all, he mostly gave free legal service anyway. Generally the question asked of him he couldn't answer anyway, because it wasn't his area of expertise, and this was no exception.

After sipping his coffee, he said over his cup, "Depends on what the arrests were for and the law where you were arrested. You planning on getting arrested a lot, Shirley?"

"No, not me, but I know someone who has and the people over at the jail, I know them and take them food sometimes, they said three times and the judge could make it a felony. Is that true?"

Charlie shrugged and said, "I don't know anything about Georgia law. I came down here to try a case with the help of a local lawyer, Steve Barclay. Ask him."

"No, it's no matter, I was just curious, thought you might know. Guess I should have figured you wouldn't, being an Illinois lawyer in Georgia and all," Shirley said with dismay.

Charlie felt her disappointment and volunteered, "Generally speaking, it's a bit more complicated than the judge arbitrarily making it a felony, Shirley. Some states, Georgia might be one, have special laws that allow a judge to sentence a repeat offender to more jail time than he would normally get."

"I see," Shirley said, even more dismayed.

"I'm not saying that would be true in Georgia or in your case, but it could be. That's generally the way it works and if the jailers say a misdemeanor can be made into a felony, then that leads me to believe that Georgia has such a habitual criminal law. Sorry to be the bearer of bad news."

Charlie watched Shirley as she retrieved his hamburger from the kitchen window. Her spirit seemed to be gone and she was deflated like a tire with a nail in it. Now it was his turn to be intuitive.

Shirley set the plate in front of him and he asked, "Known him long?"

"Huh?"

"That man you asked me about, the one who has been arrested three times in two days. Known him long?"

"Who said it was a man?"

Charlie smiled and answered, "Your eyes told me, Shirley. And the way your mouth started dragging on the floor after I told you how it works. A good friend?"

"Oh, not really, just a man I know or know of, I guess. He doesn't know of me, but I know of him and I think he's better than he gets around this town."

"I see," Charlie said as he dug into his onion rings.

"Charlie, exactly what type of law do you practice?"

"I specialize in civil rights cases, mostly religious rights."

"You mean if you heard of a civil rights case or that someone was being denied a right of some sort you'd come running?"

"Not quite. I only go where I'm led."

Shirley had been around the block a few times and she was always just a little skeptical when anyone talked about being led somewhere. *Led how*, she wondered. *What was Charlie talking about?* She decided to find out. "What precisely do you mean when you say you're led?" was the cautious question.

Charlie detected the cautious note in her voice and smiled, saying, "Oh, I don't know myself. I just get these feelings; things seem to happen to me, I don't know how or why. I wind up in the right place at the right time, defending the right person. I never know for sure until I'm there."

Shirley wasn't sure about this. She liked Charlie, but she wasn't sure about a guy who believed that he was led around the country by feelings and strange occurrences. *What strange occurrences,* she wondered.

At least Charlie didn't insist that God talked to him. That would have been more than she could take. She had met a couple of evangelists who thought that way and she hadn't been impressed. Charlie seemed genuine enough though. He really believed what he was saying, even if he might be mistaken. More than likely he just took interesting cases he happened to hear about; then, looking back, he convinced himself that he had been led to the case. *That was more like it,* she decided.

Now it was Charlie's turn to get information from Shirley and he asked, "Shirley, you know anything about Carol Harmon?"

Leaning on the counter with both elbows, she looked seriously at Charlie and responded, "Why of course. She's a big time country singer, famous all over the world in fact, she was in here yesterday, don't you remember? You was here."

"That much I know or have been told, but I mean do you know anything about her, personally, where does she come from?"

Shirley looked baffled and said, "Why she comes from right here. Born and raised on the south side of town, now she lives up above Burning Chapel Hill. I figured you knew that. Everyone knows that. That's why she's getting sued here, she lives here, she was back visiting when her man got in that wreck. I ain't been around here long, but I know the local history, never knew her myself personally, but I heard the talk.

"And the talk is she is not only a fine singer, but a fine person, too. Ain't at all what she seems first off, I guess. Real down to earth when and if she gets the chance, which she don't get much I hear 'cause of her manager. He keeps a tight rein on her. She's his money machine. He's a local, too. Name of Dan Chase, been around here all his life. Got a mean streak in him though, so they say."

Charlie persisted, "How old is she, married, kids?"

"Can't say as I know, besides those are the kinds of things you ought to ask in person, of the person, Mr. Chambers."

"From what you say, Shirley, the manager wouldn't approve of that and besides I doubt I'll see her again, I was just curious."

"You flying out tonight?"

"Yes."

"Then you'll see her again. Only one flight out of the airport over at Thomasville and that's at six o'clock. She's flying out tonight, too. She could afford her own plane I guess, but likes going commercial for some reason. Now an enterprising, sharp lawyer like you ought to be able to figure out a way to get through that barrier of men surrounding her."

Charlie did not respond, but he was thinking. The gears in his brain were starting to mesh and he felt a great anticipation. Why he didn't know. He had no reason to anticipate meeting Carol Harmon again, except to show her he really was not the obnoxiously rude person she had seen the last time they met. Although he doubted she cared and he wasn't sure why he should.

Eight

Todd and Sam were back in their office poring over more documents. This time, the documents had been obtained from the First National Bank of Georgia, Johnson City branch. Todd had just executed a court order obtaining all of Corey Merriman's bank records.

Sam tossed a stack of papers onto his desk and muttered, "Nothing wrong with this guy's finances. Looks to me like he was pretty well fixed."

"Yeah. Look here, Sam," Todd said, leaning over with his finger on a portion of a bank statement and continuing, "a deposit of twenty-five hundred bucks on the second, a thousand bucks on the fifteenth and another thou' on the twenty-fifth. Every month, just like clockwork, for the past five years. That's a mighty good retirement plan."

"Can't be all retirement, Todd, retirement plans pay a set amount once a month. This guy was getting three checks a month, must have had another source of income. A job? Investments?" Sam pondered out loud, rubbing his chin with his left hand.

"Guess it doesn't matter, Sam. He wasn't having financial difficulties and so that rules out one more motive for suicide. Unless..." his voice trailed off.

Sam perked up and asked, "Unless what?"

"Oh, nothing much. It's just that he could have been investing in some high risk securities and lost big time. If that were the case, it wouldn't show up on these statements, because he didn't live to make any records. Pretty slim, but we ought to rule it out."

"How?"

"Let's run up to Merriman's house and have another look around. Maybe something will turn up in his desk drawers or maybe there's a filing cabinet. We might turn some paperwork that would tell us if he were into investments or whether or not he had another job."

"I'm game," Sam pronounced, dropped his feet to the floor and stood.

~ * ~

"Look here, Todd," Sam said from a chair he had pulled up to a large file drawer in Merriman's desk.

Todd dropped his handful of useless, paid bills and walked across the study to the drawer Sam was indicating. As he reached the desk Sam was pulling out handfuls of paper saying, "Check stubs. Company check stubs. The amounts match the deposits. See... here's one for twenty-five hundred from Tieman Textile Mill, he worked there didn't he?"

Todd took the stub in his hand and answered, "Yeah, supposedly retired a few years ago. Yeah, this must be a retirement check, see it says retirement fund on the stub."

"Okay, but what about these others? A thousand bucks on a company called TBM, stands for Tanner Business Machines and another for a thousand from a company called Thomas T. MacIntire, Inc. They match the other deposits. Did this guy have two other jobs?"

Todd shook his head and pursed his lips thoughtfully. "Nawh, not for that amount of money. Not enough hours in the day for him to make that kind of money on two other jobs. The amounts and timing are regular enough to be payroll checks, but the stubs don't indicate that they are payroll checks. Look here..." Todd pointed to one of the stubs and continued, "This one says per invoice number three two five six. Payroll stubs don't read like that. It's almost like this Merriman was selling something to this TBM company and submitted an invoice for payment. But why the same amount every month, at the same time every month?"

"Beats me, makes no sense to me except that it doesn't look like a motive for suicide."

"Right and nothing else around here does either. What say we run up to the mill and see if anyone knows anything? Maybe someone up there can give us a lead. Merriman was pretty high up, could be the pressure got to him. Those higher ups never really retire. He could have been a consultant. Maybe that's what he was doing for these other companies."

"Wait a minute. What's this?" Sam said, holding up what looked like an accounting ledger book.

Todd took it, opened it to a random page and scanned it. He whistled softly saying, "This looks like an accounts received book, not receivable, but received and the amounts are different from the bank statements. Up here at the top is an account number, but no bank is indicated. This guy was dropping ten thousand a month into this account, sometimes more, but never less. Not recently though. The entries stop this time two years ago. Here's another account though, with recent deposits." He looked at Sam with a puzzled, questioning look.

Todd's look elicited an immediate response from Sam, "Gambling?"

Todd shook his head in the negative. "I don't think so, Sam. The figures are just too close to the same."

"But if you were gambling big and lost, that would be a good reason to dump yourself," Sam insisted.

"Maybe, but why are the entries so consistent? Gambling is a lot of things, but it sure isn't consistent. Let's go up to the mill, if he was a gambler, someone up there would be likely to know it," Todd finished, sticking the book under his arm and heading across the room.

Sam tossed the check stubs back into the drawer, slammed it shut and trailed after Todd. He knew from experience that once Todd got an idea into his head it was no good to do anything except follow along. He was like a Pit Bull with his teeth buried in the leg of an intruder—until he satisfied himself that what he had wasn't worth holding on to, he would continue to hold on.

Sam made sure the front door was secured while Todd went ahead and started the car. Just as Sam dropped into his seat and grabbed for his seat belt the car lurched forward.

It was only a short drive up to the mill from Merriman's. Probably no more than ten minutes, if you took the time to enjoy the scenery—and it was clear that Todd wasn't taking the time to view any scenery. Sam sat silently and watched as the pine trees all but flew by. Rocks spewed left and right behind the car and rattled inside the wheel wells as Todd cut the time to the mill in half.

Todd slowed and turned into the private drive leading up to the main entrance of the mill. A sign on the security shack proclaimed, "Main Gate, Tieman Textile Mill, No Trucks." A security guard stepped out of the little shack as they approached and Todd braked the car to a stop.

"Yes, sir, can I help you?" the guard asked, in an abrupt manner.

Todd flipped out his badge and said, "Sergeant Evans and this is Sergeant Pinehurst. Meridian County Sheriff's Department."

"Okay, what can I do for you?"

"We'd like to talk to someone about Corey Merriman. We're investigating his death."

The guard responded dryly, "Yeah, heard about that. Too bad, nice guy Mr. Merriman was, but do you have an appointment with someone in particular? We don't just let anyone wander around the place, you know."

Todd hesitated, then responded calmly, "Well, no. We just need to talk to someone who knew him and who might give us some information about why he would kill himself."

The guard nodded and said, "Let me make a call. Just a minute." He spun on his heels and entered the guard shack.

Todd and Sam watched as he held an animated conversation with someone. In a few minutes the guard came back and said, "The chief of security says to see him. Maybe he can steer you to the right place. Drive straight ahead and stop at the headquarters building on your right. Dan Mosley is chief of security. Tell the receptionist you're here to see him. She'll show you how to find him."

Todd nodded and said, "Thanks."

"Anytime," the guard replied as Todd pulled through the gate and slowly made his way to the headquarters building. It was a fairly long drive up to the headquarters building and Sam looked around as they drove. TTM was a good-sized place and employed a lot of people around Johnson City. Johnson City wasn't quite a company town, but sometimes it seemed so. There was little doubt that the mill was the major employer in the county and Sam could feel the power and persuasion of that position as they approached the six-story headquarters building. The mill was more than just this plant. There were two more Tieman Textile Mill facilities in the state of Georgia and the benefit to the economy was tremendous. The police and everyone else walked softly up here, but fortunately, the mill was generally cooperative.

Todd found a parking place not too far from the front door and they sauntered up as though they knew what they were about, when in fact, neither of them had ever had occasion to be here before.

Inside, the receptionist asked them to have a seat while she called the security chief to tell him they had arrived. Not two minutes later the receptionist escorted them through a set of double glass doors and down a wide hallway to a door proclaiming, "Dan Mosley, Chief of Security." The sign left no doubt in Sam's mind that this man held an important position. There was also little doubt that his reach was farther and more effective than theirs when it came to the mill and any of its business affairs.

Once through the door to Mosley's office, they encountered yet another secretary. She again asked them to have a seat until Mr. Mosley could see them. She assured them it would only be a minute or two. True to her word, in less than two minutes, her intercom buzzed and after she hung up the phone, she announced to them that Mr. Mosley would see them now.

They were ushered into a very expansive office with a large plate glass window. In front of the window was an exquisite oak desk and behind it sat a man in his middle forties dressed in a dark business suit. The man rose as they entered and extended his hand across the desk saying, "Afternoon, deputies. Dan Mosley. Please have a seat." He waved them to a pair of large leather chairs facing the desk.

Once they were seated, Mosley took his seat and asked, "What can I do for you?"

Todd began, "We're investigating the death of Corey Merriman. It appears that he committed suicide in his basement a few days ago. I'm sure you are aware of that."

"Yes. I read about it in the papers. Heard some talk around the mill, too. This is supposed to be a textile mill, but sometimes I think it's a rumor mill in disguise," Mosley finished disarmingly.

Todd nodded knowingly. Liking the way this was going, he continued, "Mr. Mosley..."

Mosley held up his hand and cut him off, "Dan. Please call me Dan. We're basically in the same business, different employers, but the same business. You're interested in security out there and I'm interested in security in here." As he finished, he made a sweeping motion with his right arm toward the window behind him that commanded a good view of the mill.

Smiling now and feeling even more comfortable, Todd started again, "Okay... Dan... can you tell us anything about Corey Merriman?"

Dan shrugged and asked, "Like what?"

Sam sat quietly as Todd continued, "We're trying to find the reason he killed himself. So far we've drawn a blank. We don't really have any reason to suspect foul play, but we just can't find a motive for suicide. He wasn't depressed, according to neighbors. His doctor says he was in very good health for his age, no bad habits. His finances look good. From what we can find he was getting a fat retirement from the mill and had income on the side from at least two other sources." Todd consulted his notebook and continued, "He was getting a thousand a month from a company called TBM and another thou' a month from Thomas T. MacIntire, Inc. Doesn't seem as though he had any financial woes. I guess he was a consultant for you and those other companies, huh? I mean that's a lot of retirement pay, even for an assistant VP of research and development."

Dan narrowed his eyes in thought and said candidly, "Yeah, that's good take home all right. About right for an assistant VP though and I suspect he was consulting on the side. Most of our retired execs do that and we don't care so long as they don't reveal any trade secrets. Corey wouldn't have done that, he was straight."

Sam now put in, "No gambling or carousing?"

"Why ask that?" Dan shot back.

Sam shrugged and responded evenly, "No reason, just checking all the angles. We can't leave any stones unturned. You know how that goes."

Dan nodded knowingly, leaned back against his high backed chair and said, "Yeah and no. I mean he wasn't a gambler or carouser. He took a lot of business trips, some I went on and some I set up security on, when he went out of the country. That's not carousing though and as far as I know he never detoured from his job on any of those trips."

Todd now picked up where he had left off. "You say his retirement payment was about right for his job?"

"Yes, he made a hundred thousand a year when he was here, so actually his retirement payment was a little low, but he had deferred some of his retirement. You know, to keep his income down. I think that later on, in a few years, his payments would have increased. When he was older and in a lower tax bracket."

A thought popped into Sam's head and he interjected another question, "Did he get a golden parachute?"

Dan looked at him questioningly, then responded, "Don't think so, he wasn't that important. The company only does that for key officers, like the Chairman of the Board Directors or the company president. Golden parachutes are big bucks. You know how they work or you wouldn't have asked the question. Surely, if you looked at his finances, you'd know he didn't get any big bonuses when he retired like you would get with a golden parachute deal."

Sam nodded in agreement, saying, "Yeah, just checking in case we missed something. Really doesn't matter, we've already established that money couldn't have been his motive, at least not money troubles."

Todd rose now and Sam followed suit. "Thanks Dan. We appreciate your cooperation. I reckon we'll look elsewhere for our motive," Todd said, as he stuck his hand out for a parting handshake.

As he took Todd's hand, Dan asked, "What if you don't ever find one?"

"It'll still be a suicide, we have no evidence of anything else. It's just that we'd like to nail down a motive for this so that we can close our file with confidence. We don't always get to do that though, so one more time won't make much difference. The sun will still come up in the east just the same."

"Goodbye, Dan," Sam said, as he turned with Todd for the door.

"So long. Sorry I couldn't help you more."

"No problem," Todd said, as he reached the door and pulled it open.

Dan waited until they had cleared the reception area before he took his seat, pulled open the top right-hand desk drawer and pushed the stop button on the tape recorder. He hit the rewind button and while the tape was rewinding he made a call upstairs.

"Mr. Tieman's office."

"Hi, Sherry. Is he in?"

"Yes, Mr. Mosley, just a moment."

While Dan waited, the tape finished rewinding and he hit the eject button. As Tieman came on the line, Mosley was just pocketing the tape.

"Sorry to bother you, sir, but I just had a visit from two deputy sheriff's investigators. They were asking about Merriman."

"Did you get a tape?"

"Yes, sir, of course."

"Good, bring it on up. Don't use a courier."

"Yes, sir. On my way."

~ * ~

"Pretty nice guy," Todd said, as they reached the car.

"Yeah, but he didn't give us much," Sam responded.

"Maybe there isn't much to give. Could be this motive for suicide is subtle. It might be that no one knew or suspected what caused Merriman to fall over the edge."

"Well, it isn't the first time we've wasted time talking to someone and not gained anything of value. I suppose if Merriman had been a gambler Mosley would have told us. He did seem pretty straight forward. What now?"

"Back to the office and comb the file again. Nothing else to do at this point. We need to find some other people who knew him."

~ * ~

Walter F. Tieman, III sat back on his couch and stared across the coffee table at Dan Mosley asking, "What do you make of it, Dan?"

"I can't say for sure, sir. They were fishing for something. Maybe it was like they said, but I'm not sure. The bait they were using sounded too specific. I don't know, but I thought you should hear it. It could be they were just looking for a motive for suicide. Still, it's not my ball park and I figured you should know about it."

Tieman leaned forward and sat in silence for a moment. He trusted Dan Mosley's opinion; Dan worked pretty much directly for him. As CEO and Chairman of the Board, he needed a sleuth like Dan to keep his finger on the pulse of the mill and the community. Dan had always served him well and his instincts were usually right on.

Tieman was no fool; he hadn't gotten to where he was just because he was the grandson of the founder. That helped, but it didn't keep the ship afloat. He knew he couldn't know it all, so he had men like Dan Mosley out there keeping him abreast of things. Walter was only fifty-five and he wanted to stay in power for a good many years. He knew a lot of people and a lot about those people, which tended to make his position secure. Walter wanted to remain secure and so he had his network of spies to keep his information up to date. Mosley was his principal spy.

Finally, he stood up and said, "Thanks, Dan. I'll think on this. Keep me posted and let me know if they show up again. The mill doesn't need any scandals. I don't like the cops nosing around up here, but we can't appear uncooperative. You handled them very well, as usual, good job."

Dan popped up on his feet immediately, saying, "Thank you, sir. Do you want to keep the tape?"

"Yes, for a while. I want to sleep on this."

"Yes, sir. Goodbye, sir."

"Bye, Dan and thanks again."

"Any time, sir," Dan said, as he made his way out of the office of the most powerful man in this community, if not the state. He liked doing things for Mr. Tieman, it made his position more tenable each time he let Tieman know how valuable he was to him. Everyone around the plant, and all the plants in the company, knew that Dan Mosley was Walter F. Tieman, III's bright young star. Not that Mosley would ever hold a position such as a Vice President or President of any division, he wasn't cut out for that. His abilities were lodged in other areas and no one except Tieman knew for sure what all those abilities were. Most of the people inside and outside TTM didn't really want to know what Mosley's abilities really were or what he knew.

Nine

It was five o'clock and quitting time before Todd wheeled the car into the sheriff's department lot. Sam got heavily out of the car with a grunt and rearranged his suit coat. He hitched up his pants and slammed the door shut. He was tired and hungry. This running all over the county had worn him out and to make matters worse, he had missed lunch.

Todd looked over at Sam and said, "Sam you have to start working out. They're going to bust you out if you don't get into shape. Then what will I do? You've only got a few years left. You want to blow your retirement?"

Sam growled as he came around the front of the car, "Yes, mother!"

Todd chuckled and Sam then said, "I know, Todd, but how am I supposed to get in shape riding around in that steel trap all day? I have things to do at home. How can I be running off to the health club every whip stitch?"

"It's like anything else, you have to want to do it. When you want to get back in shape you'll find the time and the energy. I can't make you do it and I wouldn't if I could. I just want you to know the facts. You do what you want with them."

Sam just grunted and, being one step ahead of Todd, for a change, opened the employee entrance door and held it for Todd. As he passed, Sam said, "Thanks, Todd. I'll try."

Once inside, Todd wound around the hallways toward the front of the building, stopping at the lieutenant's desk. The lieutenant wasn't there, but the blotter was and that's all Todd wanted anyway. He wanted to know who had been picked up today so that he could keep track of his snitches. He didn't have too many, but he had some and he had to know if they had been picked up. It wasn't so much that he protected them, but he used them and their constant troubles. They always paid the price for their crimes, but sometimes Todd could vary the price to get what he needed.

The blotter told him whom the sheriff's department had arrested and he didn't see a snitch on that one. Dropping the blotter back on the desk, he crossed the room to a small table. The city police dropped off a list of all people they had arrested and booked at the end of each shift. From the table he picked up the list and scanned it quickly, there was a name on that list that he recognized.

Sam had already cleaned up his paperwork and was headed home by the time Todd made it back to the office. Todd felt bad about getting on Sam like he had, but when he had seen him laboring just to get out of the car he knew he had to say something. Anyone else who said anything wouldn't be trying to help, they would be bouncing him out and Sam was too close to retirement and too good of a partner for that to happen.

Todd knew that Sam had just squeaked by his last department physical and he wasn't too sure someone didn't fudge the weight to pass him then. Another was coming up in a couple of months; Sam had to be at least improving by then. *Oh well,* he decided, nothing more to be done about that and so his mind turned back to the name on the list of recent arrestees and on going home. He had things to do at home, too, and family to see.

~ * ~

Walter sat at the head of the boardroom table, studying the small group of men scattered around the table. The chairs weren't all full, but then this wasn't a board meeting. In fact there wasn't a board member present, except for Walter, who was chairman of the board. Directly to his right was Tim Willis, President of Research and Development, then came Austin Murray, President of the Distribution

Division. At the opposite end of the table was Pete Schrage, Vice President of the Material Acquisition Department, the president was out of town or he would have been there, too. On the left side of the table sat the president and vice president of the northern plant located at the very northern portion of Georgia, they were Fred Penner and Dalton Trimble, respectively. In the very middle of the table sat a cassette player and the tape that Mosley had made had just finished playing.

Walter looked around the table slowly and asked, "What do you make of that, gentlemen?"

Pete was first with, "Corey did kill himself, didn't he? I mean, who would kill him?"

"That's not the point," Walter said sharply, "I don't give a dead rat about Merriman. What I want to know is what you people think the police are up to with their investigation?"

"Who says they're up to something?" Pete put in, having recovered from the sting of Walter's reply and risking another tongue-lashing.

Walter just glared at him this time and let the comment pass, looking further around the table to his left.

Austin looked directly at Walter and said in a matter of fact tone, "They know."

"Know what?" Tim Willis put in quickly and breathlessly. He was the least spirited of any of those around the table and he rarely spoke at any gathering, social or business. He had a great mind for organizing, but he couldn't put three thoughts together when in a room with more than one other person. When no one responded, he continued, "Know what? Nobody at the mill did anything to Merriman, did they?"

Fred rasped out, "Not Merriman, stupid! The bonus plan. Remember? The bonus plan! They're on to it. I think Austin's right. Why else would they come up here asking these kinds of questions?"

Walter put in with a calming effort, "Mosley thinks they might just be doing what they say they are doing."

"Mosley doesn't know what we know," Dalton now said and continued with his own question, "or does he?"

Walter looked sternly at Dalton and responded acidly, "No, he doesn't!"

Dalton nodded and shot back, "Just checking." He wasn't a coward and he had his own influence. Walter had more, but Dalton was no slouch in the political game. He respected Walter's position and his power, but Dalton cow-towed to no one.

Walter now looked back at Austin, to him he seemed to be the only sanity in the room. "Austin, why do you think they know?"

Austin shrugged and explained, "The questions they asked and the way they asked them. They acted too much like they didn't know what to ask or how to ask it. I've been around a lot of people who like to hide the ball and these guys are hiding the ball."

Walter nodded quietly and said, "I agree, that's why I called you all here, but the real question is how do they know and how much?"

Austin responded again, "They probably came across some papers in Corey's house and with his bank statements they put two and two together."

Fred now interjected, "So what? We all get checks from those other companies, I report mine, I get a 1099 every year and I report all my income."

Walter shook his head in disbelief and responded dryly, "It isn't that end so much Fred, as this end. Where do you think the money from those other companies comes from? Those companies don't exist. We made them up. The stockholders and the board members don't know that and we don't want them to know. TTM funnels money to the dummy companies so that they can pay us from the phony invoices. On paper it all looks good, but if someone questions it and looks into it at all, then the whole thing goes up in smoke. The stockholders will have a heyday with us. Not to mention the Feds. That money we're funneling out to those fictitious companies isn't treated as a reserve on our books. It isn't even on our books. The company doesn't pay taxes on it. They call that money laundering and when you use electronic methods to move the money, they call that wire fraud. I thought everyone understood that. We're cooking the books here, gentlemen!"

Austin piped up again, "Apparently Fred doesn't and I suspect Merriman didn't either, because he obviously left something around that got these cops interested. I don't know what that could have been. We all have the same records. Some check stubs and 1099s. What would Merriman have had to put the cops on to us?"

Walter shrugged, but said nothing.

Austin continued, "We need to nip this in the bud, Walter. Exercise some of your clout and see what you can come up with."

Walter didn't like to do that. He didn't like spending favors and he didn't like people knowing he had or used any influence. He liked being seen as the mysterious, but harmless corporate executive hiding behind his corporate shield. However, maybe Austin was right. It might be necessary to do something this time and quickly.

~ * ~

Jerry Bales left the sheriff's department where he had once again posted bail for Tommy Trenton. *This is bizarre*, he thought and the sheriff's department personnel were thinking the same thing. This time before Jerry even made his way back to his car he saw the Preacher come out the jail intake door. *That was fast*, he thought, *they must not have even put him in jail clothes. Well, not my business*, he decided and fingered the crisp new ten in the pocket of his battered suit coat, third one in two days. *Better than working*, he mused to himself.

Inside the jail, at the booking desk, another ten was changing hands, as the booking officer smiled and said, "Told ya he'd be out by supper. Aren't you glad you didn't waste your time making him change clothes and bagging and tagging his effects?"

There was no response as the losing figure waddled his way through the cellblock door and slammed it behind him with a loud clang.

~ * ~

Outside the jail, Tommy stopped to breathe in the fresh air. It was just after five o'clock and the street was pretty busy with the businesses all having just closed. Glancing up the street to the front of the courthouse, he saw a white Cadillac pull up to the curb and watched the man driving it climb out. Tommy knew who it was and he knew what he was doing. It was George Rosmund and he was picking up the queen of Meridian County, also known as Jeannie Rosmund.

The circuit clerk was a big joke around town. Even Tommy knew how inept she was and how perfect she thought she was. She lorded over her employees and any one else who gave her the chance. How she got elected he couldn't understand, but the real question was, could she get elected again? From the talk he had been hearing, everyone prayed she wouldn't get re-elected, but most agreed she had enough political savvy to get the job done. *Politics*, he grumped to himself in disgust. *You didn't have to know anything except how to get elected.*

The job must pay pretty well, he reasoned. That Cadillac was new, every year. She wore fancy clothes and her two kids drove nice cars, too. They both worked for her in the circuit clerk's office. Nepotism, Tommy recalled that being called. It was okay, he supposed, so long as the job got done, but in this case he had heard it didn't get done. At least not very well.

People thought the Preacher was just some cracker who babbled about Jesus Christ, but they were wrong. He might not have been formally educated, but he had knowledge about this community no one even suspected. He kept it to himself. Who wanted to hear anything from a crackpot?

~ * ~

Charlie had cleared security and was seated in a far corner of the boarding area waiting for the pre-board call. It was a little early yet, around five fifteen p.m. and he observed Carol Harmon on the far side of the waiting area firmly ensconced in the opposite corner with her goons in full array. *Now Charlie*, he chastised himself, *that's not nice. They are just doing their job and they get paid to look that way. A nice girl like Carol Harmon probably needs protection in her line of work, can't have just anybody walking up to her or following her around.*

Out of the corner of his eye he watched her as she casually flipped the pages on a magazine. She looked absolutely bored and he didn't blame her, not much to do in an airport boarding area, except read a book, or play hand held video games and he didn't have either.

On the other side of the waiting area, Carol was still flipping the pages of her third magazine, but ever since that irritating man had appeared and sat in the opposite corner she had gotten nothing out of the magazine. She was covertly watching him and she thought he was covertly watching her at the same time. She turned to Dan Chase, always at her side and asked casually, "Dan, who's that guy across the room, the one in the corner with the rumpled suit?"

Dan had been reading a suspense novel that he was really getting into and, slightly irritated to be interrupted, he responded gruffly, "Huh, what!"

"That guy over there across the room, in the corner. Know him?"

Dan looked up with a disgusted look on his face, briefly examined Charlie and retorted, "Some low-life lawyer from out of state, I hear. Name's Charlie or Chuckie or something like that, last name's Chambers I think or Chalmers, don't know, don't much care. He's a religious freak, works for some kind of Christian defense outfit. No money, no ambition, just sucks off some fund for a few bucks and travels around arguing religious rights for a bunch of other religious freaks."

It was obvious to Carol that she wasn't going to get any worthwhile information from Dan so with a sigh she went back to her magazine. *No matter*, she decided, *just curious.*

Charlie glanced at his watch for the tenth time in five minutes and noted the time was five fifty-five p.m. His flight was scheduled to depart at six p.m. and they hadn't even called first class boarding yet. *Must be something going on*, he decided, *but why don't they at least have the courtesy to tell the passengers what was going on? The pilot is probably late or some dumb thing*, he fumed. He was anxious to be on his way. He wanted to be home and he wanted to be away from here, away from Carol Harmon. Why, he didn't know, but he was uncomfortable here with her. It didn't make sense that he should be, but unlike in the café, he couldn't get his mind off of her and he didn't care for that. He wanted to be gone from her, but at the same time he had a notion to go over there and set things straight before they parted. To let her know he wasn't a total jerk, but to do that, he would have to be a jerk again, just to get through her guards. *What's your problem, Charlie*, he thought, *you are a decisive guy, a lawyer who is used to thinking on his feet and acting swiftly but decisively. Why the hesitation, why*—the public address system crackled and Charlie's mind focused on that instead of finishing his thoughts. "Ladies and Gentlemen, we're sorry for the delay..."

~ * ~

Johnson City didn't have an airport, so Shirley had to drive to Thomasville, which was across the county line in Blair County. It was a good half-hour from her café to the airport and she barely had thirty minutes when she left. His flight was scheduled to leave at six p.m. At least that's what he had said this morning. She glanced at her watch. Five fifty-five. As near as she could calculate, the airport was ten minutes away. Ordinarily she wasn't a speeder, but now she would make an exception. He might not agree to help, but she had come this far and she wasn't going home until she knew.

Nervously, she glanced from side to side ahead of her, looking for police cars. If there were any she was in trouble, but if she didn't take the chance then Tommy was in worse trouble. Finally, she saw the sign ahead on her left; 'Thomasville Public Airport' and she breathed a sigh of relief. On the tarmac sat the waiting DC-9. It hadn't left yet. Her watch said it should have, but it hadn't. The prayers she had said all the way to the airport had been answered. The plane had been delayed for whatever reason and she thanked God.

Her relief was short lived, because as she approached the small terminal building the jet taxied off toward the north. She whipped into a parking place, jumped out and watched the plane pass her by. The plane got continually smaller as it continued down the taxiway.

The Thomasville airport was a small one. It only had three flights arriving and departing each day, except Sunday when none arrived or departed. This was the last flight out today and no more would arrive. She looked around the little airport forlornly and passed her eyes over the north side of the terminal building. There, looking out a large window, she was sure she saw Charlie Chambers, *but how*, she wondered. *I must be seeing things, his plane just left.* As she contemplated the situation the face backed away from the window and disappeared. She hurried into the building and dashed across the marble floor to the passenger boarding area. Shirley wasn't allowed in, but she could look in and it was clear that the area was full of waiting passengers. Her head was spinning. This didn't make sense. The plane was gone, but the passengers were still here, why?

Peering carefully through the windows separating her from the passengers, she spied Charlie Chambers hunched down in a seat toward an inside wall. She made her way down toward him as far as she could and still see him. She tapped on the glass window and was rewarded by Charlie's head coming around. He peered at her for a minute, obviously not recognizing her. *Why should he?* she decided, *These aren't my usual surroundings.* Finally, he arose and came closer to the window, recognition flooding his eyes as he approached.

Shirley motioned for him to move toward the door and come out to talk to her. Charlie got a concerned look on his face, but then went down toward the door and held an animated conversation with the security guard. Shirley waited breathlessly until he nodded to the guard and walked through the door.

"Miss Becker, what can I do for you?" Charlie said tiredly.

"Oh, Mr. Chambers, I'm so glad I caught you, I thought I'd missed you."

Charlie looked at his watch in disgust and answered, "You should have, but they had trouble with the plane."

"Trouble, but I saw it leave as I drove up."

With obvious disgust, Charlie said, "You didn't see it take off though, did you? It just taxied down to the hanger for repairs. They're supposed to be bringing in another plane." Charlie glanced at his watch and said, "Should be here in about another thirty minutes."

Shirley said nervously, "Mr. Chambers would you consider not taking that flight? I mean, someone here needs your help. That person I talked to you about this morning. He needs your help. He's been arrested three times now in two days for disorderly conduct, but he isn't disorderly, he just preaches to folks along the sidewalk and passes out pamphlets. He's harmless, but Judge Ferrell is going to put him in Statesville. I just know it," she ended, almost crying.

Charlie furrowed his brow in thought and then it came to him and he asked, "Tommy Trenton, that's his name isn't it?"

Shirley looked at him oddly and said, "Yes, but how did you know?"

"I met him in the jail or at least he was being booked when I was there. He said something about giving me a pamphlet. I heard him tell the booking officer his name and the booking officer said he only knew him as the Preacher. Is that your friend?"

"Yes, he's harmless. He just likes to preach. He's never hurt anyone and never would."

"How do you know?"

"I just do, that's all," Shirley shot back.

Mumbling almost to himself, Charlie said, "Maybe he's good and maybe he's bad."

"What!"

"Nothing."

"No, I heard most of that. What makes you think he's a bad person?"

"I didn't say he was. I don't know what he is and I don't care. He's not my problem. His cause isn't my cause. Okay?"

"Well... I... I...," Shirley sputtered.

Charlie didn't give her a chance to get her thoughts organized. "Sorry, I can't help."

"Why not? I can pay, not all at once, but I can pay. The café brings in enough that I could..."

Charlie cut her off, "It has nothing to do with the money, or with you, or with Tommy Trenton. I only take cases when I have the feeling I'm supposed to and I don't feel led to this one."

"How do you know?"

"I don't know, but when it happens, I know. That's all I can say and this case isn't one. Find you another lawyer. I'm not a real criminal lawyer anyway. Call Steve Barclay, tell him I said I would appreciate it if he helped your friend." Charlie glanced at his watch and continued; "Now if you'll excuse me, I have to clear security again and get ready to leave. That spare plane should be here any minute." As he spoke, a plane could be heard roaring to a stop out on the runway as its engines were reversed.

"But..."

Charlie held up his hand, "No 'buts'. Sorry, I'm going home. This isn't my business. My business is done. Maybe I'll be back in a few months to prepare for the appellate court arguments. Hopefully by then your friend will have gotten out of this trouble."

Finished, he spun on his heels and headed through the double glass doors to be checked by the guard again and ready himself for boarding. It was almost seven now, he noted.

Shirley watched as the passengers left the terminal building. After Carol Harmon and her entourage boarded, the rest of the passengers were allowed to leave and they all walked across the ramp, ascending the steps to the plane one by one. As far as she could tell, Charlie Chambers never once looked back. Even when the doors were shut and the plane wound up both engines for taxiing, she watched. Not until the plane had taken off and disappeared into the northern sky did she listlessly walk back to her car.

One thing is for certain, she decided, *Tommy is in trouble now*. She wasn't buying what Chambers was selling. Shirley knew Tommy wasn't bad. He couldn't be. She had watched him long enough to know that he wasn't a bad person. He needed help. Help she couldn't give him or get him. Now it seemed he wasn't going to be around long enough for her to help him, not with Charlie Chambers gone.

Ten

Charlie felt badly about the way he had acted toward Shirley, but he had no choice. Still, he had been acting badly toward people lately and he didn't like that. But what he had told Shirley was the truth. The case she wanted him to take wasn't in his area of expertise and it wasn't meant to be. The feeling that he always got when he was supposed to take a case just wasn't there. He just hadn't been led to this one and he would not take a case he wasn't sure he was supposed to take. His case in Georgia was over, it was the reason he had come and that was that. He was going home.

~ * ~

The pilot keyed his intercom and said to the co-pilot, "What a lousy day. First our scheduled plane has engine trouble and we're an hour getting the replacement. Now a line of thunderstorms pops up where no one predicted it. That's what I hate about flying down here in the Southeast. You can't predict these lousy thunderstorms. They pop up everywhere and anywhere."

The co-pilot responded, "We'd better climb over this line or it's going to be mighty rough going."

"How high are they supposed to be?" the pilot asked.

"Who knows, they weren't even supposed to be here."

The pilot grumbled inaudibly into his headset, as he eased back on the stick and felt the plane start to rise ever so slowly. Already they were hitting some turbulence from the distant thunderheads.

A flash of light shot out in front of the windshield and both the pilot and co-pilot's hair stood on end, literally. It was evident that the plane had taken a lightning strike, the most dreaded occurrence for any aircraft. A lightning strike could drop you right out of the sky, ignite your fuel or knock out all your power and leave you helplessly falling toward the earth.

~ * ~

Charlie saw the flash, too. It wasn't as pronounced where he was, but none the less he knew what had happened. All the lights went out in the cabin and he heard the air vents cut out. The plane, which had been slowly ascending, now began to descend again. Charlie prayed that the descent was intentional on the part of the pilots.

~ * ~

"Thomasville control, this is Delta flight niner-four-three-eight declaring an emergency. Over," the pilot said calmly into his headset. Panic never accomplished anything, he stayed cool, that's why they had made him a pilot.

"State the nature of your problem Delta flight niner-four-three-eight and the assistance requested," the controller's calm voice responded, he too was trained to be calm, only he didn't have to do it in the face of death, at least not his own.

"Thomasville, this is Delta flight niner-four-three-eight, we have taken a lightning strike and have lost all power to lights, air circulation and auxiliary functions. We still have rudder controls, but they are sluggish and our communication circuit is weak. Request immediate clearance for landing at Thomasville. Have your fire and rescue team standing by. I'm not sure how long the power to the controls will last. We still have smoke coming from under the cockpit instrument panel and we..." the voice faded with a crackle.

The controller asked, in a still calm, but not as calm, voice, "Delta flight niner-four-three-eight, come in."

A crackling, broken transmission came through. "Comm... i... ation... al... st... go... ow. We just lost o... avigation lights."

"Delta flight niner-four-three-eight, you are cleared for immediate landing on the north-south runway, no need to acknowledge!" he spun to his right as he ended and pulled a lever on the wall. Instantaneously a bell and horn began alternating and resonating across the small field.

~ * ~

"May I please have your attention ladies and gentlemen, this is the pilot. We have been struck by lightning and lost some power. We are in no immediate danger and have been cleared to return and land at Thomasville to effect repairs."

The way pilots so skillfully lied to their passengers always amazed the co-pilot and he wondered if he would be so good when he got his own plane. Providing, he lived to get his own plane.

Delta flight nine-four-three-eight had only been twenty minutes out of Thomasville when lightning struck, but with the sluggish controls and only minimal power, it seemed to the pilot that the flight back had taken hours. Finally, he saw the runway lights and could see the constant flicker of the emergency lights on the vehicles taking up positions along the runway. Vehicles, he earnestly prayed, would not be needed this night.

"Thomasville this... Delta flight niner-f... -three-... ght on final app... we..." the voice cut off as the controller listened helplessly and watched the blip on his approach scope. Descent was a little fast and he had tried to tell them that, but they weren't receiving anymore. All he could do now was watch his scope and pray. With no navigation lights the people on the ground would hear them before they saw them. Ordinarily, at this time of day the lights wouldn't matter, but with the storms moving through the area, the sky was as dark as full night.

The blip disappeared and he looked out the tower window praying not to see a fireball on the ground. His prayer was answered and he neither saw a fireball, nor heard an explosion. He could just see the plane dropping out of the sky like a rock.

At the last second, the pilot pulled up and bumped the plane down on the runway. *Now if we just have enough control left to reverse the thrust*, the pilot prayed, as both he and the co-pilot struggled to maintain control of the rapidly moving plane.

Charlie was leaned well forward with his head on a pillow, as instructed, praying. When he felt the huge bump, he was sure the plane had crashed, but then he felt the reverse thrust kick in and he knew it would be all right. Providing there was no fire. *I may stop flying*, he thought, as the plane lurched to a stop amid the flashing red and blue lights of the emergency equipment.

~ * ~

Charlie was still shaky when he passed through the boarding area that he seemed destined never to leave. The ground personnel had already made an announcement that Delta would put everyone up in a nearby motel until a new flight could be arranged in the morning. Of course, that was providing, any one still wanted to fly Delta. The ground personnel hadn't said that.

A bus was already waiting to take the passengers to the motel by the time they made it outside the terminal. Charlie noted that Carol Harmon and her crew were already gone, waiting limousines had whisked them away almost before the plane's engines had stopped turning over.

Charlie was following a middle-aged woman when he noticed she had dropped something. He snatched it up and said, "Excuse me, ma'am, but you dropped this."

She stopped before boarding the bus, turned and took the pamphlet. "Oh, thank you, but it's nothing. Just a pamphlet I got from some bum in Johnson City."

Charlie hadn't noticed what it was he had picked up, but now he looked at it and saw that it was a pamphlet with bold letters on the face of it proclaiming, "Jesus Christ Saves!"

The woman took the pamphlet and Charlie asked, "Was he preaching?"

"Huh?"

"The bum who gave you the pamphlet, was he preaching, too?"

"Yeah, I guess. He was reciting Bible verses as he handed the pamphlets out. There was a fairly large group of people around him and he gave everyone who passed a pamphlet. Do you know him?"

"No, not really, I saw him, too," Charlie responded thoughtfully, as he climbed on the bus.

~ * ~

Dan Mosley was still at his desk, he was single and his job was everything to him. Maintaining security for TTM plants and making sure that its traveling executives had proper protection was no small task. There were very few nights that he couldn't find work right up to midnight if he chose and this one looked like just one more. The mill ran twenty-four hours a day so he was never lonely. Sometimes staying late paid off. People who couldn't ordinarily contact him during the day could get him in the evenings.

On this evening he was busy scouring a map spread out on his desk. Mr. Tieman was planning a business trip to Mexico to evaluate some new sources of materials and Mosley had to make sure no one got the idea he was an easy target. Terrorism against high-powered executives was getting very fashionable, so it was more than mere paranoia when Mosley cautioned against a certain route, time or destination. Dan hadn't lost an executive yet and he wasn't about to start now.

The ringing of his phone broke his concentration and he started. Flinging aside the map, he dug down to his phone and answered gruffly, "Mosley."

"Mr. Mosley, sorry to bother you, but this is Aaron Farmer. I'm a supervisor at the dyeing facility. I wondered if you might be able to help me or at least look into something for me?"

Cautiously, Dan responded, "Depends on what it is you want me to look into and why." He didn't jump at every request for his services. He had underlings for that and he liked to concentrate on the important fish upstairs.

"Well, I have a man in my facility who I think is being harassed by the police."

Dan's curiosity was aroused, especially considering the visit by the sheriff's department just today and he asked, "Sheriff's department?"

"I'm not sure. I just know the poor guy is being hassled. He hasn't been able to make it to work for three days."

"Why?"

"They keep arresting him on some bogus charge," Aaron said emphatically and continued, "Do you know any body down at the city police department or the sheriff's department who could find out what's going on? This guy's a good worker, he does his job and doesn't cause any problems."

"Is he a key employee?"

"Nawh, he just sweeps up and cleans around here, but he does a good job. Nobody else wants to do it. He's been doing it for a long time, before I came to work here. He's never made more than minimum wage and never asked for more."

"So, what is he being arrested for, he must be doing something? We don't want criminals working around here," Dan said shortly.

"He's no criminal! They keep picking him up because he passes out religious pamphlets and preaches to people on the street. No big deal. He doesn't do it around here, but he's been doing it in Johnson City for years without any trouble. I think they are just hassling him. Just as soon as he bails out, they pick him up again. I was hoping you knew some people who were connected to the police and maybe get them to lay off so he could come back to work," Aaron finished evenly. It really wasn't any thing to him, but Tommy was good help and he liked him.

"Wait a minute, you talking about the Preacher?" Dan was interested now, he knew this guy, a little.

"Yeah, I sure am. He's good help, been here a long time."

"Yeah, I know about him. He's harmless. I'll see what I can dig up. Can't promise anything, but he can't be in too much trouble."

"Thanks, Mr. Mosley. Good-bye," Aaron said and hung up.

After Dan hung up on his end, he contemplated the situation. It wasn't unheard of for him or his people to look into such situations, to try to make things easier for an employee, especially a loyal one. This didn't sound like much. It was curious though why they would pick this guy up so often and so fast. Sounded a lot like just plain harassment to Dan and he didn't tolerate anyone harassing employees of TTM.

Dan took out his electronic pocket telephone directory, flipped it open and typed in the search. Once the phone number came up, he picked up his phone again and began dialing.

"Sergeant Ferrenbach," the husky voice said dryly.

"Stan, this is Dan Mosley up at TTM."

"Oh, hey Dan, how's it going?" Stan perked up immediately, he liked to think he had connections at TTM, it could come in handy one day, after retirement.

"Just wondered if you knew anything about the Preacher."

"What about him? Everyone knows the Preacher."

"Yeah, but do you know why he's being picked up all the time? My information has it that he's been picked up three times in the last couple of days. He's missed three days of work and we'd like to have him back. What's the beef?" Dan asked calmly, no sense getting huffy when it wasn't necessary.

"New mayoral policy, Dan. Can't say more on this phone, but that should be enough. You know who the new mayor is and what platform he ran on," Stan answered cryptically.

"Oh, yes, I got you, Stan."

"He's out again now, Dan. He bails out within hours of getting busted, but he goes right back to his old tricks. You guys must pay him pretty good up there or he saves his pennies. He's had to have put out several hundred dollars in bond money in the past three days. Curious thing is, he doesn't put it up himself. A guy by the name of Jerry Bales always does it and won't say where the money came from. That's making matters worse. Some of the guys are starting to wonder if the Preacher doesn't have a sideline. Get my drift?"

Dan thought for a minute and said, "Yeah, I see your point, but can you guys lay off him long enough for him to get back to work?"

"Not if he keeps it up. Not unless the word comes down to do differently. Follow?" Stan said, with that cryptic inflection in his voice again.

Dan understood what the inflection was supposed to emphasize, but responded without seeming to understand, "Yeah sure, Stan, you guys got your job to do to. I'll see about keeping him out of trouble. Okay?"

"Thanks, Dan."

"Good talking to you, Stan. Hey, you're about to retire aren't you?" Dan asked, but he knew the answer, he made it a point to have the dope on every cop in the county.

"A couple of years."

"Good, keep your options open. Don't forget to give me a call if you need something after you pull the pin. I can usually scare up something to keep the wolf away from the door," Dan said evenly.

Stan's heart skipped a beat or two, he had been wanting a position with TTM after retirement and now it seemed as though it was sewn up. "Sure, Dan, if I get caught short I'll give you a call."

"Take it easy, Stan."

"You, too."

Dan hung up, chuckling at the way he sometimes had to carry on conversations with cops at work. The city police department monitored all incoming calls and it wasn't fruitful or wise to speak too plainly. What most people didn't realize was that all calls, incoming and outgoing, at TTM were monitored, all the time. Dan knew how the game was played and information was the queen.

The cryptic manner of talking didn't bother Dan, he figured out what Stan was saying. The mayor had a law and order push on and the Preacher was caught in the middle. Stan was saying that a word from high enough up at TTM might make the mayor back off of the Preacher, but Dan didn't think so. This mayor didn't play ball. He didn't like some of TTM's endeavors and it didn't seem to matter to him that TTM employed most of the people in his town. Besides, Dan wasn't about to bother Mr. Tieman with a minor problem like this. A sweeper in the dyeing facility wasn't going to impress Mr. Tieman.

Dan thought for a minute, switched off his desk lamp and stood. He grabbed his suit coat off the rack by the door, switched off his office light and left for the night. He could probably rectify this situation himself, or at least get the Preacher back to work.

~ * ~

Asher Adams was in his office late, too. It wasn't uncommon for him to be here past midnight and especially now. The November election was coming faster than anyone imagined and he was going to be ready. Maybe it was still summer, but the early bird got the worm in elections. Name recognition was the name of the game for a politician and he needed more. His opponent had plenty and she had a lot of opportunities to get more, he didn't. Still, he had another angle working. He smiled ruefully to himself at that. If everything worked out the way he had it planned, Rosmund wouldn't even know what hit her. At the same time, he was accumulating a nice little nest egg to use to get his name recognition. *Sweet,* he thought, *real sweet.*

He could hardly wait for November to arrive. Some nights all he thought about was the speech he would make on election night after Jeannie Rosmund had conceded. He could barely contain himself when he was at the circuit clerk's office filing papers. That was the hard part, he decided. In his job as manager of the Meridian County Credit Bureau, he had to go to the circuit clerk's office a lot to file new collection cases and post judgment proceedings against deadbeats. Asher hated going over there and having to put up with the inept help Rosmund had hired. He also really disliked going in there and feeling the tension in the office. All of the help, except her two daughters, hated her and knew how stupid she was. She was also a tyrant and everyone who was anyone knew it. It was all he could do to hold his tongue while he was in there. *A few months more,* he thought to himself, as he turned back to his stack of new filings he was readying for tomorrow's trip to the circuit clerk's office.

~ * ~

Sitting at his desk in the investigator's office, Todd examined the ledger book that Sam had found at Merriman's. A close examination made it clear, even to Todd, who was by no means an accountant, that a lot of money had been moved through several accounts and this ledger had kept track of it. It wasn't possible for him to accurately calculate the amount of money. However, it was obvious that the money was shifted from various companies, into separate accounts and moved back and forth between several accounts over a period of several years. If this money was all Merriman's, he certainly didn't have financial difficulties as a motive for suicide.

Just the money in his regular checking and two savings accounts would be enough to rule out financial trouble as a motive, but aside from a motive, Todd was now starting to wonder why this ledger even existed, and why Merriman had kept it. Merriman was a medium level executive at the mill. A glorified supervisor with a small office in the headquarters building. Why would he rate such a retirement, and what was this green ledger all about? Despite what Dan Mosley had said about Merriman's retirement income being consistent with his salary, Todd wasn't buying it. He had looked into enough bank records to be able to estimate a man's salary and these records didn't support the salary Dan Mosley had intimated. Something wasn't adding up, and Todd realized that instead of getting closer to declaring this case a clear-cut suicide, he was getting farther away.

Closing the ledger book and placing it carefully toward the back of his top drawer, he stood up and stretched. *Maybe what I need to do is tap another source at the mill,* he decided. *Maybe I can get a different perspective by talking to someone who exists on a different level than Dan Mosley.*

Eleven

The personnel office was closed, but Dan had a key to every lock in every plant, or knew where to get one. He also had the passwords to every computer program currently being used by TTM or any of its subsidiaries; or if he didn't, the program wasn't authorized to be in use. Dan's problem was not locked doors or secured systems, but rather he couldn't remember the Preacher's real name. A quick call to Ferrenbach settled that matter though and at the same time it let Ferrenbach know that Dan hadn't simply blown him off.

With the right name, it was only minutes until Dan had everything that TTM had on Tommy Trenton, alias the Preacher, including his address. He had no phone. This wasn't a matter for the phone anyway. Dan was more interested in the address and glancing at his watch he noted that the evening was early yet, by his standards, only nine o'clock.

Dan flipped off the computer, stood and headed out the door of the personnel office. On the way out of the building, he was going over in his mind what he would say to Tommy Trenton to get him to ease off on his preaching and get back to work.

~ * ~

Tommy was reading his Bible. He did that frequently and for long periods of time. He enjoyed reading and he especially enjoyed reading the Bible. The passages that he 'preached' to people on the street were real to him and well rehearsed. He rarely misquoted a verse and could quote quite a few at any given time. Give him a subject and he could pretty much tell you what was said on it, by whom and where you could find it in the Bible.

Tommy worked in the mill for minimum wage. Lived in a cramped two-room apartment, one of those rooms was a bath, and wore old clothes only because of happenstance, not because he was stupid. Things had just never worked out for him like they had for other people, but he was content with his lot in life. He didn't have much and he didn't ask for more.

Sometimes he contemplated what life could have been had it not been for the bad start he had gotten. If his old man hadn't been such a no-good worthless crook who used his kids and everyone else to his own gain. A man with no thought for anyone else. Had it not been for the old man, things might have been different. If he hadn't had to quit school at age fourteen and gone to work, things might have been different. If he would have had the presence of mind to go back and get his GED when he was younger and then saved his money for some college courses, things might have been different. If people hadn't been so unwilling to give a fourteen-year-old dropout a job or an even break, things might have been different. If the townsfolk hadn't held what his old man had done to them against him, things might have been different.

Yet all of that had happened, or hadn't happened, as the case may be, and there was no changing it now. He harbored no ill feelings. He was a Christian and they couldn't take that away from him, no matter how many times or how long they put him in jail.

Tommy started at the knock at the door. It was unusual for him to have visitors, at any hour. Not many people knew where he lived and even fewer cared. He put his Bible aside and walked fearlessly to the door. Except for his old man, no one had ever had reason to hurt him and he couldn't see anyone having one now.

When he opened the door, a large black man stood framed there. The man reached inside his coat and pulled out a black case, flipping it open for Tommy to see. There was little doubt what it was, a badge, a gold badge. Tommy didn't bother reading it, a cop was a cop in his book.

"Yes, sir. What did I do now? You going to take me back to jail again?"

Todd smiled and said disarmingly, "No, Tommy, I just want to talk. I'm Sergeant Todd Evans, Meridian County Sheriff Investigator. May I come in?"

Tommy was puzzled, but cooperative. "Sure, come in, have a seat."

Todd stepped into the small room and glanced quickly around. There was a couch, which very obviously doubled for a bed, one lounge chair and one straight back chair. Off to the right was a half kitchen and next to that a bathroom. That was the sum total of Tommy Trenton's home.

Todd picked the straight-backed chair, as he didn't want to sit on this man's bed and it was obvious that the lounge chair was the primary place for Tommy to sit. After both had taken a seat, Todd asked, "Do you know a Corey Merriman up at the mill?"

"Yes, sir. I mean I know the name. He doesn't work there any more; he sort of worked in my building. He wasn't my supervisor, but I knew him, pretty high up I think."

"He's dead."

"I... what... I mean, I didn't..."

Todd held up his hand to stop Tommy's babbling and said, "He killed himself a few days ago. We think. I'm not saying you had anything to do with it. I just wanted to know if you knew him and could tell me anything about him."

Tommy narrowed his eyes and responded cautiously, "Like I said, I didn't know him. I knew of him, but never talked to him. I seen him come and go, sometimes I seen him riding with Mr. Tieman, but not too much. A time or two, I happened to be looking out the window when Mr. Tieman dropped him off at the dyeing facility or picked him up. Sometimes I seen him walking over to headquarters, but like I said, he was pretty high up, that's not unusual for higher ups to hang together, is it?"

"No. Did you ever hear anything anyone else might have said about him, or overhear anything he said to anyone else?"

"No, sir. Like I said, he was pretty high up, he had no truck with me. I just sweep up and take out the trash."

"You do that just in the dyeing facility?"

"Mostly, but sometimes I get called over to headquarters or another building to clean. When the cleaning person over there didn't show up or there was an especially big mess."

"Did you ever hear anything over in the headquarters building about Merriman?"

"No, it was mostly at night when everyone was already gone, 'cept Mr. Mosley. He was always there seemed like, or at least there really late. He's a hard worker."

"Dan Mosley, chief of security?"

"Yes, sir, that's him, hard worker."

"You ever talk to him?"

"Only to say hello or ask him if he wanted me to empty his trash or sweep his floor. I don't think he knew who I was or my name, most people don't know and don't care. That used to bother me, but it doesn't anymore. God knows my name, that's all I care about now."

"And Merriman's office, did you sometimes clean it?"

"Yeah. He had an office in the headquarters building and a small one over in the dyeing facility, too. I cleaned the one in the dyeing facility along with everything else. That's what I do. I clean. It's all I've ever done."

Todd looked deeply into the sad eyes of Tommy Trenton and decided that he was looking at a wasted life. Not that the waste was Tommy's fault, but it was wasted just the same. The man seemed to be intelligent; he was clean and well groomed, considering his lifestyle. He was in his late forties or early fifties and though he wasn't clean-shaven and his hair wasn't closely cropped, he didn't have the look of filth. His hair certainly didn't have the look of constant grooming by a professional barber, but it wasn't unruly either. He was a tall man with a solid build and obviously in pretty good physical shape, probably from all the manual labor he'd done. He could have been something. He could have done something with his life, but instead he was content to clean. What caused such a man to waste his life like this? What had happened in his past that made him content to clean up after other people his whole life?

~ * ~

Dan quietly slipped through the entrance door to the apartment building at 211 Adams Street. It wasn't much and he wasn't surprised that the door was unlocked. There was no light over the entry way and very little on the stairway. Discarded papers and empty plastic bottles littered the entryway and the landing between floors.

On his way up the stairs he stopped under the dim light to double check the apartment number on his note pad and when he stopped, he heard voices on the next floor. From the landing he could just see the second floor of the apartment building and one door, 2F. That was the door he wanted, that was Tommy Trenton's apartment, but someone was already there. The door was being held half open and the apartment number was clearly visible. There could be no mistake. He couldn't make out the voices or recognize the person who stood in the half-open door. He could see the man had on a suit coat though and was definitely out of place in the building, as was Dan Mosley.

Easing back down the stairs and out of sight of the second floor, he remained on the first flight of stairs peeking around the corner at the man standing in the Preacher's doorway. Suddenly the voices ceased, the man stepped back and the door began to close. Dan only got a glimpse of the man, but as he retreated down the stairs to avoid being seen himself, he knew instantly who he was. A cop. Not just any cop either, he realized, he was one of the sheriff's investigators who had come up to the mill today. Sergeant Evans, as Dan recalled and he had a good memory for names. This wasn't a good sign, he decided. First they come to the mill and now he finds one of them talking to a longtime mill employee. Dan didn't like the feel of this. This could just be more harassment, but he was more inclined to think that the Preacher had found his own help and didn't need Dan. Whether he needed Dan's help or not, Dan had decided he wasn't going to get it, at least not right away.

Dan made it out the entrance door and around the corner to his car well ahead of Sergeant Evans. He sat in the car waiting to make sure Evans was gone before he started his own. He glanced at his watch out of habit, but didn't really care what the time was. He had another stop to make and he didn't care if he upset this person or not. In fact, he was hoping he would.

It wasn't necessary to look up this guy's address on any computer; Dan had it burned into his memory. Not because he was an important part of Dan's life, he didn't even work for the mill, but Dan used him from time to time and so he always kept his address on the front edge of his memory banks. As far as Dan knew, Jerry Bales had never worked for any one for more than a few days and especially not the mill. He was a two-bit thief, a druggie, a con artist and anything else that would garner him a buck or two. Yet, he had his uses. The cops used him, too.

Dan didn't knock gently on Jerry's door, instead, he kicked it in as a frightened Jerry Bales cautiously opened the door and peered out. When the door smashed into his face, it flung him across the room. Seconds later, he pulled himself up off the floor and was about to protest when he saw Dan Mosley step through and slam the door shut.

"Mr. Mosley, I thought you was the cops. What a surprise, what can I do for you? Need something on somebody? I can find out, I can find out anything on the street you know that, I can..."

"Shut up, Jerry!" Dan hissed.

Jerry's mouth slammed shut so hard Dan thought he would break his bottom teeth.

"Who's putting up the bond money for the Preacher?" Dan spat out.

"I don't know... I..."

"Don't give me your line of baloney, Bales! You don't want to mess with me. One word from me, and you go to the big house. With luck you'll get a fair trial first, but you'll go just the same. I've still got it locked up in my safe, Jerry. You tried to rip off the wrong place, Jerry, you remember that don't you? Now spill it!"

"I... uh..."

"Okay, Jerry. Have it your way." Dan spun around for the door and over his shoulder, he threw his last salvo, "You'll like the big house, Jerry, they might even let you live out the year, before they stick a shiv in you. Don't forget, Jerry, they don't like snitches in the slam and you're a professional snitch. I'll make sure they get the word, too."

"Okay! Okay! What's the big deal anyway? I just posted the bail for an old street bum as a favor. I'm not sworn to secrecy or nothing. It's no big deal."

"Then out with it, Jerry. My patience isn't what it used to be!"

"A cop."

"A cop what? You're pushing me, Jerry and I'm not in the mood. I'm going to send you up if you keep jerking me around."

"Sergeant Evans! Meridian County Sheriff's Department."

"Yeah, I know him. Okay, if it's straight you skate for a while longer, maybe forever. Now why is he putting up the money?"

Jerry turned dead white, held up his hands and whimpered, "I don't know that, Mr. Mosley, for sure I don't. Don't ask me to give you what I can't. Please, I don't know why. He just came and told me what to do and gave me the cash. He paid me a tenner each time. I had to, he's got me, too. Not like you, but he's got me good. Please, I'm giving it to you straight," Jerry ended with a distinct whimper.

Dan wasn't sure he believed him, but he figured Jerry had no reason to be lying. Jerry Bales was a lot of things, but he wasn't brave, at least not brave enough to risk what he was risking. "Okay, Jer, take it easy now, ya hear," Dan said amiably and flung open the door. He stepped out the door and without closing it, he was gone.

Jerry remained where he was, with the door still standing open. He was sweating, really sweating. That had been close, too close. Finally, when his legs would hold him no longer, he dropped to the floor. Dismayed, he sat on the floor contemplating his miserable situation. He was a pawn in a big game, used by the police and TTM for whatever good they thought he could do them at the time. It was nobody's fault, except his own. But that didn't make it any easier to live with.

~ * ~

The motel room was closing in on Charlie. Flying in the morning didn't appeal to him after the close call tonight. However, he bolstered himself in the knowledge that things had always worked out, through the good and the bad. There had been some really bad.

These were the good times for sure. Sometimes he wasn't so sure just what he was accomplishing. He knew he won or lost, but he always had the feeling there was some deeper meaning behind his work. Some hidden justice being worked that neither he, nor anyone else was aware of at the time.

Charlie didn't bother himself with why he was led to his cases; it was enough that he was led. The master plan wasn't his to know. He was just to do his part. Whatever that might be.

He got up off the bed and retrieved the TV remote control. Maybe some diversion was in order, but as a rule he wasn't a TV fan. Too much junk on TV for him, they just didn't run the good old movies enough and every sitcom was like the next, different town, different actors, same theme.

Leaning back against the wall with a pillow stuffed behind him, he surfed the available channels. Quite a few for a small town motel. *Must have a good cable system,* he mused, as the current image showed him another sitcom in process. Another push of the button and up popped an old favorite of his, an early episode of 'Highway to Heaven'. He remembered this one. A sad old man with nothing and no one, who wandered the streets, praying for God to take him away from the nothingness he experienced daily. God answered his prayers, but not the way he expected. Instead of taking him away, He showed him his purpose in life, his place in God's plan. He showed him how even he could make a difference and how someone with nothing, still had something to give.

When the show ended, Charlie turned the TV off. For a while he sat contemplating. *Is there a lesson here for me?* he asked himself. Was he giving something, really giving or just going through the motions? Finally, he couldn't stand being cooped up in the motel any longer and decided he would go down to the motel lounge and have a beer. He wasn't much of a drinker, but maybe tonight a beer or two would help him unwind from a most stressful day.

~ * ~

Back in Johnson City, Jeannie Rosmund was up late, too. She was wracking her brain to come up with someone to put in Gene's place. Despite what everyone in the office thought, she wasn't stupid. She just didn't know how the clerk's office ran. She also knew that her employees weren't very fond of her, she felt the tension, too. It wasn't bad enough to fire anyone. It wasn't really their fault. She had made a lot of changes and the employees didn't like the changes. They wanted to maintain the *status quo*; it was easier to work from habit than to learn something new. They were good employees, so she tolerated the tension and the snide remarks that weren't really directed at her or near her. Hopefully, they would come around.

Who to put in Gene's spot though? He was a hard act to follow. No matter who she promoted, there would be dissension in the ranks.

All of the employees were good, but she needed someone who could take charge. The election was creeping up on her and she needed to be out campaigning, not running the office. She had to find someone who could run the office while she was gone, not that her presence was all that important, but the office had to run smoothly so she wouldn't lose votes. Plus, after the election was over, she still wouldn't know how to run the office. She needed another Gene in there to run interference and keep the place operating while she kept up appearances. Jeannie was good at appearances, but that was about all. Despite everything anyone else thought, she was bright enough and honest enough to admit to herself that she didn't know how to be a circuit clerk.

~ * ~

Long before he reached the lounge, Charlie heard the music, loud music. *Maybe this won't be so relaxing after all*, he thought. *This late I figured the place would be winding down, but it kind of sounds like they have gotten their second wind.* Yet he continued on and when he reached the door, he opened it without hesitation. He had had all he could take of that motel room and was just too keyed up to try sleeping.

The lounge was packed, almost standing room only and the music was so loud it was hard to hear yourself think, let alone anyone talk. Charlie spied a little corner table for two or maybe just one. Just a small round cocktail table stuffed into an out-of-the-way dim corner. Of course, all the corners were dim. He practically fought his way over there, through the crowd and the clouds of smoke. By the time he made it to the table he was ready for bed. *Too late now*, he decided, *I'll have a beer and see if the crowd thins out*. That didn't look too promising though, this was a country and western crowd, they were dressed and ready for it. Looked to be an all night crowd or until closing time anyway and Charlie had no idea when the bars closed in Georgia.

Seated at the table, Charlie waited for the waitress to appear, but he didn't really hold out much hope of one appearing anytime soon. He was out of the way, across the room from the bar and between the bar and his table was a solid wall of people. He could just occasionally get a glimpse of the stage area where the band and a singer were performing—it was Carol Harmon. That explained the crowd. Must be a rare treat for this lounge to get a live act of her class.

Hey, she's pretty good, he thought. Charlie wasn't a country fan, but this girl had talent. It was clear to see, and also just as obvious that she enjoyed singing, enjoyed performing, at least in front of this crowd.

Suddenly the song was over. When the music stopped, the din of voices, that were drowned out just seconds before, rose in the lounge. With the music over the crowd seemed to mingle within itself without form and the mass of people became a swirling jumble of bodies. No way was a waitress going to find him now, he realized. *No wonder no one was sitting at this table*, he told himself.

He was about set to stand up and struggle his way back to the front door when out of the corner of his eye he noted that the crowd seemed to part and from his right, over the rest of the voices in the lounge, which seemed to be subsiding greatly, he heard, "I don't think this is such a good idea!"

Turning toward the voice and the parting crowd, Charlie saw Carol Harmon about three steps from his table with a middle aged man right on her heels, his face bearing a dark disgusted look. Before the realization of what was happening hit him, he heard Carol respond, "No, Dan, I don't imagine you do, you don't like any of my ideas."

Charlie jumped to his feet, almost knocking the little table over, but steadying it with his left hand as Carol stopped in front of the table, saying, "Good evening, mind if I join you?"

Flabbergasted, which was a very unusual condition for Charlie, he hesitated only a second or two, but that seemed like an eternity to Carol. She had seen him come in and decided she was going to talk to him, no matter what anyone else said or thought. Unless of course, he didn't want to talk to her, didn't want her to join him. Admittedly that would have been a thought foreign to her thinking a few days ago. No one ever turned down an opportunity to talk to Carol, have her join them, or in any way be seen with her. This man was different though and she felt that was part of her attraction to him. She was almost frightened that he would say no. Very possibly he was going to say no.

Charlie, completely at a loss, stammered out, "Please, ah please, yes, if you like, have a seat... Miss Harmon, I'm honored."

Honored? Carol thought, *now that's one I didn't expect from him. This could be interesting.* Especially since she knew she had already irritated her manager and that was one reason for her wanting to join this man. It was time Dan realized he was not 'King of the Roost' and that Carol had a mind of her own. He needed to know that she was not a child any longer.

The whole thing happened so fast that Charlie's brain barely had time to register it, but he did realize Carol was dressed 'down' in faded blue jeans and a short sleeved blue blouse, probably also denim or maybe flannel, but not silk, nothing fancy. Then again maybe this was the way she always dressed when performing, since he had not seen her perform before he had no way of telling.

The crowd had moved a respectable distance from the little corner table. It was obvious that the people in this room adored Carol Harmon so much that they would not have dreamed of interfering with anything she was doing. So they backed away, though it was hard to back away very far from anything in this room. Not so for Dan Chase, he looked around for a chair, but found none. Carol and Charlie had the only two available and no one near enough to count looked to be about to give their chair up for a middle aged man who looked fit enough to stand.

"Dan, you may not get tired of standing there, but I'm going to get awfully tired of you standing there, so how about you go over to the entertainer's table and wait for me?" Carol said sweetly, without any sweetness.

"But..."

"Dan, I'm fine, no one in here is going to kidnap me or beat me or kill me, Okay?"

"Well, I..."

"Dan... please," Carol ended rather forcefully, but not in an angry tone.

Dan turned and left. The cloud of disgust deepening on his face with each step he took from the table.

Carol turned to Charlie and said, "I'm sorry to intrude, but I saw you here and just felt I had to come and talk with you. It was very rude of me to talk to you the way I did the other day up on Burning Chapel Hill."

Charlie shook his head in the negative and put in quickly, "No, no, quite the contrary. You had every right to be upset with me. I don't know what got into me. I'm not that way ordinarily. No excuses. I owe you an apology and I welcome this opportunity to tell you that I'm sorry. I am not ordinarily such a rotten person."

"Okay, what say we just forget the whole thing?" Carol asked.

Charlie's heart skipped a beat for some strange reason, he took her question to mean she was going to get up and leave, that she had the feeling he didn't want to talk to her. Quickly, he said, "No, please stay, have drink."

Smiling with the brightest and whitest set of teeth Charlie thought he had ever seen, Carol responded, "I meant let's forget the whole incident up on Burning Chapel Hill. I'd like a drink, a draft beer."

Comprehension finally soaking in, Charlie smiled and said, "Okay, deal, now all we have to do is get the eye of a waitress. I haven't seen one since I walked in and sat down."

After another smile at Charlie, Carol turned looked over her right shoulder and ever so slightly motioned with her right hand. In a second flat a waitress stood in front of the table. Charlie didn't know where she came from, Carol could have conjured her up out of thin air for all he knew, but there she stood, smiling, waiting.

Carol said nothing, waiting for Charlie, who after waiting a few seconds for his mind to catch up once again, ventured, "Two schooners of whatever you have on draft, no light beer for me, high test." Turning to look at Carol he questioned, "Light beer, Miss Harmon?"

"High test for me, too, it's been a long day," she responded with what, for the first time, sounded to Charlie, like a tired strained voice. Then looking at Charlie as the waitress scurried away, she continued, "And please call me Carol."

Nodding his head, Charlie said, "Okay Carol, I'm Charlie, Charles Chambers, but I answer to almost anything," he ended lightly.

Carol stared at him with a frown on her face, saying nothing for a few seconds. During which time Charlie was not sure what was going on, and realized that this woman had a way of doing that to him. He also kind of liked it, for some weird reason. Charlie was always in the driver's seat, always on top of the game, always prepared, but he wasn't with her, and he found the experience rather unsettling and tantalizing at the same time.

Finally, Carol said, "You're a Charles, not a Charlie."

Smiling, Charlie said, "Whatever you like, it's okay with me."

"I like Charles, it's distinguished, respectable and you are that."

Chuckling, Charlie responded lightly, "I know a few judges that would take exception to that."

"They'd be stupid judges then," Carol said with sureness. "Anyone can see for themselves that you act, walk and talk like a real gentleman, even when fighting your way through a crowded lounge." Smiling now, she continued as if in answer to his unasked question, "I told you, I saw you come in the door. When you've spent as much time as I have up on a stage, you get used to noticing the crowd and everyone in it."

Charlie was impressed and embarrassed. He had expected a lot of things when and if he ever got to talk to Carol Harmon again, but not compliments, especially considering the way he had acted on their first meeting.

The waitress appeared with the beer and disappeared with a nervous smile. Another younger woman appeared suddenly and stammered, "Uh... Miss Harmon... uh... could I please have your autograph."

Carol turned toward her and said easily, "Glad to, what's your name?"

"Mary Turpin, Miss Harmon."

"Okay, Mary," Carol said as she signed her name on a napkin and handed it to Mary. "Will that do?"

"Oh, yes, thank you," the woman said breathlessly and left the table with a giggle.

Carol turned back to Charlie and said, "That felt good."

"Oh? I'd think you'd get tired of that."

"Maybe I would if I got to do it all the time, but I don't. This is very unusual, you see, usually my manager, or one of the stage crew, gather up things from the audience for me to sign, or I sign a bunch of different things at random and they are distributed. I never get to see a fan close-up, never get to talk to them. It's Dan's policy to keep me away from the crowds, for my safety. That's why he was so upset when I decided to sit here with you. I usually wouldn't go against him, he's a good manager, but I felt the need to rebel a little," she ended with a chuckle.

"Well, I'm glad you did. It gives me the chance to let you know I'm not the same person you met by that burned out church."

"I thought we had put that behind us," Carol responded.

"Yeah, right, sorry." Then he continued, "Say, you're a good singer, a good entertainer."

Smiling with a slight chuckle she responded, "Thanks, I take it you have never seen or heard me sing before?"

"No, I'm afraid not. I have to confess I never was a country fan, but that is changing," he ended with smile that showed faint dimples at the corners of his mouth. Carol thought those dimples very becoming.

"Glad to hear that, I can always use another fan." Carol was really enjoying herself, much to her amazement. She had come over here to just clear the air between her and this relative stranger, but had lingered and it was refreshing. The noise of the bar and the stares of the crowd were all shut out for the time being. She was a different person, a real person, something she had longed to be for years.

Charlie now asked, "How did you manage to line up this engagement so fast? I mean, I saw you at the airport and when our plane was delayed, I figured you would head back to Johnson City for the night. Your manager must be pretty good to come up with a job for you on such short notice."

"Oh, this isn't a regular engagement. I didn't feel like driving back to Johnson City and then coming back in the morning, so I suggested we get rooms here at the motel. I saw the lounge and decided to get the band together for a practice session. There were only a few people in here when we started, but that changed pretty fast. No, this is a freebie, something else that my manager doesn't like much. Which makes it all the better," she ended with a light laugh.

"You talk as if all you try to do is irritate you manager. You say he's a good one, but you keep talking as if you don't like him," Charlie observed.

"He is a good manager and I guess I like him okay, but he does tend to get on my nerves. He is too protective, too domineering. He's been with me since I started, at age eighteen, and sometimes he seems to think he is my father, mother, brother, husband and manager, all rolled into one. Occasionally, I have to let him know differently."

"I see," Charlie responded and then decided to try and find out more about Carol, stating, "I figured he was maybe your husband, a lot of singers have manager husbands."

Seeing right through his ploy and liking the fact that he was interested, Carol responded quickly with a faint knowing smile on her lips, "No, he's much older than I am, he's in his fifties! I'm not married and don't even have a steady. How could I? Dan keeps me cloistered like a nun. You are the first man I've talked to outside of my circle for I don't know how long."

"That doesn't sound to me like a very enjoyable existence. Why be rich and famous if you can't enjoy yourself, be yourself or feel normal?" Charlie responded.

"Exactly what I've been thinking lately, but only thinking. I can't get out, because I have contracts and commitments. I don't really want to get out. I just want to do a few more normal things, like this."

"So do them," Charlie stated flatly.

"Sounds good, but it isn't that easy. How about you? What makes you tick Charles?" Then chuckling she said, "Dan thinks you are just some low life lawyer with no money and no ambition who sucks off some fund for religious freaks."

Charlie saw the humor in that immediately, he was never one to consider himself better than others and generally could make fun of himself quicker than someone else. He laughed heartily and after taking a few seconds to recover answered calmly, "I'll bet it does look like that to some people. In a way it's true I guess. I get paid, but very little, by a fund that sends me around the country defending people's religious rights. He isn't that far off. Although, I do take exception to the low life part, after all I'm over six feet tall," he ended with wink.

Carol laughed in answer. She was really starting to like Charles. He had a fresh outlook, he was ordinary and normal, nice sense of humor once you got down to it and past the lawyer facade. Initially he came off as a stuffed shirt, but Carol had a feeling that was a protective mechanism he used, but was he married? He had gotten that answer out of her readily enough. *Typical lawyer*, she decided with mirth.

"No," Charlie said.

With a puzzled look on her face, Carol asked, "No, what?"

"No, I'm not married. That's what you were getting at wasn't it? After all I asked you in a round about way and you asked me in a more round about way" he ended with an impish smile.

"You read minds, too?"

"Sure, lawyers have to be able to read minds, a little anyway. Or at least they have to be good at making people think they can. Now let me cut to the chase and answer all your questions at one time. Not married. Been married, not married now. No children. No girl friend.

I'm thirty-five, six foot two and one hundred eighty pounds. I work constantly. I don't listen to country music. I watch very little TV, but I read a lot. I live in Illinois, by myself, and I make $50,000 per year plus travel expenses. I don't take any cases that aren't religious rights cases and only those that I feel destined to take."

The last part of that answer seemed a little strange to Carol, but she had to admit that he covered the basics pretty succinctly. *Typical lawyer*, she said again to herself and then immediately told herself that she was wrong in that, *Charles Chambers was far from a typical anything*.

"Okay," Carol stated, and continued, "Turn about is fair play. Not married. Been married, not married now. No kids, though I'd not be opposed to it. No boy friend. I'm one hundred twenty-five pounds and five foot four. I work constantly. I always listen to country music, but watch no TV. I read only song lyrics and I live in Georgia, with my bodyguards. I make more money than I have time to spend and travel all the time on tour," she ended, scrunching her face at him in a playful manner.

Charlie gave her that impish smile again, showing those dimples, that Carol was beginning to yearn to see and asked, "Age?"

"You don't know me well enough yet to get that answer, counselor. We aren't in court, I said turn about was fair play, but I never swore to tell the 'whole' truth."

They both laughed at that.

"Excuse me, Miss Harmon," a short, dark haired man interrupted.

"Oh, yes, Tom, what?"

"Well, ma'am, the rest of the band was just wondering if we could pack it in. The bar's about to close, it's almost two o'clock."

"No kidding!" Carol exclaimed looking at her watch to verify the time and continued, "Oh, I'm sorry, Tom, I lost track of the time." Looking around her now at the still crowded lounge, meeting the eyes of some of her expectant fans, she said, "Tom, how about just one or two more songs. I meant to play another set, but it's late. I can't just quit. They are all waiting for another song or two."

"Sure, ma'am, I'll tell the boys."

Carol got up and Charlie jumped to his feet.

"Thank you for the beer, Charles. This was nice, but I have to go back to work. I can't disappoint my fans. Maybe we could have a beer again sometime. I have to fly to Nashville to cut a record, but I'll be back in a week or so."

With genuine remorse on his face, Charlie responded, "I'm sorry, Carol, I won't be here. I'm heading home in the morning, since my case is over. Maybe I might have to come back to argue in the appellate court or work on the briefs for the appeal, but probably not."

"Well, okay, this is it then, I guess. Good-bye Charles, it was nice meeting you," she said wistfully, extending her right hand to him.

As he took her hand he said, "Good-bye, Carol. I promise I'll start listening to more country music and I'll start watching for you on TV."

Carol said nothing and let her hand remain in his. Charlie also said no more, each looked at the other's face for few seconds more and then dropped their hands as if on cue. Carol turned and walked through the crowd to the stage. Charlie retook his seat, he could at least listen to a couple more songs, he decided.

Twelve

The loud ringing jolted him upright in bed and he groggily grabbed the phone off its cradle to tell the operator that he was awake, or at least upright. Charlie hated those jarring wake-up calls, but since he didn't have an alarm clock with him, he had little choice. The airline bus was due to leave at six thirty a.m. and he wouldn't mind some breakfast and coffee first. He had been up too late last night or early this morning, he guessed and he was paying for it now. He had a dull aching in his head and his brain was foggy. He did recall why he had been up late though and he had a strange giddy feeling about him, although it left when he woke up enough to realize that he was leaving Georgia today. And so was Carol Harmon.

Across from the motel was a restaurant and Charlie wasn't long in getting over there to order breakfast. As he waited for breakfast and drank his coffee, he watched the motel awaken. People began coming out of the rooms, loading cars and moving off toward the office to check out. He wouldn't have to worry about that, this night was on Delta Airlines.

With little interest, he watched a truck pull up and two men unload a very tall ladder. They stood the ladder up against the building and one man climbed to the roof. Must have developed a leak during last night's storm, Charlie decided and continued to watch, as he finished his breakfast. He was hoping to catch a glimpse of Carol and her entourage, but she was not to be seen, in or out of the restaurant.

After breakfast, he collected his belongings from the motel room, walked up to the entrance to the motel office and waited for the bus. The men were still working on the roof and Charlie decided to pass the time of day with the worker manning the bottom of the ladder.

"You guys hit it mighty early," Charlie stated amiably.

"Not always, rush job," the man said with a facial expression that clearly stated his distaste for this early rush assignment.

"Developed a leak in the storm, huh?" Charlie opined.

"Nawh, stupid lightning bolt fried the satellite dish. Must have been the first bolt of lightning in the storm. Knocked the cable out in the whole place. They wanted us to come out last night, but we told them they were crazy. Could you imagine what would happen to us if lightning did strike twice in the same place and we were holding on to the feed wires on that baby!" the man ended, jerking his left thumb up toward the roof.

"I see your point," Charlie sympathized and continued, "But what's the big deal? I watched TV last night or did it not go out until late?"

"Went out about six o'clock or before. You could watch the local channel without the dish. If you disconnected the cable feed from the TV. The internal antenna would pull in WFTV easy enough."

"I didn't unhook anything. I had several channels to choose from and I finally settled on 'Highway to Heaven'."

The man looked at Charlie queerly, shook his head in disbelief and said, "You must have been dreaming. When lightning fried that dish the only channel any TV in this motel would pick up would be WFTV in Thomasville and for as long as I can remember it never carried no episode of 'Highway to Heaven'. Shoot, a bunch of us even tried to get them to carry it a few years ago, but they wouldn't, not even the old syndicated reruns."

Charlie didn't bother arguing. It didn't matter, the bus was coming and besides, he'd been in similar situations before. He once had heard a sermon he couldn't have heard; yet he had heard it, every word and it had had a profound effect on his life.

~ * ~

Dan Mosley sat in front of Mr. Tieman's desk and waited. He had been summoned upstairs before he had a chance to pour his first cup of coffee. Something was up.

Tieman took off his glasses, leaned back in his chair and began unconsciously twirling them in his right hand as he asked, "Dan, what are your theories on why the sheriff's department was here the other day?"

Dan shrugged slightly and answered, "I can't figure it, sir. They said they wanted to make sure Merriman had a motive for suicide, but they were really ranging far and wide on their questions. They didn't seem to have a focus. Maybe that's why they came; to get a focus."

Tieman narrowed his eyes, leaned forward in his chair and responded, "I don't buy it, Dan, I think they were looking for something in particular and only wanted it to seem like their questions had no focus."

"What?" Dan asked innocently, he knew some things went on in a plant this size, but nothing the sheriff's department would be interested in investigating. Maybe the Feds. There were always some corners cut in the area of anti-trust, to make a little better profit, but it did no real harm. Still, the Feds wouldn't look on it that way, but the sheriff? No way would the sheriff care. Besides, the sheriff knew where his bread was buttered.

"I won't put you on the spot and spell it out for you, Dan, but you know how the system works, for the most part. Anyway, what I want to know is how the sheriff's department got on to anything we might or might not be doing. We run a pretty taut ship here and I don't like the sheriff's department having an insider or at least a source. What do you make of that?"

The light bulbs went off in Dan's head. Not that he had the slightest idea of what Tieman was talking about, but he did know how the information was being passed, whatever it was. "I might just have that for you, by pure accident." And Dan went on to explain his almost visit with Tommy Trenton and why he aborted the visit. He also recounted his visit with Jerry Bales.

Dan then pointed out the significance of his findings, "Now why would a sheriff's investigator put up the bond money for a guy like

Tommy Trenton, a bum in anybody's book? Why would the city pick him up three times in less than two days? The answers are simple. That sheriff's investigator wouldn't and the city police wouldn't, unless there was something else going on. Like that sheriff's investigator asked that the city police pick up the Preacher and while he was in the county jail, Evans visited him or he was brought to where Evans could talk to him in private. Then Bales was sent in to bail him out."

Tieman nodded approvingly and asked, "Why three times, why not just once?"

Again Dan shrugged and answered, "Could be so that the Preacher wouldn't be seen talking to Evans for any length of time, or maybe they needed an update, or maybe he was sent out to get more details."

"How would this Tommy Trenton get any information for the sheriff's department, he's a glorified janitor, not smart enough to do anything else?" Tieman argued.

Dan smiled and responded confidently, "Janitors clean up. Generally when no one else is around. They have plenty of time to snoop and they have plenty of garbage to snoop through. He cleaned up at the dyeing facility and over here. Not always over here, but enough. He cleaned Merriman's office and your office, mine, too."

Tieman didn't go dead white, but it was obvious to Dan that the message had been received. Tieman was very quiet for several minutes and Dan could almost hear the gears turning in his head. Watching him, Dan could tell when Tieman had made a decision and he had made one now.

Nodding in agreement, Walter now said, "Yes, I believe you have the situation sized up about right, as usual. Thanks, Dan," he ended in dismissal.

Dan rose and without further comment, left the office. Just what decision Tieman had reached was beyond Dan, but there was little doubt he had reached it and that Dan's information had done the trick. Dan liked being helpful, but for some reason Dan wasn't sure he liked being helpful in this matter. He couldn't put his finger on it, but something was going on here that he didn't think he was going to like when he found out. Dan always found out, sooner or later. It was his job.

~ * ~

Shirley was almost through the breakfast rush when she heard a voice say, "Coffee, Miss Becker."

She was busy and didn't pay much attention to who had said it. It was just another customer who wanted fast service with no nonsense. She grabbed the pot, a cup and spun around to face Charlie Chambers sitting at the counter.

"Is that decaf? I have to have decaf," Charlie said with a disarming smile.

Shirley spun back, set the regular coffeepot down, grabbed the decaffeinated pot and spun again. "Thought you were leaving last night?" she asked, as casually as she could manage.

"I was, but something changed my mind."

"Oh, what was that?"

"A TV show."

"A TV show!" Shirley exclaimed and continued, "You don't strike me as the kind of person to be influenced much by TV."

Charlie smiled and responded cryptically, "Only when I see a show that no one else could see."

"Huh?"

"Never mind. When will you have some time to tell me all you know about the Preacher and his problem?"

Shirley's bottom jaw went slack and almost hit the counter. After she recovered, she asked, "You mean you're taking his case? You'll help?"

"Looks that way, if he'll have me. What do you think, will he have me?"

"Not sure. He's an odd one, but I bet he'll come around." Motioning him to follow she said, "Over here, let's sit in that corner booth and talk."

Charlie followed with his coffee and slid in opposite Shirley, saying, "Okay, now what about the Preacher. Who is he? Why does he preach?"

"I'm not sure. I don't know that much about him."

"Wait a minute," Charlie said. "You come out to the airport and beg me to help a man you don't know anything about? This isn't starting out well," he ended cynically.

Shirley took a deep breath and said, "I've been in Johnson City about ten years. I started working in this café as a waitress and when the chance came up I bought it from the owner when she retired. I'm still paying on it every month."

She continued, "You see, I'm pretty new around here, but I've watched the Preacher work the streets out front for all of those ten years, rain, snow or shine. I've asked some questions and gotten very few answers. No one around here really knows him or wants to know him.

"He works up at the mill and he lives downtown in an apartment, when he isn't on the street. His name is Tommy Trenton and he's forty-nine years old. As far as I've been able to learn, he has never hurt a flea, he works hard and he's dependable. He likes to pass out religious pamphlets and tell people about God. Where I go to church we call that evangelism and we don't put people in jail for doing it," she ended with conviction.

"And you like him, a lot," Charlie stated seriously.

"So? Does that make a difference?" Shirley replied stubbornly.

Charlie smiled and retorted, "Not to me, just stating an obvious fact."

Avoiding the topic, Shirley continued, "Lately he's been arrested three times for his evangelism. In all the years I've known him, or rather known of him, he's never been arrested and never been hassled. Now all of a sudden the new mayor goes on an anti-crime campaign and sweeps up harmless Tommy Trenton the first thing. What irony, Tommy preaches against the very thing that the mayor wants to clean up.

"I've talked to some of my friends over in the jail, I take them rolls sometimes," Shirley smiled impishly. Then on a more serious note she continued, "I told you what they said and the way you explained it, Tommy's in real trouble. If the state's attorney tries Tommy separately and gets three convictions, old Judge Ferrell will send him to the state prison. That would kill him, he just couldn't survive there," Shirley ended, dismally.

Charlie didn't respond immediately. What he didn't say was that he doubted Statesville would kill a man who, from all indications, had lived on the streets off and on his whole life. A man who was used to the hardest of the hard life. He didn't say it, because even though true, it wasn't what Shirley needed to hear. At least not yet, and hopefully never.

Instead, Charlie stated firmly, "They have to get the convictions first, Shirley. Your information indicates that he was arrested for disorderly conduct and I've seen very few disorderly conduct statutes that could hold up to a constitutional challenge."

Shirley was in rapt attention. The constitution was some holy grail to her. She wasn't stupid, in fact, by most standards, Shirley was very bright and capable in business. But the law always left her a little cold and intimidated. Yet to hear this man speak so easily of a law being unconstitutional, she could imagine laws falling before his arguments like wheat to the scythe. This was a great man, she sensed. How could Tommy lose? She thanked God for having sent Charlie Chambers her way.

"There's one problem, Shirley. I can't just represent Tommy because I want to be his lawyer. He has to want me. Unless he asks me to represent him and unless he is willing to talk to me and cooperate, my hands are tied. Now, do you think he would be willing to do that?"

Shirley thought for a few minutes and answered, "I'd like to think he would, but I don't know for sure. He's an independent cuss. If he knows what's good for him he'll be glad to have the help."

Charlie pressed the issue, "Some people don't know what's good for them, that's the problem. Could you talk to him, or would you be willing to go with me and talk to him? It can't look like I'm soliciting him. That's not strictly ethical, although in this case I'm not asking for a fee and that makes a difference. Still, I have to be careful. Okay?"

Quietly, Shirley responded, "Okay, I'll try."

"Do you know where he lives or where we could find him?"

"Yes."

Charlie liked this spunky lady and he was already feeling good about this case. He was doing what he did best and besides, he might just still be here when Carol got back from Nashville.

~ * ~

Mark Fribley had never been summoned to the executive offices before, he wasn't sure he liked it. He was a computer guy, he generally stayed in his little office in the basement and played with his computers. He transferred corporate data, wrote and rewrote programs and fixed programs when they crashed. Upstairs had always been an abstract place to him. As long as they paid him to play with his computer he was okay, but he didn't like the limelight. He didn't want to be noticed.

The elevator stopped at the sixth floor and Mark knew you didn't get any higher in Tieman Textile, at least as far as the physical plant went. Following the directions he had been given, he stepped off the elevator and turned left. At the far end of the hall he saw the door he was looking for. It was hard to miss, the name was in large bold letters 'Timothy J. Willis, Director of Research and Development.'

Mark entered the door and was immediately in the center of a large reception area where the lone secretary looked up and inquired, "May I help you?"

Mark was slightly nervous, now that he was here and also because he knew this secretary. Not personally though. He had seen her arrive at work this morning and she had on that becoming blue skirt that showed off her shapely legs quite well and that sensuous white, not overly transparent, short sleeved blouse. "Yes, ma'am, my name's Mark Fribley, I'm supposed to see Mr. Willis at nine o'clock." Sheepishly, he finished, "I'm a little early."

The secretary smiled at Mark's nervousness. She had seen it before, a lot of people were nervous up here on six. She also recognized Mark. She had made it a point to find out about him and she had seen him occasionally around the mill area, watching her. She knew he was the hottest thing around—on a computer keyboard. A first class brain, she had heard, not bad looking either. She had noted that first. This might just be the opportunity she had been seeking.

Giving him a comforting smile, she said, "Have a seat, I'll tell Mr. Willis you're here."

"Thank you, ma'am," Mark said still nervously, he was a fish out of water and knew it.

"Janet."

"Huh?" Mark responded absently, as he dropped heavily into a chair.

Smiling again, Janet responded sweetly, "My name is Janet, not ma'am. I'm not an old maid. I'm just not married."

Embarrassed now, Mark said lamely, "Oh, yeah, sorry." He knew her name, of course, but didn't want to seem forward.

Janet immediately decided that she liked this bashful young man. She usually met the brashest of people up here and almost all of the men either figured she was just some dumb blonde or fair game. Mark Fribley was refreshing. He was interested in her, too, she knew. He still watched her arrive every morning and had for quite some time. This could definitely be the break she had been wanting.

"Would you like a cup of coffee, Mister Fribley?" She put a lot of emphasis on the 'mister' to see what would happen. Her expectations were met.

"Mark, my name's Mark. I'm not a 'mister' I mean, I just work downstairs, I'm nobody in particular. I don't even know why I'm here. Yes, coffee would be good, black with sugar, but you don't have to get it, just show me where it is. I get my own coffee downstairs and at home."

Good to his word, Mark got his own coffee and when he returned to his seat, he watched Janet Longrade. He watched without letting on that he was watching, he thought.

While Mark was getting his coffee, Janet popped a breath mint in her mouth, just in case and informed Mr. Willis that Mark Fribley was here, but it was still only eight thirty so he had told her to have Mark wait.

"Oh, rats!" Janet exclaimed from in front of her computer.

Mark perked up and asked, "What's the matter?"

In disgust, she responded, "This stupid word processing program is giving me an error message again. It does it all the time. I lose half the stuff I type with this stupid thing."

Mark got up and walked around the desk to look at the screen and as he leaned over Janet's shoulder to examine the screen, his nostrils filled with the sweetest perfume he had ever encountered. It took him a few seconds to regain his bearings. Being this close to a beautiful woman was something he didn't often have the chance to do, but staring at the computer screen brought him back to reality. His life was computers.

"Hit the tab key and then return, I want to read the details."

"What?"

Pointing to the screen, he explained, "See there, in the error window there are two buttons. One says 'ignore' and the other says 'details'. You are on the 'ignore' button, you need to hit the tab key to move to the 'details' button and then hit the return key to show the details of the error."

It was all Greek to Janet, but she was so frustrated with this word processing program she was willing to try anything, besides this might be the best error she had ever gotten on this stupid computer. At least she had gotten Mark's attention, or hoped her perfume would.

She did as she was told and the screen suddenly filled with lines and lines of letters and numbers interposed with colons and commas. "Oh, I'm sorry, what did I do now?"

Mark chuckled and said calmly, "Nothing. Those are the details." Pointing again to the screen he explained, "See, these symbols tell us what part of the program erred and why."

Janet shook her head in disbelief that anyone could make heads or tails out of the mess of numbers, symbols and letters on the screen. As her head shook, her hair lightly brushed Mark's cheek, by pure accident, of course.

With difficulty, a few seconds later Mark tuned his mind back into the computer. "I can't save what you were typing, but I can keep this from happening again," he pronounced firmly, as he reached across in front of Janet and turned off the computer. After a few seconds he switched the computer back on and began typing commands as rapidly as a trained secretary types words on a page. He was still reaching across Janet and was having a little difficulty typing in such an awkward position, but he didn't really want to ask her to move and for some reason she wasn't volunteering to move. Mark saw that as a good sign and continued to type.

When he was finished, he restarted the computer once again and straightened, saying, "There you go. Every once in a while these complex programs drop bits of command data, sometimes whole command files and they have to be reconfigured. It should be okay now. If it acts up again, you call me and I'll come up and reconfigure it, but I don't think it'll give you any more trouble."

Janet was impressed. Mark was all she had heard he was and a nice guy, too. Trying to strike common ground with him, she said, "Could it be a virus?"

"Nawh. I check every program before it is put into use, it's part of my job." Then as an after thought he asked, "You know about viruses?"

Janet smiled disarmingly and confessed, "Not really, I know about them from hearing about them, but I don't understand them. They don't make sense to me, a virus is biological and computers aren't biological. I know it's just a metaphor, but I don't see how a computer virus compares to a biological virus."

Sharp, Mark thought, *this girl is sharp*. He smiled and responded, "You're quite right, but if you understood how a computer virus worked you'd see the similarity to the biological virus and you'd understand why the metaphor is so appropriate."

With her best pouting look, she said, "I'm too dense for that."

Smiling broadly now and feeling more comfortable around a woman than ever before, he said, "Now don't give me that. These stuffed shirts up here may treat you like some dumb blonde, but I know better. I could tell you were a lot more than that after five minutes. Truth be known, you could out smart and out think more than half the guys on this floor. I'll bet you have to do it on a regular basis anyway."

Janet was stunned. Mark was complimenting her in a very refreshing manner and it impressed her immensely. He had a way of making her feel important, very important. She liked that. And him. He was right, too. It took quite a bit to stay ahead of the letches around here.

The intercom buzzed and broke the unspoken chain of communication between their eyes. Janet reached for the phone as Mark turned back toward his chair.

"Yes, Mr. Willis, right away, sir." She hung up the phone and turned toward Mark saying, "He'll see you now, Mark."

"Thanks... Janet," he mumbled, as he moved toward the door that Janet was holding open for him and got a last whiff of her tantalizing perfume.

Inside the office, he was nervous again; a fish out of water once more. The inner office was huge and contained more furniture than Mark had in his small house. In front of a large picture window was a large mahogany desk and behind it sat Tim Willis. To the right of the desk was a computer desk and Willis was staring blankly at it. Without offering to rise, he waived Mark to one of several leather bound chairs facing the desk.

Mark took a chair and nervously leaned slightly forward as Willis said, "Here at TTM we transfer money directly to and from various accounts in several local banks. Right now I'm trying to access the Johnson City branch of the First Bank of Georgia, but I'm not having much luck. I'm told you are the best of the best when it comes to computers and computer programs."

Mark shifted uneasily in the chair and stated honestly, "I know my way around them pretty good, Mr. Willis. It depends upon the machine and the program. I know all the machines at TTM. I set them up when they first come in. You have an IBM PC three thirty-five with a three hundred megahurtz Pentium two processor. It's one of the fastest on the market right now. Your machine has forty-eight megabytes of RAM and two gigs of memory. Your modem is a three thirty-six and your 'on line' service is America Online, utilizing the new Microsoft Internet browser four point oh. I can do anything you want done with that machine. What do you want done?"

Willis was impressed and he didn't impress easily. He knew an expert when he saw one and this Fribley was definitely all he was supposed to be. He leaned back in his chair, folded his arms and said, "I want to access the First Bank of Georgia and transfer some funds from TTM to our accounts, but I can't get in to the bank's computer. I thought I had the latest password, but I'm not so sure now. I've been trying all morning and I tried last night, but I can't get through."

Mark stood up and moved around behind the computer desk for a closer look at the connections, saying, "Everything looks good on the hardware end, now suppose you tell me exactly what you are getting on the screen?"

"Access denied," Willis said with disgust. "That's all I've been getting and I'm getting tired of getting it."

Coming back around in front of the desk, Mark said, "If you'll lend me your chair, I'll have a go at it, sir."

Willis got up and came around the front of the desk as Mark went behind it and took the chair. He slid up to the computer and started the modem, "What's the password, sir?"

"Branson Lake," Willis said unemotionally.

Mark performed all the necessary steps, put in the password when requested and got the message, 'Access Denied'.

"See what I mean?" Willis said in satisfaction that it wasn't operator headspace causing the error.

Mark exited the program, typed in several commands, examined the screen display and said, "Your password is wrong. Can't be anything else. Nothing wrong with the computer."

"So what now?"

"Contact the bank and find out what password they are using now. They've changed it on you."

In disgust, Willis said, "I don't have time for this. Do you know the paperwork we have to go through to get a password out of those bureaucrats? By the time we get it they've changed it again. They're supposed to give us the new password two weeks before they change. I have to move some money and move it today, not next week!"

Mark shrugged and explained, "Sorry, sir, but without the password I'm helpless, it isn't a computer problem."

Willis blew up, "You're supposed to be a computer expert! You mean to tell me there's nothing you can do! What good are you?"

Mark was stung by the reproach, even though he knew it was unjustified. Willis didn't know that and Willis was a big shot at TTM. After a moment's thought, he said, "I can try to hack my way in, but that could take some time, too."

"What do you mean?" Willis asked.

"I can try to crack their system by deciphering their password. It's hit and miss, but I can usually do it if I try long enough. You want me to try?"

"How much time?"

"Couple of hours, maybe most of the day, can't say for sure. Sometimes I get lucky and crack a password in a few minutes. A lot of these places stupidly use common names or phrases for passwords, something that their employees can easily remember."

"So, I can't use my office until you're done?" Willis still wasn't happy.

"Well, no, sir. I can work on it from my computer downstairs and when I get the password I'll let you know and then you can access the bank from here. Okay?"

"Okay," Willis said, his anger somewhat abated.

~ * ~

Trooper John Greanias glanced into the Commander's office on the way by and noticed Commander Pinkerton waving him into the office. John stopped, backed up a pace or two and slipped into the office, saying, "Yes, sir?"

Pinkerton shuffled through a stack of papers on this desk and came up with the one he was looking for. Waving it in the air, he said, "Thought you'd like to know. The department of transportation has graciously decided to put up flashing yellow lights over those quarry road intersections on AA. Plus they are putting a flashing yellow light on the 'trucks entering the roadway' signs and adding signs that say, 'Caution dangerous intersection ahead'."

"That should help," John answered and continued, "But I still say they need to either reduce the speed limit along there or reroute those quarry roads so that they enter AA in areas of good visibility."

The commander tossed the sheet of paper on his desk and said, "Put that in writing and I'll see it gets kicked up the ladder. They may not listen to the patrol officers upstairs, but it isn't because I don't pass on your opinions. I personally think one patrolman's opinion on traffic conditions is worth a whole hat full of traffic studies by a bunch of over paid and under worked engineers."

This commander was pretty new and John didn't really know him, but he was starting to like him.

Pinkerton then continued, "Just for the record, even these signs wouldn't have helped your Georgia couple one little bit. The accident reconstructionist says the brake lines were as dry as bones in the Sahara. Near as they can tell so far, the main line separated from the master cylinder sometime before the accident. How they can tell that stuff is beyond me, but they seem pretty good at it. Now your idea to reroute those roads might have helped him. He might have had time to evade, but there was no way he was going to stop in less than five miles. Mechanical failure is something no traffic study can predict."

John nodded solemnly, but made no response. It was all they could do to reduce accidents. No one ever tried to fool himself into believing that all accidents could be prevented, there were just too many variables.

Thirteen

Todd was sitting at his desk going over the Merriman file once again, including the little green ledger book which had yet to officially make it into the file. The numbers in the upper right-hand corners of the pages had to be account numbers, but none matched any of the accounts that Merriman had in his own name. In the upper left-hand corner of each page were numbers and letters. He wondered what they meant. Maybe it was code for the bank in which the corresponding account could be found. He didn't really care, he was just curious, it had nothing to do with his discovering a motive for Merriman's death, he didn't think.

Sam Pinehurst came in and asked, "Did the sheriff talk to you?"

"Yeah," Todd responded dryly.

"And..."

"He wanted to let me know how important TTM was to the community, employing all those people and all. Wanted us to take it easy up there. Put a lid on this Merriman thing and stop bothering those nice folks up on the hill."

Sam nodded in the affirmative and said, "Same speech I got, almost word for word. What do you make of it?"

Todd shrugged and responded calmly, "Who cares? Nothing up there for us anyway. The sheriff didn't need to talk to me. I wasn't planning on going back. Curious though how the word came down so quickly. They must really be sensitive up there. No doubt they've got the clout around the county though, probably the state, too."

Sam nodded again in agreement and said, "Yeah, but what if it had been something really important? What if we'd been called off of something really big up there? That ain't right, Todd."

Smiling thinly, Todd responded, "It's politics, Sam. You've been around here longer than I have, you ought to know that much. Big isn't up to us to decide, we just do our jobs, when and where we're told. That's all."

"And if it had involved a burned out church?" Sam said pointedly.

"It didn't," Todd shot back.

"But if it had? Would you be so ready to pack it in?"

Clearly irritated, Todd asked, "What's your point, Sam?"

"No point, just that it ain't right is all."

"So it ain't right! You going to jeopardize your retirement to make a point when there's no point to be made? Let's save our fight for a battle worth fighting, partner."

Sam dropped heavily into his chair and answered, "Yeah, I guess you're right, no sense fighting city hall when there's nothing to be gained."

~ * ~

Tommy walked cautiously across the room to the door, he couldn't ever remember having had two callers in less than twenty-four hours.

He opened the door slowly and to his surprise he saw Miss Becker standing in the hall and she wasn't alone. He didn't know the man with her, but since he knew Miss Becker he opened the door all the way and said, "Morning, ma'am... I mean Miss Becker... I..."

Smiling, Shirley said sweetly, "You can call me Shirley and this is Mr. Chambers. May we come in?"

"Oh... yeah sure. Come in," he said lamely, as he stepped away from the door and they both stepped through. Immediately he said, "Sorry for the mess, but I don't get many visitors up here. I've never had so many visitors as lately."

Charlie glanced around the tiny apartment, which despite the protests of Tommy, looked very neat. It was sparsely furnished and small so there was little to mess up. It was obvious that this man had very little and needed less. Charlie immediately noted an open Bible lying next to the only recliner in the room. Charlie decided this man didn't just talk the talk.

Charlie was waiting for Shirley to start the conversation and he glanced her way. She was taking in the tiny apartment, too, with a strange look on her face that Charlie interpreted as pity and more. But what more, he couldn't quite figure. He suspected that Shirley had a flame for this itinerant, self-proclaimed preacher, but why he couldn't fathom. Maybe she had watched him from afar for so long that she knew him better than she let on and she might have become more attached than even she realized.

"I have another chair over here by the table, let me get it. Miss Becker you can sit on the sofa if you like," Tommy said very hospitably. It was obvious he was nervous in the presence of Shirley.

Tommy took a seat in the recliner, picked up his Bible, closed it and carefully laid it aside. He turned and looked at Charlie with an appraising look and then at Shirley, saying, "What do you want?"

Shirley began, "How many times have you been arrested in the last three days Tommy?"

"Three, but it wasn't my fault."

"I know, but what are you going to do?"

"I don't understand, what is there to do?"

"Are you going to get a lawyer? Do you know they could send you to the state penitentiary if you get convicted three times?"

"No, I didn't know that, but it doesn't matter. God is everywhere and His work is everywhere. If God wants me to go to the state prison then that's where I'll go. There must be work there, too."

Charlie liked this guy's style. He might be poor in worldly wealth, but he was rich in spirit.

Tommy continued, "You see, it doesn't matter, because there's nothing I can do about it anyway. I wasn't doing anything the last three days that I haven't been doing for the last twenty years. They didn't put me in prison then, why now?"

Shirley continued, "There is a different mayor now in Johnson City. He wants the streets cleaned up and he has decided to start with you."

"Why? I don't do any harm. I just spread the word of God, that's all. What's wrong with that? Doesn't the new mayor like God?"

Charlie chuckled inwardly at that.

Shirley was not amused however and continued, "I don't know and there's nothing wrong with what you do, but now you're going to need a lawyer or go to state prison. Do you want to do that?"

Tommy thought for a minute and answered honestly, "No, but I could if I had to, I've been worse off, I'll bet. And like I said, I can't do anything about it. How can I afford to hire a lawyer? I don't have any extra money. I only get minimum wage up at the mill. Oh, I know I could get a court appointed lawyer, but I don't think that would help me. I know enough about life to know that no court appointed lawyer is going to take a serious interest in the likes of me. Right?"

Shirley persisted, "A court appointed lawyer maybe, but what if you could have a lawyer that wasn't court appointed and you still didn't have to pay?"

"Okay, I'd do that, but where am I going to find someone like that?"

Charlie put in, "Me."

Tommy took real note of Charlie for the first time. He was dressed in a nice suit, not flashy, just nice. He was quite a bit younger than Tommy, but he looked older than Tommy figured he was. It was clear to see that he had had some hard times, too. Clean cut, smooth shaven, short-cropped hair with no sign of gray. *He could be a lawyer*, Tommy thought, then said, "Why would you want to represent me for free? Lawyers get big bucks. I'm poor, but I'm not stupid. What's in it for you?" Tommy ended skeptically.

"Good question," Charlie responded and continued, "You just said you would serve God even in prison, right?"

"Sure."

"Well, I do pretty much the same thing. I go where I feel God wants me to go and I do what He wants me to do. Usually that is defending people who are being prosecuted for their religious beliefs or actions. Sometimes I file lawsuits for people who are being discriminated against because of their religion or who have been prevented from exercising their religious rights.

"You're willing to go to prison to serve God, don't you think I might be willing to come to Georgia to represent someone for free so that they could continue to serve God? Does that make sense to you?"

Tommy thought for a few minutes, studied Charlie carefully and responded, "Yes, it does. Say, you aren't saying God talks to you are you? I'm pretty skeptical of people who think that way."

Charlie smiled and said, "No, I just get feelings is all and things happen to convince me to go or stay. I don't hear voices. I'm as sane as you are."

"Okay, but I still don't see what can be done, the law is the law."

Charlie replied, "Leave that up to me. I can tell you for starters, though that I think the law they used to arrest you is unconstitutional. Now that isn't going to be as easy as it sounds and it will take longer than a few weeks. It might take months. The main thing is that you have to stay out of trouble for the time being. You have to be careful not to continually get arrested for the same thing. It will only make matters worse. I think I can get the three existing cases consolidated, but not if you keep getting more."

Tommy shook his head in the negative and said, "I thought you understood, Mr. Chambers. You seemed to understand. I can't do what you ask. I have to be preaching the Word, no matter what the cost. Can't you do something to make that possible? Can't you do some of that lawyer stuff and make them leave me alone?"

Charlie shook his head in the negative and said, "No."

Tommy shrugged and said, "Okay, then next time I better not get bailed out, because I can't quit. I just can't."

Charlie now asked, "But you bailed yourself out. How can we stop that?"

"Not me. Look around you. Does it look like I have the money to bail myself out of jail? Three times?"

Charlie readily agreed with him and it hadn't occurred to him that someone else was bailing the Preacher out of jail. Who would do that? No one cared about the Preacher, or so it was said. Charlie narrowed his eyes and looked directly at Shirley.

Shaking her head, she said emphatically, "Not me! I don't have the money to throw around on bail. Why, I can barely pay my bills at the café. I don't mind trying to help, but I don't have the money for bail, not that I wouldn't have done it if I could, but I couldn't."

Curious, Charlie thought, but in the end it really didn't matter, he had to figure a way to keep Tommy out of jail. After a few moments of silent defiance by Tommy, Charlie said, "Okay, Tommy. I won't ask you to stop preaching, but will you give me one day before you start in again? Is that asking too much? Just one day?"

"What for?" Tommy questioned.

Charlie pursed his lips and furrowed his brow. "I'm not sure, but give it to me anyway, okay?"

After a moment Tommy responded dryly, "Okay, one day."

"Good. Now when is your first court appearance scheduled?"

"Tomorrow, I think."

"You think. Didn't they give you some papers when you were released?"

"Yeah, sure. Every time."

"Your court date is on those papers. Do you have them?"

Tommy nodded and opened the drawer on the end table near his chair. After a moment of digging he came up with several sheets of paper, got up and handed them wordlessly to Charlie.

Charlie scanned them, put them in chronological order and said, "The first one is Friday morning. Courtroom B, Judge Seymour at nine o'clock. I'll meet you there a few minutes before nine. I should be able to get you arraigned on all three charges at once and save you a couple of trips to court. That doesn't mean the cases will be consolidated, not yet. I'll have to work on that later." Rising now he handed the papers back to Tommy and finished, "You keep those with you all the time. They prove you are out on bond and they prove how much bond you put up, or was put up for you. Don't lose those receipts whatever you do. Sometimes the circuit clerk loses things so you hang on to your receipts. Okay?"

"Sure, okay."

"Good. See you in the courthouse just before nine."

"Yes, sir. And thank you, sir."

"Charlie. Just call me Charlie."

~ * ~

Austin Murray fiddled nervously with the pencil in his hand, staring at the pages in front of him, without seeing them. Finally, he turned and picked up his phone to dial Tim Willis' direct line, not his secretary.

"Willis." After one ring.

"Did you get that little matter taken care of?" Murray asked bluntly, without any preliminaries.

Tim recognized the voice immediately and responded briskly, "Sure. Easy as pie. That boy really does know his computers."

"Good," Austin said and hung up, leaving Tim still holding the receiver of his phone up to his ear in expectation of something more.

Austin had no more than hung up on Tim when he opened his upper left-hand drawer and took out a stack of checks already filled in with the name of the payee and the amounts. He detached the check stubs and put them in his right-hand suit pocket. In the left-hand breast pocket he put the checks.

He grabbed up his telephone and buzzed his secretary.

"Yes, sir," came the prompt response.

"I need a donut or something, Tess. Came in too early without breakfast again. Would you please run down and grab me a couple before they're all gone?"

"Sure, Mr. Murray, be back in a minute."

Austin hung up and waited a full minute. He got up, crossed to his office door and slowly opened it to see if Tess had left yet. She had and he quickly stepped out into the outer office and crossed to the paper shredder. At the shredder he took out the check stubs and quickly shredded them one at a time. Finished, he went back into his office and took up a busy posture behind his desk long before Tess returned with two chocolate cake donuts.

After finishing the donuts, he stood up and donned his light overcoat. It looked like it was misting out again and besides, when he toured the plant, he liked to have something on to protect his suit from the dust and dirt.

It was Austin's custom to take a foot tour of the plant occasionally and at this particular time he was glad that it had become his custom. He could kill two birds with one stone this time.

On his way across the expanse between headquarters and the dyeing facility, he took the checks out of his pocket and began rubbing them gently to give them a handled look, but not enough to deface them. By the time he reached the dyeing facility the checks were back in his pocket and well handled. Shortly after he entered the building, he slipped into the employee locker room and after making sure no one was around, he quickly found the locker that he sought. Stopping only momentarily, he slipped the checks into an air vent slot, letting them fall into the locker. A quick glance around to confirm he hadn't been seen and he continued with his regular tour of the plant.

He abbreviated his plant tour slightly because he wanted time to locate Dan Mosley and have a talk with him before lunch. Once back in his office, he called Dan Mosley and in short order Dan appeared in Austin's office.

"Yes, sir, Mr. Murray. What can I do for you?" Dan asked, as he took the proffered seat across from Austin's desk.

"Something has come to my attention and I'm not sure I like it. I want you to check into it and if there's anything to it let the police in on it."

Dan sat up attentively now, it was very unusual that any one at TTM would even suggest inviting police scrutiny. *This must be serious*, Dan decided and responded, "The police? Usually we like to keep them at arms length up here, sir. Is it that serious?"

Austin raised his hands and spread them in the universal 'I'm at a loss' sign and said, "Wish I knew Dan, I want you to look into that for me. Anyway, I have it from several sources that there has been quite a bit of petty cash missing from some of the departments. Mostly over here at the headquarters building, but also some of the others. Now, I'm head of distribution, but I also have the additional job of working with the auditors on an ongoing basis. Not my cup of tea, but I'm stuck with it. Anyway, that's what I'm picking up."

Dan hadn't heard of this and wondered why he hadn't picked up on it before Murray. He didn't say anything and waited for Murray to continue, which he promptly did.

"Also, there have been some checks stolen. Checks already made out to TTM from other companies, not large amounts, but it adds up to a nice little sum. The checks were logged in, but never deposited. As near as I can tell it has been occurring over a two or three year period, maybe longer."

Dan couldn't contain himself any longer and asked, "How did you hear about this? I never got a sniff and it's my job."

Austin shrugged unemotionally and said, "Just bits and pieces here and there. Mostly from conversations with the auditors, they really noticed it first. You wouldn't have regular contact with them or the financial data that I have."

Dan was somewhat comforted by that. *Yes*, he decided, *it was true that he didn't generally get involved in the financial end of the business, except to insure that physical security was tight.* He didn't feel quite so much like he had dropped the ball and it didn't seem as though Murray thought he had either. Then the investigative side of Dan took over and he began quizzing Austin.

"I don't suppose you know who is doing it?"

"No, but I want you to find out."

"Okay, what departments have missing funds?"

Austin ticked off several names and Dan quickly took out his note pad and began writing.

"And the checks, what departments were they stolen from, what companies did they come from and how many?"

Dan continued writing as Austin answered.

"Any information on the time of day or night when the thefts might have taken place?"

Murray leaned back in his chair and answered evenly, "I'm not one hundred percent sure, but most probably at night. We deposit any checks that come in late in the afternoon the first thing the next morning, so there could be some in or around desks over night. Most other times there wouldn't be any checks lying around. I'm just speculating there, of course."

"How much are we talking about here Mr. Murray? A few hundred? Thousands?"

Austin leaned forward, placed his elbows on his desk and contemplated for a minute and then he answered, "All totaled, probably a couple of thousand over a couple of years. Not a big deal when you consider that TTM deals in millions, but it's the principle. Plus, it could easily escalate if we don't stop it."

Dan nodded in assent. "Yes, depending upon who is doing this, it could get into the tens of thousands pretty quickly."

Austin knew better than that, of course, but pretended he didn't. He knew who was doing it, too; or rather, whom it was supposed to look like was doing it anyway.

"Any guesses at this point, Dan? I won't hold you to them," Murray asked nonchalantly.

Dan thought for a minute and responded evenly and cautiously, "If I had to guess, with no more than I've got to go on now, I'd say it was someone on the night shift. Someone with access to headquarters at night. But not an executive, at least not a high executive. The amounts are too small for that. No, this is the work of a penny ante crook, not big time, not yet."

Murray raised his eyebrows and nodded affirmatively. "Yes, that would be my guess. Maybe even a janitor or the like, but then I'll leave the master sleuthing to you," he ended abruptly, stood up and extended his hand to Dan.

Dan knew this was a dismissal and besides, he had work to do. Maybe he hadn't been the first to pick up on this breach in security, but he would be the first to know who was doing it.

Fourteen

Todd put down the phone and looked oddly at Sam.

From across his desk, Sam noted the look and asked, "What?"

"Weren't we just chewed out for going up to the mill and asking questions? Something about not rocking the employment boat, I think?"

Sam shrugged and took another sip of his coffee before saying, "Yeah, so what?"

"That was Mosley, chief of security, you remember him?"

"Yeah, he was probably the guy who complained about us asking questions up there. He giving us more grief today?"

"On the contrary, my dear Mr. Pinehurst, he wants us to come back. It seems he has a problem and wants us to help. Someone has been dipping into the till up there and he wants us in on it," Todd retorted sarcastically.

Sam nodded and then asked, "Do we go?"

Emphatically, Todd shook his head in the negative. "Not on his say so we don't. That's asking for trouble. We don't work for TTM, as much as they'd like us to think we do. How about we report this to the shift commander and let him decide whether to send a patrol car out to take a report? Proper procedure dictates that we don't go on cases that haven't been assigned to us." Todd smiled thinly.

Sam smiled back and agreed, "Yes, of course. We don't make those kinds of decisions, do we?" he asked rhetorically.

Todd picked up the phone and dialed the inside line to reach the shift commander, Sergeant Walker. Shift commander was really a misnomer since there were only two deputies on this shift and they certainly didn't need a commander. Still, the proprieties had to be observed.

"Commander Walker," came the all-business answer.

"Bill, Todd Evans here. I just got a call from Dan Mosley up at TTM. He wants us to come up about some thefts he says he has uncovered. Thought you should know in case you wanted to send a patrol up there to take a report. We can't go before you guys clear it."

"You trying to get me put back on the jail detail, Todd?" Walker said lightly and continued, "The sheriff has put a 'hands off' sign on the mill. You know that as well as I do."

"Didn't know patrol couldn't go up there. Sam and I just figured we weren't supposed to go up there, because we asked too many questions the other day."

"Well, it may be because of you, but it applies to everyone. The sheriff kind of wants to get elected at least once more."

"So what do we do? The chief of security at TTM is asking for the sheriff's assistance," Todd said evenly.

"Okay, okay. I'll run it up the flag pole and see who salutes it, but I'm not sending any deputy out there without approval," Walker said, clearly irritated to be put on the spot like this. He didn't like calling the sheriff for advice on command decisions. Commanders weren't supposed to have to ask every time a decision came up. But then, this was a little different, so he called the sheriff.

~ * ~

Dan couldn't figure out why it was taking the sheriff's department so long to get there. He had called the investigators directly to speed things up and that had been hours ago. He wanted to get this ball rolling quickly. He had already pretty well identified who the culprit was and he needed the sheriff in on the clincher. Where were they? It was getting on to quitting time at the mill and he wanted this done today.

Maybe a phone call would speed things up, he decided and grabbed for his phone.

~ * ~

"MSO Ten, Meridian county," came the somewhat hurried voice of the dispatcher and both investigators gave each other a knowing look. This could be a hot one, the dispatcher didn't generally show any emotion unless something big was up.

Sam quickly responded with his blood racing just a hair, "MSO Ten, go ahead Meridian county."

"Ten-one-seven," the dispatcher's voice crackled over the radio and went silent.

"Ten-four," Sam said with plain disgust in his voice. They were ordered to return to the station. But why the hurried tone of the dispatcher, what was up?

They had no more than entered the back door of the sheriff's department when they both found out. Walker met them at the door and pointing down the hall, said, "The sheriff wants you two, on the double."

They were really puzzled now, but didn't waste any time. When the sheriff called, deputies hopped.

The sheriff was livid and his face looked like a storm cloud brewing in the west on a hot summer's day. He arose slowly from behind his desk as they entered. As he reached his full height, he exploded just like a summer thunderstorm, "Don't you guys like me? Are you trying to get me booted out of office? Just because we are under the merit commission system doesn't mean I can't give you two clowns the boot! I can always figure a way to do that!"

Sam was flabbergasted and stammered out, "What did we do Sheriff?"

"Don't play coy with me, Pinehurst and lose that dumb-founded look, Evans! You guys got a call from the chief of security at TTM and passed it off to the shift commander. Are you guys just trying to get this department in hot water with TTM or what?"

Todd started, "Sheriff..."

The sheriff cut him off with a wave of his hand and boomed, "You two best shake your tails on up to the mill and do it right quick. Mr. Tieman himself called me a while ago and he wasn't happy. I told you guys not to stick your nose in up there at TTM, but I didn't mean you should ignore them when they ask for assistance. Passing it off on the shift commander was really cute, Evans, but don't pull that again. Now get out of here and go up there to TTM and act like you're enjoying yourselves. If I hear another complaint on you two, or either of you, from any one at TTM, including the guard at the back gate, I'm going to take real pleasure in finding some way to toss you both out on your ears, merit commission notwithstanding. Now move!"

It took less time to get back to their car than it had for the sheriff to chew them out for the second time in twenty-four hours. As Todd backed the car out and spun around for the street, Sam said, "It ain't right, Todd."

"What are you talking about now?" Todd asked roughly, he was preoccupied with his own thoughts and wished Sam would just shut up for a while.

"The way the sheriff favors TTM I mean. I know he gets a lot of votes up that way and I know that company employs a lot of people around here, but this bouncing around at every TTM whim isn't right. Walter Tieman isn't God."

"That's a fact and it's a good thing he isn't. Don't sweat the small stuff, Sam. Me, now I just go with the flow. If the sheriff wants to cow tow to TTM that's okay with me. Nothing illegal about a little favoritism. If there's something else to it then that may be their problem some day, but not mine."

Mumbling under his breath, Sam repeated, "Ain't right."

Todd laughed for the first time in the last twenty-four hours and said, "Sam, you're a peach. When you get something in your craw you don't let it go do you? You complain about me not letting go of a burned out church and you're just as bad."

Bitterly, Sam responded, "At least my trails aren't cold! When I get something in my craw it's a more recent injustice than a fire that happened thirty-five years ago and about which no one cares!"

Todd was silent for a few moments and so was Sam. He was already sorry he had let his temper get out of hand. He wasn't mad at Todd, it was the system he was fed up with and he decided it was a good thing he was close to retirement.

After some time Todd said evenly, "I'll take it that you didn't mean what you said, or the way you said it, Sam. I figure you're just as frustrated as me about injustice. It's just that we have a different perspective on injustice and its degrees." As he turned down TTM's private drive and scooted past the gate shack as if the guard wasn't even there, he finished, "I don't believe that no one cares about that burned out church. Even if no one else cares, I care, Sam. And you do, too. I can hear it in your voice when we're up there and I can see it in your eyes when we leave. You try to hide the fact that you care, but you care. Maybe you don't care the way I do about it, but you care. You can't hide from me, partner, no matter how hard you try."

Sam was relieved. The bad air between them passed like a rain cloud and the sun had come out again. He knew that no apology was necessary or any further explanation. His partner understood him— almost completely—and he understood his partner. He also understood why Todd had blown by the gate guard without bothering to stop. It was one way, a small way, to let someone at TTM know that not everyone danced to their tune, not all the time.

Before the gate guard even had time to report a vehicle failing to stop, Todd had whipped the car into a parking spot in front of the headquarters building and killed the engine. Sam rolled out of the car. There just was no other way to describe how Sam got out of a car.

Todd was at the main door and on the way in by the time Sam got his legs under him and started moving on his own power. He knew Todd was right, he had to do something about his weight. Providing the sheriff cooled off and let him stay to retirement, he wouldn't pass his physical if he didn't do something. That would also be an excellent reason for the sheriff to dump him, he now realized.

Todd was through the double glass doors, having blown past the receptionist, just as he had blown by the guard at the gate, before Sam caught up with him. Todd smiled wickedly as Sam approached, not at Sam, but at the fact that they had already passed two main checkpoints at TTM and not bothered to stop and play the game. Although Todd had flashed his badge at the receptionist, he figured she was already calling security and it gave him a wicked sense of delight at how the TTM apple cart was being upset this late afternoon.

He didn't really care about the sheriff's threat and he didn't believe it either. If he were wrong, who cared, he was as fed up with the system as Sam was. If he could just solve the church burning he would be tempted to quit.

When they reached Mosley's office they did stop for his secretary. No sense being too overbearing. Up to this point they could always explain their failing to stop as haste to come to the aid of TTM, but to barge into someone's private office without a warrant or a good reason, well, that just wasn't done.

Dan Mosley opened his inner office door, stepped out into the secretarial area smiling broadly and said with obvious mirth, "I knew it was you guys. As soon as the gate guard called I knew it was you two. The receptionist is about to have kittens. She was all for calling the sheriff when I explained that two deputy sheriffs probably just walked by her." He chuckled and continued, "Come in, please."

Todd and Sam entered at his beckoning and once the door was shut Dan said, "I'm sorry if I got you two in hot water. I just wanted to get some action. I didn't want to get anyone in trouble, not really. Up here at TTM we're used to getting what we want promptly, at least most of us are. Not me. I only wanted to get this thing nailed down today, before it was too late. I'm afraid if we wait any longer the evidence will disappear, if it exists now."

Todd softened just a tad. Mosley seemed genuine to him, but yet he wasn't sure. *Could the chief of security at TTM be a real down to earth guy? How could you get to be chief of security at any organization without taking on the characteristics of the organization?* Still, he decided to reserve his judgment for a time yet.

Sam put in his two-cents worth for the first time, "Suppose you tell us what evidence you expect to find. Where you expect to find it and what you expect it to prove?"

Todd smiled to himself, Sam had a way of getting to the point, even when it might be better to beat around the bush for a while.

Dan leaned forward slightly in his chair and adjusted a note on his desk. Leaning on the desk with both arms, he summarized his notes for them, which basically consisted of the story Austin Murray had told him and his own investigation of the shifts that various people with access worked. Once he was done summarizing his notes, he leaned back in his chair and concluded, "The best time to see if there is any evidence that one of these people committed the thefts, is right now, before they come on duty tonight. This is a textile mill, but it doubles for a rumor mill and I'm afraid that after tonight any evidence will be gone."

"What about some surveillance?" Todd now asked.

"Sure, we could try that, if this doesn't turn up anything, but that will take a little time to set up. I have a feeling that if we waste too much time we will take a really big hit and the culprit will either disappear or cover his tracks so well we won't find him."

Todd persisted, "Okay, so we hold off on surveillance awhile, but I still think it is the best shot for solid evidence in a case like this. Unless we find direct evidence elsewhere, surveillance is always the best bet. We know enough about the pattern of conduct and we have a narrow enough list that we could watch them all for a week and nail this down really tight."

"How about we try my way first?" Dan asked.

"Okay with me, what do you think, Sam?"

Sam shrugged and responded, "Couldn't hurt. Let's go."

Dan nodded his assent, rose and showed them out the office door.

Out in the hall, Dan took the lead and walked them to the elevator. Once on the elevator, he pressed the button for the basement, explaining, "The night shift maintenance people all have lockers in the basement. We'll have a look in them to see if anything is there."

Todd raised his eyebrows and asked, "What about a warrant? Anything we find won't be any good without a warrant."

Dan expounded, "Every employee of TTM who maintains a locker on the premises signs a waiver allowing us to check his or her locker at any time we deem necessary, for any reason."

Sam put in, "Maybe they do, but that's only okay for you. If the guy gets a sharp lawyer he'll claim you were an agent of the police and the search will be no good. Your waiver only keeps you from getting sued, it doesn't help get evidence into court."

"Good point," Dan said and continued, "but what judge would give us a warrant on no more than we have?"

Todd nodded. "Also a good point. So, I assume we are just looking for PC here. We find something that links an employee to the theft and use that as our probable cause for a warrant to search his or her home, etc."

Dan smiled and winked without commenting further.

Sam said, "That works for me, how about you, Todd?"

"Close enough for government work," Todd responded dryly.

Dan stepped off the elevator first and led them through the dimly lit basement full of pipes, electrical conduit and ductwork. They wound around the basement until Dan turned into a small room containing several lockers. No one was there and Dan walked up to the first locker, pulled a ring of keys from his pocket, checked the numbers and inserted a key in the lock.

"All the lockers at TTM have standard internal locks and we issue the keys," Dan explained, "that way we know which key fits which locker and we always have a key."

Handy, Todd thought, but wasn't sure he would like his employer having that kind of access to his locker. Even though there would be nothing incriminating in it, there might on occasion be something embarrassing. *Guess I won't retire and work for TTM*, he thought flippantly, *as if they would have me.*

Dan rummaged carefully through the first locker as Sam and Todd looked on with disinterest. Todd, for one, wasn't expecting any evidence to be uncovered in this search. Who would be dumb enough to keep evidence of a theft from his employer in a locker to which the employer had easy access?

They watched as Dan picked his way through each of five lockers to no avail. There were dirty clothes, odds and ends of personal effects and some left over food, but nothing else. *What a waste*, Todd thought.

When Dan slammed the last locker door closed, Todd said, "No soap. Well, what about surveillance?"

"One more place to check first," Dan said and waived them to follow him again.

This time he took the stairs to the ground floor and exited at the side of the building. He led them across the parking lot to a building with a large sign proclaiming it to be 'Dyeing Facility #1' and they followed him in the door. This time they entered a locker room on the main floor and Dan walked along the rows of lockers, stopping at number three oh two.

Todd's breath caught for a second as he read the name on the locker—Tommy Trenton—and he watched with puzzlement as Dan opened the locker.

Todd asked, "I thought you had it nailed down to a maintenance man in the headquarters building? What's this?"

"This guy does maintenance work over there sometimes. I've seen him there myself. You know him?"

"Yeah sure, sort of, I mean... every one knows the Preacher. He's harmless. Can't feature him stealing anything from anyone. What makes you think he did it?" Todd questioned.

Dan pulled open the door as he responded with another question, "What makes you think he didn't? You know something I don't?"

Before Todd could respond, several pieces of colored paper tumbled out on the floor and as Dan stooped to pick them up, Todd read one that had landed face up. It was a check on a company called TBM. He had heard that name before; it was all over the little green ledger book found in Merriman's house.

Dan exclaimed, "Got you!" Turning now with the papers, he held them out to Sam and Todd saying, "Checks from companies we deal with. No reason he would have those unless he stole them. See, the check indicates the amount and the invoice number being paid. All TTM invoice numbers. This Trenton took the checks and some how was going to negotiate them."

"How would he negotiate checks made payable to TTM?" Todd asked defensively. He liked the Preacher.

"Don't know, but first we need to prove he did it. With this you should be able to get a warrant to search his apartment and seize his bank records. Right?"

Grudgingly, Todd agreed, "Yeah, sure." This hadn't turned out quite like he had expected. Never in his wildest dreams had he even faintly thought that the Preacher would do something like this and then keep the evidence in his locker at work. *Stupid, real stupid, too stupid, too pat*, Todd immediately decided, but didn't know why.

~ * ~

Jeannie sat in her private office casually looking out the large picture window across from her desk. Ordinarily she had the curtains drawn on that window, she liked her privacy, but today she had opened them and continually observed her employees. She was hopeful that one of them would catch her eye or somehow do something that made him or her stand out. She needed some indication from one of them that they could handle Gene's job, but none had done so, especially not her daughters. Jeannie had to admit to herself that if anyone in this office was more inept than she was, it was either or both of her two daughters. But they needed the jobs and there were enough competent employees to cover for them. Never even in her weakest moment had she seriously considered putting either of her two daughters in charge of anything, including taking out the trash.

A knock on the door disturbed her and she snapped out, "Yes!"

"Sorry to bother you, Mrs. Rosmund, but the files haven't been pulled for tomorrow morning's setting. Gene usually did that himself," a dark haired young girl squeaked out from behind the edge of the door.

"Have Julie do it, she's been doing it with Gene not here, hasn't she? Tell her to pull up the cases on the computer for each courtroom, beginning with traffic at nine o'clock. Print out the list and then pull the files. Stack them in a prominent place and then Tim can take them around first thing in the morning, no time left today."

"Julie's off today, ma'am."

"Then you do it, just like I told you."

"Yes, Mrs. Rosmund, sorry to bother you," she finished lamely as she backed out and quietly shut the door.

Not five minutes later there was another knock on the door and Jeannie barked, "Yes, what is it!"

It was the same girl again, Betsy something-or-other. "I'm sorry, Mrs. Rosmund, but I can't get the list to come up on the computer."

Jeannie rose abruptly from her chair and flashed past the girl on her way to the counter where several deputy clerks stood in total frustration. *It's beginning*, Jeannie thought, *I have to find me another Gene and quickly.*

Reaching the counter, Jeannie brushed past the crowd, scanned the computer screen and said, "No, no. You have to hit the 'control' key and the 'enter' key at the same time. Not in sequence. That's not too hard is it? Here, see." She punched in tomorrow's date, hit 'control' and 'enter' simultaneously and the screen filled with a list of names, courtrooms and times. "Nothing to it. Now print it and pull the files."

"Print it?" Betsy questioned.

Sighing heavily, Jeannie responded, "F10 to 'actions,' select 'file' and then select 'print'. Nothing to it." Raising her voice now and looking around the room, she finished, "You people have to get up to speed on these computers. They aren't going to go away. I know it's new and different, but it's here to stay and you have to learn how to cope. Would it help if I called the software company and had them bring someone back for a training session or two?"

Everyone smiled and nodded in unison and Jeannie said, "I'll see what I can do." Turning to Betsy, she said, "You help pull these files, we're about out of time today. And from now on it's your job to pull the files. Only you, no one else. Understand? No one pulls files for court except you."

Betsy responded, with uncertainty in her voice and with a fearful look on her face, "I'll try, Mrs. Rosmund."

"No. Don't try, do it. It isn't difficult and pretty soon you'll be doing it in your sleep. Okay."

"Okay, I guess."

The Preacher   Robert James Allison

Fifteen

His apartment lease had not really ended when he had left the other day so Charlie talked to the owner, who had no other prospects anyway, and the owner agreed to continue renting to Charlie on a month-to-month basis, just as he had. Charlie didn't really figure he would need it for another month, but in his line of business you never knew. If something couldn't be worked out with the state's attorney or an order to dismiss obtained, then he would have to stay long enough to go to trial, and that could take some time.

Gazing out the window into the street, Charlie contemplated his day. Not much to it at this point. He wanted to see Tommy again, but not until this afternoon, he had some stops to make this morning. First off he was going to Shirley's and have some breakfast. Eggs and bacon, he smiled inwardly and said out loud to no one, "Take that, doc."

Out on the street, it was a lazy summer morning and Charlie felt good about himself. He was on another case and he was really getting to like this Georgia weather and this town. He wasn't at all sorry not to have left. He could live here, he decided, if his base wasn't already firmly established in Illinois. Slowly, relishing the morning walk, he made his way to Shirley's, thinking the only thing that would make his day brighter was to see Carol in Shirley's, but he knew that wasn't going to happen. It slightly amazed him that he even had such thoughts. Carol was a nice woman and he had to admit that he was attracted to her for some strange reason, beyond her good looks, fame and talent, which was saying a lot. Yet he couldn't fathom the reason for his attraction. He felt like a high school kid anticipating his first date whenever he thought of her and he had absolutely no reason to feel that way.

Shirley hurried over to the end of the counter where Charlie had parked himself, just as soon as he had settled onto the stool. "Morning, Mr. Chambers."

"Charlie, just call me Charlie."

"Okay, Charlie, any news?"

"Shirley, you are supposed to ask customers what they want, not if there is any news," he said evenly.

"Okay, what do you want?"

"Eggs, bacon, toast, decaf coffee."

Shirley turned and barked out the order to the kitchen, turned back and asked, "Any news?" Charlie smiled, stifled a laugh and said, "I have no news, not yet, but I'm going to make some inquiries this morning. Maybe I can get in to see the state's attorney."

"He won't help," Shirley said in disgust and continued, "he's up for election again this fall and he isn't going to rock the mayor's boat. The mayor and him are tight on the political circuit."

"Can't hurt," he responded to Shirley's back, as she hurried away toward the kitchen.

Charlie caught himself looking across the room to the corner where he had seen Carol and her group eating that day, a lifetime ago. His mind was going over that day and the day he had met her up on Burning Chapel Hill… and at the motel lounge.

"Heard you were seen talking intimately with Carol Harmon at the Super Eight motel lounge in Thomasville," he heard Shirley say, and his mind snapped back to the present.

Shirley put his plate on the counter and said, "She lives up above Burning Chapel Hill, you know."

"So?"

"So, I just thought you might like to know, just making conversation. She's not there now though, gone off to Nashville, I hear, to make a record or something. So is it true?"

"Is what true?" Charlie asked as he heavily salted his eggs, in direct opposition to what his doctor wanted him to do.

With an exasperated look, Shirley fumed, "Is it true that you were in intimate conversation with Carol Harmon in Thomasville at that bar?"

"I talked to her, yes. I wouldn't call it intimate. There was a lounge full of customers within speaking distance. No big deal, we just chatted for awhile, nothing to it."

Smiling now, Shirley responded, "My dear, Mr. Chambers, Miss Carol Harmon does not just stop and chat for awhile for no reason. The word is she incurred the wrath of her manager, Dan Chase, for just sitting with you. I hear the talk and I'm telling you that the word is she doesn't incur his wrath without a mighty good reason. I think she's scared of him and I think she wanted to talk to you mighty bad."

Charlie liked the idea of Carol wanting to talk to him so badly that she incurred the wrath of Dan Chase, but he didn't like the part about her being afraid of her manager. What kind of influence did he have on her and why did she put up with it?

Shirley was still hanging around the end of the counter. It was slow this morning and Charlie asked, between bites of toast, "What's the deal there, Shirley? Why would she be scared of him? Why would he care who she talked to anyway?"

Of course Shirley had an answer. She had almost all the news that was worth having, a café in a small town was even better than a barbershop for gossip. You got it from both sexes in a café. Pursing her lips, she ventured, "I hear Dan Chase was born and raised here just like Carol. He had nothing until she came along and he isn't going to let anyone take his meal ticket from him. He guards her like a jealous husband guards his wife. I don't think she gets to see anyone he doesn't approve of. He doesn't want anyone influencing her decisions except himself. All of the men who guard her and all of the so-called servants around her are loyal to Dan. The guards are there to keep an eye on Carol, as much or more than, to protect her. He's an odd duck and I hear he has a real mean streak."

Charlie's head snapped up from over his plate at that and he said hurriedly, "He wouldn't hurt her, would he?"

"Nawh, he's not stupid, just greedy and well... like I say... mean, or so I hear."

Once breakfast was finished, Charlie felt he had some time to kill. He didn't want to see Tommy until that afternoon and it was too early to try to get in to see the state's attorney. He would be in morning traffic call until just before noon. Having rented the same car from the airport that he had earlier in the month, he decided to take another drive. This time though, he wasn't going to just wander aimlessly around. He was going to drive by Carol's house, just to see what it looked like. He had wormed out of Shirley the directions, using his lawyer skills and she had smiled a knowing smile, having seen right through his questions. *I do believe that woman should have been a lawyer*, he ruefully said to himself.

The road up Burning Chapel Hill, to where Shirley had described the location of Carol's home, was a lot better than the washed out gravel road up to the old church. This road was on the opposite side of the hill and was paved all the way to the top. Not just a one lane road either, two wide lanes all the way. The house was easy to find, it was off the blacktop about a hundred yards, but the wrought iron gates gave its existence away. However, the house was just too far off the road and had too many pine trees between it and the road to be easily seen. Charlie was a bit dismayed; he had hoped to get a good look at the place where Carol lived. Why that seemed important to him he didn't know, but it did. He wanted to feel a closeness to Carol in her absence and yet he chided himself for acting and thinking like a high school freshman.

No matter, he said to himself, *she isn't there anyway, but it would have been nice to get a good look at her house, just to know what it was like and maybe get a glimpse of what Carol was like by looking at her house.* That even sounded silly to him, but that's the way he felt. *Stupid thought*, he decided, *especially for a supposedly educated adult man*. After passing the gate and seeing practically nothing, he turned the car around and came back slowly, peering out of the right hand window. He was just able to make out a portion of the front of the house through the trees and then he noticed that there was a gate guard in a little shack, just off to the left of the gate, alongside the woods. Charlie straightened up, accelerated slightly and headed back down the hill. He felt like a stalker. He was more than a little embarrassed to be seen by anyone driving by Carol's house.

When he reached the bottom of the hill he turned along the base of the hill and came back around to the gravel road that led to the old church. For some unexplained reason he was being drawn back to that church, so he turned on to the steep road. The little car was skipping and sliding in the gravel and barely able to pull itself up the incline. However, the same as the last time, the little car made it and Charlie turned into the grass-covered parking lot. He stopped under a large pine tree and again noticed the little dilapidated brick shack alongside the woods. Out of curiosity and for lack of anything better to do, he walked over to it and looked in the window. There was plenty of light. The roof had numerous holes and he could see the interior clearly, but there was nothing to see, just bits and pieces of junk. It looked like someone might have actually lived there or stayed there at one time or another for a rather long period of time, but it was obvious that that had been a long time ago.

Turning his attention from the little shack, he walked toward the church ruins, remembering what Carol had said about hallowed ground and not totally disagreeing with her. He felt as though he were in a church instead of viewing a burned out building. It seemed as though he could almost feel the pain of the people who had died here, feel their fear, hear their screams, share their terror—a crackling sound startled him and he turned toward the woods to see a shadow emerging from them. It was a few seconds before he could see the figure clearly and when he did his heart skipped three times in rapid succession.

"I thought that was you," Carol said from the edge of the trees.

Charlie was flabbergasted, speechless. *How come I always feel speechless and inadequate around this woman*, he wondered to himself.

"Carol! I thought you were in Nashville."

"And I thought you were in Illinois," she responded gaily.

"I was going, but I found a new case to work on, so I'll be here a while yet. Hey, it's good to see you," Charlie ended, and he knew he meant it too. It really was good to see Carol. He had wanted to see Carol, that's why he went by her house and maybe why he came up here. "And what's your excuse?" he continued.

"Got a call from the record production company. They had a foul up in their schedule and over-booked the studio. I probably could have pressed the issue and gotten in anyway, but I decided a day or two off would be nice and now I'm glad I decided that way. It's good to see you Charles, and I haven't said that to anyone, and meant it, for a long time."

"Well now, I'm flattered," Charlie responded and he felt a quickening of his pulse.

"It's true," she said and moved off slowly to her right toward a large fallen tree.

Charlie followed, noting her hair was pulled back in to two long braids today and liking the look. But then again, he figured he would like Carol's look, no matter how she wore her hair, but it never hurt when a woman tried to be attractive and succeeded.

When Carol reached the tree she sat down, beckoning him to join her.

Settled on the tree trunk, Carol looked at him deeply and said, "Not married, was married, not married now, that leaves a lot out of the equation, Charles. Are you divorced?"

Slightly uncomfortable at the question, Charlie responded simply, "She died five years ago. How about you? As I recall you answered my question the same way."

"Divorced, I was eighteen and he was a drummer in the band."

"Drummer," Charlie put in and continued, "what is it with singers and drummers anyway?"

Carol laughed and Charlie liked the sound, it was deep and throaty, but soft at the same time.

"Oh, I don't know," she said with a smile and added, "like cops and nurses I guess, birds of a feather and all that, you know."

"A drummer," he stated again.

"Yes, he was a nice kid, just like me I guess. Just kids and that was the problem. I was seventeen and he was eighteen, it just happened, but it didn't last six months. There was nothing substantial to it, but it still hit me hard when it ended. He's somewhere out west now, herding cattle and working as a part time DJ."

"Sounds like you are over him now."

"Yeah sure, now I am, but it hit me hard at the time. It was right after that my mother and father were killed in an auto accident on their way to watch me perform at the Grand Old Opry. I was devastated. It almost ended my career before it started. That's when Dan Chase entered the scene. He picked me up and dusted me off. He kept me going and got me some great gigs, before I knew it I was in the big time, on a roll, with more money than I could spend, literally."

"Dan sounds good for you," Charlie ventured and felt a twinge of jealousy.

"He was, but now I'm not so sure. Oh, he's still a good manager, but like I said the other night, he's domineering at times. I'm so big now, and I don't mean to brag, but it's a fact, that I could have my pick of managers equally as good or better."

"So why not get another one?"

"Not so easy. I was eighteen, almost flat broke and quite naïve when Dan picked me up. I didn't know anything about the law, lawyers or contracts. He had his lawyer draw up a real tight contract. Oh, it was fair to me, but it was for twenty years and no early termination clause, short of my death and then he still gets a percentage of royalties from my estate. Plus, he has the option to renew for another ten years. So I'm stuck with him and I do my best, but sometimes I could strangle him. After Jim, that's my ex, left me flat, I never got a chance to get close enough to another man to get involved. Dan keeps me so isolated I hardly get to see or talk to anyone outside the business and even then he limits my contacts. I sometimes feel like a slave and I just don't seem to be able to enjoy myself anymore. I don't enjoy performing like I used to, it's just a job, just money and I have all I need. But not Dan, he always wants more."

"The other night at the motel you seemed to be enjoying yourself."

Charlie could see her eyes light up as she answered, "I was! That was great wasn't it? But I don't get to do those impromptu performances anymore. That was the rare exception. Dan says they don't pay and I shouldn't do anything that doesn't pay."

"Sounds tough all right," Charlie sympathized.

"Oh, I know I sound ungrateful, but there's more to life than making money and being famous. You know you are the first man I've been able to have a real conversation with in... oh, I don't know, years. And I've never talked to anyone like I'm talking to you now. Why is that do you suppose?"

Charlie thought for a second and admitted, "Don't know, but I like it," he ended with a smile.

Changing the subject now, Carol asked, "So what brought you back to Burning Chapel Hill?"

With a sheepish look on his face that aroused Carol's curiosity, he responded, "Well, if you must know, I came up here to stalk you."

Carol burst into laughter, flinging her head back and exposing a soft white neck. Charlie smiled broadly. "It's true. I found out that you lived up here and I decided to drive by your house to get a look and to... well... feel your vibes, to put it bluntly. But you weren't there, of course, or I didn't think you were and I couldn't even see the house from the road, or not much of it. So I came here, where I had seen you once before, to see if any vibes were here, but they weren't here, you were and that's much better."

"Now, I'm flattered."

"You? Nawh, I'll bet you get stalked regularly," Charlie responded, only in half jest.

"Yes, but not by a handsome lawyer."

Charlie felt himself flush just a tinge, not enough to be noticed, he hoped and said lightly, "This is a much better meeting than the last one we had up here, but we will have to stop meeting like this or people will talk."

"Who cares what people say?" Carol asked rhetorically.

"You should. You make your living off of entertainment and you need to maintain your popularity or no one will pay to hear you sing," Charlie responded seriously.

Just as serious, Carol stated flatly, "I told you, Charles, I already have all the money I need. If I never made another dime, I wouldn't starve for the rest of my life. I don't have to sing another song in public, write another song or cut another record. I can live off the royalties of what I already have and what I have in the bank. That's one thing Dan does not control and never will. I have complete control over my finances, my bank accounts and my investments. I'm not overly smart maybe, but I've seen what managers have done to others and my money is mine."

"Sounds pretty smart to me."

"Okay, so that's settled. We can meet here anytime we want."

Charlie wasn't sure how to take that, so he left it alone and instead inquired, "So when do you have to go to Nashville?"

"I'm not going."

"Oh, I thought I heard you say earlier that your trip was delayed a couple of days, not off."

"I did, but now I've decided it's off."

Charlie's mouth dropped open and he asked, "Why? Won't your record company be mad? Won't they assess a penalty for breaking your record contract?"

"Probably."

"Carol, that's not sounding like the smart girl I was just talking to," Charlie chided.

"Oh, don't give me that lawyer attitude, Charles. I'll give them their record. When I'm ready, maybe next month or the month after that. They'll get over it. I want to stay here a while."

"Why?"

"I would have thought that was obvious. Because you are here, at least for awhile and I want a chance to get to know you a little better. I like talking to you and I need the rest."

Charlie was flabbergasted again and replied, "Won't that upset Dan a little?"

Smiling broadly now, Carol winked and said, "Yes, won't it now? You don't suppose he will get mad and quit, do you?"

"Not much chance of that," Charlie stated flatly.

"I'm afraid you are right on that score, but there is always hope."

"Not much," he said, even flatter than before.

"Are you always so encouraging to your clients?" Carol good-naturedly fumed.

"You aren't my client."

"I could be."

"No."

"Why not for heaven's sake? I've got money to pay you."

"I don't represent friends or relatives. Bad business."

"Well, in that case I don't want to be your client, I'd rather be your friend and you mine."

"I can do that."

Carol stood up now and Charlie hastily arose also. Looking at her watch, she exclaimed, "Oh! Look at the time, it's almost noon. I have to get back. I didn't intend to stay away this long. If they find I've left the grounds without protection, I'll never hear the end of it."

"You really mean to say you can't just leave home and wander off by yourself if you want to?" Charlie asked, incredulous.

"Not and get caught. Dan would have a fit. That's one reason you are the only man I've been able to have a real conversation with in years. Although I have to admit it was worth the wait."

Charlie blushed slightly again when he heard that and said, "In that case I'm glad Dan Chase keeps you sequestered, maybe without any competition I'd have a chance."

Laughing now, they both turned toward the edge of the woods. "Shall I walk you home?"

"No, it's okay. I'm really just over the hill and I can sneak back on to the grounds easier by myself. I know all the concealed paths." Hesitating, she added, "Sounds horrible, doesn't it, I have to sneak out of my own house and I'm twenty-nine years old. Oops, I told you I wouldn't tell you my age."

"That was before we knew each other. I think you said you don't know me well enough to get the answer to that question. Now I do, don't I?"

"Sure," she said simply.

Going back to their previous conversation, he now answered, "It does sound unusual to have to sneak in and out of your own house, I'll admit."

When they reached the edge of the woods, they both stopped and Carol turned to look at Charlie's face. Charlie looked into her deep blue eyes and his heart began racing. She was more than just beautiful, he decided, she was absolutely ravishing, and a good personality, too. He was tempted to bend forward slightly to see if she would be receptive to a kiss, but he dismissed that thought almost immediately. He was a cautious man, he liked to know how deep the water was before he dove into it. He had not told Carol, but she was the first woman he had had more than a passing interest in since his wife had died.

Carol, on the other hand, was studying Charlie's face and finding it even more handsome in the daylight. She didn't know what had drawn her to him initially, maybe it was his utter indifference, almost contempt of her at the outset. But she knew what was drawing her now. He was handsome, intelligent, understanding, reserved, but not stuffy and she was willing to bet he had a real humorous side. She hadn't been kidding when she had told him he was worth the wait. Normally, she would not think of being so forward in any relationship, not that she had had much experience at relationships, but she had been around enough to know her way around. However, she had a feeling that if she was going to get to know this man and determine if she wanted to know him better, she was going to have to make some of the moves first and fast. Between her career and his, she was willing to bet there would be little time for getting acquainted. So time was not a commodity to be wasted.

After a few moments of awkwardness, while each stared at the other with their own deep thoughts, Carol finally broke the silence and asked, "How about coming up to my place tonight for dinner?"

Taken completely aback once again, he thought, *is there no end to her surprises?* Charlie responded, "Dan wouldn't like that."

Smiling now, Carol responded, "Exactly and I don't really care, do you?"

Returning her smile, he winked and said, "No, and yes, I'd be honored, what time?"

"Seven sharp."

"It's a da…" stopping before he finished the word 'date' he blushed again.

With a broad impish smile that showed her gleaming white teeth, Carol chuckled and finished his sentence, with a question, "Date?"

"Okay, date," he answered, slightly embarrassed.

Then before he knew what was happening, Carol rose up slightly on her toes, steadied herself by grabbing his shoulders and kissed him lightly on the lips. Before he could even react and almost before the kiss registered, she was in the woods and gone.

Charlie just stood and stared at the foliage hiding the path she had taken. His heart rate was way up and he felt as though his feet were going to leave the ground. He hadn't felt this way in a long time and he liked it, liked it very much. Feeling his heart rate continue to rise at just the thought of Carol, what had just happened and the anticipation of dinner with her tonight, he said out loud as he turned for his car, "Take that, doc!"

~ * ~

Charlie was still trying to recover from the events of this morning and to quiet his anticipation of tonight. He was trying hard to get his head back into his game, but it was very hard. He was sitting along the wall, in one of several chairs provided for the attorneys who were waiting for their case to be called. This was Judge Seymour's afternoon call of criminal cases and Charlie wanted to see how the system worked here.

He had talked to the state's attorney right after lunch. He had missed him this morning and Shirley had been right about that, too, it had done no good at all. Next to Charlie was his ever-present accomplice, Steve Barclay, looking bored. Charlie smiled to himself and decided that Steve had a right to be bored. Traffic and misdemeanor court was a boring place. Yet to Charlie it wasn't so boring. because every jurisdiction did it a little differently and there was always plenty to learn from how someone else did something.

This afternoon, though, things weren't going so smoothly. He continued to watch and listen as the latest case was called from those in the custody of the sheriff. Five men were lined up in the front row of the jury box, attired in blazing orange jumpsuits. One of the men rose as the judge said, "Ninety-seven TR Four-oh-two, The People of the State of Georgia versus Frank Spittler. Step forward, Mr. Spittler."

The man walked slowly toward the bench and stopped in front of it, looking up at Judge Seymour, who was studying his file. The man started to talk, "Ah Judge..." but Seymour wasn't ready to hear from him and he held up his hand to stifle the comment, saying, "Just a minute."

The man waited while Seymour continued to study the file.

Finally the judge said to Frank, "You're here because you failed to pay your fine on time and then you failed to appear in court to explain why you hadn't paid. Now what is your excuse for not being in court last week when you were supposed to be?"

"My fine was paid, Your Honor," the man said calmly.

"That's not what the file shows, do you have a receipt for it?"

"I lost it, I had it, but I lost it," the man said meekly and continued, "but I did pay it, sir. I did."

The judge turned to the clerk to his right who was seated in front of a computer screen and asked, "How much does he owe and what is his bond?"

The clerk had a confused look on her face and answered, "He doesn't owe anything, Judge. I don't know why his file was pulled for court last week, but he was paid in full two weeks ago."

In disgust the judge retorted, "Then why wasn't that caught last week when he failed to appear? Why was a warrant issued for his arrest on a failure to appear when he was paid? The computer should have indicated he was paid in full last week. Can't anyone read those things?"

The clerk made no response and the judge looked at the correctional officer asking, "What else is he being held on, Sheriff?" A lot of judges called the correctional officer in charge of the prisoners 'sheriff' it made it simpler, they didn't have to remember all the different names of the officers.

"Nothing, Your Honor. Just this failure to appear. That's all."

Turning back to his clerk, the judge asked, "And how much bond does he have up?"

"Three hundred," the clerk answered timidly.

"And he owes no fine, no court costs, nothing?"

"Yes, sir, that's right."

"You're absolutely sure? There's no paper in the file to indicate that he posted any bond. Nothing to indicate he paid his fine. The last docket entry is that a warrant issued for his arrest with bond at one hundred. Why does he have three hundred up?"

The clerk made a few more keystrokes and replied rapidly, "Two hundred is from a prior case, Judge. It should have been refunded, but wasn't. Part of that bond was applied to his fine in this case and that's why he is paid up. I don't know why that wasn't caught last week."

With an audible sigh the judge said, "Show the Defendant present in the custody of the sheriff, assistant state's attorney, Mr. Princeton, present for the state. The court finds that the defendant has paid his fine in full, four-oh-two dismissed and stricken, the clerk is directed to refund the bond of one hundred dollars." Turning back to the clerk, he asked, "What's the case number with the other bond?"

"Two-six-three."

"Ninety-seven, traffic?" the judge queried.

"Yes."

"Fine. Show two-six-three is called for hearing, the same parties present, dismissed and stricken, two hundred-dollar bond to be refunded to the defendant. Defendant is ordered released from the custody of the sheriff. Okay, Sheriff?"

"Yes, sir," the officer responded snappily.

Looking now at Frank, the judge said shortly, "Good-bye."

Frank turned and went back to the jury box to await his release later in the morning.

Charlie couldn't help but notice the confusion in the files of this court system. It had been like that all afternoon. *They sure ought to be thankful they have those computers*, he decided. Without the computers to track payments and bonds they'd have people in jail forever in this county. For sure the right paperwork wasn't getting in the court files. He was very glad he had told Tommy to hang on to his receipts, very glad.

~ * ~

Todd sat forlornly at his desk shuffling through the file, studying the skimpy reports and flipping through the faded black and white photographs. It seemed that every time he was depressed he always retrieved the same file from his bottom desk drawer. There was nothing to be gained by it, but he did it anyway. It was, in some manner he didn't understand, therapeutic. For the thousandth time he read the list of people who had died and with every fiber in his body wished there was some way that he could get at least one of them to talk to him. He was sure that one or more of the people on the list knew who had committed this horrible crime or could give him some lead.

It was a vain hope, he knew, the crime was too old and the people were too long dead. Yet each time when he reached a low ebb in his life, he pulled the same file—the burned out church—and searched it in vain for something, he knew not what. Solving this crime had become his sole purpose in life; it gave him direction when life seemed to be without direction.

Sam was off talking with the state's attorney about a warrant to search the home and bank records of the Preacher. Todd couldn't bring himself to accompany him, he would not allow himself to believe that Tommy Trenton had ever stolen anything, for any reason.

Todd had read through the file twice by the time Sam returned with the warrant. Though he could duck going along to get the warrant, he knew he couldn't duck the search.

"Ready Todd?"

"No," he answered honestly, but stood up anyway.

"Yeah, I know, but it comes with the territory. It's a lousy job, all in all, and I'm glad I'm about to retire."

Todd did not respond as he followed Sam out the door and down to the car. Neither spoke during the short drive to the Preacher's apartment. Though it was mid-afternoon, they both secretly hoped not to find the Preacher at home and more than that, hoped they wouldn't find any corroborative evidence against him.

The Preacher answered the door, dashing their hopes. Sam, handing him a copy of the search warrant, said, "Tommy Trenton, by order of the Circuit Court of Meridian County, Judge James Ferrell, we are hereby authorized to search your residence for the following items: Currency in any denominations, bank drafts, check stubs, bank records and ledgers recording financial transactions."

Tommy was stunned and overwhelmed. For a few moments he said nothing, but stood back so as not to appear to bar their entrance. Finally, he said, "I don't have any checks, I never had a checking account. I have a savings account at the First Bank of Georgia, but that's all. I have cash, because that's how I pay my bills. I don't have any bank records. They send me a statement once a month, but I don't keep it," he ended simply.

"We have to look, Tommy," Todd put in, as Sam started to nose around the apartment, being as unobtrusive as possible.

"What's it all about, Deputy?"

"We can't say, Mr. Trenton," Sam said, as he continued his search.

Tommy didn't understand and just stood by watching as the other deputy also began to rummage carefully around the small apartment.

In a kitchen drawer Sam found a plain white envelope containing three hundred and twelve dollars.

Tommy immediately asked, "You going to take that? That's my rent money and grocery money. I can't pay the rent without that. Can you take that?"

"For now we have to, Mr. Trenton. You'll get it back if everything checks out," Sam responded.

"When?"

Sam shook his head and said, "I'm not sure."

The search took only a few minutes. There just wasn't much to search. It was Todd's opinion that Tommy Trenton wasn't stealing any money, or if he were, he certainly wasn't spending any of it on furnishings. Sam wrote out a receipt for the money and left it with Tommy as they exited the apartment. Tommy closed the door and sadly took his seat in the lounge chair. He absently picked up his Bible and began reading, although his mind wasn't on the words.

~ * ~

"He's clean as a hound's tooth, Sam."

"Yeah, looks that way so far. I hated to take his money, but that's what the warrant said to do. I hope he isn't thrown out before we can return it to him."

As they climbed into the car, Todd responded, "Well if he is, it wouldn't be the first time the Preacher was on the streets."

"Yeah, but that isn't much comfort."

"Yeah."

On their way back to the sheriff's department they stopped at the First Bank of Georgia. They had one more warrant to serve.

It took them longer to get a copy of Tommy's bank records for the last five years than it did to search his apartment, but finally they had them and were headed for the sheriff's department. On the way Sam was flipping through the records and he commented, "My memory isn't what it used to be, but I don't think these deposit amounts correspond with his pay. I may be wrong. I hope so. The amounts are too varied and much more than his pay would account for in the job he holds."

Todd did not respond, but he had a cold, sinking feeling in his stomach.

Back in their office, the worst was confirmed. The *coupe de grace* would be obtaining other already negotiated original checks from the same companies as the checks found in Tommy's locker. An examination of the endorsement and the date of negotiation would confirm everything. Someone might even remember the Preacher having cashed them. He was toast and they both knew it, but neither took any pleasure in the fact.

~ * ~

Charlie knocked on the door and waited as the shuffling footsteps came closer. The door opened and Tommy stood framed in its opening, looking as sad as a rumpled suit.

"Good news, Tommy," Charlie said.

"I need some. The police were here just a little while ago with a warrant and they took all of my rent money."

Charlie felt as though he had been slapped by a baseball bat and exclaimed, "What! Why!"

"I don't know. They showed me the warrant and took my money. They gave me this receipt, see." Tommy finished, handing him the receipt he had been clutching in his hand ever since Todd and Sam had left, as if it would magically be transformed back into his money. Then he added, "It won't pay my rent though."

Charlie took the receipt and asked, "What were they looking for, exactly?"

"They gave me a copy of the warrant, it's over here," he responded, as he moved toward the kitchen table to retrieve the copy of the warrant. Following him to the table, Charlie took a seat and began examining the warrant.

"This doesn't make sense, Tommy. It has nothing to do with why you were arrested. It looks like they were looking for evidence of illegal financial transactions, money laundering, or outright theft. You make any sense of that?"

"No, sir," Tommy said forlornly.

"Who were the policemen? City or county?"

"Deputies. I've talked to one of them before, not too long ago and I seen them both around. They are sheriff's investigators. The county only has two so they won't be hard to find."

"Why would the county worry about someone in the city?" Charlie asked without really directing the question to Tommy and Tommy didn't attempt to answer.

"Let me check this out, Tommy."

"Can you get my money back? My rent's due in a couple of days."

"I'll do what I can," he answered simply, without any real commitment in his voice. He knew how long these things could drag out. Tommy might get his money back, but by the time he did, his rent would be long over due.

Charlie headed for the door when Tommy's next question arrested him, "What was your good news?"

"Huh... oh yeah. Well, I talked to the people who run the homeless shelter over in Thomasville and they said they need some help over here at the Johnson City shelter. It doesn't handle the volume they do, but I talked them into letting you help out. You can do some preaching in there and pass out your pamphlets, they said that would be fine. That way I hoped you might see your way clear to stay off the streets for a while until I can see about your disorderly conduct charges. Deal?"

"Okay. I'll try it, but I have to work you know. I can't be tied down there."

"No problem, they said whenever you wanted to help was fine. Set your own hours and do what you want. Sounds too good to pass up."

For the first time this day Tommy had a glimmer of hope and his eyes showed it as he responded, "Yes, it does. Those people really need the Word. I could maybe do some real good there. Thanks, Mr. Chambers."

"No sweat, Tommy. I'll let you know about this other thing as soon as I can find out."

~ * ~

Todd was back on the church fire file when a strange voice broke his concentration, "Detective Evans?"

Todd looked up to see a well-dressed man in his thirties standing in the doorway to the office. *A lawyer*, he immediately decided. People always said they could spot a cop a mile away and Todd could do the same with lawyers.

"Sergeant Evans, and I'm not a detective, just an investigator. Same thing I suppose, but less pay."

"Okay, sorry, I'm Charlie Chambers, I represent Tommy Trenton."

"The state's attorney is over in the next building, but then you know that."

"Yes, I wanted to talk to you."

"I can't talk about active cases unless the state's attorney says it's okay, you should know that. Copies of reports you get from him, not me. Unless you've got a subpoena issued by Judge Ferrell or Judge Seymour that is, and I doubt you do," Todd said shortly and leaned back over his file.

Not to be deterred, Charlie persisted, "I don't want any sensitive information, just generalities. Like why you wanted to search my client's apartment and the reason for your search."

Charlie had eased himself into the office and was standing beside Todd's desk. He had hopes of glimpsing something on the desk that would give him the information he sought, he had a feeling Evans wouldn't tell him a thing. It was to no avail though, all that was there was a file of faded photos and a list of names. The file was old, too old to be Tommy's.

"Sorry, no can do, Mr. Chambers. When and if your client is formally charged, then you know the system as well or better than I, and how to get your information. Until then I can't release information that might jeopardize an ongoing investigation."

"Do you really think the Preacher is stealing money?" Charlie took a shot in the dark or made an educated guess, fishing for a response.

"No," Todd shot out, without thinking and then bit his tongue. Then he said, "Okay, Mr. Chambers that was cute, please leave, I have work to do. Before you leave though, let me ask you this. If Tommy Trenton is so innocent and so poor, why did he hot foot it out and hire a fancy lawyer like you right off the bat?"

Charlie nodded and said, "A fair question. Lots of people hire lawyers before they are formally charged. They want the lawyer to nip the matter in the bud before it gets out of hand. It's a natural response. They are smart enough to know that early prevention is better than a late cure."

"Is that why Tommy hired you? Early prevention?"

"Actually no. I represent him on the disorderly conduct charges. I just happened to be talking to him today about those charges and he said you had been over to search his apartment. When I left him, I promised him I'd find out what I could, but I really didn't expect to find out anything, and I didn't. I already had a good idea you suspected him of theft, but of what and from where I didn't know and still don't."

"How does the Preacher come off being able to afford a high-priced lawyer like you?"

"What makes you think I'm high-priced?"

"I know who you are now. I recognize the name. An Illinois lawyer in Georgia, now that doesn't happen for nothing. Takes money to bring an out of state lawyer in on your case. I think you guys refer to yourselves as hired guns."

Charlie chuckled and responded, "That is the term usually applied to such a person, but I'm not one. Sorry to disappoint you. In fact, I'm not even hired, let alone a gun. You see, I'm primarily a constitutional law attorney. I work for an organization that defends people's religious rights almost exclusively. I rarely dabble in the criminal law field, except as a peripheral matter in a civil rights case. The long and the short of it is; I work for nothing. Oh, the organization pays me, not a lot, but enough, but the clients don't pay, not a penny. I hope that doesn't shock you, Deputy or shatter your illusions about every lawyer being on the take and out to grab all he can from the unfortunate."

Todd felt a little embarrassed. He had to admit he did think all lawyers were just out for a buck. He kicked out a chair by his desk and said, "Have a seat, Mr. Chambers."

Charlie took the proffered straight-backed wooden chair and waited.

"You want to know about the Preacher's latest troubles, you go nose around up at TTM. They are the complainants. I won't tell you any specifics, but I will say that it involves money in the form of checks that TTM says disappeared at the hands of one Tommy Trenton. I don't buy it, but I can't tell you why, or I won't. End of story, and I didn't tell you even that much. Wouldn't have told you anything, but I like your style. I like Tommy, too, and I hope a nice guy like you can help him out."

Charlie nodded and said, "Okay, thanks." Then gesturing at the file on the desk, he said, "That file looks older than you."

Todd looked at the file and back at Charlie and said, "Not quite, but close. This one I can talk about. Thirty-five years ago, a person or persons unknown, torched a church up at a place known as Burning Chapel Hill. The name is no coincidence. At the time of the fire, the church, known as Little Flock Baptist Church, Negro, happened to be full of people and not a one survived. No one cared to look very close at it at the time. It was a sign of the times we lived in back then. The sixties weren't good times for the South, in a lot of ways. Anyway,

I've always thought there ought to be a clue in these pages somewhere, but I never found it. Someday I hope to solve this one."

"Why? I mean other than the fact that a lot of innocent people died."

"I'm black and so were they, every one of them."

"Aw, baloney!" Charlie almost exclaimed, "Don't give me that. I've got you figured for better than that, Sergeant Evans. Maybe you're black and so were they, but that isn't the end of it, not for you. You've got a reason for digging in to this so deep for so long. Maybe it's because you're a good cop, or maybe it's the injustice of it that eats at you, or something else, but being black is too simple, too shallow. You don't strike me as being that transparent. Thanks again," Charlie ended, as he got up to leave.

Todd just watched him go. Here was a guy he had just met and he had already figured out that there was more to Todd's interest in the burning of Little Flock Baptist Church, than just being black. Not even Sam could get that through his head and he had known Sam a long time. He wasn't right about the reason, but at least he recognized the fact that there was a reason other than color.

Turning back to the file, he fingered the photos again, each one in turn, hesitating longer on some than on others, as if they could talk if he just held them correctly. But they couldn't and they didn't. He was where he always was at the end of the file—nowhere. The people on the list and in the photos were still dead and he was no closer to knowing who killed them.

~ * ~

My man has come through again, Asher thought, as he counted the cash from the envelope. His campaign fund was growing very nicely. An additional one thousand brought it up to just short of twenty-five thousand. Almost enough to put on his campaign advertising blitz and get his name recognition. Once he had his name out there in the public's eye, he was a shoe-in.

Asher had made a trip to the courthouse today, appearing on some collection cases and he had heard about the fiasco in Judge Seymour's courtroom. This was working out even better than he had hoped. Not only was he accumulating a nice little nest egg, but at the same time Jeannie Rosmund was looking more and more incompetent.

Her computers were going to be her ruination. It was a noble idea to bring Meridian County in to the twentieth century, but she didn't appreciate the wizardry involved in such an endeavor. Asher did and he had the solution all ready to go. He had him a first class computer expert all lined up. In fact, he was all ready making good use of him. In the past he had never had much use for TTM, but he was glad they had trained this guy so well. Inside of two weeks or less of his taking office, he was absolutely certain the computer glitches would be a thing of the past. *They might even give me a medal,* he thought with a smirk.

Sixteen

Steve Barclay was sitting at his desk, pressing his head between his hands and massaging his temples, when Charlie walked in and sat down.

"Headache, Steve? I hope it isn't brought on by me," Charlie said lightly.

Steve looked up and answered, "No, it's just been a long day. After you left today I appeared in front of Judge Ferrell and he had a piece of me. The lawyer on the other side was J.L. Harper, one of the biggest jerks this side of the Atlantic. He knows all the law, all the time and likes to wax on eloquently for hours in his arguments. He'd like to be a judge, but the people have never been stupid enough to elect him."

"If he's such a jerk, why did Ferrell chew on you?"

"After J.L. explained the law of the case, from the beginning of time to the present, the judge was so tired of hearing about it that he lit into me for holding up his golf date. It was only three-thirty, but Ferrell likes to have a beer or two before his tee time. Why he didn't shut J.L. down earlier I don't know, but anyway that's why the headache and for once you had nothing to do with it." Steve went back to massaging his temples.

"Did you win or lose?" Charlie asked as an afterthought.

"He took it under advisement. Ever since he took your case under advisement he's been doing it regularly now. I think he decided that not having to face the lawyers when he rules is easier. You started something, Charlie. He still hasn't ruled on your case. You really put him to thinking," Steve said, with more humor than he felt.

"Well, I'm glad I didn't give you that headache, but I might make it worse."

"Spare me," Steve said dryly, not bothering to look up.

"I stayed here to help out the Preacher. He had a little trouble with the city and some disorderly conduct statute that is most likely unconstitutional. Right?"

"So what's the point? You can handle a Dis Con statute."

"Yeah, but I'm not a real criminal lawyer. I only delve in the criminal law to get to the constitutional issues. The Preacher needs a real criminal lawyer or may soon."

Steve popped his head up and grimaced at the pain he got from the sudden movement. "Why?" he asked, but didn't really want to hear the answer.

"Seems as though the place he works, TTM, has decided he is the prime suspect in the theft of some money. I don't know the 'ins' and 'outs' of it, but I have information suggesting that the sheriff's department is looking at him. They just finished searching his apartment and seizing some cash."

Narrowing his eyes, Steve asked, "Has he been charged yet?"

"No."

"Then what do you want from me? You want me to talk to the state's attorney and try to nip this in the bud?"

"No, we don't know enough for that yet. A source close to the investigation told me that I could get the full scoop from TTM. Also that the 'powers that be' up there were the complainants. They know what's going on and why, because they complained. Trouble is, I don't know anyone up there and I need you to run interference for me. Go up there with me and let's see if we can steam roll our way into some information. Then you can go to the state's attorney with some hard information that might help the Preacher."

Steve just gave him a blank stare, nodded his head in the affirmative and said dismally, "You're right, you did make my headache worse. You're crazy, Charlie! You don't fool with TTM in this town or this county! The state for that matter. TTM has more clout than a hat full of senators. If we go up there and bull our way through, we'll get information all right, but nothing we'll like."

Charlie shrugged, he always had been a rebel and his newfound vocation suited him well. He said, "Okay, so we don't bull our way in, who do you know up there?"

Steve leaned back in his high-backed chair and rested his head in his right hand. After a moment, he responded, "No one. I know names, but not the people associated with them. Not to call up and talk to anyway. I've met them here and there at formal doings, but not really socially. I have no business contacts up there. I leave that to the partners, maybe they do, but I don't."

"Maybe I should talk to the partners."

"Go ahead. They think more of you than they do me. I'm just a 'go-fer' to them. I do the work and they spend the money."

"Are you sure you don't know anyone up there to help us?" Charlie persisted, he didn't really want to rattle the cages of the partners, after all, they put up with him and gave him an office for free. No sense rocking the boat.

"Us!" Steve grabbed his head again.

"Okay, me."

Quietly, to keep his head from falling off, Steve responded, "No, just names. Like Dan Mosley, chief of security, but he wouldn't help, even if I knew him personally. He probably turned the Preacher in anyway. There are several in-house lawyers, but I don't know them, just their names, like I said. There's Phil Stellar, Dale Bukker, Milo Tanner and another I can't put my finger on. Head hurts too much, but they're just names. I don't know the people and if I did they wouldn't help. They are loyal to the bone to TTM."

Charlie said nothing and contemplated the situation for a few seconds and then asked, "This Phil Stellar, do you know if he comes from around here?"

Carefully Steve shook his head and said, "I don't know, why? Who cares?"

Ignoring the question Charlie asked, "Do you have a Martindale Hubble?"

"Huh? Yeah, sure. It's in the library, why?"

Charlie hopped up and said, "Be right back," over his shoulder, as he scooted out of the office and down to the library.

In seconds, so it seemed to Steve, he was back holding a huge book in his hand, which Steve recognized as just one volume of Martindale Hubble, a directory of lawyers in the United States.

"Here it is," Charlie said and as he walked toward the chair he had formerly occupied, he read aloud, "Stellar, Phillip P., born on 12-9-52, Bachelors degree in Social Justice, Sangamon State University, Springfield, Illinois, in 1978; he was awarded a Juris Doctorate from the University of Illinois, Champaign, Illinois, 1980; admitted to practice in Illinois 1981 and in Georgia 1985; currently chief counsel for Tieman Textile Mills, Johnson City, Georgia."

"So?" Steve said gloomily. His head was not up to heavy thinking or any thinking for that matter.

"So, I know him, or at least I used to know him. Back in Illinois he was a local lawyer for a while, then he drifted."

"Yeah could be, he's been here a few years, I think," Steve said.

With a look of deep concentration, Charlie hesitated a moment and then said, "It's worth a shot."

"What shot?" Steve asked again, cradling his aching head in his hands.

Charlie didn't answer, he was thinking out loud, "I'm going to make a phone call and then we'll see." He turned for the door and when he reached it he turned back and said, "You really ought to take something for that headache."

He was gone before Steve could tell him that the headache probably would have been gone by now had it not been for Charlie.

Charlie was seated in his office, which had been graciously provided for him by the law firm of Speck, Mansard, Little and French. He picked up the phone book and began thumbing through the pages. Without difficulty, he found the listing for Tieman Textile Mills and various subheadings under it, one of which was for the office of the corporate counsel.

Charlie reached for the phone, dialed the number and after a couple of rings a pleasant sounding woman answered, "TTM, corporate counsel, may I help you?"

"My name is Charlie Chambers and I would like to speak with Phil Stellar," he said, as he leaned back in his chair and gazed unseeing out the window.

"One moment please, I'll see if he is available."

"Thank you."

Charlie watched the sparse traffic on the street and sidewalk from the third story window. This was the tallest building in the town and he was on the top floor.

"Phil Stellar," the deep voice fairly boomed into the phone, but cordially.

"Phil, this is Charlie Chambers. We knew each other in Illinois a few years ago."

"Yes! Sure, been a long time, Charlie. You still practicing?" Phil asked pleasantly.

"Sort of, I move around a lot now. Right now I'm in Johnson City."

"Georgia?" Phil questioned.

"Yes, down here on a case and your name came up. I didn't know you were around the area. Thought I'd give you a call."

"Glad you did. I just came back from lunch or I'd take you to lunch. You going to be around for a while yet?"

"Looks like it as of now," Charlie answered truthfully.

"Hey, how about coming up to the mill and we'll shoot the breeze? Talk over old times; or I could come into town. Where are you at?"

Rapidly, Charlie responded, "I don't want to put you out, Phil. You're busier than I am right now. How about I just come up and see you? Would that be all right?" Charlie wanted to get into the mill for a look see anyway. He always argued a case better when he had visited the area involved.

"No problem, glad to have you. I'll leave word at the main gate. You know how to get up here?"

"Can't miss it, Phil. They say in Johnson City that all roads lead to TTM," Charlie responded seriously.

"That's true," Phil stated in return and continued, "How does two o'clock tomorrow suit you? Or we could have dinner tonight."

"Can't do dinner, but I can come up at two tomorrow. I'll see you then, Phil."

"Okay, bye."

"Good-bye," Charlie ended and hung up with satisfaction. That had been easier than he had anticipated. He and Phil had never been buddies, but they had known each other professionally and had shared a cup of coffee or two at the courthouse snack bar. They hadn't done any socializing together, but that was mostly because Charlie wasn't much of a socializer, especially with other lawyers. He still wasn't, he preferred his own company and the company of non-lawyers.

~ * ~

Carol had been sequestered in her room all afternoon, by choice. She had bathed, put on make up, perfume and primped the whole afternoon. She had brushed her hair probably a thousand times and was now trying to decide if after all that she should put it up in a bun. Sitting at her dressing table, staring half-heartedly at her reflection, she was feeling like a kid in high school getting ready for prom. Though Carol had not been able to attend prom, she was sure it must have felt something like this.

Leaning her head on her hands and her elbows on the table, she pouted into the mirror and recalled with distaste that she didn't really get to do anything in high school that the other kids had gotten to do. Her singing was already pretty much a vocation by that time. Although she had not hit the big time, she was being kept pretty busy and very secluded by her manager father. Suddenly she realized that she could not recall a time when she was not kept secluded by someone, in some manner or another. *No wonder I feel so empty*, she decided, *I've never been allowed to live. Well, I've had enough of this seclusion. I'm really going to start breaking away.*

With that resolution firmly established, she decided to leave her hair down and brush it more. Glancing at the clock on the bedside stand she noted the time to be only five thirty and absently ran the brush through her hair again while she tried to recall every detail on the face of Charles Chambers.

~ * ~

Charlie was sitting in his apartment going over some notes on the Preacher's case, killing time. His heart, or his mind, wasn't in the case right now. He was on pins and needles anticipating his 'date' with Carol. He was just trying to keep his mind off of the time. *This is silly,* he told himself, *I'm thirty-five years old. I've been married. I'm a well-educated man, a lawyer, a self-sufficient adult and I'm as nervous as a newlywed.*

~ * ~

At six o'clock Carol left her room, having decided that if she brushed her hair one more time it would all fall out. She wanted to check with Maria, to make sure the dinner she had planned was on schedule, though knowing Maria, it would be, with or without Carol's interference. At the bottom of the long staircase she saw Dan lurking, that's the way she saw it anyway. Actually, he was just sitting on the sofa, drinking a beer and reading the paper. He had his own wing of the very expansive house, which he shared with the guards, but he felt free to use the common areas of the entire house, which irritated Carol to no end.

He heard her come down the stairs, looked up and asked, "Where've you been hiding all day?"

"In my room, resting."

"You look mighty dolled up, the rest must have done you good."

"Actually, I'm expecting company for dinner," Carol stated nonchalantly.

"Oh, I didn't know about any dinner party, why wasn't I informed? Who is it, what record company?" Dan asked, assuming it was business. There would be no other reason for a dinner guest.

"Because it is my guest, not yours. He'll be here at seven."

"He? He who?" Dan asked in an irritated tone.

"Charles Chambers."

Dan thought for a minute and then he said hotly, "Charles Chambers, that guy you met at the bar the other night? That creepy lawyer? What are you doing inviting him here, without my okay?"

"Your okay! You don't okay my friends!"

"Since when? I've been watching out for you since you were eighteen and not dry behind the ears. I know what's best and who's best for you, you know that," Dan retorted.

"No, I don't. You don't own me, Dan! You are my manager, not my guardian! This is none of your business!"

"Oh yeah, we'll just see about that. I know this clown's type, he's only after your money. Let's just see if he can get by the guards at the main gate after I make a call. Now you go on upstairs and rest some more. I'll take care of this, you ain't having a dinner party, not tonight you ain't," he finished hotly and walked over to grab the phone off the nearest end table.

Carol exploded, "Dan Chase! You touch that phone and I'll never sing another note, never!"

"What's that supposed to mean?" he shot out, but his hand stopped reaching for the phone.

"It means exactly what is sounds like it means. You are my manager and I'm stuck with you. I have to pay your contract, but I don't have to sing, write songs or make public appearances and I won't. That should cut into your take quite a bit, Dan. Thirty percent of nothing is nothing. All you will have is a percentage of what is already coming in and that will diminish when I stop singing. You have a contract to manage my business. But that does not include my personal business. You may be able to force me to pay you your percentage, but you can't make me earn any money, and I won't!"

Dan was caught completely off guard. He didn't know what had gotten into Carol. He had never had any trouble controlling her before this. Now all of a sudden she had grown a backbone and Dan didn't like it. What he liked least of all was the fact that what she had said was true. He couldn't make her sing and perform, if she didn't he was going to be short on cash and his gambling debts wouldn't allow for much of that. He decided to take the safe course until he had time to properly appraise the situation and answered, "Okay, Carol, have it your way, but I'm warning you, he's no good, he's only after your money. He'll only hurt you just like that drummer kid did. I'm only interested in your best interests, Carol."

Snidely, Carol responded, "Sure, Dan. Just as long as my best interests put money in your pocket." And then she hit him with the one-two punch. "And while we're having this little heart to heart talk about my best interests, I think it is in my best interests to stay in Johnson City for a couple of weeks and rest. Maybe more than a couple of weeks." She held up her hand to cut off the response she could see Dan's mind forming and continued sternly, "And it is also in my best interests that you not be seen tonight in my house! You go to your wing with your goons and you stay there, or you go for a walk or a drive or jump off the mountain, but you stay away from Charles and me or this little songbird is done for good. Understand!"

It took Dan a moment to compose himself; more anger from him was not going to help. He didn't need to make an angry retort, he needed reason, but she seemed to be beyond reason tonight. *That lawyer*, he said to himself, *he's been talking to her, putting ideas into her head.* Finally, he said calmly, more calmly than he felt, "Now, Carol. Be reasonable. If you break that recording contract it'll cost you money, they'll hit you with a big fat penalty and you may get the word put out on you that you aren't dependable. That could be real expensive in the long run."

Carol replied calmly, almost nonchalantly, "I can afford it. Can you, Dan?"

Dan bit off the harsh reply he wanted to make, spun on his heels and headed into his wing. *That lousy lawyer*, he said to himself, *butting in where he don't belong, he's going to have to be dealt with and soon. I can see that right now.*

Carol had amazed herself. She didn't think she had it in her to stand up to Dan like that, but it had felt good and she was quite sure now that she had done it once, it would be even easier the second time. Just how she had mustered the nerve to do it she wasn't sure. Maybe it was because she wanted to see Charles and she was prepared to fight for that privilege, now and in the future. *Future?* she rhetorically asked herself.

Another thought came to mind. Dan had been right about calling the gate and now she walked over, picked up the phone and dialed the gate extension. When the call was answered she said, in a no nonsense tone, "This is Miss Harmon, I'm expecting a Mr. Charles Chambers at seven. See that there's no trouble passing him up to the house."

The guard responded, uneasily, "I don't know, Miss Harmon. Dan... er... Mr. Chase never said nothing about it."

Carol shot back instantly, "What's your name?"

"Steve Schenk."

"Well, Steve Schenk, do you like your job?" Carol asked calmly, a little too calmly Steve thought.

"Oh yes, ma'am, I sure do."

"Then in that case Mr. Chambers had better not tell me he had any trouble getting through that gate or you won't have a job in the morning and that's a promise. I don't give a hang what Dan Chase says and you can bet your bottom dollar I'm going to ask Mr. Chambers when he gets here if he had any trouble. Don't forget, Steve Schenk, I still sign the paychecks around here!" she ended, her voice rising with each new syllable. She was on a roll.

"Yes, ma'am, of course, ma'am, whatever you say, ma'am," Steve responded hastily and heard the phone disconnect. He was sweating when he hung up his end and it wasn't from the summer heat, the gate shack was air-conditioned.

~ * ~

At five 'til seven Charlie drove up to the main gate that he had passed twice just this morning, thinking that at the time he never dreamed he would be coming here with the expectation of getting admitted. He stopped the car and a muscular looking man stepped promptly from the gate shack inquiring, "Mr. Chambers?"

"Yes," Charlie answered from the car, his window was already down. Unlike the gate shack, his car didn't have any air-conditioning.

The gates immediately started to swing open and the guard said, "Go right on up, Mr. Chambers, Miss Harmon is expecting you. She just called and said you were to be admitted promptly, park anywhere up by the house you want."

"Thanks."

"Yes, sir. You have a nice evening, sir."

Charlie tooled the little car up the drive rapidly and found ample parking. He was impressed. No, he was overwhelmed by the size of the house. A main house with tall stately columns and two wings. There were three stories on the main house and two on each wing. He decided it looked a little like the White House and figured it must contain thirty or forty rooms in all. Slowly, still a bit overwhelmed by his surroundings, he made his way up the ten or so stone steps to the massive front porch. The front porch alone probably had more square feet than his home back in Illinois. *Nice digs*, he mused, *real nice.*

Before he even reached the door, it opened and Carol stood there in all her beauty. Her jet-black hair hung down around her shoulders. She had on a light colored pleated dress with a blue flower pattern. The dress hung slightly off her shoulders amplifying her full bosom. The dress itself was cut just low enough, but not too low and it carried just below her knees, showing off what Charlie thought was a nice portion of her shapely legs.

Charlie had on a suit. He always had a suit on when he went anywhere for any reason. It was the only thing he knew how to wear. It was second nature to him, but he felt under dressed now. This suit happened to be his best summer weight suit, but he still felt inadequate.

"What's the matter, Charles?" Carol asked, after Charlie stood in the doorway without moving or talking for a full minute.

His mind catching up with the events, he responded, "Nothing, just overwhelmed by your beauty."

She blushed and said, "Why thank you, Charles. Come in, please."

Charlie promptly did and as Carol closed the door, she said, "Dinner will be served in the dining room, shall we?"

Nodding, he responded, "Of course." While he followed her down a hallway to the rear of the house, he tried to take in the magnitude of the house and its furnishings. "Nice house."

"Too big actually, it's an old historic Georgia home that I bought a few years ago and had remodeled. At the time it seemed like a good idea with all the staff and everything, but now it just feels too big. I don't feel I need it. It's just not me. I grew up on the other side of Johnson City, in a little five-room house. That's the kind of house I belong in."

"Any brothers or sisters?"

"No, only child, spoiled to death by the time I was twelve and being a good singer made it even worse. I was incorrigible by the time I was seventeen, which is probably why I got hooked up with my first husband."

They had made it to the dining room and it was expansive to say the least. There was enough room to throw a real party, plus some. On the far end of the room was a sitting area with large, overstuffed leather chairs and two overstuffed leather sofas. End tables and coffee tables abounded.

"How about we sit over here for a while before dinner and have a drink," Carol suggested, motioning toward the sitting area.

"Fine with me," Charlie answered and, following Carol's lead, dropped into one of the chairs.

Almost magically a woman appeared in a servant's uniform and Carol said, "Bring us some coffee, Mary, and ask Maria how long before dinner will be served, please."

"Yes, ma'am."

Then as an afterthought she turned to Charlie and asked, "Coffee okay, I mean we have all sorts of liquor, beer, you name it."

"Coffee's fine, I don't drink too much when I'm driving anyway. I don't need that kind of trouble. I generally find enough without that," he answered lightly.

"Like getting thrown in jail by Judge Ferrell, for contempt."

"Ah, you heard about that. Yes, that's kind of what I mean. For some reason judges don't warm up to me, and I think if they did I would get worried. I get paid to irritate judges and make my client's case, not win friends and influence people."

Changing the subject Carol now asked, "Do you have any family anywhere, Charles?"

"A mother in Illinois, my dad died a few years ago, a brother in New Mexico, but I don't see him much."

"So what do you do for entertainment?"

"Entertainment? Nothing to speak of really. I read a lot, but that's about it. I'm too busy generally to think much of entertainment. Although lately I've been thinking I might become a country and western music fan."

Carol chuckled at that and said, "Always good to have another fan."

Now it was Charlie's turn to change the subject. "So how did Dan Chase take the dinner news?"

"He was hot, I mean real hot, but I told him he could put up with it or I would stop being his little songbird. As I told you, I don't need to sing another song to live the way I want to live, but Dan can't say that. He needs every dime he can get through me."

"That's good thinking. You can't break his contract, but you can starve him into compliance, to a certain degree. I'd be careful though, some people take drastic measures when the heat is on, especially financial heat, when their financial needs are great."

"Yeah, that's a fact. The financial heat is on him, all right. In fact, he said you were only interested in me for my money," Carol said off-handedly, but she studied Charlie's face carefully when she said it just to see if there was any reaction. After all, Dan wasn't stupid, he could be right about that. However, there was no reaction.

Carol waited for more, but none was forthcoming, she did note that Charlie's face had taken on a serious frown, as if he were pondering something far away.

"Why the frown? Something I said?"

Charlie snapped back to his present surroundings and replied seriously, "You know I told you my wife had died."

"Yes."

"Well, my baby daughter died, too. At the same time, in the car crash. There was a defect in the steering system. The company knew about it and ignored it. A lot of people around the country were killed as a result of the same defect. Back then, the type of law I practiced was product liability, holding manufacturers liable for just such conduct. At the time of the accident I was in California trying a products liability case. I hated myself for that and all the other times I had gone off to court in one state or another leaving my wife and daughter alone, not having the time to spend with them, not taking the time to appreciate them.

"To make a long story short, I took out my anger at myself on the car manufacturer and won. Not only for me, but for all the others who were injured or killed. After that I never tried another product liability case. I realized all I was doing was obtaining money for people in an attempt to replace something or someone in their lives that couldn't be replaced. It seemed stupid. After that realization, money never seemed important to me. I get along just fine. I don't need or want your money. I'm fine the way I am.

"That was just over five years ago, I started down a different path and I'm happier for it. I don't get stressed out anymore. I do my job and I go home. I manage to pay the bills."

Both Carol and Charlie lapsed into silence until it was broken by the tentative voice of Mary announcing dinner.

"Thank you, Mary," Carol answered and stood.

Charlie hopped up quickly and they crossed the room to the table. It was huge and only two places were set on one end directly across from each other. Several candles were adorning the table and the lights in the room were dimmed appropriately. Charlie was not used to such a formal setting for dinner, a small café was more to his liking, but Carol was *here*.

Over dinner there was small talk, nothing serious, nothing earthshaking, just two people trying to get the feel for each other, testing the waters to see if they were compatible, or at least could tolerate each other. Charlie felt he could do much more than tolerate Carol, but he thought it a bit early in their relationship, if that's what this was, to get pushy.

Carol, on the other hand, had little doubt about their compatibility. She just felt it was there, with no logical explanation. Of course wasn't that the way it went when you found someone you liked? Didn't it just click? The trouble was, time was wasting. She had commitments. Despite what she had told Dan, she had no intention of blowing off her singing career. She enjoyed singing, or used to, and she intended to begin enjoying it again, if she had to give free impromptu performances like she had the other night, every week. She knew Charles had his business too, and that he probably would not be around here much longer. So if she was going to convince him that they were compatible, at least enough to see each other regularly when their schedules permitted, then she had to get moving, or rather, get him moving.

The only real fault she had discovered, no not a fault, an oddity. That thing about being led to his cases. She had heard talk and had to admit it was a little odd, but people had a lot worse things wrong with them and she wasn't yet admitting to herself that this was a 'wrong', just different. After all, she used to be a frequent churchgoer, when she was young. She should go now, but it wasn't very practical.

"So what are you doing Sunday?" Charlie asked out of the blue.

"Sunday? Nothing I guess. Why? Do you have something in mind?"

"Church," Charlie answered in a matter of fact tone.

Can you believe that? Carol asked herself, *is this guy a mind reader, too?*

Charlie noted the hesitation and said, "I've been attending a little Baptist church on the south side of town off and on and I thought you might like to give it a go. Don't tell me you don't go to church. The way you talked up on Burning Chapel Hill I figured you to have some religion in your background."

"Oh, no, it's not that, it's just that it isn't very practical for me. I mean how? What would it look like if I showed up with all my bodyguards? Going to a restaurant is one thing, but church?"

Charlie responded in a serious tone, "So don't take your bodyguards. You don't need them anyway, not here. This is your hometown; do you really think anyone is going to molest you here? These people love you; they would never allow anyone to hurt you, not in their town. Have you ever stopped to think what kind of impression they get from you when you go everywhere in your hometown with a gang of bodyguards? I'm not from here, but if I was, I think I'd be offended that you didn't trust me enough to appear in public without guards. In Chicago, maybe or New York, but Johnson City, your hometown, where everyone worships the ground you walk on, I don't think so."

The thought had never occurred to Carol before. Charles was right though, no one was going to bother her here and if they did there would be a hundred men volunteering to assist her at the drop of a hat.

Why had that never occurred to her before? The answer was simple, Dan Chase. It had always been his insistence that she be guarded, but guarded from whom? Dan probably insisted on the guards more to keep her in line and keep an eye on her than out of fear for her safety. The more she thought about it the more sense that made and she finally answered.

"Okay, Charles, I'd love to go to church with you. What time?"

"Ten o'clock, I'll pick you up at nine thirty. It's only a ten minute drive."

"I'll be ready then. Now, how about dessert?"

"No thanks, my doctor doesn't want me eating too much dessert, bad for my cholesterol."

Carol screwed up her face and said, "You don't strike me as a person who cares too much about what a doctor tells him is good or bad for him."

Chuckling, Charlie said, "You're right of course, but sometimes I do heed his advice just so that the next time I go see him I can say I'm trying. But mostly I do thumb my nose at him. What's for dessert?"

Dessert turned out to be a huge slice of apple pie with ice cream on top and Charlie enjoyed it almost as much as the company.

After dinner they had more coffee in the sitting area and time seemed to stand still for Charlie. He couldn't remember the last time he had enjoyed someone's company so much, unless maybe with his wife. But for some reason he couldn't recall that and that disturbed him. He felt as though enjoying another woman's company was somehow being unfaithful, not so much to her, but to her memory. That was stupid, he decided. Had it been the other way around, he would want her to find solace in someone else and not pine away for the rest of her life.

Carol was having a good time, too, but she noted a certain reserve in Charlie, he just wasn't loose. Something seemed to be bothering him, maybe the surroundings. This house could have a rather imposing effect on people. Another good reason to go to church with him on Sunday, aside from the fact that Dan would go berserk again. She smiled to herself.

Time seemed to be standing still for Charlie, but of course it wasn't and Carol finally glanced at her watch. "Eleven o'clock, I can't believe it! I haven't had such a relaxing evening in... I've never had such a relaxing evening." She wanted this night to go on forever, but she knew it couldn't.

"It has been nice," Charlie remarked, in what Carol thought was still a very reserved tone.

Rising slowly, Charlie said, "Well, I guess I had better be going. Dan can probably only tolerate so much," he ended lightly.

"Oh, who gives a hang about what Dan can take or not take. I've been down that road for too many years and I've decided I'm getting off that train."

With a seriousness, Charlie responded, "You be careful there, Carol. I have a feeling Dan could have a bigger bite than you think."

"I don't believe it. He'd never do anything to hurt me. I'm his meal ticket."

"Maybe. I hope you're right, but I'd go easy if I were you. I don't really know Dan Chase, but I just have a feeling about him. I've learned to trust my feelings over the years."

As they talked about Dan, they were making their way toward the living room and across to the front door. No one else was in sight and Charlie wasn't surprised. He figured Carol had not exaggerated laying down the law to Dan earlier in the day. Charlie had said he didn't know much about Dan Chase and he didn't, but he figured him to be smart enough to know when to back off.

At the door Charlie suddenly turned to Carol and asked, "Have I seemed a little distant tonight?"

Smiling at his uncanny ability to seem to know what she was thinking, she responded honestly, "Yes, a little reserved I thought, especially after dinner. Was it something you ate?" she ended with a chuckle, but wanted a serious answer.

Charlie thought as much, he felt he had been unknowingly telegraphing his mood, but he had to be sure, he didn't want the night to end on this note. He glanced around and crossed to a sofa and, with his eyes, implored Carol to join him.

The Preacher   Robert James Allison

When Carol was seated beside him on the couch, he explained, "It wasn't anything I ate and it isn't you, not personally anyway."

At Carol's confused look he continued hastily, "I mean, it's me, or my memories I guess. You have to understand, I was very much in love with my wife and I worshiped my daughter, not that you could tell it by the way I acted, but that's beside the point. At the same time I am very attracted to you and have been since our second meeting. I discount the first.

"So there is my dilemma. I can't understand it. I tell myself I'm crazy, but I feel like I am betraying my wife by enjoying your company. It's stupid. I know my wife is dead and that she would want me to be happy, but I can't help the way I feel. So if I seemed a little distant tonight that's what it was. It's not your fault, it has nothing to do with you."

"How do you figure that, Charles? It has everything to do with me. I'm the person you enjoy being with, you say, and that makes you feel guilty. Sounds to me like it has something to do with me." She could see by the anguish in his face that he was going to make some apologetic response so she quickly continued, "It's okay. I understand and I'm not taking it personally. It will pass, I'm sure of it. I had similar feelings after my mother and father were killed. I felt as though I should be sad all the time; that I should not be allowed to be happy. For a long time after they were killed, whenever I performed and enjoyed it, I felt guilty. I told myself that my being happy and successful in my singing career was just what they would have wanted and that was true. But I still felt that since they had died and I had lived that, for some reason, I should not be happy.

"It passed. It took a long time, but it passed. I just kept getting up there in front of those crowds and kept having a good time. I kept laughing, kept joking and one day I realized it didn't make me feel guilty anymore. I can't say when it stopped bothering me, but one day it just did. The same will happen for you, Charles, if you let it. If you don't bottle it up inside, if you don't hide away in some corner. Which is what you have been doing up until now, isn't it?"

Charlie thought about what she had said and it made sense to him. He had said most of the same things to himself on more than one occasion, but coming from Carol it seemed to take on a different meaning. Nodding, he studied her face, noted the slight creases around her eyes. Whether from smiling a lot or squinting in the bright stage lights, he didn't know, but he liked them. They added character to her already beautiful face. He saw the light dance in her eyes and watched as she nervously brushed the dark bangs from them and then he said, "Carol Harmon, you are really an amazing woman. You're right of course, I always knew it, but as you can see by the way I acted tonight, it is easier said than done."

Shrugging, Carol said, "It takes time, Charles. And in case you haven't already figured it out, I may just be willing to wait."

"May I kiss you, Carol?"

Carol was astounded, what a class act this guy was, he was almost too much of a gentleman for his own good. Without the right woman he'd never get to first base. Fortunately, Carol decided, he's with the right woman, he just doesn't know it yet. Then she said earnestly, "I thought you were never going to get around to that Charles Chambers."

Charlie leaned forward tentatively and their lips met. Not once, but several times and each time with a little more energy than the last.

Finally, Charlie pulled back and said, "I'd best be going. It really was a *nice* night. I just had to make you understand before I left that I was not being distant because of something you did or anything. You do understand?"

Carol stood as Charlie stood and responded firmly, "Charles Chambers, didn't those kisses answer that question?"

Blushing slightly, Charlie nodded and said with an impish gleam in his eye, "Yes, as a matter of fact I think they did. But in case I forget the answer, can I ask it again?"

Playfully Carol slapped him on the right thigh and answered with another kiss and then said, "Anytime, anytime at all." Thinking to herself, *he's getting better already.*

Seventeen

Promptly at two o'clock the next afternoon, Charlie walked in to the outer office of the chief corporate counsel for TTM, still half-floating from his date with Carol the night before. He hadn't felt this happy in years and he was relishing the feeling. Life could really be good. Seconds later, he was ushered into the inner office of Phillip Stellar. Phil looked older and slightly heavier, but he was definitely the Phil Stellar that Charlie remembered.

Phil stood as Charlie came in, greeted him warmly with an extended hand and waved him to a chair opposite a sofa where Phil planted himself.

"Coffee or a soda?" Phil inquired, as they took their seats and the secretary hung in the distance awaiting a reply.

"Coffee, black, no sugar please," Charlie uttered.

Phil nodded wordlessly to the secretary and she scampered off to get the coffee.

Charlie had a few seconds to look closely at Phil while he settled into his sofa and he saw immediate differences in this Phil from the old Phil. His suit was very expensive and perfectly tailored. It was neatly pressed and spotless; too neat for having gone through a morning of work in the office. Either Phil didn't work that hard or he had just put on a fresh suit. Charlie suspected the latter since even no work could soil a suit in no time, especially a light colored summer weight suit like the one Phil wore. *Why put on a fresh suit for me?* he asked himself, *or did he change suits every day after lunch?* The latter was quite possible and bespoke of wealth beyond anything that Charlie had known Phil to previously have. Back in Illinois, Phil Stellar had been a hard working, sharp, lawyer of moderate means.

Charlie had also noted how the secretary jumped at Phil's beck and call. He got the distinct impression that Phil was used to giving orders and having those orders immediately carried out, with no nonsense. Again, a contrast to the lawyer that Charlie remembered, the old Phil had been easy going and rarely raised his voice to anyone. He had the feeling that this Phil could and had raised his voice a lot around here. Just why he had that feeling he wasn't sure, something in the look of the secretary or the way she moved to get the coffee.

Before his thoughts were completed, the secretary reappeared with the coffee in hand, "Oh, thank you," Charlie said pleasantly as he took the proffered cup.

He noted that Phil didn't speak to dismiss the secretary, but rather just made the same curt nod as before and she rapidly retreated out the door, closing it softly behind her.

Smiling now, Phil asked, "So what brings you to Johnson City, Charlie? You said something about a case?" The smile was too good, too genuine looking to be real.

"Yes. I do mostly Con Law these days and I travel around the country defending people whose constitutional rights are being infringed, religious rights generally," Charlie responded without detail and sipped his coffee.

"ACLU lawyer?" Phil asked.

Chuckling, Charlie responded, "No, in fact we're on opposite sides most of the time."

"So you freelance then?"

"Yes, in a way. I'm supported by an organization headquartered in Illinois, but I try to be as frugal as possible. I get a salary, but it isn't that large. I get by though, and the work is important to me."

"I see," Phil said with a tone that said he didn't see at all why a lawyer would pass up big bucks just for a cause.

Charlie decided to plunge into the deep end of the pool and said, as off-handed as he could manage, "I think my latest client is an employee of TTM."

"Oh," Phil stated in surprise, but like the smile it was just a little too genuine to be real.

Charlie pressed forward anyway. "Yes, a fellow by the name of Tommy Trenton. I think they refer to him as the Preacher, because he likes to preach to the people on the street and pass out religious pamphlets. He was arrested for Dis Con several times and I think the statute is unconstitutionally overbroad with a chilling effect on free speech and religion."

Phil nodded his understanding and said, "Spoken like a true constitutional law professor."

"Maybe you could help me, Phil. I could use all the information I can get on my client. He's a bit of a recluse and no one knows much about him. I like to be well versed in my client's life when I argue a case. It makes it more personal to me, and I do a better job of arguing. What can you tell me?"

Pursing his lips in contemplation, Phil rose and crossed to the desk. He pushed his intercom and without awaiting a response, said crisply, "Julie, bring me the personnel file on Tommy Trenton, ASAP!"

Crossing back to the sofa he settled in again and said, "Glad to help any way I can. TTM is always trying to better the lives of its employees." Smiling again.

"Good. Do you know of any trouble he's been in either on or off the premises? I don't like to be surprised in court."

"What has he told you?"

"Says he's clean."

Phil shrugged and responded, "Far as I know he is. I don't know janitors on a first name basis and I don't socialize with them, but as far as I know he's clean."

"You do know him though?"

"Never met him, first I heard of his name was when you mentioned it. I only say he's clean, because if he wasn't, I'd know about it, and I don't."

"I see, sure, that makes sense," Charlie responded absently, thinking that the old Phil would have socialized with a duck if it had been buying the coffee.

A moment of silence passed between the two men and Charlie noticed that Phil had picked up the habit of jerking his chin up and away from his right shoulder every few moments.

At the same time he would almost grimace and a moment or two later the gesture would be repeated. It didn't matter if he was talking or walking or just sitting, he jerked. Nerves, Charlie knew. A nervous tick taken to the extreme was the result of too much pressure, too much stress, too much work and not enough time off. Phil lived an intensely hurried life from daylight to well after dark, Charlie guessed.

The personnel file appeared at the hand of the secretary about as quickly as the coffee had and after another curt nod from Phil she disappeared just as quickly.

With Phil's consent, Charlie scanned the personnel file and found out very little that he didn't already know, which was almost nothing. The personnel file had very little information in it and that in and of itself said something. A personnel file with no reprimands or other disciplinary records meant more than volumes of 'atta boy' letters. The other data was just that, data about Tommy Trenton. His address, next of kin 'none,' telephone number 'none,' date of birth 2-14-48. Employment began on 2-14-66, on his eighteenth birthday. *Makes sense*, Charlie decided, *probably had to be eighteen to work at this plant under the Georgia labor laws.* It seems from the day he started to the present he had held only one job, he was a sweeper in the dyeing facility, a janitor by any other name.

Charlie closed the file and handed it to Phil. "Not much there, I guess he is clean."

Phil shrugged in a noncommittal way as his nervous tick kicked in once again and he said, "Like I said, I don't know him and that's good news for any employee of TTM."

Changing tacks, Charlie said, "Hey, I was talking to some of the cops in town and they spoke highly of your Dan Mosley. He's a pretty sharp cookie from what they say."

Nodding, Phil responded, "You can't become head of security at TTM unless you are. Dan's a good man. Honest as the day is long."

Somehow, Charlie wasn't overly impressed by that statement, considering it came from Phil. He wasn't impressed with Phil either, at least not near as much as Phil was impressed with himself. He had gotten the distinct impression that Phil Stellar would say and do any thing if it benefited Phil Stellar and TTM. Conversely, he seemed ready to not say or do any thing that would harm TTM or himself.

Charlie realized that no information was going to be forthcoming about Tommy Trenton or the theft of any money. He made a little more small talk and then excused himself. Charlie had come to see an old acquaintance, with an ulterior motive, but he had come just the same. What he found was a stranger in the body of an old acquaintance. He didn't like what he had found. He didn't like what had become of Phil Stellar. Quite obviously, Phil had traded a mediocre life as a well-liked, average lawyer for the high priced, high-pressure job of corporate counsel, with the power to make people jump and cringe at his every word.

Charlie knew Phil had come out on the short end of the trade, but he doubted Phil would agree, at least not today or anytime soon. Someday, he might see what he had become before it was too late. Charlie prayed he would, he had liked Phil Stellar, once upon a time, in another world.

~ * ~

The comptroller slowly walked around the conference table and scanned the sheets of paper scattered around its edge. Pursing her lips, she was obviously in deep concentration, as she hesitated over each sheet and examined it.

In a far corner, Leon Semple stood silently by, as the examination continued. After several more minutes of silence, the comptroller finally declared, "What a mess. You're right, Leon, these books don't even come close. The shortfalls are quite evident."

Leon now added, "Yes, Mrs. Carpenter. Everything is properly documented, but the disbursement side is way out of whack. I mean, it's also properly documented, but a blind man could see it isn't going to balance. Whoever did this made no attempt to cover it up. Either they weren't smart enough to cover it up or they didn't think we were smart enough to find it.

"Taking into account the whole system, there are correlating entries to justify the disbursements, but the disbursements are more than came in. For instance, a bond would be shown posted on cash receipts at one hundred dollars. That's an income, but when refunded, the same bond would increase to three hundred. Yet the program tracking the bonds would agree that the bond on file is three hundred and that three hundred should be refunded. That's two hundred dollars going out that shouldn't have. Anyone can see that. The same thing happens on fines. A fine is posted at five hundred, but the money might never actually come in, yet the fine is shown paid. That isn't a disbursement in the actual sense, but it is a loss and it amounts to the same thing as a disbursement. The public is still shorted money it should have gotten."

"How about child support? I don't see any discrepancies in that area. Am I missing something?"

"No, ma'am. Child support checks out right on the money and so is the civil side. Oh, a few bookkeeping errors here and there, but they are just posting errors. No pattern like I noted on the criminal side."

Rubbing her chin in thought, Lisa Carpenter asked, "Do you think this is intentional? Could it be a bad bookkeeping system or maybe just incompetence?" She was pretty sure Leon wouldn't help her in this area, but she wanted to try. Leon was smart and she had often thought of moving him up into her administration, but he wouldn't come out of his shell.

True to form, Leon nestled himself deeper into his shell and answered, "I don't know. I don't think about that. My job is to see if the books balance, not to decide if someone did something wrong."

Lisa persisted, "According to your report this has been going on for almost four years. There seems to be a thirty thousand-dollar shortfall each year. Around one hundred twenty thousand in four years. Intentional or not, that's a lot of public money unaccounted for and something needs to be done. If it isn't intentional, then it's grossly negligent. Either way, the situation has to be corrected. Surely you have some indication of whether or not there is criminal activity afoot?"

"No, ma'am, not really. I mean it could be, but it could just be lousy bookwork, too. It's just not my expertise to know the difference. I just know if they balance or not."

"Don't give me that, Leon. You're more than an accountant. You've got a real gift for sniffing out these things. Take a risk for once in your life and give me your gut feeling."

Leon was beside himself. He didn't want to be placed in the position of judging others. That was for people better than he was.

"Leon," Lisa said, firmly.

After another moment of inner turmoil, Leon answered weakly, "If it is criminal, and I'm not saying it is mind you, I don't see the benefit."

"What do you mean?"

"I mean, who's getting the money? I didn't find any evidence of improper transfers. Any disbursement was made to the person the computer indicated should get it. The only people who benefited from the fines not being paid were the ones who owed the fines. If someone was playing with the figures they had to have a reason. Generally, that reason would be that they stood to gain money. No one did, except the people the computer said should gain. No one in the office got any money, no cash hoards were accumulated. Every transaction had a paper trail, an easy to follow paper trail. You see my point? Why risk jail to alter the books, but not gain anything?"

"Of course! I see your point. That doesn't sound right does it? There isn't any evidence of theft, just poor bookkeeping that resulted in hundreds of people getting what amounted to windfalls. Right on, Leon. See, I knew you had it in you. Someone in the Meridian County Circuit Clerk's Office may be incompetent, but they aren't crooked."

Pacing the floor now with unseeing eyes, Lisa asked, "So what do we do about it?"

Once started, Leon decided to plunge on ahead, "Check out the system first, then check out the individuals who are responsible for entering data. Either the system is all balled up or the people inputting the data don't know what they are doing."

"Do it," Lisa stated flatly.

"Huh? Me? I'm not a cop, I'm..."

Lisa cut him off, "Yeah I know, you're a number cruncher and a number cruncher is what we need right now. We need someone to go in there who can ask the right questions about how the system works and how data is managed. Someone like you. Some dunderheaded cop or assistant attorney general wouldn't have the foggiest idea of what to look for, but you would."

"But, I don't have that kind of authority," Leon almost whimpered, he was in over his head and drowning fast.

"No problem. I'll make some calls. You'll have an investigator from the attorney general's office to accompany you."

"I... but..." Leon stammered.

Lisa smiled sweetly and said, "I've got you, Leon. You'll have to come out of your shell now. I won't take 'no' for an answer. If you want to stay on in the comptroller's office, you'll take care of this for me."

He was stuck and he knew it. There was no sense arguing with Mrs. Carpenter, he was no match for her mind, which seemed to move at the speed of light.

~ * ~

Charlie was scanning the inside of the café looking for a likely spot to park himself for supper, when he spied Sergeant Todd Evans in a corner booth by himself. Hesitating, he decided to ease over that way. The café was pretty crowded this time of evening. It was the prime supper hour for Johnson City, so seats weren't all that easy to find. For a small town, Charlie was amazed at the crowd that Shirley could attract at mealtime, but then again the food was excellent.

"Mind if I join you?" Charlie asked Todd.

Todd looked up, somewhat surprised to see this lawyer again and so soon. He didn't cotton much to lawyers anyway, but he didn't see the need to be rude, after all, it was a public place. The sixties weren't so far out of Todd's mind that he didn't recognize the significance of a white lawyer asking to sit with a black cop in the Deep South.

"Sure, why not. It's a free country," Todd said lightly.

Charlie took his seat and responded, "Not as free as it used to be, but freer than most."

Todd thought about that a minute and said, "Yeah, I see your point." Then changing the subject, he asked, "Go up to the mill today?"

"I did."

"Learn anything?"

"Not much."

"I'm surprised they even let you in. They're a closed mouth bunch up there," Todd said flatly.

"It just so happens that I discovered I used to know one of the corporate lawyers. I called him and he invited me up to see him and talk over old times."

"A friend in the enemy's camp, huh?"

"No," he corrected Todd, "Phil Stellar was never a friend, just an acquaintance. I knew him back in Illinois a few years ago, always wondered what happened to him. As it turned out, I'm glad he wasn't a friend."

With arched eyebrows, Todd responded, "Why say that?"

"I don't like losing friends. Good friends are hard to find. Had Phil ever been a friend, I would have lost him today. He's turned into something I don't like. I can't put my finger on it exactly, but his style isn't mine and he wasn't friendly. He tried to act friendly, but he wasn't being friendly."

Todd thought about that a minute and nodded in the affirmative, saying, "I understand that. I see that a lot in my line of work."

"Anyway, I'm glad he was never a friend. You can't lose a friend you never had," Charlie said dismally and turned to greet the waitress who had just arrived.

Todd stirred his coffee and asked, "I thought you'd be heading home. Why are you still hanging around? Don't you have a family back in Illinois?"

"A mother is all, she was a little disappointed that I canceled my flight back home the other day. I couldn't help it, though. I had to do it. I just got a feeling that the Preacher needed me."

Todd thought that an odd statement and asked, "A feeling?"

"I don't expect you to understand it, but it happened. It happens a lot. I'm driven to be in certain places at certain times, to help people defend their religious rights. It started a few years ago. There's no doubt though that things seem to happen to me. I get feelings and I sort of get pushed to one place or another. I don't know how else to explain it, but things just seem to work out.

"You ought to understand, a man like you, I see it in your face and your eyes." Staring now at Todd's face, he continued, "Something drives you, too. Where it's driving you or why, I don't know, but I see it."

"Don't see it myself," Todd stated.

"You don't see your family much either, do you?" Charlie asked.

"No, it doesn't fit in too well with being a cop," Todd answered simply.

"You know why?"

"No, but I'm sure you're going to tell me," Todd said dryly.

Charlie smiled and answered, "It's because you're driven. You don't have room in your life for anyone else, not now. Driven people are like that, they focus on one goal, one path and nothing else.

What's your goal? What path do you take that takes you from your family?"

Todd was uncomfortable with the stare he was getting from Charlie and this conversation.

Changing the subject, Todd asked, "You said you didn't learn much at the mill. Did that mean you learned something?"

Charlie contemplated the question for a minute and answered, "Something's odd up there. I was given a look at Tommy's personnel file and it was as clean as a hound's tooth. No disciplinary action documented, no reprimands, nothing. He's been a steady employee up there for thirty years. Why would he start stealing from them all of a sudden?"

Not waiting for an answer, he continued, "Tommy doesn't strike me as a man who would be disloyal. I don't really know him. I only know about him, but it doesn't add up. He's a driven man, too, you know. There's little doubt in my mind that God is driving him, somewhere, for some reason."

Back to the driving, Todd thought, *this guy's got a one-track mind* and again he tried to change the subject. "I like the Preacher, too. He's been a part of my work on the streets for a lot of years. Ever since I was just a green deputy on patrol duty, the Preacher has always been there. He's never hurt anyone and never caused any trouble. For what it's worth, I don't believe he's stolen anything, ever. He's honest to the bone."

With a wistful look on his face, he continued, lost in the past, "I've never admitted this to anyone before, but I've always kind of looked out for the Preacher. I didn't do a lot, just little things from time to time. Back when I first started out on the streets, he was pretty much living on the streets. He had his apartment, but he didn't always stay there. He was still so used to being out on the streets that he couldn't stay cooped up for long.

"Sometimes when I heard bad weather was coming I'd hunt him up to make sure he knew it. I'd make sure he had enough warning to find cover if he could and when he couldn't, I'd lend him an extra blanket. I'd slip him a fiver every now and again to make sure he had a meal.

"He was working at the mill then, but he sometimes spent his money before payday. I suspect he gave some away to other less fortunate people and got caught short himself. He'd never admit it, but I'd bet he did it. Hard to imagine someone worse off than the Preacher, but he didn't, and doesn't, think that way. You know to hear him tell it he's had a pretty good life, or at least he's satisfied with what little he has. I think if he had a million dollars he'd just give it away," Todd ended, still staring off into space.

Charlie thought about what Todd had said, and how he had said it, while he drank a whole cup of coffee. Neither spoke for several minutes and finally Charlie said, "Is that why you bailed the Preacher out of jail those three times?"

"Yeah, I..." Todd stopped when he realized what he was admitting then continued, "You'd make a good cop, Chambers. How'd you figure that so fast?"

"No, I wouldn't. I'm too much of a bleeding heart liberal, but to answer your question. I just put two and two together and it felt right. You strike me as the kind of cop who would be concerned about the plight of his fellow man; a man who wouldn't forget the less fortunate when he was in a position to do something about it. Why though? You should have known he would just go out and do the same thing again, it's in his nature."

"Like I said before, I've known him a long time, I've watched him out on the streets now for years. Out on the streets he's free, or used to be. What was that you said when you first sat down? The country isn't as free as it used to be. Well, that's true for Tommy. Once upon a time he was free to roam the streets at will and preach to anyone, anywhere, but not now. Now they lock him up and I couldn't stand to see that.

"You can't understand, I guess, unless you've practically grown up watching the man like I have, but he has to be free. He's a little like wild deer. You can see them sometimes from afar and maybe even get close enough for a good look once in a while, but that's all. You can't possess them, because if you do, they aren't wild anymore. And if they aren't wild it's no fun watching them.

"If you lock one up it won't live in captivity, not like when it was free. It may survive, but it won't live. There's a big difference between surviving and living. So anyway, that's why I did it."

Charlie nodded and said with genuine admiration, "I like that. You've confirmed my early assessment of you, Sergeant Evans. You're good people. I wish all cops had your heart."

Todd smiled thinly and said, "It has its price."

"Yeah, I know. It eats at you doesn't it? Seeing the injustice in the world and not being able to do anything about it. It eats at me, too. That's why I do what I do, even when I sometimes suffer for it. You understand now, don't you?"

Nodding over his coffee cup, he answered seriously, "I do. I guess I always did, but I've so long been antagonistic toward lawyers that I didn't want to believe there were actually lawyers out there who cared more about justice than a buck."

Shrugging, Charlie said, "Yeah, that's a common problem. I guess that's what I disliked most about Phil Stellar. He's only after the buck now, at any cost, to any one. It's a mighty sad thing.

"Speaking of Phil Stellar, he did say something today that didn't make sense to me at the time, but now I'm thinking he told me something, without knowing it. You're a cop, maybe it would mean something to you. Anyway, when I asked Phil if he knew whether or not Tommy had been in any trouble he said, no, but that he didn't usually socialize with janitors."

"So?"

"Wait now. After that, a few minutes later, he told me that before I had told him Tommy's name he had never heard of him."

Todd furrowed his brow and said without being asked, "Yeah, I got it. If he didn't know him or his name, how did he know he was a janitor?"

"Exactly. It didn't hit me until just now, but he slipped up didn't he? I've seen people do that on the stand in cross-examination, when I was looking for it, but I wasn't looking for it today. What does that say to you?"

Todd thought a minute and answered, "Lots. First, he knew of Tommy before you got there, but for some reason he didn't want you to know that. He probably knew that you were Tommy's lawyer or were looking into the charges against him and he was trying to throw you off the scent. He wanted you to think that the mill didn't know anything about the trouble Tommy was in, or at least that he didn't. You were playing against a stacked deck. They knew you were coming and they knew why. It was Stellar's job to appease your curiosity so that you would go away without discovering anything of value and be satisfied enough not to come back. The only reason they would do that is that they know something that would help Tommy, or that if you found out, would make it possible for you to help Tommy."

"But what?"

"That's the sixty-four thousand dollar question, but the fact that you had to ask it means that there is something up there which will help Tommy." Todd cleared his throat and asked, "Can you help Tommy?"

Thinking for a minute before he answered, Charlie said quietly, "On the Dis Con, yes. On the theft charges, maybe. I'm not a criminal lawyer, not the kind he needs. My best hope is like I told you earlier, nip it in the bud. I need to find out the truth of the matter before the state's attorney decides to file formal charges. I don't know how much time I have before that happens. Not much, I suspect. I have a feeling that the mill wants this done quickly and that the mill usually gets what it wants. So far the state's attorney has not been overly cooperative."

Disgustedly, Todd put in, "They do get what they want, all the time!"

"That won't help any then. I need time to find out what it is they are hiding and I'm not going to get much. I'm getting stonewalled at every turn."

Defensively, Todd said, "I can't help that. I have a job to do to."

Holding up his hand in a gesture of needing to hear no more, Charlie said quickly, "Oh, I know that. I wasn't talking about you. You have your job and I wouldn't ask you not to do it. The mill might, but I never would. Things will work out, they always do, but sometimes I forget and get impatient to see the end.

"You don't by any chance know anyone up at the mill who could shed some light on this matter do you? Someone who might be able to tell me what they are hiding?"

"No, they don't like cops up there. Like I said, they are a closed mouth bunch. They all seem to have a single mindset up there, protect their job and that means protecting their employer. To a point I can't fault them there, but only to a point."

~ * ~

Janet was trying her best to get an error message out of her computer, but couldn't. Mark had fixed it too well. She wanted to see him again and the only way she knew to do that was to have her computer act up again, but it wouldn't. She figured she was wasting her time this night anyway. She had worked late trying to get that error message and now it was past six o'clock. Mark would be gone anyway so she might as well forget this quest for tonight.

Gathering up the papers on her desk she put everything in its proper place and set her purse up on the desk. She got up and made sure that the inner office door to Mr. Willis' office was locked, grabbed her purse and flipped off the light on her way out the door. She didn't lock her door; the janitors would just have to unlock it to clean anyway.

In the silent hall, she pushed the elevator call button and waited—and waited—and waited. *This elevator sure is taking a long time*, she thought. No sooner had she processed that thought than the elevator doors suddenly opened and in the middle of the elevator stood Mark

Fribley. Stunned, she wished she had brushed her hair before leaving the office. *Just my luck*, she thought.

"Hi," Mark said nervously, he was just as shocked to see Janet as she was to see him. He had also worked late on the off chance that she might have more trouble with her computer. For once his skill in fixing computers was a drawback. He had done too good a job.

"Oh, hi," she said, as she stepped onto the elevator and continued, "I wondered what was taking the elevator so long. I must have called it just after you did and it went to the basement first."

"It did. I thought the stupid thing was busted when it passed up the first floor. Usually, I don't ride the elevator because it's quicker to take the stairs up from the basement, but tonight I didn't figure it would take long. I'm glad I was wrong."

Smiling as sweetly as she could manage, she said, "Me, too. Working late, huh?"

Enthralled by the aroma of her perfume in the close confines of the elevator, he almost forgot to respond, but then said, "Yes. A little catch up. I do it frequently since there's no one waiting for me at home. Us single guys can get away with being late for supper," he ended lightly.

"Me, too," she said, for lack of a better response. She wasn't sure what he meant by his statement, but felt he meant more than the words conveyed. Maybe he just wanted to make sure she knew he was single and alone.

"How about you," he said and continued, "I figured your social calendar would be pretty full. How do you get away with working late?"

"Oh, I didn't have anything planned for tonight," she responded, not adding that her social calendar wasn't all that full and that she didn't find that many men to whom she was attracted. She felt it better to let him think she wasn't all that available, all the time. It had been her experience that appearing to be readily available was sometimes counter-productive in the dating game.

The elevator reached the ground floor and he held the 'open' button for her while she stepped off. She didn't want to step off, she knew when she did that they would be leaving the building and their conversation would end with the workday.

Silently they traversed the lobby, Mark unlocked the door and held it for her, deep in thought. Clearing his throat as they stepped out into the warm night, Mark braced himself for rejection and said, "I don't feel like going home to a TV dinner tonight. Could I interest you in a steak dinner over in Thomasville?"

Janet felt her response was too quick, while Mark was sure the time delay meant she was framing a tactful refusal. After all, she was awfully pretty, and what would such a pretty woman want with a plain computer nerd like him.

"I'd like that."

"I understand... I..." Mark stammered and stopped. Suddenly he realized she hadn't said no, and then he tried to make his last half statement conform to her acceptance. "I understand that the Black Angus serves a mighty fine filet."

Smiling broadly now, Janet said, "I've heard that, too."

Walking side by side to the center of the parking lot Mark wished he would have had the presence of mind this morning to have shaved a little closer and worn some better clothes. *Why not?* he decided and said, "I don't know about you, Janet, but I've had a long day and could use a shower and a shave. How about we each go home and I come by and pick you up about seven thirty?"

Janet had been thinking about the same thing. Her makeup was long spent and her hair was a mess. A more comfortable dress would be nice, too. And maybe a little more alluring also. She smiled to herself.

"That's a great idea, I was just thinking the same thing myself. Do you know my address?" Without waiting for an answer, she continued, "Sure you do, I'll bet the computer in personnel is easy for you to access." She smiled mischievously.

Mark's face turned crimson and he stammered, "Uh... I... ah..." Then with a smile like the cat that had eaten the bird, he answered, "I've forgotten it, though. I didn't write it down and if I don't write things down, they're gone. Computer stuff I remember, but anything else is a bust."

Janet said nothing, she had confirmed her suspicions, or more accurately, her hopes. She had gone to the trouble to look him up and she had hoped he had done the same for her. He had. *This is going well*, she decided, as she continued to smile sweetly.

Mark was hypnotized by her bright and mischievous smile. She was so pretty it almost hurt. In a way it did hurt, he couldn't make himself believe that this girl could really be interested in him, but she seemed to be. Finally, he admitted, "I remember the street is Bower Street and I saw your car parked there one time, but I don't remember the house number." As an after thought he added, "I was over that way a few months ago and happened to recognize your car. You know."

Still smiling that irresistible smile, she responded, "Yes, I know." Deciding not to play too coyly with him, because he was too timid and might run for the hills, she added, "Do you still live on Sixth Street?"

Mark's eyes widened, but before he could say anything, she continued, "I get around town too, and I happened to recognize your car once... or twice." She smiled again with those sparkling and perfect white teeth.

Nodding his understanding, he reached into his right-hand suit coat pocket and pulled out several scraps of paper, saying, "I keep notes to remind me of important things, but I sometimes forget to look at them." Smiling sheepishly, he continued, "Let me have your address again and I'll jot it down on the back of one of my notes." Finishing, he pulled a pen from his shirt pocket.

Flashing that mischievous smile again, Janet asked, "Sure you won't forget to look at it?"

Without batting an eye, Mark shot back, "Not on your life. In fact when I get home I'm going to frame this one."

They both had a good laugh, the banter had clearly broken the ice and they were starting to get comfortable, that was always a good sign in any relationship.

Eighteen

It was eight o'clock by the time Mark and Janet made it to the Black Angus, but neither seemed to mind a late supper. Actually, they both thought it was rather unique to dine when almost no one else was eating. Janet had heard talk from the other girls at the office, some of whom had worked in Atlanta, about how almost no one dined before eight or eight thirty. In the big cities everyone seemed to go out late and stay out later. She had never been impressed with big cities, but this dining at eight o'clock could get to be a habit with her, especially with the right company, and she had the right company now. All she had to do was figure out a way to keep this company coming. The dress she had changed into was helping and the new makeup couldn't hurt any. Mark hadn't taken his eyes off of her since he had picked her up.

What Janet didn't realize was that Mark wouldn't have cared if she had worn a suit and tie to dinner. He saw an inner beauty in her that no amount of clothes or makeup could cover up or increase. It was that inner beauty he couldn't take his eyes off, not the dress, although it was pretty nice, too.

By way of small talk Janet asked, "Did you get Mr. Willis' computer fixed the other day?"

Mark's mind snapped back to the present, someone had mentioned his only love, until tonight that is. "It wasn't his computer, not really. He was having trouble accessing some bank accounts. All he needed was the right password. Nothing wrong with his hardware at all, I checked it all out. Apparently the First Bank of Georgia dropped the ball and didn't send out the new password when they changed it the last time."

"Password?" Janet asked, curiously.

"Yeah, to access their data base and the TTM accounts. Willis was trying to move some money into or out of some TTM accounts and couldn't access the bank's database. He explained that to save time, money and manpower that they had an arrangement with First Bank of Georgia to access their accounts directly and make deposits and withdrawals.

"Anyway, he hadn't gotten the new password like he was supposed to and I had to crack the code for him. It took me a couple of hours, a piece of cake really. Hacking is what I do best. That's how I tapped the personnel computer and got your address, which I promptly lost." He wasn't the least bit embarrassed this time. The time was right, he now wanted Janet to know how interested he was. Mark only hoped she wanted the same thing.

Janet furrowed her brow into a deep frown, but said nothing.

He saw the frown and when she made no response, he wondered if he had said something to upset her. After a moment, he asked, "What's the matter?"

Shaking her head back and forth, she answered, "Mark, we don't directly access TTM accounts at First Bank. Willis is giving you a snow job."

"What! You're kidding. I mean, Willis said they did. You ought to know, you're his secretary and he's pretty high up, he..." The realization of what he had just said caught up with him and he continued, "That's right, you would know, but you don't. That means TTM doesn't directly access its accounts or at least Willis doesn't do it. Willis lied. Why?"

"I don't know, but I don't like it," Janet said, with concern in her voice.

"Me either, and I'll tell you why. Not only did Willis lie to me, but he used me as a patsy. Hacking your way into a system that you legally have access to, is one thing, but hacking your way into one that you don't have legal access to, is something else. Something criminal. Willis made me an accessory to whatever he was doing. I don't like that."

Janet's face fell and she said, "Could you get into trouble?"

He nodded and said seriously, "Big trouble, depending upon what Willis was up to through me. Do you have any idea what he might have been doing in First Bank's database?"

Quietly, she answered, "No."

Mark was silent for several moments and she could see that he was in deep thought. Finally, he said, "Janet, can you get me into his office, when no one else is around? Like tonight?"

With alarm, she responded with a question, "But why?"

Calmly, he answered, "Willis isn't too smart when it comes to computers and not too fast. My bet is that if he did some fancy footwork with some bank accounts, he didn't do it on line. An employee working in the database at the same time might notice that. My bet is that he downloaded some account information into his computer and then at his leisure he reworked them."

Janet didn't understand much about computers, but she admired Mark's knowledge, so she asked, "So what? How does that help?"

Smiling without humor, he said, "When you download files into your computer and then upload them to another computer, they are still on your computer, unless you erase them. Chances are that Willis downloaded those files into a Temp file and he isn't smart enough to know what that is—or where it is on his computer—so he couldn't erase the files. More than likely he didn't even think about it. I need to get in there before he thinks of it. Most people are under the impression that when they upload a file from their computer, it's gone, but that's not always true.

"The bottom line is that if I can get to his computer I can find those copies on his hard drive and examine them. If I find out what he was up to, then I can download the files to my computer and print them out. Then I'll take them to the cops to make sure they know I'm on the up and up and had no part in all this.

"Janet, if you can get me into his office, then I'll activate his modem and access his computer from my computer in the basement,

Once I have the data, I'll go back in and shut his computer down. He'll never know what hit him."

Mark was going too fast for her. When it came to computers it was clear she was no match for him, nor ever would be. She wasn't thinking of a match in that regard anyway. She wanted to be his match, but not in computers. "Okay," she said simply.

"Now, I don't want you to get into trouble, Janet. You just get me a key to his office and I'll take it from there. I don't want you involved. I can take care of myself, I don't want to have to worry about you."

Janet smiled that beguiling smile again and responded sweetly, "Sorry to hear that. I was thinking that it would be nice to have you worry about me, at least just a little."

"Well, I... you know what I mean... I..." This is some woman, he decided, but couldn't put his thoughts into words.

~ * ~

It was eleven o'clock when they arrived at the mill. At the gate, Mark pitched the story he had rehearsed during the long drive back to Johnson City. Janet smiled sweetly, as she snuggled close to him and peered out the driver's window at the guard. The guard seemed glad to have someone to talk to, even if it was only for a few seconds. Mark and Janet knew the guard by his first name and he knew them, too. It wasn't a problem to convince him that Mark had computer work to do at a time when the Internet was at its low ebb. TTM needed some software downloaded and if he did it during Internet peak hours it could take hours. This way he could knock it out in thirty minutes and have his date home before midnight. Janet did all she could to convince the guard that she was Mark's eager date and her non-act was very convincing.

As the car pulled through the gate the guard thought to himself that they made a nice couple. He had always liked Janet, and she deserved a steady guy like Mark Fribley, not some bar fly who couldn't go a week without changing girl friends twice.

Janet was more familiar with the upper reaches of the headquarters building than was Mark. He was glad she was along, for more than one reason. Artfully, Janet dodged the last vestiges of the cleaning crew and they slipped easily into her office. She quietly opened the inner office door and in they slipped.

"It would be best if we didn't turn on any lights, Mark. Can you do it that way? Mr. Willis' window can be seen from the main gate and a lot of other places. The cleaning crew has already been on this floor, so the guard would know it wasn't them."

"Good thinking. Right. No, I don't need a light, I don't think. I won't turn on his computer screen, it would give off light, too. I only need his box and the modem turned on."

~ * ~

The gate guard was just settling back with his book in hand, when more headlights appeared from the road. A quick glance at his watch told him it hadn't been ten minutes since Fribley came through and now someone else was coming. He was coming to an interesting part in his book, too. *Just my luck,* he thought, *a busy night.*

He stepped out of the guard shack as the headlights came closer and he immediately recognized the car. "Good evening Mr. Willis, working late, too?"

"Too?" Willis questioned.

"Yes sir. Mark Fribley just went in ahead of you. Said he had to download some software while the net wasn't busy. Too deep for me, sir, but he had your secretary with him. Needed some company I guess," he finished with a wink.

"Janet was with him?" Willis stated, more than questioned.

"Yes, sir."

"Where were they going?"

"To Mr. Fribley's office, sir. That's what he signed in for and I expect he had to use his computer for whatever he was doing."

With a concerned look on his face, the guard asked, "It was okay, wasn't it, sir? I mean, Mr. Fribley works in the building and he has to work some strange hours sometimes."

Waving a dismissal with his left-hand, Willis mumbled, "Yeah, sure. Okay." Then he dropped the car into drive and sped off toward the headquarters parking lot.

Approaching the building, Willis scanned the top floor and as his eyes passed his office window he thought he caught a faint flicker of light, but when his eyes retraced their route he saw nothing. Nervousness, he decided. It had hit him after he had already gone to bed that he had some unfinished business at the office. Talking with a friend of his at supper, who was very computer knowledgeable, had made him realize that he needed to make sure there were no remnants of the bank's files left on his computer. He had realized that he had downloaded them, but not erased them when he had finished uploading them again. He wasn't all that computer literate and it hadn't occurred to him that there was something left to erase, at least not at the time.

~ * ~

"Okay, let's go. The box is on and so is the modem."

"What now?" Janet said nervously.

"Out the door quickly. The light from outside will shine through, so open it fast and close it just as fast. I didn't think about it until you mentioned the light showing."

They both flashed out the door and closed it quickly, but quietly. Breathlessly, Janet said, "Your place?"

Mark chuckled and responded, "Yeah, in the basement."

"That's what I meant," Janet said lightly.

"I knew that. Let's go," he said with a chuckle.

Out in the hall, Mark said, "Let's take the stairs. Be just our luck some janitor would decide to use the elevator and there we'd be," he finished and guided Janet toward the back stairs, leading the way down.

Outside in the parking lot, Tim was in a hurry to get this over with and get back to bed. He would have loved to have stayed in bed, but he knew he couldn't have slept while this remained undone. His big concern was whether he was smart enough to find those files and erase them. Hurriedly, he shut off his car and flung the door open as he tore his keys from the ignition. Swinging out with the keys in his right hand, he lost his balance and tried to catch himself with his left hand.

He did manage to catch himself, but the swing of his body caused the keys to fly out of his right hand and arch into the night. It wouldn't have been so bad except that he had parked near the front door and the keys landed in the heavy bushes fronting the building. There was some light from the parking lot lights, but not much.

Tim ducked back into his car and fished his flashlight out of the glove compartment. He headed for the bushes and flipped his light on, but it gave him no light. The batteries were dead as a doornail. He decided to try his luck finding the keys before walking all the way back to the gate guard to borrow a light. It certainly wasn't his desire to create an incident leading to a lot of talk about his visit tonight, and the gate guard was sure to tell everyone the story if he had to loan Tim a light.

~ * ~

Mark's computer screen flashed and blinked as his hands flew over the keyboard. Janet stood pensively behind him and marveled at his speed. The man loved his computers and she wondered if a woman could compete with that kind of devotion. She was willing to bet that she could.

Mark was not oblivious to Janet. That would be impossible. Especially with that fresh dose of perfume she had very obviously put on just before he had picked her up before dinner. *What kind is that?* he wondered. *Good stuff whatever it is.* With half his mind on the woman behind him and half on the computer in front of him, he completed his task in record time. It really was a simple task for him, even though Janet thought it was nothing short of miraculous. His only problem at the time was keeping enough of his mind on his work to get the job done correctly, the first time. Janet was a distraction, but one he would gladly put up with any time.

Finally, he reached up and pushed a button that caused a small disk to pop out of the front of his computer. He switched off the computer and turned to Janet saying, "Okay, that's that. Here, put this in your purse for safekeeping."

She took the proffered disk and asked, "What's this?"

"Not sure, but it's what Willis was fooling with, all right. I didn't study the files. I just called them up to make sure I had bank files and then I downloaded them to that disk."

"I thought you were putting them on your computer."

"No way, then I'd be in the same boat that Willis is. That disk is the only copy of those files outside of Willis' computer, I don't want them on mine where someone might find them. No sir. Those babies are going home, we'll study them there on my home PC, at our leisure. Okay?"

"Tonight?"

"Not if you don't want to go."

"Oh, I want to go. I couldn't sleep knowing there was something on this disk, but not knowing what. Not after all this cloak and dagger stuff."

"Okay then. Let's get upstairs and shut that computer down so we can get to my place and have a look at that disk. I'd like to know what Willis tried to get me in to before it's too late."

Out in the hall, Mark said, "Okay, you stand by here and I'll run up to the office and shut everything down. I know the way now."

Janet pouted and said adamantly, "No way. I'm in this all the way. I'm not letting you out of my sight until this is over."

After all the weeks of imagining a date with Janet, Mark wasn't inclined to separate himself from her if she didn't want to be separated, so he said, "Okay, but it's up the stairs again. We can't risk the elevator."

"Good, I need to lose some pounds anyway," she responded lightly.

He stopped and stared at her approvingly and said, "What pounds? You look just fine to me."

She just blushed as he smiled and turned for the stairs.

~ * ~

Willis was highly irritated at having wasted a good ten minutes digging around in the bushes for his keys, but he had found them. *Lousy bushes, whose idea was it to put those monsters there anyway*, he grumbled to himself as he pushed the elevator call button. Since they were programmed to wait at the lobby floor when not in use the elevator door opened immediately. On the elevator, Tim pushed the sixth floor button and tried to rearrange himself on the ride up. He still felt like he had pieces of that evergreen bush inside his pants.

~ * ~

With the computer shut down and the inner office door locked, Janet and Mark headed for the hallway. Just as Mark opened the door for Janet they both heard the elevator bell sound and the unmistakable noise the opening elevator doors make. Janet jumped back inside the room, flipped off the light and grabbed the door. She eased it closed, leaving just a crack to peer through, and to her horror she saw her boss step off the elevator. Closing the door completely, she whispered urgently, "It's Willis. Quick, under my desk. Hurry."

Mark's heart stopped momentarily, but he followed Janet. Actually he had no choice, she had a grip on his left hand like a vise. Under other circumstances he would have liked holding her hand, but right now handholding was about as far from his mind as it could get.

Opening the outer door and stepping through, Willis flipped on the light and thought to himself that Janet must have really spread the perfume on big time today. He could still smell it, just like she was in the room.

It was close quarters under Janet's desk and they were well concealed, but as Willis entered the room and walked by the desk, Mark felt as though they were sitting in the middle of Main and Main for the whole world to see.

Willis passed by the desk and entered his office, but he didn't close the door. Mark whispered into Janet's ear to be careful not to extend a hand or leg out from under the desk. She pressed herself closer to him, and they remained crammed under the desk holding on to each other for dear life. Fortunately, the desk faced the center of the room and not the door so that only the left side was visible from Willis' office. If he didn't look too closely, he wouldn't see them. Though they were both fearful of being caught, they were strangely comfortable wrapped in each other's arms.

They sat as still as possible, trying to not even breathe heavily for fear of discovery. Mark tried to concentrate on what Willis was doing in the other room, but he could only hear faint sounds and having Janet in his arms wasn't helping his concentration. *What is that perfume?* he kept wondering.

A few minutes after Willis began working on his computer, he slammed his hands onto the computer board in disgust and began mumbling to himself, "Lousy stinking computers. Can't figure this. Can't figure this. What's wrong?"

A slam or two later and Mark clearly heard, "Aw, forget it! Stupid piece of junk!"

The distinct sounds of the computer power switches being roughly snapped off could easily be heard from under the desk, as well as a rustling sound, as Willis got up from his desk. A light switch clicked off and the inner office door slammed shut as Willis stomped past Janet's desk, roughly flipping off the light. He slammed the outer door and they were alone again.

Mark chuckled and Janet asked, "What?"

"I moved the files to my computer's floppy disk. Unlike Willis, I didn't copy them, I moved them. Before I loaded those files back onto his computer, I put them in what's called a hidden directory. I'll bet he came in here to erase them, but he couldn't find them."

"Why do that?"

"I figured I might want to be able to prove that those files were on his computer at some time in the future. Just a notion I had."

"I see. Can we go now?"

"Better wait another hour or two," Mark said lightly, snuggling the right side of his face against Janet's.

With a giggle Janet responded, "If you wanted to hug me you didn't have to drag me up here and put me through all this. You and Willis cook this up just for me?"

"Sure, we're old buds, Willis and I. We do this sort of thing regularly. It's the only way I can get a date," Mark fired back and Janet responded with a good-natured punch in the ribs as they began crawling out from under her desk.

Nineteen

Good to her word, the comptroller had arranged for Leon's escort from the attorney general's office in short order. At eight o'clock the next morning, Leon and Attorney General Investigator, Brett Simms appeared at the circuit clerk's office just as it opened.

The circuit clerk didn't arrive until eight thirty and when she did, she was informed that there were two 'official types' waiting for her in her office. As if she didn't have enough problems with Gene gone, now she had 'who knows what' camped in her office.

Brusquely, she entered her office, dropped her purse on the desk and cast a critical eye at the two men seated across from her desk. Still standing, queen of her domain, she spat out, "What can I do for you gentlemen, or do you just like intruding into private offices?"

Leon had no idea what he was doing and didn't have a reply even close to formulated when Brett said, "I'm from the attorney general's office and this is Mr. Semple from the comptroller's office. The latest audit of your office indicates that you are short some one hundred and twenty thousand dollars and we want to know where it went. We can do this the hard way and go get a warrant, which will cause a lot of undue publicity or we can do it the easy way with your cooperation and maybe no one will have to go to jail!"

Shrinking down slightly in his chair, Leon thought that Simms had said it plain enough. It was obvious he wasn't prone to beat around the bush.

Jeannie was thunderstruck. All of the haughtiness gone from her tone, she fumbled for her chair, sat down and said, "I knew there were some minor discrepancies, but I never suspected that kind of money was missing. I just thought we had some posting problems. Do you really think someone stole that money? From my office?"

Steeling himself against the horror of speaking to a stranger in a strange place, Leon finally found his voice, "That's what I... we, need to find out. I'm the one who performed the audit and I noted the discrepancies. Your office is short right at thirty thousand dollars a year and that's a lot of posting errors. It isn't big money when you consider what goes through this office in a year, but it's big enough to get the attention of the comptroller and the attorney general."

Jeannie was still humble; her mind was spinning. She kept thinking that this couldn't be happening to her. Wishing with all her heart that Gene were here to take care of this, she said, "Gene was checking out the problems, but I don't know what he had found."

"Gene who?" Leon asked.

"Gene Petrowski. He is... was, my chief deputy."

"Was?" Brett asked now.

"He died. He and his wife were in a car accident over in Missouri a little over a week ago. The office has been in a state of shock ever since. Gene was almost irreplaceable, in fact he hasn't been replaced yet."

Simms now continued, "Did this Gene say anything to you about his findings?"

"No. I don't know that he had found anything."

"Did he have his own office?"

"Not really, but he had his own desk, over there in the corner. It's just the way he left it, pretty much."

Turning now to Leon, he said, "I'll have a look to see if he left any notes."

When Simms was gone, Leon said, "Just to ease your mind, I'm not convinced there is anything criminal going on here. It may just be very sloppy bookkeeping or a computer glitch. Certainly no one in this office is targeted for criminal investigation. I'm not a criminal investigator." Motioning with his head to the outside of the office and the corner desk where Simms had gone, he continued, "Simms there, he's the criminal investigator, but he's only here to assist me. I'm just here to find out what happened to the money and how. If it's a computer glitch, I'll be all the more happy to find it, if I can. If it's just poor training, then the comptroller's office will see you get training assistance. Okay?"

Jeannie was much more at ease with that having been said and responded amiably, "What can I do to help?"

"I need to go over your posting system. Someone needs to explain to me how your employees do their jobs. I know numbers and what makes them balance, but I don't know beans about how a circuit clerk's office runs, and I need to know that."

Me, too, Jeannie thought to herself, but responded, "Okay, no problem."

Rising, she went to the office door, stuck her head out and said, "Tess, would you come in here, please?"

Before Jeannie had made it back to her desk, Tess was popping her head into the office and saying, "You wanted me, ma'am?" as she timidly glanced over at the strange man sitting across the room.

"Yes, Tess. This is Mister Semple... is that right?" she said to Leon.

"Yes, ma'am, Leon Semple."

Turning back to Tess, she said, "He needs to be shown how we do our job around here. Posting money for bond, child support and fines. Entering court dates, new petitions, new criminal cases, bond refunds, the works. Everything he wants, he gets, okay?"

"Yes, ma'am," Tess answered meekly.

For the first time, Jeannie took a good look at Tess. Her medium length light brown hair was slightly disheveled and she looked as though she would faint at the sight of her own shadow. She didn't come off as any mental giant, yet she knew her job, made few mistakes and was always ready to do more. She came in on time and never left early. Not married, no boyfriend to distract her and, from her appearance, that didn't surprise Jeannie. She wasn't homely, but she was no more than plain at best.

Turning back to Leon, Jeannie said, "Here you are, Mr. Semple. If I can do anything, please let me know. I want this cleared up more than you do. My reputation is on the line."

Rising now, Leon said, "Yes, ma'am."

"Please, call me Jeannie."

"Okay," Leon mumbled as he followed Tess from the office. This situation was getting worse, he decided. Not only did he have to talk to people, real people, but he had to assert some authority, too. That didn't come easy to him. And now he had been confronted with the *coupe de grace*. He was going to be forced to interact with a pretty woman, not just casual talk; he was going to have to communicate with her.

~ * ~

Charlie had just returned to his apartment from the corner flower shop, where he had ordered a dozen long stemmed roses to be sent to Carol. The clerk was all ears and probably would have read the note that Charlie languished over for several minutes, had it not been securely sealed in the envelope. Had he read it, there would have been nothing earth shaking in it anyway, but it was the best Charlie could do at the time. He had not romanced a woman for a long time, but he dearly wanted to be successful at romancing this one. He thought the feeling was mutual, last night it certainly seemed to be mutual.

But it had been a long time and he wasn't sure how to read the signals anymore. He might just be acting on wishful thinking. After all, she was quite a bit younger than him, extremely attractive and talented. She was famous, rich and seemed to have it all. Why would she bother with a rambling lawyer who wore rumpled suits more often than not?

As he stood gazing out the window, thinking of Carol and relishing the slim hope that she might actually care for the likes of him, the phone rang. He turned from the window and grabbed the phone off the wall hook. "Hello."

"Mr. Chambers, this is Sergeant Evans, Meridian County Sheriff's Department."

"Oh, yes, Sergeant Evans, what can I do for you?"

"I just wanted to let you know that our department just received an arrest warrant for Tommy Trenton. The charge is grand theft and it's signed by Judge Ferrell. Since I know you represent him, I thought I'd give you a call and ask if you wanted to have him voluntarily surrender. Say by noon. If so, I'll tell the shift commander and he'll hold off having the warrant served."

Rapidly, Charlie responded, "Yes, he'll surrender voluntarily and before noon. Thank you for the courtesy, Sergeant Evans. I'll see to it immediately."

"No problem. Good luck, Mr. Chambers."

"Thank you, Sergeant," Charlie finished and hung up the phone with his mind already racing ahead to the upcoming events of the day.

Quickly, he finished his coffee and roll, then he was off to the bathroom for a quick shave. Inside of fifteen minutes he was ready to go, and he had decided to go directly to Tommy's apartment to see if he was home. He knew he hadn't been scheduled back to work yet. Undoubtedly, his supervisor had been told not to schedule him for work.

The weather was very pleasant, so Charlie decided to make a relaxing walk out of the short jaunt to Tommy's apartment. While walking, he kept a look out for Tommy, just in case he was back on the streets, even though he had promised to do his preaching in the shelter for a while. *The shelter*, Charlie decided. *That's where he would be, no doubt about it.* He made a slight detour to the east for two blocks and found the shelter's front door standing wide open. The unmistakable voice of the Preacher was drifting out the door onto the morning air.

Charlie entered slowly and found three men listening to the Preacher in rapt attention. He had a way about him, Charlie realized. If anyone was born to preach, it was Tommy Trenton. Too bad he had never pursued the ministry; or maybe he had just never had the means.

Moving through the common area of the shelter toward the back, Charlie took a seat at a small dining table. The shelter wasn't large; it was just a branch of the larger shelter over in Thomasville. Yet they had felt the need over here in Meridian county, and since Johnson

City was the county seat, they thought it the appropriate place. Actually, there were only two or three people who could even be classified as homeless in this small town, if that many. Most of the people who took advantage of this homeless shelter were transients with car trouble and no money or who were afoot. Then there were those who occasionally came in for a free meal.

Soon Tommy broke away from the small group of men and came over to the table to sit with Charlie. "Good morning, Mr. Chambers. I want to thank you for getting me this position. It's what I've always wanted to do. I can care for people and spread the Word of God at the same time."

"It isn't really a position, Tommy. What I mean is that it doesn't pay anything," Charlie responded evenly.

"I know that, but it's the opportunity to witness, inside, out of the weather and in a quiet surrounding. That's what's important, not the money."

Charlie steeled himself, took a deep breath and began, "Bad news, Tommy."

"Oh?"

"Yes, it's about the trouble at the mill."

"I don't have any trouble at the mill, I told you that. I didn't do anything and if I didn't do anything then I'm not in any trouble."

"I'm afraid it doesn't always work that way, Tommy, and you should know that. If you don't, it's time you learned. We don't have to do anything to be in trouble. Sometimes trouble just follows us," Charlie said earnestly. He had a feeling Tommy knew what he was saying, but was trying to ignore the realities. That would only make things worse. He needed Tommy's assistance to be able to help him. He continued, "Anyway, the sheriff's department called me, a Sergeant Evans. Do you know him?"

"No."

Curious, Charlie thought, *or maybe it isn't*. It is possible that a cop could help someone and them not know the cop's name. Again, he continued, "He wanted to let me know that Judge Ferrell issued an arrest warrant for you. The charge is Grand Theft and he said they would hold off serving it until noon. I told him you would voluntarily surrender before then. Was I right?"

Dismally, Tommy responded, "Yes, sir, of course. No sense in not surrendering, I suppose?"

"No, there isn't. Not surrendering might only make things look worse."

"Whatever you think, Mr. Chambers," he said, without emotion.

"Tommy, do you remember a cop, a deputy sheriff, who would lend you a blanket once in a while? He'd warn you when bad weather was coming and sometimes he'd give you a little money on the sly?"

"Yes, sir. I do. He's a big black guy, but I can't help him."

"What do you mean you can't help him? Did he ask for your help?"

"No, sir," Tommy said flatly.

Charlie waited for more, but it didn't come and finally he asked, "What did you mean you can't help him?"

"Nothing. It's just that he likes to have people who can tell him stuff now and again. I can't. He did help me sometimes and he was nice, but I can't help him."

"Maybe he didn't want your help, Tommy. Maybe he just felt you needed some help and he liked you."

"I don't see why he would like me. I never did anything for him," Tommy said adamantly.

Charlie thought Tommy's attitude was strange, but it didn't really matter. Obviously Tommy thought that the only reason a cop would help him was that there was something to be gained from it. *Can't say as I blame him*, Charlie decided, *I doubt anyone ever did anything much for Tommy*. Still, Charlie knew that Todd had helped out of the goodness of his heart, but it would do no good to try to convince Tommy of that.

Changing the subject, Charlie asked, "Tommy, why would anyone up at the mill want to get you in trouble? My guess is that they are framing you, though I can't prove that yet."

"I don't know, sir. I never told anyone anything and I wouldn't," Tommy stated evenly.

"Told what?" Charlie asked.

"Nothing."

"Tommy, I can't help you unless you cooperate," Charlie said in exasperation.

"I am. I told you I don't know why anyone up at the mill would want to get me in trouble. I never tried to get them in trouble."

"Could you if you had tried?"

Tommy was silent for a few moments then finally he said, "I can't say."

"Tommy! I need some help here. Give me a lead."

"No, sir, I can't."

"Can't?"

After a moment of silence Tommy responded dryly, "Won't."

"I don't know what you know, Tommy, but why protect the people up at the mill? They aren't interested in you, they want you in jail for something you didn't do."

"It's not about them, sir. It's about me."

"Are you telling me you're guilty of stealing from the mill?"

"No, sir, I never stole a thing from the mill, never."

"What are you hiding then?"

"It isn't important, sir. Not to this. It has nothing to do with what they say I did. I didn't steal from them and I won't tell."

"Tell what?"

"Nothing."

"If you won't tell me what, then at least tell me why you won't tell?"

"It wouldn't help you. I don't know why anyone would want to get me into trouble. I can't tell you more," Tommy ended with finality.

In disgust, Charlie said, "Okay, fine. Well then, let's go over to the sheriff's department. I doubt anyone will be able to bail you out on this one, Tommy. This is a felony and bail will probably be at least twenty thousand dollars. Even with the ten percent cash deposit rule, that's still two thousand dollars somebody has to put up for you, and I don't think that will happen. Sure you don't want to sit back down and tell me what you know?"

"There's nothing I know that will help you and I'm not worried about jail. I like it here, but I'll go where God decides I should go. You don't say 'no' when God calls."

That's the first thing he's said that makes sense, Charlie said to himself. "Yeah, I know about that. Okay, let's go then."

~ * ~

Todd was sitting at his desk. *I'm always sitting at my desk*, he thought, *or some place else. Sam's right, we sit too much in this job.* It was just before noon and he was going over the old church file again. It was strange, but he had never really thought of the file being all that old until Chambers mentioned that the file looked older than him. To Todd, the file was as recent as yesterday. It didn't age. There was no reason for it to age.

So here he sat, going over the old file again. As usual it was acting as therapy. He was upset about Tommy and he had to have something to do. The Merriman file wasn't going anywhere so he was back to his old standby, the church burning.

"They said you were in and that I could come back."

Todd looked up to see Chambers standing in the doorway and asked without emotion, "Is Tommy in jail?"

"Yes, and for quite a while this time, I'm afraid. The judge will have to set bond on the theft charges, maybe tomorrow. Doesn't matter though, bond will be too high for Tommy to get out, even with your help," Charlie ended dismally. He always got too involved with his clients. It helped him argue their cause more strenuously, but it didn't help his stomach any.

"Have a seat," Todd said and kicked a chair toward Charlie.

"Thanks," Charlie said, as he dropped into the proffered wooden backed chair next to Todd's desk. Glancing at the open file on the desk, he said, "Back to the same old file, huh?"

Nodding wearily, Todd answered, "Yes, but it's only therapy for me. I'll never solve it, I know that now."

Shrugging, Charlie said, "Never is a long time. Once I thought I'd never love again." At Todd's curious look, he went on to explain. "My wife and daughter were killed a few years ago, and I've not looked at another woman with romantic interest since. Until recently. So much for the word 'never'."

"You've had a tough life," Todd responded with sympathy.

"Had some rough times, but a lot of good times, too. Like most people. Like you and Tommy, not much difference."

"Why say like me? You don't know me."

"I read upside down pretty good; years of practice. I remember things, too, like our last conversation in this room, about this fire. Remember that I told you I knew it wasn't about being black, but about justice. At the time I didn't know why, but now I do."

Reaching across the desk in front of Todd, he picked up a sheet of paper with a list of names typed on it. He held it up and said, "This is the list of the people killed in that fire, isn't it?"

"Yes," Todd said simply.

Flipping the paper around so that he could read from it, Charlie read, "Jack Evans, wife Betty, son Fred. Your mother and father. Was Fred your older or younger brother?"

"Lots of Evans around these parts."

"Sure there are, but these happened to have been related to you, didn't they?" Without waiting for an answer, he reached across the desk again and picked up an old faded photo. Studying it and then turning it for Todd to see, he said, "I'd say you were about seven in this photo, the resemblance is unmistakable, I see quite a bit of your father in your face." Turning the photo back around so that he could see it, Charlie continued, "Ah yes, your brother was older. About three years I'd say."

"Four," Todd said quietly.

"Okay, four. Why weren't you in church that night?"

"I was sick. I stayed with my Uncle Burrell and his wife Ginney. After the fire they raised me like their own. They didn't have any kids of their own, and since their last name was the same as mine, most people just got used to me being theirs and so did I. The school didn't care and when it came time for permission slips my uncle just signed as my dad and that was that."

"Not quite. All these years it has eaten on you, hasn't it? Is it justice you seek in that old file, or absolution for not dying with your family?"

"To be perfectly honest, it's probably both. Sure I feel bad about being the only one who survived, but I know that's not right. My dying in that fire would have gained nothing. I know that now. Once maybe I didn't, but I know it now."

"But, still you search in vain for the person or persons unknown, who killed your family. That's why you are obsessed with this crime," Charlie pronounced.

"Almost. Once that was totally true. When I was in college and when I first started on the streets, I only wanted to find the killers of my family. But somewhere along the line that changed. Somewhere along the line I realized that a lot of other people's family members were killed in that same fire and that I didn't have a corner on the grief market. I also realized that no one else was interested in finding out who killed them. That's when it became a search for justice, not vengeance, not absolution, but justice. A hopeless search, I guess. For years I've hoped to find something in this file that I've missed, something to give me a lead, but it isn't there."

Charlie shrugged and said, "Maybe it isn't there because it's somewhere else."

"What do you mean?"

"Only that things aren't always where they ought to be. Look, I only know that if it is meant for you to find justice for these people, you will and not a minute sooner or later than you are supposed to find it. Keep in mind, though, that there isn't any justice this side of heaven, not real justice.

"Someday you might find the clue that breaks this case open. The clue might be in that file and it might be somewhere else. If it's meant to be, you'll find it. It won't bring those people back, though. It won't give you your family back and you might be surprised at how little satisfaction it actually gives you. I've been there. I've lived through the type of justice you seek and it didn't give me back the empty years I suffered through. After the fact, I realized that the empty years were empty only because I let them be. I focused on my loss so much that I missed life as it passed by my window. Don't do that, Evans. You deserve more than that. You've got a family now. It's a different family than the one you lost, but it's still a family. Don't lose that family because you can only see the family you lost. Don't ignore your family for your work, no matter how important it seems to you at the time. That was my mistake, don't make it your mistake, too."

Todd said nothing, but it was clear that he was giving what Charlie had said some serious consideration. The truth was, that he was tired of pursuing the elusive thing called justice, at least for these people.

Charlie continued, "Did you ever stop to think that all those people died in church? What better place is there to die? They are all in a better place than we are and have been for a good long time. Go ahead and seek justice for them if you want, but don't expect too much. My guess is they couldn't care less about our justice.

"One thing has me puzzled, though. Why did I see the connection between the fire victims and you, but no one else did?"

Todd looked up and, with an even stare, said, "No one else ever bothered to look. That's part of why I keep looking. No one else cares."

"Surely your partner has looked, surely he cares."

"Maybe he does, he says he does, but he has never looked. This has always been my case. This isn't even an official file. The official file has almost nothing in it. Just a fire report. Not even a list of the names of the dead. This fire occurred in 1962 in Georgia. No one cared about a bunch of blacks that burned up in a church. Just consider the name and you'll see what I mean. Little Flock Baptist Church, Negro. *Negro!* By the time things changed to the point where someone would care, it was too late. Too much time had passed and the trail was just too cold."

Charlie responded evenly, "I see what you're saying. But you know, I can't help thinking things worked out pretty well for you. You went to college. You have a good job where you can at least try to find justice for all people, not just for those who died in that fire."

Todd considered that for a minute then responded, "Funny thing about college. My uncle was as poor as a church mouse, or at least I thought he was, but when I wanted to go to college he had the money. I worked some, but he always sent me money and my tuition was paid. It cost thousands of dollars to send me to college and when I pressed him about it he finally confessed that he had been receiving money each month without fail for years. He had put it in a bank account for me to use for college.

"The money always came in the form of cash, never anything that could be traced. It was just left at one of many places and my uncle never knew who left it. After a while he didn't even try to find out. He just put it in the bank for me. He continued to send me money when I was in college, sometimes as much as one hundred a week. After I finished college it stopped coming. My uncle says he hasn't gotten any money now for years. He's still alive up in the hills. In fact he lives on Burning Chapel Hill, but my aunt Ginney is dead," Todd ended sadly.

"Amazing," Charlie said in puzzlement, "What do you make of it?"

"Don't know really. Somebody felt sorry for me. Somebody who knew my mom and dad were killed and that my uncle was poor."

Charlie nodded, deep in thought and finally said, "Yeah, somebody felt sorry, for sure."

Twenty

Locally, the Preacher was a well-known character. His arrest three times for disorderly conduct hadn't drawn much attention, but his arrest for the theft of several thousand dollars from TTM did. The local newspaper picked it up from the jail intake blotter and although it wasn't front-page news, it did rate a fairly sizable article on page three.

Mark Fribley was scanning the paper before leaving for work when he came across the article. It was pretty straight forward reporting without embellishments.

~ * ~

Tommy Trenton voluntarily surrendered to Meridian county sheriff's deputies yesterday just before noon. Judge James Ferrell had issued an arrest warrant for Mr. Trenton early yesterday morning and when his attorney was notified he said his client would voluntarily turn himself in by noon. True to his word, Charles Chambers appeared midmorning with Mr. Trenton at the Meridian County Jail, where Trenton was promptly booked for grand theft.

Information derived from sources close to the case suggests that the sheriff's department has in its possession the bank records of Mr. Trenton. Those records show that there were deposits of money corresponding exactly to checks written by companies TTM did business with and paid to TTM. Other checks recovered from Mr. Trenton's locker at the mill match invoices sent by TTM to the same companies. Other deposits correspond with the dates that cash was stolen from various departments of TTM.

Speaking through his attorney, Mr. Trenton denied the thefts and stated that the activity shown on his bank records has to be in error; that he made regular deposits of his paycheck and nothing more. He added that the proof would come as soon as copies of Mr. Trenton's records were found, but that they had been temporarily misplaced.

~ * ~

Mark Fribley put the paper down, picked up his cup of coffee and went over to his computer desk across the living room. He picked up several sheets of paper and began to scan them again. These were the printouts of the account information he and Janet had transferred from Willis' computer the other night. At the time, he didn't see the significance, but now he did. Why this was being done he didn't know, but he knew he couldn't remain silent. He had to keep Janet out of this though; it could backfire on them both.

~ * ~

"Sergeant Evans?" Mark Fribley asked timidly from the doorway.

Todd, sitting with his feet propped up on his desk, sipping his morning coffee, growled, "Yes!"

Sam kept skimming the reports he was working on without even looking up.

"Uh, they said I could come back and see you."

Todd was in a bad mood today. The Preacher was in jail to stay and he had to help keep him there. To make matters worse, he was still suffering from the realization that his parent's murders were never going to be solved. After a long icy stare at this slim man in the doorway, he responded dryly, "So you've seen me. Is that all you wanted?"

"Uh... no, sir. I have something you might want to look at, sir."

Todd rolled his eyes and said, "Don't call me, sir. I'm just a cop, okay?"

"Yes, si... sorry," Mark ended, tongue-tied.

Waving with his left hand, but leaving his feet propped up on his desk, Todd softened and said, "Come on in here and have a seat. What can we do for you?"

Holding out a sheaf of papers, Mark said, "Take a look at these, sir."

Todd looked over at Sam who had finally looked up and shrugged. He took the papers and scanned them quickly. When he was finished, he said, "So? I don't know where you got these, but you probably shouldn't have them. Bank records are confidential. I don't know what significance you place on them, but it isn't news to me. I've seen a copy of these records."

Reaching for a file across the desk without dropping his feet, he opened it and pulled out a copy of Tommy Trenton's bank records saying, "See, I have a copy, too."

"Yes, but you don't have these," Mark said with a little more confidence and handed Todd a second stack of papers.

Todd scanned them and about half way through them he dropped his feet from the desk with a thud and bolted upright in his chair.

Sam set his cup down and stared at Todd with rapt attention. Something was going on here. This joker had gotten Todd's attention in a big way.

"Where did you get these?" Todd blurted out.

"From the same place I got the others. A computer hard drive at TTM."

Todd was still reading and he commented almost to himself, "Different dates, different amounts, but the same period of time. Same account number, same bank, same man." Looking up at Mark, he said, "Okay, tell me exactly where you got these and how."

Mark did, but was careful to leave out any reference to Janet. When he had finished, both Sam and Todd were all ears.

Todd was the first to speak when he asked, "How come the old records were still there if he changed them?"

Mark explained easily, he had thought this one through before he arrived, "He downloaded the records from the bank so that he would have time to alter them without anyone at the bank knowing he had accessed the account. He converted it to Word Perfect six point oh, but the old ASCII file was still there. He didn't delete it or move it, he just called it up and converted it. In short, the original file remained intact and a copy of it was altered in the word processor.

Todd put in quickly, "How do we prove this? I mean aside from your testimony, not that it won't be enough, but, you know what I mean?" Todd ended lamely.

"Yeah, I know and that's easy. The files are still on Willis' computer. I can show you or anyone else. Piece of cake."

Sam now put in for the first time, "But, what if he erases them or has already? He tried once already."

Mark just smiled and responded, "He can't find them. I hid them in a hidden directory." Smiling broadly, Todd looked at Sam and Sam nodded in the affirmative. Then Todd said to Mark, "Okay, let's go see the state's attorney. You tell him the same story you told us and show him these records. I think he will be impressed, too."

Mark hesitated, saying, "I'm not going to get into trouble, am I? I mean for hacking into the bank like that? I didn't know TTM wasn't supposed to be in there."

Todd said firmly, "No way! You didn't have the criminal intent necessary for computer theft or piracy. Don't worry about sneaking back in to TTM the other night either. You work there. You didn't do anything you couldn't have legally done in the daytime; it was just convenient and important to do it immediately and at night. Okay?"

"Yeah, sure. That makes me feel a lot better," Mark confessed. He was feeling better about this all the time and the fact that Janet didn't have to be involved made him feel even better. He could still smell that perfume of hers and feel her golden hair next to his cheek. *What an adventure*, he decided, *what a first date.*

~ * ~

"What's going on over at the clerk's office?" Barclay asked Mike Princeton, who was sitting at the opposite counsel table waiting for the judge to enter the courtroom.

Charlie sat with Tommy and listened half-hearted, his mind mostly on the matters at hand. He couldn't totally block out thoughts of Carol and he was wondering what she thought of the flowers he had sent. He was sure she was used to getting flowers and he was prepared that they might not have much effect on her, but he knew no other next step to take.

"Don't know for sure, Steve. Couple of guys from the attorney general's office or something. Looking over the books on the computer system. I'm not sure what it's all about. We weren't informed and when Lamont inquired, he was told nicely, it wasn't his business."

Steve continued, "Maybe they are trying to figure out why the computers are so fouled up around here."

"Nawh, not those guys. They wouldn't know any more about computers than me. Something to do with the money is my bet, but I don't know what. The clerk just went through an audit and it's my bet they are following up on that."

"Could be both, the way the bonds get messed up when they go into that computer system. I don't know who dreamed up that system, but it sure isn't doing something right. Something has to be done about the bonds and the fines in this county. No one can keep them straight anymore. I never know if my clients have a bond up or not, if they don't keep their receipts," Steve ended.

Tommy leaned over and whispered something into Charlie's ear and Charlie asked, a little louder than necessary, "You're sure, Tommy?"

Mike and Steve looked up and Charlie said, "Tommy says the bonds in this county don't mean a thing. If you know the right people you can get anything. Fines cleared or bonds increased."

"What's he talking about?" Mike blurted out. "He's a fruit cake."

Tommy shrugged and said, "I live on the streets enough to know, more than you, what goes on in this town. You want a bond increased or a fine cleared, all you got to do is know who to see."

"How?" Mike asked.

"How I don't know, but it'll happen. You pay the right guy and he'll fix it for you. Guaranteed, for a fifty percent fee. I've known guys who started with a one hundred dollar bond and a thousand dollar fine who came away with two hundred in their pocket and no fine."

"Who?"

"Won't say."

Steve now asked, "How come none of us ever heard about it?"

Tommy smugly replied, "Cause you are part of the system and I'm not. I'm a nobody who preaches to people on the street. None of the people out on the street have anything to fear from me. They tell me anything I want to know, and some I don't."

Light bulbs were going off in Charlie's head. He was just starting to figure a way to trade this information for a deal in Tommy's theft case, when the door to the right side of the judge's bench opened and out strode Judge Ferrell.

Charlie rose from the counsel table and tapped Tommy on the shoulder alerting him to rise. The judge took his seat, picked up the file and announced the case, "The People of the State of Georgia versus Tommy Trenton. This case comes on for arraignment. Show the State present by Assistant State's Attorney Mike Princeton." Addressing Charlie, he continued, "Mr. Chambers, are you entering your appearance for the defendant?"

"Yes, Your Honor, with the court's permission."

"Very well, counsel, the court will allow your appearance on behalf of the defendant. Is the defendant personally present?"

Charlie chimed in, "Yes, Your Honor, he is, in the custody of the Sheriff of Meridian County."

"Very well, the record shall so reflect..." The judge was interrupted by a commotion in the rear of the courtroom. The State's Attorney, Paul Lamont, entered noisily, accompanied by Evans and Pinehurst. Paul motioned Todd and Sam to take a seat at the rear of the courtroom and continued toward the front of the room saying, "I apologize for the interruption, Your Honor, but I have to ask permission to speak, before this matter goes any further."

Judge Ferrell was not happy. He didn't like being interrupted. He ran a taut ship. "This had better be good, Mr. Lamont."

"Yes, sir, again I apologize. But I have, just at this moment, received evidence from the sheriff's department, that reveals that a fraud is being perpetrated upon the court."

Judge Ferrell raised his eyebrows in interest and said, "Okay, let's have it."

"First of all, Your Honor, the state of Georgia moves to dismiss all charges against Mr. Trenton arising out of his arrest for theft. The evidence I have conclusively proves that personnel at TTM framed him. I will be asking Your Honor to issue an arrest warrant for Timothy Willis on charges of obstruction of justice, manufacturing false evidence and computer theft. I anticipate more charges once I've had the opportunity to investigate the matter further."

Everyone in the courtroom, including Judge Ferrell, were stunned into silence, as Lamont sketched out the story as it had been related to him, and then produced, for the judge's examination, the two sets of bank records.

Judge Ferrell cleared his throat and pronounced, "The state's motion is granted. The defendant is ordered released from custody immediately. Mr. Lamont, I believe the balance of the court's business is better conducted in chambers. This court stands in recess." Ending, he stood up and Paul Lamont, after motioning for Todd and Sam to accompany him, followed the judge into his chambers.

It took Charlie a moment to gather his senses, but when the courtroom was cleared he turned to Tommy and clapped him on the shoulder saying, "Who says there's no justice in the world?"

Tommy just smiled and nodded as the bailiff approached to return him to the jail and process his release.

"I'll be waiting for you outside the jail, Tommy. I'm buying coffee."

"Yes, sir. Thank you, sir."

"Don't thank me, thank those detectives in there," he said motioning toward the judge's door and continuing, "apparently they uncovered the evidence that set you free."

"Thank God," Tommy now said.

"Yes, thank God indeed," Charlie responded earnestly, as he followed Tommy and the bailiff out of the courtroom.

Before they cleared the courtroom, Mike caught them and said, "Charlie, I'd like to hear more about what your client was telling us before the judge interrupted us."

Charlie nodded and said, "Let me talk to him about it first and then I'll contact you or Lamont. Okay?"

"Soon?"

"Soon."

Outside the courtroom, Mark Fribley stood in the hallway waiting for the state's attorney.

Behind them, the courtroom door swung open and Paul Lamont came out saying, "Okay, Mr. Fribley, we didn't need you after all, not today anyway. Oh, Charlie, this is Mark Fribley, he's the computer guy that came up with the records that sprung your client," Lamont finished, motioning toward Mark.

"Thank you, Mr. Fribley. My client will be forever in your debt. Good citizens are hard to find these days, I'm glad you're one"

"No problem, sir, I'm just glad I didn't get into trouble."

~ * ~

Steve was back on the main gate again; at least it was an air-conditioned job. He had had a lot worse jobs. His little baby boy had an ear infection and the doctor's bills were getting pretty high so he was more than happy to stand this gate in the air-conditioning and get paid well to do it. The noise from an approaching vehicle woke him from his musings and he noted the local flower shop's delivery van coming to a stop by the gate. As he stepped out of the shack, the driver rolled the window down and said, "Hey, Steve, how's it going? Got a delivery for Miss Harmon, of course."

"Okay, Jake let me check to see if they want them left here or up at the house."

Stepping back into the shack he called the house and when Dan answered he asked what he was supposed to do with the flowers.

"Who they from?" Dan queried.

"Dan wants to know who they're from, Jake."

"Ah, let me see here, a Charles Chambers paid the bill, the card's sealed, but probably him."

Steve relayed to Dan and Dan said, "Take them and throw them in the trash."

"Huh?" was Steve's shocked answer.

"You heard me, we don't want any flowers from that crooked lawyer. You throw 'em out."

"No, sir," Steve responded.

"What do you mean? I told you to throw them out, and if you like your job, you will follow orders."

"Yes, sir, I do like my job and that's why I can't do that. Miss Harmon told me last night that I was not to interfere with Mr. Chambers, coming or going and I think that goes for flowers, too."

"That kind of attitude with me will get you fired."

"No, sir. Miss Harmon pointed out to me, at the same time, that she still signs my paycheck. She finds out I helped trash flowers from Mr. Chambers and she won't sign no more. I need that money, Dan, I got a sick baby."

Taking a different tact, Dan responded calmly, "You're right, Steve, send him up to the house, I'll accept delivery, Miss Harmon is unavailable right now."

"Yes, sir." And then to the driver he said, "Go on up to the house, Jake," as he flipped the lever to open the gates.

The driver made his way rapidly up the drive, he had a lot of deliveries today and this was just one of them, although his most important. He felt privileged to bring flowers to Carol Harmon, even if they were from someone else. Like most people in the town and the whole area for that matter, as Charlie had guessed, Jake worshipped the ground she walked on.

At the house Dan made short work of accepting the delivery and as soon as the delivery van had turned around he walked around the side of the house and tossed the box of flowers in the dumpster, slamming the lid closed with a vengeance, and saying to himself, *Not long now hot shot, not long now.*

~ * ~

Janet was going about her morning as usual, but couldn't get her mind off of Mark. She was hoping her computer would lock up so that she would have an excuse to call him when the outer door opened and in walked Mark with two other men she didn't know.

The first man, a black man, walked up to her desk, displayed a badge and said, "Is Mr. Willis in?"

In alarm she looked at Mark who winked at her before she responded, "Yes, sir, may I say who's calling?" The response was automatic. She didn't know what else to say or think.

Todd responded calmly, "No, we'd rather you didn't." At that he walked to the inner office door and opened it roughly.

"What's the meaning of this?" Willis yelled.

Todd produced his badge again, as Sam stepped around him and produced a paper saying, "This is Sergeant Evans and I'm Sergeant Pinehurst, Meridian County Sheriff's Department. This is a warrant for your arrest. Stand up, walk to the wall and lean against it, please. You are under arrest for obstruction of justice."

Todd moved around the desk, helped the stunned Tim Willis out of his chair and guided him toward the nearest wall.

Mark stood just inside the doorway with Janet who was visibly shaken. He put his arm around her to steady her and whispered. "It's okay, hon." The 'hon' just slipped out by accident, but he was glad that it had, and Janet didn't seem to mind either. He doubted she even heard it.

Sam took over the custody of Willis after Todd had placed his handcuffs on him and Todd turned to Mark saying, "Okay, Mr. Fribley. Please check the computer to insure the files are still intact."

Mark released Janet and scooted around the desk. The computer was already on and his heart skipped a beat as he called up the files from the hidden directory. What would he do if Willis had lucked on to them and wiped them out? That he hadn't, became evident as first one file appeared and then the other, listed in the directory right where they had been. While he half listened to Sam informing Willis of his rights, he called up the files one by one and pronounced, "They're still here, Sergeant Evans. Just like they were."

"Excellent," Todd said and continued, "shut it down and secure it. We're taking it with us."

Turning to Janet who was still reeling, but recovering rapidly, he produced another paper, laid it on the desk and said, "This is a search warrant and we are seizing this computer as evidence. We'll give you a receipt."

Hesitating while the latest pronouncement sunk in, she finally answered, "Yes, sir, of course."

Todd now said to Mark, "We appreciate your help, Mr. Fribley. We'll secure this computer at the department. Is there anything special we need to do to make sure its integrity is preserved?"

"No, except other than store it in a temperature controlled environment. No temperature extremes. A rapid change in temperature can damage the hard drive. Room temperature is fine. Don't get it wet and keep it out of dusty areas."

"Okay. Now exactly what do we need to take?" Todd asked.

"Just the box. You can leave the monitor, keyboard and modem. I'll disconnect it for you. When it comes time to read the files all you need to do is hook up a compatible monitor and keyboard."

"I expect you'll get to do that. When it comes time, I imagine the state's attorney will ask you to testify and read the files in court. Okay?"

"Yes, sir, whatever you need," Mark stated calmly.

Todd then added, "Oh, and if anyone at TTM gives you any guff about all this, you let me know. I think any pressure put on you up here would constitute tampering with a witness and the state's attorney doesn't take that lightly."

"Thanks," Mark responded simply and smiled.

Nodding, Todd picked up the computer box and left with Sam leading Willis by the arm.

Mark and Janet watched them go from the inner office and then Mark became aware of the fact that Janet was trembling. He looked around and guided her toward a sofa along the far wall. He sat next to her on the sofa to comfort her and she reached out and took his right hand in hers. A strange tingling coursed through his body as she touched his hand, and he put his left arm around her shoulders to ease her trembling.

After a few moments, she asked quietly, "What was all that?"

Mark explained, "Those records we got off of Willis' computer were Tommy Trenton's bank records. Willis altered them to make it appear that he was stealing money from TTM. I saw an article about Trenton's arrest in this morning's paper and realized what we had. I took it to the sheriff's department. You see, there were two sets of files on that computer, one file contained the real records and the other contained the altered records. They clearly prove that Trenton was set up, but I don't know why. Tommy threw his copies of his records away, or so Sergeant Evans says. He can't prove that, but the records are missing. Anyway, after I told them what I had found they took it to the state's attorney, along with me, and used the evidence to spring Mr. Trenton. Then they brought me along to make sure they got the right computer. I was glad to come, it gave me another chance to see you."

"Hon?" Janet asked as if she had just awoken from a dream.

"Huh?" Mark was puzzled, *she must still be in shock,* he thought.

"You called me 'hon' a while ago. That's a term of endearment," Janet said simply.

With a reddening face, he responded, "I'm sorry... it just slipped out... I..."

"Why?"

"I don't know, it just did."

"No, I mean why are you sorry, I'm not."

"You're... I... " Mark stumbled.

Smiling, she squeezed his hand and said, "I can't believe how bashful you are." Then continuing, she said, "Don't worry. If you hang around me very long that'll change. No, don't change. I like you just the way you are," she ended and leaned over, gently brushing his lips with hers.

~ * ~

Leon watched her fingers fly over the keyboard and listened as she explained the posting procedures. As it turned out, Tess did most of the bond posting and disbursements, so she was very familiar with the procedure. It seems that the bonds taken by the sheriff's office were transmitted to the clerk's office for entry into the computer and Tess did that. The money was deposited after being posted by someone else, who then posted the deposit to a different set of books.

In a matter of hours, Tess had given Leon a complete tour of the office and explained everything to him. He was impressed with her knowledge and articulation. At first she seemed not to want to talk, but later on she loosened up. Leon got the feeling that she had been out of her environment until she started explaining the office procedures.

Like him, she didn't seem to be socially competent. More interested in her work than anything else, also like him. Now though, he wasn't so sure. He was starting to get into this interacting with people thing. Especially pretty ones. Maybe there was something in the real world for him after all.

"Okay, Tess," he used her first name easily after several hours of interaction, "now let me tell you what I found. The bonds coming in looked okay, but when the same bonds were dispersed, they were often for more money than came in. Maybe two or three hundred more. Now tell me, how that could happen in your system as a posting error?"

With a pouting look that Leon thought was quite attractive, she responded, "It couldn't, not a lot. Someone might make a mistake once in a while and misread the screen, but not very often. I post almost all the bonds myself and I can tell you I don't post them for less money than is in the envelope. Each bond is sealed in a separate envelope with the cash and bond information sheet. I keep the sheets." Moving to her right, she reached a filing cabinet and pulled open a drawer. "In here are all the bond information sheets for the past five years and in alphabetical order. You can check them all and you'll find the amount on the sheet will correspond with the computer."

"But it won't, Tess. That's the problem. Somehow the information is getting scrambled in the system."

"But..." Tess began and Leon cut her off, "I'm not accusing you or anyone in this office of anything. I'm only trying to figure out what is happening. I'm telling you that if you check those sheets, there will be some that don't match. They can't match. If the entry you made when you input the data was the same as the disbursement, then there wouldn't be a problem. But it isn't, not always. I don't know why that is, but I'm going to find out.

"If you are putting the data in correctly..."

"I am!"

"Okay, you are. Then something is happening after that to change it. Either someone is intentionally changing the data or it is happening through some computer program glitch. The fact remains, that it is being changed or the disbursement wouldn't be for more than you posted. The same with the fines. If they were actually paid the money would be there, but it isn't. So someone, or something, is changing the data."

Unknown to both Leon and Tess, Simms had walked up behind them and now put in, "It's being changed."

Leon spun and said, "What?"

"It's being changed in the system, somehow. I found some notes in Petrowski's desk suggesting that he believed someone in the system was changing the figures. Nothing in his notes about a computer glitch, he thought someone was changing the figures after they were entered."

"Inside the office here?" Tess asked.

"Who else? You've got a closed system here, don't you? No modem access, right?" Brett asked.

"Yes."

"Then it's somebody on the inside," Brett pronounced.

"And Petrowski was on to them," Leon now tossed out.

Brett thought for a second and agreed, "Yes, and he's dead."

Twenty-one

Charlie was making good his promise of buying the coffee at Shirley's. The jail personnel were so used to releasing Tommy that they had most of the forms already filled out before he had his clothes changed. Consequently, Charlie and Tommy made good time getting to the coffee shop. Steve had excused himself, citing pressing business at the office.

Charlie commandeered a corner booth and he sat with Tommy as Shirley took their orders. When the coffee came, Charlie said to Shirley, "It looks like business is a little slow now, Shirley, how about you join us?"

Glancing around the café, she had to agree with Charlie and besides, she still had her morning waitress on to cover for her. She decided she needed a break and she wanted to hear how it was that Tommy was out of jail again. Tommy sat opposite of Charlie in the booth and when he didn't offer to slide over for Shirley, Charlie moved over and said, "Here you go, Shirley. Have a sit down."

Smiling, she said, "Thanks, I do need a rest."

"Coffee?" Charlie asked, reaching for the carafe.

"Yes, thank you," she responded amiably, turning over a cup which was already on the table.

While Charlie poured her a cup of coffee, he watched Tommy out of the corner of his eye. He was very obviously nervous. It happened whenever Shirley was present, Charlie noted. In Tommy's apartment it had been the same. Maybe he was that way around all women. He was a loner and probably had never developed the social skills necessary to feel familiar in the presence of women. Some men were that way their whole lives, they just never got used to socializing with women.

"So, tell me in detail how you got Tommy off?" Shirley asked, stirring sugar into her coffee.

Charlie shrugged. "Wasn't me. The cops stumbled across the evidence that cleared him. Sergeant Evans came into court along with his partner and the state's attorney himself. The state's attorney strolled right up to the bench and proceeded to explain to Judge Ferrell that someone up at the mill had framed Tommy. I think they are going to be heading up there pretty quick to make an arrest. Maybe they're already there. The state's attorney really seemed to have a burr under his saddle. I'm not really sure of everything they had, but it was plenty to spring Tommy. We didn't hang around to give them the chance to change their minds."

Tommy was sitting in silence, still clearly uncomfortable at being this close to Shirley. Charlie watched them both out of the corners of his eyes and he could see that Shirley wasn't herself around Tommy either. Something was going on here and he wasn't at all sure that Tommy was aware of it. Perhaps Shirley wasn't either. There was something between these two, he decided. They were about the same age, Shirley probably a few years younger. They had both had a pretty hard go in life to date, yet they both seemed to have an inner endurance that sustained them.

In Tommy's case, that inner endurance took the form of his faith in God and he was quite willing to let God's will be done. Nothing upset him, except Shirley.

As for Shirley, her inner endurance wasn't all that clear. She did seem to be religious. He recalled she had talked about being active in her church, but there was something else to her. Some driving force beyond what sustained her in her times of troubles. He could sense it, but he couldn't identify it.

As he sipped his coffee and covertly watched them, he could see Shirley watching Tommy without letting him know she was watching. Tommy, on the other hand, hardly raised his eyes to her level. This surely wasn't a match, Charlie predicted. He knew the old saying about opposites attracting, but these two weren't just opposites, they lived on different planets.

"So, what about this bond fixing deal, Tommy?" Charlie asked.

"It's like I said. You know the right guy and it's a done deal."

"What guy?"

"Oh, I don't know his name or nothing like that. I just heard of him is all. It's the truth. Like I said, I know a couple of guys who used his services. It's on the level."

"How does it work?"

"I'm not sure about that either. Some computer deal. The guy's a computer whiz I hear. Even works up at the mill, but I don't know him. I never asked around up there, 'cause it wasn't my business. I don't stick my nose in where it doesn't belong."

Charlie thought for a minute and asked, "That's all you know?"

"Yes, but that's how come the bonds and stuff are so messed up in this county. Don't you think?"

"Yes, sure sounds like it. Okay, I'll have a talk with the state's attorney and tell him what you told me."

"Why?"

"Because I don't think this is over yet, and you might need some good will in his office," Charlie ventured, still remembering his conversation with Tommy yesterday morning, before heading for the jail to surrender.

Tommy brought his head up at that. Shirley stopped with her coffee cup half way to her mouth as Charlie continued, "There has to be a reason they framed you. You must know something that they don't want out. I don't think they are likely to quit at this point. I'd be willing to bet that there are others involved in this and that if what you know is really serious, they won't quit."

Getting no response, he continued, "Tommy, yesterday morning you talked about knowing something. What was it? Not this bond fixing mess. Something else wasn't it?"

Tommy set his jaw and said, "Has nothing to do with this. I told you that. It only has to do with me and mine."

"What do you mean by that? You don't have any kinfolk around here, do you? What do you mean by mine? You got a girlfriend or something? Who are you protecting?"

Tommy stared icily at Charlie and answered, "Got no kinfolk anywhere I don't guess, but that doesn't mean I've forgotten the ones I had."

Charlie softened slightly and asked, "You had relatives around here once? I guess I just thought you were raised an orphan. What happened to them?"

"Don't know. I was raised an orphan, pretty much. I raised myself from about fourteen on."

"Why?" Charlie asked.

"My business, but I'll tell you this much. I left home when I was fourteen and I never went back. I didn't run away, there wasn't much to run from. I just struck out on my own and stayed on my own." Then taking a deep breath, he continued, "I don't know what happened to my mother and father. Had a sister, too, but they moved away and I never heard from them again."

Though he had said it was his own business he decided to tell a little more. For some reason it made him feel better, "My old man was no good. He was always thieving and conning people. He used to use me to shoplift for him. In case I'd get caught, he made it look like it was my idea and he'd lay into me hard. Usually I got off with his promise to whip me good, but he was the one who really got off. For every time I was caught, there were a hundred that I wasn't. The old man made a good living off of me and the stuff I stole. He dragged me all over the area from one town to the next.

"Finally, I realized that I was eventually going to get caught and they weren't going to let me off. I was fourteen then and old enough that I was going to do the time, not my old man. Not too long after that, I left and I never went back. The old man probably never even looked for me.

"My only regret was that I couldn't take my sister with me. She was four years younger than me and he was just starting to use her in his schemes. I loved her more than anything else in the world, including my mother, who never seemed to be able to help. She was afraid of the old man, too, I guess, but somehow I wasn't sure of that. I sometimes got the feeling that she approved of his tactics. It did put food on the table."

Wistfully, he ended, "I only pray that my sister had the brains to get out before he got her into trouble. She was my only regret in leaving."

Charlie caught a movement from Shirley and noted she had tears in her eyes. *It was a sad story,* he thought.

Shirley wiped her eyes with a napkin and said, "I didn't know that."

"Know what?" Charlie asked.

"That Tommy regretted leaving me. I thought he left because he hated me, that's what Dad said anyway. For years I hoped he'd come home. I didn't realize that he was avoiding trouble by leaving. At least not at the time I didn't."

Tommy was the first to react. Charlie's bottom jaw was still on the table by the time Tommy stared across the table at Shirley and asked, "Patty?" Then continuing to stare at her as the tears welled up in her eyes and rolled down her cheeks, he said, "Yes, it is you. You are Patty." And then with awe in his voice, he said, "My word, I thought I'd never see you again."

Charlie was stunned into silence and that took some doing. He kept looking back and forth between Tommy and Shir... Patty, but could not see the resemblance. He had seen it right off in the photos of Todd Evan's family, but not these two. Not even now that he knew they were brother and sister, could he see it. Maybe it had something to do with the difficult lives they had each led, but the resemblance just wasn't there. At least not enough to tell, without being told.

He now realized why Shirley had been so interested in the Preacher and why she had been watching him without him knowing it. Why she had come to the airport, what seemed to be years ago, and begged him to help. She had probably been looking out for him the past several years without him even suspecting it. Watching him from a distance, the brother she thought had hated her. Hated her so much that he had left home at fourteen.

Patty had moved around to Tommy's side of the booth now and they sat quietly holding hands. Just staring at each other's face and smiling. Patty still had a tear or two on her cheek, but the flow had ebbed. Now they seemed content just to know that they had family and that the family loved.

"What happened to the rest of your family, Patty? Where were you all those years before coming back to Johnson City?" Charlie asked.

Patty looked at him with emotionless eyes and answered, "Like I said, I didn't realize the trouble Tommy was avoiding by leaving. I just thought he didn't like me, like Dad had said. The truth of the matter is that Dad used me like he had used Tommy, but I wasn't smart enough to see where it was leading. By the time I was in high school I was stealing more for him as each day went by. I was finally caught, just like Tommy feared he would be, only they didn't let me off that time. They sent me to juvenile hall. I stayed there until I was twenty-one and I learned more bad habits while I was there.

Fighting back the tears, she continued, "When I got out I went back to the only thing I had learned from Dad, how to steal. It wasn't long until I was caught again. This time it wasn't juvenile hall, it was prison. I was twenty-eight when I got out that time, but I had learned something in prison. I found God and Jesus Christ. I changed my name and my ways. I was a born again Christian and I became active in church. I knocked about making minimum wage for a while, here and there. Going to church and making ends meet where I could, but it was honest work. Then, quite by accident, I was passing through Johnson City and heard of a job here in this café. I took it and a few months later, when the owner wanted to retire, I offered to buy it on contract. I've been here ever since and I've watched Tommy from a distance, never knowing how to approach him, never believing he wanted to know if I were alive or dead."

Tommy looked up coldly and said, "He did that to you?"

She responded, "No, I did it to myself, Tommy. I could have left, like you did, but I was too weak. It was different since I was a girl. Girls couldn't just up and leave like boys could. I couldn't have done what you did, not in a million years. I'm not bitter, not anymore. It wasn't so much his fault, as mine."

"You're wrong, Patty. You don't know the whole of it. The old man was rotten clean through. After I left home, I lived where I could for as long as I could and then I'd move on. I stayed in school for a while and worked odd jobs. Mostly cleaning up the stuff no one else wanted to clean up.

"Well one of the places I stayed was a little building up at a place now known as Burning Chapel Hill." Looking at Charlie, he asked, "You know why they call it that?"

"Yes, Sergeant Evans told me, he has a file on it. It was a church, a black church, which was burned to the ground in the early sixties. Everyone in it died and they never rebuilt it."

"Yes, that's right. Only it wasn't just in the early sixties to me, it was much more precise than that. It was 1962. May 12, 1962, and I was fourteen. Next to the church was a little brick building used for storing lawn care equipment. It was never locked and hardly ever used. I used it more than anyone else, to sleep in. That night I was there. It was about eight o'clock and I had just finished work. I was trying my best to read a book by the light of a small candle. I made sure I kept the candle shielded, because they were having services that night and I didn't want them to know I was using their shack.

"There was some commotion outside in the parking lot and I blew my candle out in case someone was approaching the shack. I stood up and looked out the little window that faced the parking lot and the church. There were several men circling the church, but I couldn't tell what they were doing, nor could I see their faces. It was too dark and they were a little too far away. I thought it curious though, so I continued to watch.

"It wasn't a minute later that I saw a ring of fire spring up around that little church and to my horror, the flames climbed the sides of the building before any one inside could even react. The men backed off a distance then, and I could see they were white men. Still, I couldn't see any faces, but in the flickering light from the flames I could definitely tell they were white. My impression was that they were mostly young men, but I couldn't say for sure.

"It wasn't long before the flames had completely engulfed that little church. There was a roar as the flames climbed higher and higher and the heat reached to the little brick shack. The men took off then and ran through the trees to my left. The heat from the fire was so intense that I was afraid that the building I was in would catch on fire, too. So when the men ran off, I snuck out the door and eased into the trees. Even from the woods where I was hiding, I could hear screams over the roar of the flames. I still hear those screams in my sleep.

"Then I heard cars coming and thought surely someone was coming to help, but the cars contained white men. The same white men, I'm sure. They had driven their cars back to watch the total destruction of the church. There were no more screams by then, just the roar of the flames and a mountain of sparks flying every which way. I was sure the woods would catch fire, too. But by God's mercy, the rain began to fall about then. It wasn't enough rain to stop the church fire or help the people inside, but it saved the woods and cooled the fire.

"When the church finally collapsed in on itself, the men climbed calmly into their cars and drove away. Only one even looked back and he didn't hesitate long." Tommy ended sadly.

Charlie was thunder struck. "You saw the fire! You know who burned that church? Why didn't you come forward? Why remain silent all these years? Those people's ashes cry out for justice!"

"I had my reasons. Number one, I was fourteen and a runaway. Who would believe me? They'd more than likely accuse me of setting that fire than anything else. Number two," he hesitated and looked at Patty, saying, "my old man was one of the white men who set that fire."

Patty's mouth opened wide and she stifled a scream with her hands, as Tommy continued, "I couldn't turn in the old man. If I had, what would have happened to Patty? He wasn't much, but he put food on the table, and she was only ten. Mom wouldn't have been able to take care of her; she never could take care of herself. That was part of the reason my old man got away with what he did. Mom was a puppet under his control. Had I known what he was going to do to Patty, I would have turned him in, but I didn't know, so I didn't."

Charlie interjected, "I thought you said you couldn't see who burned the church, just that they were white?"

"That's right, at first, but when they came back, I had moved closer to the road. I saw the old man right enough, passing a bottle with the others. I recognized his old car, too. The others I saw, but didn't know. One other car I recognized, but not the man driving it, at least not at the time. I've seen that car since though, and I know it's the same car. I'd recognize that car anywhere. At the time it was a brand new 1962 Ford Mustang. A Convertible. Like I said, I've seen it since the fire, it's a classic."

"You're sure you didn't recognize any of the other men?" Charlie asked.

"Just my old man," Tommy said without emotion. "I saw him for sure."

"Does your father know you know of his involvement?"

"No way. He couldn't know. I never told anyone before today. I wouldn't have told today except for Patty here. Realizing what the old man did to her and how he ruined her life made me decide it was no use protecting him to protect her, not anymore. He isn't worth it, he never was."

"I understand a lot now," Charlie said. "You've lived with what you knew for thirty-five years. That did something to you, didn't it?"

Tommy shrugged and answered, "Yeah, but it was good in the end. You see, from that little shack I could just see inside the church windows. I could see that preacher standing up in front of his congregation. He was preaching away, even as the flames rose higher. The last I saw of him through the flames, he was still preaching, undaunted. I never knew whether he wasn't aware of the fire or if he was just bound and determined to go down preaching. Either way it didn't matter. That vision left a lasting impression on me, and ever since that night, all I've ever wanted to do was preach the Gospel. I wanted to live my life preaching and go down preaching, just like the preacher in that little church.

"Knowing what I did about the fire made me even more determined to see God's word spread. I knew, better than anyone else, the evil in this community and how quickly it could strike. I had to tell people about Jesus while there was still time. The 'Jesus people' who came and set up their tent on Burning Chapel Hill helped me to do that better than ever before. When they left, I stayed and carried on even more fervently.

"I know people think I'm crazy, but it isn't so. I'm different, but I'm not nuts. As long as they let me preach, I don't care what they think about me."

Charlie now said, "Sergeant Evans has to know about this. He's been tracking the killers of those people for twenty years and getting nowhere. Little did he realize that the key to his quest was within his grasp on many an occasion. He lent you blankets, gave you food and money, never realizing you were the key he was seeking. Will you come with me and talk to him? Will you tell him what you told me? It'll give him peace at last."

Patty now put in snidely, "Peace? He's a cop. That's a funny word to use about a cop solving a crime."

Charlie said flatly, "Tommy wasn't the only one affected by that fire. Todd Evans lost his mother, father and brother in that fire. Yes, Patty, peace is the right word."

Twenty-two

Todd was back at his desk again, reviewing reports and files. *Still at my desk*, he grumbled to himself. He missed the streets, but he knew that crimes weren't solved on the streets. Reviewing reports solved crimes, along with the information gathered on the streets. He was back on the Merriman file again. In particular, he was looking yet again at the green ledger. Todd sensed that there was something to this book, other than the figures found between its covers.

Starting again at the first page of the book, he flipped through it slowly, one page at a time. He examined each page, but they revealed little. The same old numbers at the upper right-hand corner that looked like account numbers and the letter number combinations in the upper left-hand corner that he figured to be code for bank names. Yet the columns didn't seem to be organized like a bank account record. There weren't debits and credits, just a single column of figures.

The left-hand column contained dates. That was clear, but the corresponding figures were just figures. However, the column with the figures was lined and there was a darker line two numbers from the right that had to denote a decimal point. He knew enough about accounting to know that all ledger sheets had a similar line denoting the decimal point, but no commas for thousands and there appeared to be plenty of thousands in this ledger.

All of this was speculation though. The ledger could be accounting for anything. Bushels of wheat, pounds of cotton—or money. He couldn't prove one way or the other what was being counted and tracked in this book. Very possibly it had nothing to do with Merriman's death, probably didn't, but Todd was continually drawn to the book just as he was drawn to the church file.

He started at the front of the book again with the sole purpose of examining the dates. The first entry dated back to May 12, 1964. Close examination revealed several pages with the same numbers in the upper right and left-hand corners and the dates ran all the way forward to June 13, 1977. It was obvious to Todd, that these pages were all a record of the same account at the same bank.

The next set of records also all bore the same numbers in the upper right and left-hand corners, but was different from the first, set denoting them as separate accountings. This second set had larger numbers in the columns next to the dates and the dates were subsequent to the first set of pages. The subsequent sets of pages were all of the same date range as this set, but had different numbers in the upper right-hand corners signifying different accounts.

Except for the first set of pages, all the sets had numbers in the thousands. He noted the first set contained numbers ranging from one hundred to four hundred, and Todd only assumed them to be dollars, they could have been anything.

He flipped back to the first set again and examined them closely. The dates were evenly spaced, about a month apart for several years. Assuming the figures denoted dollars, the first few years recorded one hundred dollars on each respective date. On January 6, 1970 the amount increased to two hundred dollars each month. Then on January 6, 1972o the amount increased yet another hundred, to three hundred dollars and stayed constant. On September 2, 1973 the amount increased again to four hundred dollars per month where it stayed constant until June 13, 1977, and ceased.

Pulling his calculator over toward him, he added up the figures. In no time he was finished and was amazed at how quickly the one hundred dollar increments added up to twenty-nine thousand six hundred dollars. If in fact they were dollars and if they were, that was a sizable amount of change. Almost a year's salary these days and two years' salary in the 70s. Enough to buy a new car today and enough to buy a small house or send a kid clear through college in the 1970s.

It struck him like a thunderbolt. He flipped to the first page and read the dates again. May 12, 1964 was quite obviously the second anniversary of the burning of Little Flock Baptist Church. He had graduated from college on June 13, 1977. He was pretty sure that he had begun college in September of 1973. He wasn't sure of the date, but he was willing to bet it was on the second. His birthday was January 6, 1955, making him eighteen on January 6, 1973.

Slamming the book shut, he opened his bottom desk drawer and tossed it in. Closing the drawer, he jumped up and hurried out the door. Five minutes later he was in his car and headed out of the parking lot. His uncle still lived up on Burning Chapel Hill not far from the burned out church. The same place where he had always lived, and where he would probably die.

Todd saw his uncle sitting under a large shade tree in his front yard as he pulled up. Since his aunt had died a few years ago, it seemed his uncle rarely moved from under that tree. He was just sitting and waiting for God to call him to his Ginney Ann. He was old and had stooped shoulders, his hair was dead white, but he was mentally pretty sharp yet. Todd stepped out of the car and walked slowly over to sit by his uncle. On his way up here he had been anxious to arrive, but now that he was here he wasn't sure he wanted to know what he thought his uncle knew.

"Hi, Unc," Todd said easily, as he dropped into a chair next to his uncle.

"Good ta see ya, boy. You don't come around enough anymore," the old man drawled easily.

"Yes, sir, I'm pretty busy. Crime doesn't take a vacation you know."

The old man looked at Todd with admiration in his eyes and said, "I still can't believe I gots a nephew that's a policeman. When I was your age, I never even dreamed of no black man getting to be a policeman. Them was white jobs, us black folk did the jobs the white folk didn't want to do."

Todd had heard this speech many times before and though he appreciated his uncle's admiration, he had other things on his mind this day. This wasn't a social call and he responded, "Times have changed, Uncle."

"Don't I knows it," the old man now said. "Why I remember when I had to beg to go to grade school and you got all the way through college. Got yourself a fine job and..."

"Uncle Burrell," Todd cut him off gently and continued, "it's about college. I came to talk about college and some other things. Okay?"

The old man stopped and stared carefully at his nephew's face and asked, "Sure, son, what's a bothering you?"

Todd smiled and said, "You always could read my mind."

"It comes from rais'n a young'n. You get to know them so much you almost become them. You raise 'em up to do what you couldn't do and along the way you become part of them and they part of you. Ain't no magic to it, son, it's just natural. It's just family. Some families is closer than others. We was always close, you an' me, we had to be to survive them days."

Gently leading his uncle back to the topic he was interested in, Todd asked, "Uncle Burrell, you remember when I started college..."

Burrell cut him off and said with a smile, "You bet I do. It was the proudest day of mine and Ginney's life, that day was. Except for maybe when you graduated."

"Yes, but what I mean is... do you remember how I had the money for college?"

"Sure, I told ya it was from the fund. I told you about the fund. Don't know where it came from, it was just there. Different places from time to time, but always there, just when you needed it. It was the answer to my prayers for you to do better than me and better than your folks, God bless their souls."

"Sure, I remember you telling me, but I want to know if you remember how much money was left each time for the fund."

"How much?" the old man questioned and wrinkled his brow in thought before continuing, "Wasn't no reason to really add it up. I just puts it in the bank whenever it came. I never used a dime of it for'n myself. It was for you, from God. I don't know how much, but it was always enough. When you needed school clothes it was there, when you needed books and a car for high school, it was there, just like for college, it was always there."

"Yes, but do you know how much was left each time?" Todd asked pointedly.

"Lands sakes no! I just puts it in the bank. I didn't count it, the bank took care of that. It was more'n I ever seen."

Boring in, like his uncle was a witness to a crime, Todd continued, "Was it a hundred, two hundred, four hundred and how often was it left?"

The old man was beside himself. His memory was not what it used to be and besides he really never had counted it. It wasn't his money so why count it. It was for Todd, let the bank count it. He did sort of remember when it was left though and answered, "I seems to remember it was almost always there after Communion on Sunday."

Todd thought about that for a minute, realizing that his uncle tracked time differently than most people, hill folk had their own ways of tracking time. Finally, he said, "Communion was always on the first Sunday of the month."

Smiling, the old man responded, "Yep, still is. First Sunday of every month, only have Communion oncet a month at our church.

You know that, you still come, but not like you used to," the old man ended, in a gentle scolding tone.

Todd let that roll off and asked, "Was the money there every first Sunday or just some?"

"Every Sunday."

"When did it start? What year?"

The old man was deep in thought and finally answered, "I can't say for sure, couple years after you come to us I reckon."

"Was it summer time?" Todd persisted.

Clearly trying to remember the old man responded, "Not so's you'd know it. I mean it was warming, but not blistering hot yet. Not real summer yet I'd say.

"I remember the first time I come upon it. Like I say it was warm and we had just come home from church, so I heads for the well over yonder," he said pointing toward his right to where the same well still stood and was still in use. Then he continued, "I decided to get me a cool drink, best water in the county that there well, still is, I..."

Todd didn't want to be rude, but his uncle liked to reminisce and he needed him to stay on track for a while. "Please, Uncle Burrell, tell me about the money."

The old man got his hackles up, he didn't like being interrupted when he was reminiscing. "What's so all fired important about that money? It got you through school all right and God knows I couldn't have done it without that money. That's why He sent it. What's eat'n you, boy?"

"Sorry, Uncle, but I just need to know about it. It's important. Okay? Trust me, if what I think is right, then I'll tell you all and maybe more. More than you ever dreamed of knowing, or maybe wanted to know."

The old man was mystified, but he could see how important this was to his nephew, the son he never had and always wanted, so he continued, "Well, like I was saying, I went to get me a cool drink and when I picked up the bucket to lower it into the well I seen this envelope a lying there on the edge of the well, right under the bucket. Luck was I didn't knock it into the well. But anyway, I opens it up and, my word, I almost fainted when I seen that money.

"It was more money than I ever seen before in one place. Must a been a hundred dollars or more. I never counted it. I just dropped right then and there and thanked God for it. I'd been a stewing over how to make ends meet and get you a proper education. Well, there was a whole lot of money, maybe not enough, but enough to get you your school clothes.

"Next month after Communion I just naturally went over to look under that bucket again. I don't know why, but I did and there it was. More money. Went on that way for some time till the weather got bad and started to rain'n a lot. Then there weren't no money there and I was sad. Later in the day I went out to the barn to feed the horse and found an envelope in the feed bin. There was other places it was left, too, but mostly in the feed bin after that. I just don't know how much though, boy. I'm sorry."

Todd nodded and said gently, "It stopped the month I graduated from college didn't it?"

Burrell thought a minute and answered, "Yes, I never give it no thought before, but it did. I didn't need no money after you graduated, not for you, so I never give it no thought. But no, I never found no money again after that."

Todd was thinking now and finally he said, "You said you put that money in the bank. Which bank?"

"Johnson City State Bank."

"It isn't open any more is it? I mean some other bank bought it out and closed it didn't they?"

The old man nodded his agreement and said, "Bout the time you got out of college. Yes. Why?"

"Well, I thought I could look at the old records and find out how much you deposited and when, since you don't know."

The old man said haughtily, "Never said I didn't know. Said I didn't count it, let the bank count it."

"But, if you didn't count it, how are you going to tell me the amounts?"

Smiling shrewdly, the old man responded, "Gots me the bank books, all five of 'em. Yes siree, I ain't stupid. I let the bank count it all right, but I had me a book showing what was in there so I'd know how much I had for you to use. The books, now, they'd show you how much was put in and how much was taken out; and when, right?"

Closing his mouth from his slacked jaw, Todd responded, "Why didn't you just tell me you had the books?"

"You never asked. For a high-powered policeman you ain't so good at ask'n the right questions," Burrell said amiably and winked.

Todd just nodded his agreement. There was nothing to say, his uncle had pretty much hit the nail on the head. Besides, his uncle was already halfway to the house, presumably to get the bankbooks.

When he returned, Burrell carefully took the books out of a small metal box as if he were afraid they would break. They were magical things to him and represented a power he had only dreamed of having. These books, or the money they had recorded over the years, held the power to educate a small black boy and make him into a man, a man ten times better than his parents—or uncle—for that matter.

Todd quickly scanned the books and from what he recalled of the green ledger his suspicions were confirmed. The green ledger for some unknown reason, recorded, to the dollar, on the exact dates, the money that was left for him via his uncle. Money his uncle had used to support him and educate him when his dead parents couldn't. Merriman must have kept this ledger of the payments made. But why would Merriman leave money for him? And what of the other pages in the ledger? Was Merriman giving others money, too? If so, why and to whom?

It became clear to Todd now, that the numbers in the upper left-hand corner didn't denote banks, but people. People who were paid money. But for what purpose and by whom? Merriman? He didn't have that kind of money, did he?

"Uncle Burrell I need to borrow these books for a while, okay?"

The old man's face took on a look of apprehension and he squirmed in his chair, as he grunted, "What for?"

"I need to compare them with another book I have and make some notes." Seeing his uncle's look, he continued, "I'll take good care of them, I promise. You'll get them back in good shape."

"I don't know... I... those is the fund books. I never let them go anywhere before. I don't know what I'd do if they was lost."

"Uncle Burrell, they're just old bank books. There's no money left and no bank left. They aren't worth anything now."

"That's where you're wrong, boy. Those books made you what you are. They's important."

"The money in the bank that the books represented sent me to school, Uncle Burrell, not the books. The books were just used to keep track of the money. By themselves they mean nothing, except for what I can learn from them now."

The old man was clearly not convinced. All he knew was that those books had always represented the answer to his prayers. Maybe the money was gone, but the books themselves represented to him how a small black boy could become more than anyone had ever imagined. Yet he trusted his nephew, he was a policeman and a fine man. If Todd said the books would be safe, then Burrell guessed he had to believe him, and he finally relented. "Okay, I guess, but you be careful with them and I want them back as soon as you're finished with them. Nobody ever touched them before, not even my Ginney."

"Sure, I promise. I'm going to copy them and study them and then I'll return them."

Todd was so excited on the way back to the sheriff's department that he could barely contain himself. Too bad Sam was off today, he could use another set of eyes on this. Twenty years and he might finally have a lead worth something. If Merriman had been the one to leave the money for him, there could only be one reason. What had Chambers said? "Somebody felt sorry, for sure." Todd had always just figured someone felt sorry for him since he had lost his parents and his uncle was poor, but there was more to it than that. Chambers had seen it, just like he had seen the resemblance in the photos when no one else had.

For someone to feel that sorry for a little orphaned black boy in the sixties, there had to be a good reason. To feel sorry to the tune of over twenty-nine thousand dollars would take a whale of a reason. The only reason he could think of, which could make someone give that kind of money away, was that they had something to do with the death of his family. Someone was carrying a powerful lot of guilt. Guilt, because they had something to do with the fire.

Merriman? Who else? Had he helped start the fire or had he just known who did? If he knew who did, was he killed because someone feared he would talk? Was the money that was recorded in the book hush money? That would explain where he came up with so much money to send an orphaned black boy to college. Why would someone be afraid Merriman would talk after all these years of silence?

A lot of questions, Todd mused, but he was excited to be asking them. Prior to today all he had was pure speculation. Now he at least had a focus to his questioning. He had a focus to his investigation. Merriman was his lead, except that he was dead, just like all the other leads up on Burning Chapel Hill. Still, he was more recently dead and the trail wasn't near so cold.

For the first time, in a lot of years, he had hope. Despite what his uncle thought about him having drifted from the faith, he was wrong. Todd had prayed daily over the last twenty years for a break in this case and now he thanked God that his prayers might finally have been answered. Now he could put his education to real use. Ironically, he would put to work the education given to him by Merriman, to prove that Merriman had killed a hundred people thirty-five years ago.

~ * ~

After having briefed the circuit clerk on what they suspected was going on, based upon Gene's notes, Leon was still not willing to quit. He was still wondering if there wasn't a break down in the system and that Petrowski had been wrong. However, it wasn't helping that Brett had used his credentials to get a copy of the accident investigation faxed to him and immediately noticed that there had been something wrong with the brakes on Petrowski's car. Brett was cooking up a conspiracy theory now, and he was going to include anyone in the office he could possibly imagine having been connected with this fraud, as he now called it. Tess was high on Brett's hit list, and for some reason that bothered Leon more than he wanted to admit.

Leon continued to go over the office procedures with Tess and she continued to dazzle him with her knowledge. He was also getting over his initial shyness and opening up to her as they bantered back and forth between bursts of work. Tess could not be part of this, he knew, deep down he knew she couldn't be, but he had to have evidence. He had to find out what was wrong in the system, to make it look like someone in the office was playing with the figures, when they weren't. Of course, it could be someone other than Tess, but he doubted that, too. After talking with all of them, he got the impression that they were being truthful about their actions. But then, he was a number cruncher, not a cop.

Twenty-three

Sunday didn't come fast enough for Charlie, but finally it came. He was on pins and needles pacing around his tiny apartment waiting for the appointed time to leave for Carol's. He hadn't tried to call her and she hadn't called him, so he was hoping the trip to church was still on, no news was good news in this case, he figured.

When he couldn't stand it any longer he finally ran a comb through his hair one last time, wiped his shoes with a rag for the twentieth time and headed down to the street. It was a little early, but close enough, early was better than late and in this matter he was not about to be late.

Not even ten minutes had elapsed when he rolled to a stop at Carol's front gate. A call to the house by the guard, not the same one as the other night, gained him immediate and friendly access. His heart was pounding from just the thought of seeing Carol again and by the time he made it to the front door his palms were sweating. Not good, he decided, he needed to calm down and take things a little easier, but for some reason he could not make himself feel calm. It was silly. He was a grown man, not some kid on his first date, but he felt like a kid on his first date, just the same. What a powerful effect just the thought of seeing Carol had on him, a complete contrast from his feelings the first time he laid eyes on her in the café. *What a difference a few days can make, and a few kisses,* he wryly thought.

The door opened before he got to it again and there she stood, Charlie was in awe again and hoped he always would be, if he got the chance. She was in a white light cotton dress with a red flower pattern. In contrast to the dress from the other night this one was well up on her shoulders and revealed nothing except the rise in her bosom, which Charlie doubted could be hidden, or should be. In short, it was very appropriate for church attendance and Charlie had had no doubt that it would be. From what he could tell, in complete contrast to his earlier hasty and incorrect assumptions, Carol was nothing but proper in all manner and ways.

"Morning, Carol, you look lovely," Charlie said and he meant it too, her hair was pulled back into a bun behind her head, she had on just a touch of blush and her lips were adorned with just the right amount of lip gloss, peach shade, he decided or close to it. Very inviting.

"Why thank you, Charles, I tried my best," she responded with a smile revealing those perfectly shaped and gleaming white teeth.

"You succeeded very nicely."

"You look dapper yourself, Charles," Carol commented on their way to his car.

"Thanks," he replied and wondered when she would mention the flowers; he didn't want to bring it up. *Too pushy*, he decided, but he was surprised she hadn't mentioned them. She may get a lot of flowers, but he, at least, thought she would mention having gotten flowers from him.

"Sorry about the air-conditioning, there isn't any," Charlie said as he drove out the gate and turned on to the blacktop.

"It's okay, I dressed for the heat, I'm Georgia born and raised, you know. You get used to dressing for the heat and humidity."

"Sure you can do that, but lawyers have to wear suits and ties all the time, no way to dress cool in a suit and tie, that summer weight suit stuff is all baloney. They never made a suit that was comfortable above eighty degrees."

During the short drive to church they made continuous small talk and Charlie kept wondering about the flowers. Did she get them? Did she like them? Why wouldn't she mention them? Was he not reading the signals correctly? Probably so, he decided.

At the church, the whole congregation was clearly thrilled to have Carol in attendance, but as Charlie had predicted, she was not molested, she was not bothered in the slightest. People only greeted her cordially, no one asked for her autograph and everyone respected her right to be in church, with them, and to her privacy.

It was a novel experience for Carol and she thoroughly enjoyed herself. She was out amongst people, with no shield around her, no wall between her and the world; and she loved the feel of it. She had not been able to interact with people like this in years, how she had let herself become so isolated she didn't know, but she was determined not to let it happen again. Protection had its uses, but Charles was right, not here, not in her hometown. This was the one place she could and should freely associate with other people, without barriers.

Carol was feeling so good about being out, without her protection, that after church, she suggested they stop at Shirley's for an early lunch and Charlie whole-heartedly agreed. He had admitted to himself that he wanted to be with Carol anytime, anyplace, but it was even better if the place was not that imposing mansion of hers where he felt Dan Chase was always lurking.

Unlike at church, the appearance of Carol at Shirley's caused quite a stir, but once the other patrons realized she was just there to eat, they again respected her space. She was enthusiastically greeted of course. More so than at church where people tend to be a bit more reserved. Still, her presence was accepted and she was treated, given her status, as just one more of the town folk out for lunch after church.

Charlie guided Carol to a corner table as far out of the way as possible in the little café, not to protect her from the other customers, but to have her more to himself. He was being a typical male, he was trying to keep his female companion for himself. He didn't want any competition and he was sure there was plenty to go around when it came to Carol Harmon, maybe too much. *The flowers, what about the flowers?* The thought kept creeping into his mind, but he kept dismissing it, telling himself it wasn't important, but a part of him always replied, that it was important. *What about the flowers?*

Shirley popped over rather spryly Charlie thought and took their orders with no nonsense, other than to tell Charlie that Tommy was ready to talk to Evans.

"Good, Shirl. I'll set it up for tomorrow. I'll let you know."

"Work on Sunday, Charles?" Carol inquired with a smile.

"A little, got to make a buck when you can," he said lightly.

"I thought money didn't matter to you?"

"It doesn't, just pulling your leg," and then glancing under the table with an impish smile, he finished, "such nice legs, hard to resist pulling them."

Carol chuckled and blushed slightly, clearly pleased with his banter, and before Charlie realized what was happening, she took his right hand in her left hand, squeezed it gently and brought it up to her lips for a kiss. She didn't let it go either, she lowered it to the table and hung on to it, glancing around the room at the other customers, some of whom were covertly watching, and smiling sweetly as if to say, *take a good look, we don't care who knows.*

Charlie's blood pressure went clear to the roof, his heart raced and he felt as giddy as a kid who had just gotten his first kiss from a girl he had admired for years. *Take that, doc,* he said to himself. *What a way to go*, and then he added, also to himself, *who cares about some silly flowers, whether she got them or not. Things, seem to be going pretty good right now.*

When Shirley brought their order, Carol was still holding Charlie's hand and vice versa. With a knowing smile, Shirley artfully deposited their order, let her eyes wander to the clasped hands and left, saying, "Enjoy."

Charlie was hungry, but not for the food, he was hungry to hold Carol's hand, but he couldn't and still eat so he had to let go of her hand. He got the impression she wasn't all that thrilled about eating either, but then again there was always time for hand holding, or was there? He had thought that same thing about his wife and then she had died. He was not going to waste opportunities again, if Carol turned out to be his second chance at love, he was going to make the most of it, but how? He wasn't the only one who traveled the road. She traveled too, almost year round. *How could that work out?* he asked himself and then decided to ask Carol, in a round about way.

"So, when do you hit the road again?"

"Next Friday for sure. I have to get that record cut in Nashville and then I am supposed to sing with some other country performers at a charity concert in San Francisco. I go from there to Seattle for another concert and then a short road tour around the southwest."

"You're a hard person to keep up with. No wonder you married a drummer, he was probably the only guy you could see on a regular basis," Charlie stated with a smile.

Carol looked at him for a full minute with a confused look on her face and then her face took on a look of understanding and she said, "Charles, for a lawyer, you sure telegraph your thoughts. Do you do that in court, too?"

Charlie blushed mildly and responded, "No, I'm very good in court at sneaking up on a witness, but you seem to know what I'm thinking, so I haven't had much success with you. That could be a good sign, I guess."

Smiling broadly now, she bent toward him and lightly brushed his cheek with her lips, saying, "Don't worry, Charles, it can be worked out."

"What?" Charlie responded.

"Now don't be coy, Charles, I know what you were getting at. How can we get to know one another or have any time together if I'm on the road all the time and you are, too? Isn't that the question you were really asking?"

Caught, Charlie had to honestly respond, "Yes, the thought had crossed my mind. I enjoy your company and I hope you enjoy mine."

"I do," Carol shot out.

"Good, but when do we find the time to enjoy one another's company, if we decide to in the future? You are a country singer and I'm a lawyer, we're both on the road a lot and probably never the same road, so where does that leave us? You don't want to quit and I don't blame you and I don't want to quit, because I feel called to do what I'm doing and if I don't do it who else will? So what do we do?"

With a twinkle in her eyes she said with mock seriousness, "Charles, did you ever think about taking up the drums?"

Charlie was in earnest conversation and thought Carol was, too. It was a shock to his system, when she said that, and when his brain had made the transition from seriousness to fool-hardiness, he burst out laughing. Carol chimed in and they laughed until they were almost crying. The whole café looked on in amazement, most of the customers smiling and glancing around at the others as if to say, *look at the lovers, we're happy for them, you should be, too.*

When he had recovered and while he was wiping his eyes with his napkin, Carol was still laughing softly, trying to recover, too, Charlie said, "I guess I deserved that." Then he bent toward her took her chin lightly in his right hand, turned her lips toward him and kissed her lightly.

Still holding her chin, their lips having parted by a few inches, he studied her face and finally said, "One day at time."

"Yes," Carol responded softly, "One day at a time."

After they had finished their lunch they left the café hand in hand. The balance of the afternoon was spent driving around the countryside while Carol explained the area to Charlie. He was falling in love with this area, this state and with Carol, he finally admitted to himself. He never thought he would be in love with another woman. He had loved his first wife so deeply that he was sure his love had been all used up. But not so, he realized, there was plenty left and it was, if anything, even more fierce than the love he had shared with his wife. Although, he decided, probably not, it was just that time tended to rob the mind of those acute feelings, the sharpness dulled and memories faded.

The intenseness of love eased over time, it almost had to, no one could stand to live on that emotional high forever. Companionship took over in time and the character of love changed from desire and yearning to peace, tranquility and comfort. He surmised that the trick was not to let comfort and companionship turn into complacency and thoughtlessness, he didn't know how he would do on that score. He had not had the time to get to that point with his wife, but he had ignored her to a certain degree and he vowed that would not happen this time, if there was a 'this time'.

Carol was enjoying the afternoon. She loved showing off her hometown area, because she loved it so much herself and she wanted Charles to love it too, and her. It was hard for her to admit that to herself, because she had only known this man for a few days and the first meeting was hardly productive. Still, it is what she wanted. *What difference did the length of the relationship make?* she asked herself. If it's right, it's right, one day, one year, one week, if it's right, it's right.

Toward evening, Charlie rolled up to the gate at Carol's house and the guard immediately moved to open the gates. As the car passed the shack slowly, the guard, the same one from the other night, said politely, "Evening, Mr. Chambers, your flowers arrived."

Charlie gave it no thought, but Carol asked, "What did he say, Charles?"

"He said my flowers arrived."

"What did that mean?"

"I guess he was on duty the other day when my flowers arrived is all I can figure," Charlie said, not the least bit concerned about the flowers any longer.

"What flowers?" Carol said in a confused tone.

"The flowers I sent you the other day, a dozen long stemmed roses. I know you get a lot of flowers, but I figured you would at least remember when you get them," he responded in a matter of fact tone.

"Turn around, Charles."

"Huh?"

"Please, turn around, I want to talk to the guard. I didn't get any flowers from you, I would have remembered that and I would have thanked you for them the next time I saw you, first thing."

"I wondered about that," Charlie responded honestly, as he completed the circle in front of the house and took the drive back to the gate.

Steve stepped out of the gate shack rapidly when the car approached for the second time in less than a minute and asked, "Everything okay, Miss Harmon?"

"Steve, did I get flowers the other day from Mr. Chambers?"

"You don't remember?" he replied and then wished he hadn't said it quite that way when he saw the look on Carol's face and he added quickly, "I mean, yes, sure you did, was something wrong with them?"

"Did you accept delivery of them?" Carol asked in a no nonsense tone.

"No, ma'am, they were delivered to the house." Then realizing that there was no sense in sugar coating the matter at the risk of his own hide, he added, "Mr. Chase told me he would take care of them." He did not at this point see the need to tell the whole story, it was obvious that the story would come out anyway and unless he were directly asked what Dan had said he was going to hedge his bet just a little.

"Apparently he did," Carol said, clearly agitated and then to Charlie, "Let's go up to the house, Charles."

Charlie spun the little car around with a grunt of acknowledgement and headed back to the house.

Carol was fuming. Charlie could feel the heat building in the car. He would not have wanted to be in Dan Chase's shoes when Carol lit in to him, and he could tell that's just what she had in mind.

"Could have been a mistake, Carol. Might have been a misunderstanding," he said in an attempt to calm her fury.

"Oh, there was a mistake all right and Dan Chase made it. But, don't worry. I won't make a scene. I won't even mention it to him, but there will be a payback. I guarantee it," she said firmly and pursed her lips together.

Ouch, Charlie thought, *I hope I never get on her wrong side*. He had no idea what she had in mind for a payback, but he knew he didn't want to be on the receiving end.

At the door, Carol said, "I'd invite you in, Charles, but I'm afraid I wouldn't be too good of company right now, my mood has changed."

"I suspected as much," he answered and took her in his arms and kissed her deeply. Carol responded in kind, her mood may have changed, but her desire to make Charles desire her had not. She let her body mold to his and yielded to his embrace, her heart pounding and her head swimming. *For a stuffy lawyer this guy can really kiss when he puts his mind to it,* she thought, through the haze of emotions welling up inside of her.

Charlie didn't want to let her go, didn't want to stop kissing her. But knew he should. It had been a great day and despite her discovery of the chicanery with the flowers, it had been a good ending to a good day.

~ * ~

Charlie was putting his suit coat on and filling its pockets with his necessities when the telephone rang. "Hello."

"Charlie?"

"Yes."

"Hey, it's John Bullock."

"John, what causes you to call this early Monday morning? I didn't think you criminal lawyers got into the office before ten on Mondays."

"Very funny, Charlie, but I called to give you a heads up."

"Oh."

"Yes, what have you been up to down there?"

"Same old stuff, court, civil rights, something you know little about," Charlie ended with a chuckle.

"No, I'm serious Charlie. I have friends over at the state supreme court and they tell me that a complaint was received on you late last week. The word is that you've been seen carousing bars, half-blasted and driving erratically. That you got slammed for contempt of court and that you have been harassing a famous country singer, name of Carol Harmon."

Chuckling, Charlie responded, "Yes, sure John, but you forgot the six fights I was in and the murder I committed."

"No, I'm serious Charlie, this is on the level. The Attorney Registration and Disciplinary Commission is sending out a response notification letter to you, probably be forwarded to you by your office up here. They're taking this seriously."

"Who made the complaint?" Charlie asked seriously.

"Don't know, couldn't find that out, but who ever it was had some real juice. This got fast tracked. I suspect because of its connection to Carol Harmon."

"Well, it's all bull, John, take my word for it."

"Hey, I'm on your side, but it isn't me you have to convince, you know that. Once the ARDC gets a hold of something they go after it like a dog on a fresh bone."

"Yeah, I know. Those clowns haven't the foggiest idea what it is like to practice law, but they sure can tell everybody else how to do it. Aw, don't worry, John, it'll be okay. Just a misunderstanding, somebody trying to throw me off the scent."

"What scent?"

"I'll fill you in later, and thanks for the tip, John."

"No problem, you need anything you give me a holler, if this thing goes to hearing and you want me, you just say the word."

"I appreciate that, John, but don't worry, it isn't going anywhere, I guarantee it. See you."

"Take care," John responded as he hung up.

~ * ~

They were in the interrogation room, as it was the only room large enough to accommodate Charlie, Tommy, Patty and Todd comfortably and also give them some privacy. Todd listened to Tommy's story stone faced, but at times it was hard for him to remain objective. Especially when Tommy described the fire and how it engulfed the church, along with the entire congregation. He had long since stopped thinking of the members of that congregation as people. People who cared, cried and screamed. It made it easier to live with for all these years, and it made it possible for him to be objective.

Now though, he was seeing them again as people. People with feelings, hopes and aspirations. He was seeing his mother, father and brother. With great effort, he remained emotionless and calm throughout the story. Only when Tommy was completely finished did Todd venture to say anything and he only asked, "You didn't actually see the faces of the men when they started the fire did you?"

"I saw them later, my old man was one for sure, and that car is still around town," Tommy stated flatly.

Todd persisted; it was his job and his profession. "Yes, I understand that, but you didn't actually see who started the fire. You didn't see the faces of the men who started the fire. You only saw the men who drove up in their cars after the fire was burning."

Tommy was silent, but you could read in his face that he was adamant about his story.

Todd looked at Charlie and said, "Tell him, Mr. Chambers. Explain to him what I'm getting at. You know it as well as I do. We aren't talking just a story here, we're talking evidence. Right?"

Charlie nodded and said, "That's right, Tommy. What Sergeant Evans is trying to get at is that you can only assume that the men who drove up, after the fire was burning, were the same ones who started the fire."

"Right, that's right. It was them," Tommy stated firmly.

Charlie responded, "No, you just think it was them. A judge and jury couldn't make that connection, not without more. It would never hold up. Don't you see?"

Tommy thought for a minute and finally admitted, "Yeah, I guess I see what you mean, but we all know it was the same men. Couldn't be two groups of white men up on that same hill that same night."

Todd now put in, "I agree, but we have to prove that. Can you give me something more to help me prove it?"

Tommy shook his head in the negative and said, "I don't know anything else. You can stop the man that's driving that 1962 Ford Mustang."

"No, that doesn't mean he had anything to do with the fire. He could have lent his car to someone that night or it might have been stolen. Besides, there are several people in this area who drive classic cars. Probably more than one of them have Ford Mustangs of that era."

Patty now asked, "Why not talk to our father?"

"He's still alive?" Tommy interjected.

"Yes, he lives a couple of counties over, near Bushville. He isn't well, but he's still alive. Mom's dead, been dead for several years now."

Todd shook his head in the negative again, saying, "No good. I can't go two counties over and talk to anyone without permission from the Meridian County Sheriff and the sheriff over there. That could take forever."

They all sat around the table not saying a word. Each had his own private thoughts about how justice should be served.

After some length of silence, Todd asked Tommy, "You once told me you knew a guy by the name of Merriman who worked up at the mill."

"Like I said, I heard tell of him. Might have run into him once or twice when I was cleaning. Why?"

"As it turns out, he had something to do with that fire, too. According to some records he kept, he was making, and maybe taking, some payoffs to keep quiet."

Charlie perked up and asked, "How do you know that?"

"You remember I told you about my uncle receiving money for my education?"

"Yes."

"Well, it just so happens that Merriman was where the money came from. I tracked the payments recorded in a ledger he kept at his house. They correspond exactly with the bankbooks my uncle used to record the money he received. I figure you were right, Mr. Chambers, about someone being really sorry. He was so sorry, he left money for me all those years. You suspected something like that, didn't you?"

"I did, but I wasn't sure," Charlie admitted.

"Well, I'm sure. It doesn't stop there either. There were other payments or receipts recorded in that book, too. Much more than my account, but I don't know to or from whom. He had something to do with that fire though. I was hoping I could use him as a lead. Even though he is dead, his trail would be warmer than anyone else's."

After another moment of silence, Todd said, "Thank you all for bringing this to me. It may help. At least now I know two people who were involved. Merriman and your father. It's a lot more than I had yesterday. I'll just keep on digging for proof. I've been doing it for twenty years, I can do it a while longer."

Todd rose from his chair, and the others took it as their cue to leave. Each filed out of the room in silence. Todd turned back toward his office as the others turned to leave the building.

Outside, Tommy said to Charlie, "Can I leave the county?"

"Why?"

"I'm going to find the old man. I'm going to talk to him about this. Maybe I can learn something that will help."

"Why would you do that?" Patty asked. "He's never meant anything to you but trouble. What makes you think he would talk to you?"

"Because I know what he did, and at least when I'm done, he'll know I know. Besides, for thirty-five years I've heard those screams in the night, screams the old man caused. For thirty-five years I've sat by, knowing who killed those people, and I did nothing."

Charlie responded, "But you couldn't do anything. Like you said they probably would have blamed you."

"I can do something now. Can I leave the county?"

"Sure, you just can't leave the state," Charlie answered.

"Okay, Patty, you tell me all you know about where he is."

"Bushville is all I know. That's the last I heard of anyway. I haven't seen him for years, but I heard he was living near Bushville. I did hear, not too long ago, that he was ill, but that was all. Maybe he is dead by now."

Charlie now volunteered, "We'll take my rental car and we'll drive over that way and nose around."

"I'll go, too," Patty said.

"No," Tommy and Charlie said in unison and Tommy continued, "You stay and tend to your business. The old man has ruined your life enough already. That café is your last chance. I'll go, there's nothing for me to lose."

"He's right, Patty. Besides, he might clam up if you both dropped in out of the sky. Let Tommy try. I'll take Tommy over there and see if we can find your father."

~ * ~

While waiting for the one thirty p.m. court setting to start, Todd sat in the back of the room contemplating what he had learned from the conference with Tommy. Not much, but it was more than he had first thing that morning. As he contemplated the burning chapel case, he absently watched and listened as Mark Fribley set up the computer taken from the office of Tim Willis.

"Mr. Lamont, I'm not going to be able to set this computer up over here in the witness stand. There's no screen or keyboard. Won't do any good to have the box running with no screen and no keyboard," Mark said.

Lamont responded from the counsel table, "What do you suggest? Can we get a monitor and keyboard or what?"

"I can use the clerk's monitor and keyboard sir. If she won't be using hers during court."

Looking at the clerk, Lamont now asked, "What do you say, Mary? Can we use your monitor and keyboard or do you need to be up and running during court?"

"I'm usually on line with the main office during court, but I don't have to be today. This is the only case, so it isn't essential that I'm up and running. The problem is that my keyboard is screwed down to the keyboard shelf and the base of the monitor is attached to the table."

Mark now put in, "That's okay. I can just disconnect the box and hook in this box. I don't have to move anything, but I'll have to be over there when I show you or the judge what is on the computer."

Lamont shrugged and said, "Okay. The judge will go along with that. He doesn't care where you are when you testify. This is just a preliminary hearing anyway. At trial though we will have to have a separate keyboard and monitor. Okay, set it up. With Mary's permission?" he ended with a question to Mary.

"Sure, okay," Mary said, as she moved out of the clerk's cubicle to make room for Mark.

Mary watched closely as Mark rearranged the desk to make room for the extra computer box.

"I'll have to shut your computer down and disconnect it so that I can hook in this one. Okay?" Mark asked.

"Yeah, I guess, but make sure you don't mess me up. I want to be able to get back on line with the main office as soon as you're done. You won't mess up the network will you?"

Mark smiled at her limited understanding of computers and responded easily, "No chance. When I'm done, I'll restart your computer myself just to be sure you are back on the network. Okay?"

"Well, I'm not sure. I mean, if you disconnect me, won't I lose the network for good?" she responded with concern.

A real novice when it comes to computers, Mark thought then said, "Guaranteed. I'll show you." At that he flipped off the power switch on the computer box and unplugged the data cable along with the power cable.

"Okay, now I'll hook them back up and restart it, just to show you that there is nothing lost," he ended, plugged the data and power cord back in and rebooted the computer.

The screen lit up and the computer box hummed, making soft clicking noises as the system powered up. Finally the network information came up showing each station on the net as it was read by the computer and aligned into the system.

Mark read each line of information as it came up to make sure the computer was responding correctly and that the data shown was as it should be. Almost all networks came up the same so he would have a pretty good idea if this one was not coming up correctly. Of course, he knew it would, there was absolutely nothing that could be affected by disconnecting the cables. Yet, something didn't look consistent, and he asked, "How many stations are on this net?"

"Huh?" Mary asked.

"How many server units, you know, other computers like this one in court?"

Mary furrowed her brow and contemplated for a couple of minutes. Finally, she answered, "Seven."

"You're sure?"

"Yes. This one, one in courtroom 'A' and five in the clerk's main office. Why?"

"Because it looks like you have eight on the net. Wait and I'll show you." With that said, he flipped off the computer again, rebooted it and when it reached the server 'sign on' screen he paused the computer, pointing and saying, "See there. Eight, but one appears to be a duplicate. At least that's what it looks like at first, but it isn't.

See there," still pointing, "number one server is on there twice, but with a different spelling of 'server' each time. The first number one server is spelled without the last 'e' and the second number one is spelled correctly."

"So?" Mary asked, clearly puzzled.

"So you have eight servers where you are only supposed to have seven. Who set this system up for you?"

"Can't remember his name. He works at TTM, too."

"Barry Moran?" Mark now asked.

"Yes, that's it," Mary answered.

"Well, either he can't spell or he can't count, because you have one too many servers on this network."

"Is that bad?" Mary asked.

"Not for the net, no. This net can probably handle twelve servers, but the real question is where is the extra server? You say there are only seven on the net and I say there are eight. Where is that extra server and what is it doing on the net?"

Both Lamont and Todd were standing at Mark's elbow now, all ears. They had both heard enough of this conversation to arouse their interest, especially since they were both aware of problems with the clerk's computer system and the county money.

Lamont spoke first. "Mr. Fribley, are you sure that the extra server is active? I mean, couldn't it just be an erroneous message on the start up?"

"It could, but it isn't. All servers are responding when the main frame queries them. A dummy server or an error message wouldn't respond. The main frame wouldn't even bother to query it, because the command to query it wouldn't even be in the main frame's program. Sorry, sir, but it's no mistake, you've got an unaccounted for server on this net and if I was at the mill, I'd be real worried about a security breach."

Todd now put in, "Security breach? Like how?"

"Like someone has tapped into your system and hooked himself up a server. He can do anything you can do, at anytime you can do it."

Lamont now interjected, "Mr. Fribley, what if I told you we have been having problems in the clerk's office? How about I told you that bonds were being increased or decreased without paperwork to support the changes? Fines paid, but insufficient money in the bank to support the payments? Would that tell you anything?"

"Yes, sir. You got yourself a first class computer tampering case here. That's why 'server' is spelled wrong on the number one server position. That's why the number one is used twice as a server identification. To a casual observer it wouldn't be noticed. The highest server number is still 'seven' and without close examination everything looks normal."

Todd, always the investigator asked, "Can you locate that extra server?"

"Maybe."

"Will you try?" Todd asked.

"Sure, but you have to understand that it is a physical search. No way the computer can tell us where the physical location of that or any server is. Computers don't care about physical location, they only care about connections and data transmissions."

"Okay, Mr. Fribley. When would you have time to try this physical approach and where do you start?" Paul Lamont now asked.

"Soon as court is over, I guess. I'm off all afternoon because of this court thing. I do have a date tonight though, and I'm not going to miss that."

With knowing smiles, both Paul and Todd nodded in the affirmative. Couldn't ask a single young man to miss a date.

~ * ~

Tommy was silent as a stone all the way to Bushville. Charlie didn't try to drag him into a conversation, he figured Tommy was sorting out the jumbled years of his life and needed solitude.

What Tommy was really doing was replaying the night of the fire over and over in his mind. Every detail was as clear as if it had happened yesterday. He wanted it that clear when and if he found his old man.

Patty hadn't had any address, just that she had heard he was near Bushville. It wasn't such a big place, but big enough. The city limit sign said Bushville had a population of fifteen thousand and that was a big enough haystack for this needle.

"If he's here, then someone will know of him," Tommy said, speaking for the first time since leaving Johnson City. "The old man was always well known wherever he went. Mostly by people anxious to avoid him. He was trouble with a capital 'T', always was and probably still is. He's an evil man, Mr. Chambers, as evil a man as you'll ever likely see."

Charlie couldn't remain silent any longer and said, "From the perspective of a fourteen year old who left home, yes, but what about from your perspective now? You don't know him now. Maybe he's changed, or maybe he'll look differently now."

"How could any man involved in the murder of a hundred people look different?" Tommy asked.

"Time has a way of changing people. You might be surprised."

"For two cents, I'd turn around and leave right now. I never wanted to lay eyes on him again. I hope we don't find him, or if we do, we find him dead."

"What about that speech about the screams you've lived with for thirty-five years?"

"I've lived with them for this long, I could live with them some more. I'd rather live with those memories than come face to face with the devil."

Charlie said no more. He was half-afraid that if the conversation continued, Tommy would want to turn back. He guessed he couldn't really blame him. What a dismal life he had lived, on account of the way his father had treated him. Who would want to confront the cause of a ruined life? What good would it do? It certainly couldn't bring back Tommy's life, and it couldn't bring back any of those lost souls on Burning Chapel Hill. No, those souls weren't lost, that was the one sure thing about this whole affair. *Maybe that was the only important thing*, he decided. *What good was justice on earth to people whose souls were already in heaven?*

"Stop at the police station," Tommy said. "If anyone knows about my old man, they will."

That made sense to Charlie. Now all he had to do was locate the police station.

As it turned out, the police station was on the main drag and they drove right to it without even trying to find it. It was a small affair, but not a small town station. Probably quite a few policemen were employed in this town, Charlie mused on the way inside. He only hoped that the town was still small enough that the cops would know most of the people by name. After all, this wasn't New York City.

The station house was old and laid out just like the old precinct houses in the big cities. Inside the double doors was a large assembly area that had chairs along the walls and a massive elevated desk straight ahead. This was obviously the desk sergeant's desk, no receptionist, no information window, just the desk sergeant.

Charlie led the way up to the desk as the man in uniform peered over the top and watched them approach.

"What can I do for you, gentlemen?" a police sergeant asked, seated behind the desk, but high enough to look over at the two men standing before him. The desk reminded Charlie of being in court with a judge, looking over a massive desk at him standing below. The scene was also reminiscent of the old time police movies containing all Irish cops. This desk sergeant definitely spoke with an Irish brogue, even though it was watered down with a southern accent.

"My name is Charles Chambers. I'm an attorney and this is Tommy Trenton. I represent Mr. Trenton and we are trying to locate his father. We were hoping you might be able to give us some information."

"How long's he been missing?" the desk sergeant said and reached for a pad of paper on which to take notes.

Charlie put in hurriedly, "No, you don't understand. He isn't missing. We just want to locate him."

The sergeant furrowed his brow and, with a half scowl, responded dryly, "Being missing in my book is when you can't be located, but you say he isn't missing. You aren't making much sense to me."

Charlie smiled at the humor of the situation and how it must have sounded to the sergeant. He had to admit it didn't make much sense the way he had put it. He tried again, "He isn't a missing person. It's just that Mr. Trenton hasn't had any contact with him for many years. A long time ago they had a falling out and haven't communicated since. We heard from Mr. Trenton's sister that he might be in this area, but she hadn't seen him for years either."

The sergeant raised his eyebrows, rolled his eyes and with the sarcasm that only years of being a cop can create, he said, "Real close family there, huh?"

Charlie smiled again and let that pass. "His name is Herman Trenton. He's about seventy years old by now. What type of build, Tommy?" he finished, looking at Tommy.

For the first time, Tommy spoke, saying, "Medium height, slim, about a hundred fifty pounds. He had dark brown hair last time I saw him, but that was thirty-five years ago."

The sergeant's mouth fell open and he shook his head from side to side in amazement. Finally, he said, "This is some kind of a joke, right? I mean you guys are puttin' me on, aren't you? How am I supposed to help you locate a guy with a description dating back to the sixties?"

Charlie admitted, "It's a long shot, we know."

"Long shot! Mister this ain't no long shot, it's a moon shot. I'd have better luck walking out that front door and yelling for him to come home for supper!"

Both Charlie and Tommy looked at each other and nodded their assent. There had to be another way, maybe the phone book or something. As they turned to leave, a thought struck Charlie and he turned back. "You record the addresses of people on probation don't you?"

"If they are in our area and are being serviced by the county probation department, yes. You telling me this guy's a felon and he's on probation? You haven't seen him for thirty-five years. How do you know that?"

Charlie answered, "I'm not saying he is or isn't. He might be. If he is, then your records would show it, and if they don't, then we'll try something else. Could you check?"

Hesitating, the sergeant finally said, "I suppose that information is kind of public, but it's sort of confidential, too."

"We'd appreciate it," Tommy now said.

Hesitating yet another moment, the sergeant stared at Tommy and said, "Okay." Then he turned to a computer on his desk and asked, "Trenton, T-r-e-n-t-o-n, Herman. Any middle initial?"

"I," Tommy responded.

The Sergeant finished typing in the name and asked, "Date of birth?"

Tommy answered quietly, "No, sir. Sorry, we weren't close."

Smiling without humor, the sergeant said, "Oh, that's okay. I don't really need any information. I just ask those questions to pass the time."

Tommy and Charlie said nothing, as the sergeant turned back to the screen and waited.

"Woah! Herman I. Trenton, born May 12, 1927, address 1134 N. Bowser Avenue, Bushville. Man oh man, has he ever been a bad boy. Just got out of the slam last year. Did ten out of fifteen for aggravated burglary and is on intensive court probation until 2001. That ain't all either. His rap sheet is two and a half pages long, in summary. This guy's spent more time on the inside than on the outside for the last thirty years. I'm surprised he wasn't put away for life as a habitual criminal. This can't be the guy you're looking for. About the right age, though."

Tommy answered calmly, "That has to be him. Sounds just like him. I'm surprised someone hasn't shot him by this time."

The sergeant just peered down over his desk and made no response, but his eyes spoke volumes.

Charlie now asked, "What was that address again?"

The desk sergeant repeated it and added, "You didn't hear that from me."

"Yes, sir," Charlie said, and added, "Thanks for nothing, Sergeant."

"You bet," the sergeant said as they walked toward the door.

Charlie hadn't bothered to ask the sergeant where Bowser Avenue was, because he had noticed the street on the edge of town as they drove in on the main street. Even if he hadn't known where it was, he wouldn't have pressed his luck with the sergeant.

Tommy was extremely sullen as they drove back through town to Bowser Avenue. Charlie turned north on Bowser Avenue and scanned the house numbers. They were only in the two hundred block, so he concentrated on his driving for a while. Neither spoke a word as the blocks ticked off and in the eight hundred block the area started to deteriorate rapidly. By the time the eleven hundred block rolled around, the houses were nothing but shacks with trash strewn front yards.

Eleven thirty-four was on the right-hand side and Charlie eased the car over to the curb. It was evident that this was the poor side of Bushville, and a rough side at that. A man sat on the front porch eyeing them as the car came to a stop. Charlie held his seat as Tommy stared at the old man on the porch and eased his door open, saying, "Might be best if you stayed here."

"You might want a witness if he does say anything. If it really is him," Charlie said.

"It's him. My old man always was the meanest looking thing on two legs a man ever did lay eyes on. It's him all right. He won't talk if you're there. I know him that well. He's a cagey old coot, always was."

Charlie didn't respond, he just watched as Tommy got out of the car and made his way up the broken sidewalk to the porch.

~ * ~

The old man watched him come with disinterest. He'd checked in with his probation officer just last Monday. *Wonder what they want now*, he thought and then he decided this guy didn't look like a cop. His clothes were too rumpled and old. Cops liked to impress people and this guy didn't look like he would impress a rat if he were a pound of cheese.

Then again, maybe someone else sent these people. The deaths of those Johnson City residents of recent past, crept into the old man's memory now. He fidgeted in his chair and began to glance nervously around. A feeling of dread and fear swept over him and he began to wonder if it wasn't his turn. By then the stranger was mounting his porch.

~ * ~

"You a huntin' something, mister?" Herman Trenton said with caution.

"Yeah, you," Tommy responded dryly as he made it to the porch and leaned against a post.

"You found me," the old man said and glanced furtively around, his gaze ending on the car and the lone man left sitting inside.

"You're Herman Trenton aren't you? Used to live over in Johnson City about thirty years ago."

Something was familiar about this guy and Herman's mind was reaching back to who he might be, and why he might want him. Herman knew a lot of people would like to have a piece of him. One in particular, and his dread increased. Finally, he asked cautiously, "So what if I am?"

"My name is Tommy. Tommy Trenton."

The old man was stunned into silence. After a moment, very cautiously, he asked, "How do I know that?"

"You know. I'm your kid, all right. But, I'm not a kid anymore."

The old man was silent a minute longer then responded dryly, "No, you ain't." And with disinterest bordering on boredom, he asked, "What can I do for you?"

"Come to get some information."

"I'm no information booth," the old man said with disdain.

"Never-the-less that's why I'm here, and the information I want, you have."

"Humph."

"Thirty-five years ago on May 12, 1962, on your birthday, you and some others burned down a church over in Johnson City. A whole lot of people died in that fire. I saw you do it and now I want to know who was with you," Tommy said evenly.

The old man's face turned ashen. He was scared. It took a lot to scare Herman Trenton after all he'd seen, but he was scared now. Maybe this was judgment day, after all.

Tommy was amazed to see fear in the old man's eyes. He had seen a lot of things in his father's eyes over the few years he had known him, but never fear. He was strangely sorry for the old man, but it was only a fleeting feeling. This was the man who, with others, had burned a hundred people to death thirty-five years ago.

"Leave me alone. I can't hurt you no more," the old man croaked and started to rise from his chair.

"Sit down!" Tommy rapped out, and the old man dropped as if hit by an axe handle.

"I watched you help kill a hundred people and I said nothing. Nothing for thirty-five years, but that's over now. Now, I want to know the truth. I want to know who was with you and I want you to tell it to the world!"

More calmly, he continued, "Look at yourself. You've spent your life taking and taking and taking. You've ruined more than your own life. You ruined Patty's life, mother's life and who knows how many other lives, not even counting the one hundred black people you fried in that church. In a church! Do you understand that? A church! It's time you gave something back! You can't take and take in this world, not forever. Comes a time when you're called on to give something back, and now's the time. I'm calling and so are all those dead black people and their families. Pay up, old man, you've had your ride," Tommy ended bitterly.

The old man didn't even ask how Tommy had seen what he had said; it didn't matter to him. "And if I don't? What are you going to do, kill me?" the old man responded with a sneer.

Tommy shook his head in the negative and calmly responded, "I don't have to kill you. You're already dead. You killed yourself years ago. You've never been anything and you never will. I'm offering you a chance to do something right for once in your life. You take it or leave it. I don't much care which."

"I can't leave the county. I'm on probation, you fool."

Tommy laughed with genuine mirth and said, "Who are you trying to kid? I'm offering you a chance to go back to Johnson City and confess to murdering a hundred people. If they don't fry you in 'old sparky', they'll never let you out of jail again. Do you think jumping probation is going to amount to a hill of beans? You're nuts, old man, nuts!"

The old man sat defiant, staring at Tommy for several minutes and just when Tommy was about to turn and leave forever, he noticed the old man's eyes looked moist. As he watched in rapt attention a single tear rolled down the old man's left cheek, and he choked out, "I... never... mea... meant to hurt... nobody. It was my... birthday and I was drunk. I... met up with some other guys at a local tavern. We started bad mouthing the Negroes and how they was getting too uppity for their own good. Next thing I knowed we was up at that church with a can of kerosene each, and a hand full of matches. I'm sorry as I can be. I've done a lot of rotten things in my life, but I really never meant no harm to those people. I was drunk I tell you, drunk!"

Tommy sighed and responded calmly, "I don't care what caused you to do it, you did it and it's time to fess up. It's time you told the world who was with you so that the families of those people can have some justice. Not that it's going to bring any of them back, but the families deserve to know."

The old man looked deeply into Tommy's eyes, his own eyes still shedding tears, and he said, "I done some bad things in my life. Been thinking of them lately. Ain't got much else to think about on this old porch, all alone. When a man gets old his life sort of catches up with him. He starts to realize what he did and didn't do with what he had."

In genuine remorse that surprised Tommy yet again, the old man asked, "Can you forgive me, Tommy? For what I did to you and to Patty. Can you forgive me?"

Tommy hesitated for a long time, the years of bitterness welled up inside of him and the disdain he felt for this man was apparent in his tone, "I should say yes, but I can't, not now. Maybe later I'll feel differently, but not now. I'm a Christian, no thanks to you, and I know I should forgive anyone who asks me, but I just can't do it. Not yet. I'm only human. In time, maybe I can forgive you. I'll try, but even at that, I will never forget, never."

"I guess I don't deserve more," the old man said quietly.

"You don't deserve anything," Tommy said icily.

~ * ~

Carol was reclining on the sofa in the living room flipping nonchalantly through a magazine waiting for Dan to appear. She didn't have long to wait; she knew she wouldn't. Dan always went to town about this time of day; he liked to hang out in one particular bar.

"Going to town, Carol. You need anything?"

"No, thanks. Call Paul, I'm sure he'll be glad to drive you in."

"Now why would I want Paul to drive me anywhere?" he answered irritably, he was still steamed at Carol and her new attitude of independence.

"Probably because there's no other way to get anywhere."

"What are you talking about? I'll take the 'Vette. I'm quite capable of driving my car."

"What car, Dan?" Carol said flatly and continued, "That 'Vette is, was in my name and the insurance, too."

"Was?"

"That's right, was. I sold it this morning to a dealer in town. He gave me a good price and I didn't need the car, Paul takes me wherever I need to go."

"You what!! That was my car, you had no right to sell it!"

"No, actually it was my car, Dan, and I had no trouble at all selling it. Like I said, I didn't need it anymore," she answered sweetly.

"But, I always drove it, it was my transportation. It was part of our deal."

"No, I looked over our contract last night. There's nothing in there about you having a car supplied by me, and now you don't. If you want a car then you take some of your money that I earn for you and you buy one, don't forget to insure it, too," she ended harshly.

"But that 'Vette was a classic, one of a kind, I'll never find another like it."

"Go buy it from the dealer if you liked it so much! I'm sure he'll be glad to sell it to you and make a nice profit. I'll give you the dealer's name if you're interested."

Dan spun on his heels and headed back toward his own wing of the house.

Before he had taken six steps, Carol's voice arrested his movement, "Dan!"

Turning back quickly with a hateful expression on his face, he looked at her and said hotly, "What!"

"You interfere with me and Charles Chambers again, like tossing flowers in the garbage or anything else, and that car won't be the only thing you'll lose. I may have to keep you as my manager, I may have to pay you, but I don't have to like it and I don't have to treat you nicely. You'll find yourself sleeping out under the stars the next time I hear about any interference from you, and that will only be the beginning."

Dan said nothing, he just swallowed hard and his eyes were hot with anger.

"Do you understand me, Dan?" Carol said firmly and when no response was made she said again, "Dan. I asked if you understood me!"

Weakly, Dan croaked out, "Yes."

"Good, now run along to your end of the house while you still can," Carol ended with disdain in her voice.

Dan left and while he was leaving he was thinking, *this isn't over yet, I've a few tricks you don't know about. And as for Mr. Chambers, I'm going to take care of him.*

Twenty-four

The drive back to Johnson City was tense for Charlie. No one spoke even one word and it seemed like an eternity before the Johnson City lights appeared. It was well after dark when he turned his car down the main street.

Finally, he could hold his silence no more. He had to know their exact destination, "Where to Tommy?"

"Sheriff's department. Mr. Herman Trenton has a few things to say to them. Right, Mr. Trenton?"

Tommy could not bring himself to say 'dad' or 'father' since it was in his mind that those labels denoted familiarity and he was certainly not familiar with this man. Respect didn't even enter into the equation; he had none for this man. Perhaps someday he could forgive him for what he had done, but as he had told him, he knew he could never forget.

From the confines of the back seat came a barely audible, "Yes."

Charlie glanced at his watch and was amazed to see that it was far past suppertime. He hadn't even noticed missing supper, or lunch for that matter, but all of a sudden he was ravenously hungry. He doubted he would get the chance to eat for awhile yet.

~ * ~

Todd had missed supper, too. He was finishing the reports on his latest effort to question employees at TTM. For the past couple of hours he had been interviewing people who worked at the mill in an attempt to discover why Willis had worked so hard to frame Tommy

Trenton for theft. As near as he had been able to determine, either no one had any information or they were unwilling to cooperate. Considering the fact that he was dealing with TTM, he suspected the latter was most probably the case. Talking with Willis had gotten him nowhere. Willis wouldn't talk without his lawyer and that lawyer was the general counsel for TTM, so it was a given what kind of advice he was giving his client. Todd had hoped that Willis' arrest would loosen some tongues, but it had had the opposite effect. If something was being hidden up there, and he was sure there was, then it was high up.

Actually, he wanted to be at the clerk's office with Fribley and Lamont, but the state's attorney didn't want him in on it just yet. Too bad, this computer scheme had him intrigued, but he could see the state's attorney's point of view. It wasn't really a case for the sheriff's department, not yet.

The intercom on Todd's phone buzzed, breaking his concentration and he punched the hands-free button, saying, "Sergeant Evans."

"Sergeant Evans, there is an attorney by the name of Charles Chambers here to see you, along with two other men, both by the name of Trenton, I believe."

"No fooling!" Todd exclaimed at the phone and continued, "I'm on my way, Sherry."

His heart was racing as he rapidly made his way down the hallway and out to the reception area. He realized this could be the break he had always prayed for in the Burning Chapel case. Stepping through the door to the reception area, he recognized Chambers and Tommy immediately. The other man, older by many years and tattered in appearance, he figured must be Tommy's father. *I wonder how he got him to come in here?* he asked himself. Stopping just short of the group, he said in a pretended nonchalance, "Evening, gentlemen. What can I do for you?"

Tommy spoke calmly and evenly, "Sergeant Evans, this is Herman Trenton. He has a story to tell you about a fire thirty-five years ago up on Burning Chapel Hill."

Todd looked at the old man whose eyes were dull and lifeless and asked, "Is that correct Mr. Trenton? Do you want to talk to me?"

The old man spoke strongly and bitterly, "No, but I will. Don't like cops, never have, but I'll talk to you. Tommy here says it's time I talked," he finished nodding toward Tommy.

Cautiously, Todd answered, "Okay. Come with me. We'll use the conference room down the hall. There was no conference room down the hall, but Todd didn't want to call it an interrogation room. He was afraid this guy might spring for the door given the slightest reason.

Todd opened the door, after Sherry pushed the button releasing the lock electronically, and the three men followed him down the hall. Todd ushered them into the room and offered them seats all around the rectangular table. Not long before, this same table had accommodated himself and Willis. He hoped this meeting would reveal more than the last one.

After taking their seats, Todd began, "Mr. Trenton, your son tells me you know something about a fire thirty-five years ago, on what is now known as Burning Chapel Hill. Is that correct?"

With a scowl evident on his face, the old man replied, a bite in his tone, "Don't got no son. Ain't had one for a long time and, yeah, I know a little something about that fire."

Todd was surprised by this man's brazen statement about having no son, even though his son sat silently across the table. Refusing to be deterred from his task though, he shook off the man's statement and his mean-spirited attitude, asking, "Okay. What about that fire?"

The old man looked at Tommy now, not with a questioning look or one asking permission to speak, but with a look of contempt for his having put him in such a position. He was being forced to confess to a crime he knew would rob him of his freedom for the rest of his life. What the force was, he couldn't clearly identify, but it was present. Finally, he shifted his gaze back to Todd and said, "I started it, me and some others."

Todd was all business now, and he immediately put in, "In that case, Mr. Trenton, I am placing you under arrest for arson and murder. It is my duty to inform you of your rights. You have the right to remain silent. If you give up your right to remain silent, anything you say, can and will be used against you in a court of law. You have the right to have an attorney present with you during questioning. If you cannot afford an attorney one will be provided for you without cost to you. Do you understand your rights as I have explained them to you?"

"Yeah."

"Do you wish to have an attorney present during questioning?"

"No."

"Do you wish to make a statement and answer questions?"

Sighing heavily, the old man said, "Yes."

"Very well, Mr. Trenton," Todd continued as he slid a form toward Herman, "this is a waiver of your rights, you need to initial by each line, date and sign the form at the bottom."

When the form was completed, Todd examined it and looking now at Charlie Chambers, Todd asked, "Mr. Chambers, am I correct in assuming that you do not represent Herman Trenton?"

Charlie's deadpan response was, "Correct, Sergeant Evans."

"Very well," Todd responded, in a very business like manner and continued, "Now, Mr. Trenton, tell me about Corey Merriman and his part in all of this."

The old man had a confused look on his face, as he responded, "Mister, I think you must be smoking funny weed. I come here to tell you about a fire up at that there Little Flock Baptist church in 1962, not no fairy tale about some guy you dreamed up."

Todd was stopped cold and, after some hesitation, asked, "You mean to tell me Corey Merriman didn't have anything to do with that fire?"

With a nasty scowl, the old man replied, "Mister, I'm telling you I came here to talk about a fire, but I don't know no Merriman and if that's what you want, then I'm done talking."

Todd shot back, "No. I want to hear about the fire. I guess I just had some wrong information about who was involved. You said you and some others started the fire. Who were the others?"

"I ain't all so sure," he replied and Todd's heart sank again. *Another dead end*, he thought.

The old man continued, "I mean, I knowed them, back then, but only met them that once. I know there was no Merriman," he said adamantly, trying to make the point that he wasn't recanting what he had said earlier, then continued, "There was six counting me. I ran into them in a bar in Johnson City and it come upon us to burn out some blacks. One guy said he knowed of a good place to find a bunch of them. Up at the Little Flock Baptist Church, he says. 'Having 'em a get together tonight.' So we grabbed us up some number two kerosene, some rags and sticks and headed up that way. Wasn't long we had a nice fire a going up there. Heard tell later there was a hundred of 'em in that there church." The old man was telling it like it had happened yesterday and with absolutely no emotion.

The lack of emotion shown by this old man shocked Tommy. It wasn't possible for him to bring himself to even think of this man as his father. He had known that the old man had helped to burn to death a hundred blacks, but it had always been an abstract to him. Though he had seen it, he had never heard the old man speak of it and now that he had, and with such a lack of emotion, Tommy wondered if the old man was really ready for forgiveness. It seemed to him that the old man was totally lacking repentance and without repentance there could be no forgiveness. Tommy had preached that most of his life. He knew that principle very well. Yet this was the same man who had shed tears on the front porch of a run down shack in Bushville this very day. It was almost incomprehensible to him that anyone could change so much in so little time. Perhaps the tears had just been part of an act. The old man had always been a good actor.

Todd was also astounded at the coldness of the tale. Though he had investigated this crime for years, it had never really occurred to him that the men who did this terrible deed would be so cold and calculated. Deep down inside, he knew that cold and calculating people generally committed such crimes, but for some reason he had not associated that mental state with this crime. He reasoned that, in this particular case, the people committing this crime had to have had some deep emotional reason.

Apparently, he had been as wrong about that as about Merriman. Todd had been certain he had been involved. If he hadn't, then what was the reason for the payments? Had he been wrong about them, too? Couldn't have been, the payments coincided too closely with the dates of his life, but if Merriman had not been involved in the fire, then why the payments? This case was continually getting worse instead of better. Each time he thought he had uncovered a major clue it turned out to be another wall.

"So you don't remember the names of any of the others who were with you that night?" Todd asked.

"Didn't say that," Herman responded, decisively and antagonistically.

A thought struck Charlie, at the same time that it struck Tommy. Todd was a black cop and he was questioning an old white man who was raised in a different time period. Questioning him about the murder of blacks. The old man was naturally being overly antagonistic. To this old man, Todd was no different from the people he had helped to murder. He was an uppity black who didn't know his place. Tommy looked at Charlie and they seemed to communicate the thought without a word. The realization of what was happening and the communication of it to each other took only seconds. Before Todd could respond to the antagonistic remark, Charlie interrupted, "Sergeant Evans, could I speak to you for a minute? Outside?"

Todd was more than a little irritated at having his interrogation interrupted, but he owed these people something. But for them he would be no closer to solving these murders than he had in the last twenty years. Finally, he grunted, "Okay."

Looking steadily at Herman Trenton, Todd said, "You sit tight. I can see you through the window even though you can't see me."

Herman made no response, he just sneered as Todd disappeared out the door with Charlie. Tommy said nothing as they sat there alone. Herman didn't seem to be in the mood to talk.

Outside the room, Charlie was giving his opinion to Todd, "I think you might want your partner in on this one. I have a distinct feeling that this man isn't going to open up to you. I think he knows something, but he isn't going to tell you."

Defensively Todd answered, "What can Sam do that I can't!"

"Don't you see it?" Charlie asked, then continued when he got a defiant look from Todd. "That old man in there hates blacks so much he helped to kill a hundred of them. You're black, Todd! He sees in you what he destroyed in that old church so many years ago. He was drunk, sure, but that wasn't his only reason for what he did. He's one of the old school whites who were raised to hate blacks and treat them as less than human. Now you sit in there, a black cop and question him about the murders of blacks."

"Shouldn't make any difference," Todd responded stubbornly.

"You're right, it shouldn't. With most people it doesn't, not anymore. But, not with that man. He never learned that there isn't any difference. Equality to him is white. Blacks don't even enter into the picture. You need your partner in here, Todd, or someone like him."

"White like him, you mean."

"Yes! But not because of me." Gesturing with his thumb back toward the table that was visible through the viewing window, he ended, "Because of him and people like him. There are times to stand up and say, 'It doesn't make any difference. I'm not going to let you change the course of events by your bigotry', and there are times to back off. This is a time to back off, Todd. That bigoted old white man in there has something you want and something that justice demands. He has information and maybe, just maybe, some names. But he isn't going to give them to you, or any other black."

Todd was furious. Not at Charlie, but at a world that allowed attitudes like the one that old man harbored to exist. He was also frustrated. For years he had pounded on this case to get a break and now that he had one, he had to hand it to someone else.

Nodding resignedly, he finally admitted, "Okay. I see your point. I'll call Sam. It may take him a while to get here. We need to keep this guy loosened up while we wait. I don't want to slap him in a cell. I don't want to give him a chance to decide he doesn't want to talk to anyone."

Charlie responded, "I'll talk to him, just casually. Maybe Tommy and I can carry on a conversation or two and keep his mind off of the fire until you get your partner in here."

They did just that. Charlie talked and Tommy responded in kind. It was nothing, but it was something. They talked about the days Tommy had spent on the streets and the nights he had spent up at the mill. Not noticed by either of them was a softening in the old man's eyes when the conversation turned to what life for Tommy had been like at fifteen, with no car, no job and no future.

Todd was listening, too, from the viewing room, although he had stopped the tape recorder. It opened his eyes a little, too. He knew Tommy had lived a rough life, but hearing it told in the first person was different. There was a realism to it not felt before. He was listening intently when the intercom buzzed on the phone next to the little desk in the viewing room. "Evans," he announced as he picked up the receiver.

"What are you dragging me in here for at this time of night, Todd?" the voice of Sam Pinehurst bellowed.

"Got an old white guy in the interrogation room who may know something about the fire."

"What fire?" Sam responded. He thought he had missed something that happened earlier in the day.

"The fire at the Little Flock Baptist Church. You know up on Burning Chapel Hill."

"Oh, that fire. You still on that? When you going to give it up, Todd? You'll never find anyone who knows anything about that fire. The trail's too cold."

"This guy might," Todd persisted. "He won't talk to me though. He won't open up to a black. Give him a try will you, Sam? This is important."

Sighing audibly, Sam responded, "Okay, partner. For you I'll do it. Be just a second."

"Good. There's two other guys in there with him. One is that lawyer Charlie Chambers and his client. The guy I'm interested in is the oldest. You can't miss him."

"Rights?"

"Gave them to him and he waived."

"In writing?"

Todd answered, "Of course. I'm not just out of the academy."

"Okay, okay. You have to settle down, boy. Take this stuff more objectively," Sam chided him and thought to himself that he was probably the only person in the world who could call Todd, a cop with twenty years on the beat, a 'boy' and get away with it. The only reason he could, is because Todd knew he didn't mean any racial slur by it. It was, in fact, a term of endearment between partners. Black or white didn't enter in to it.

Sheepishly, Todd responded, "Yeah, you're right."

Todd waited eagerly for Sam's arrival and as he heard the door to the interrogation room open he flipped on the tape recorder.

Sam walked across the room to the table and eyed Chambers and his client, Tommy Trenton. Sam looked dispassionately at the old man and dropped into a chair.

The old man watched Sam carefully and studied his face. Suddenly the old man stood up, catching everyone by surprise and facing the viewing window, which he knew to be a one-way mirror, said loudly and viciously, "Boy, if you don't take the cake. You expect me to talk to a black about killing blacks and when I won't, you drag in a guy who helped me set the fires."

There was absolute silence in the room as what Herman Trenton just said registered. Sam looked hard at the old man and the blood could be seen draining visibly from his face. He sat stock still, as if turned to stone. Charlie's mind was spinning as he forced it to catch up to the events rapidly unfolding in this room.

Tommy said nothing, he just watched his old man standing there gloating at the mirror. Behind that mirror, Todd was the first to react. He grabbed up the phone and called the dispatcher. Two uniformed deputies were already in the building and in seconds they were on their way to the interrogation room.

Todd stepped out into the hall and entered the interrogation room just ahead of the uniformed deputies. No one asked what Herman had meant, they all knew. Sam wasn't denying anything. He just remained seated, not believing what was happening and studying the face of his accuser.

Todd came around the table and said, "Unless you've got a good explanation for what this man just said, Sam, you'd better stand up and hand over your gun real careful-like." The uniformed deputies didn't know what was going on. They had just been told of trouble in the interrogation room, not the nature of the trouble. All they could do was follow Todd's lead.

Sam looked from Herman to Todd and then to the deputies. Slowly, he stood up and pulled aside his coat to expose his nine millimeter automatic in a holster strapped to his side. Todd walked around the table and removed the gun from its holster.

Holding the gun, Todd looked at Herman and said harshly, "You're sure about this? This man was one of those who helped you start that church fire thirty-five years ago? Absolutely sure?"

"He's one all right. Still don't remember his name, but I seen his face before all right. I knowed him as soon as he sat down. Thought you was pulling something on me."

"You're under arrest for arson and murder, Sam," then looking at the deputies, he said, "Take him down and book him. Make sure you read him his rights." Reaching down and scooping up the forms on the table, he looked at Sam and continued, "Make sure if he waives any of his rights that you get it in writing. You can use these forms."

Once the deputies had Sam outside, Todd reached down, grabbed the straight-backed wooden chair Sam had been seated in and flung it across the room. The chair smashed against the far wall and broke into several pieces. Turning back with a fury he had known only a few times in his life, he said coldly to Herman Trenton, "You're going to wind up like that chair if you don't stop playing games. I'm a cop. You killed a lot of people. Forget black, forget white. I'm just a cop and now I want to hear what you know, or I'll see you put in the darkest cell we can find and you can rot for what's left of your miserable life. That's if they don't fry you first. Georgia still electrocutes people, you know. I witnessed an execution once. It was quite a sight, poor sap twitching and jerking, forever it seemed; and the smell, oh, what a smell. You'd look good strapped in 'old sparky', you surely would," he finished, with a sneer.

Herman said nothing and just when Charlie figured the whole deal was over, Herman said, "I know two other names."

Harshly, Todd said, "Spill it!"

"Walter's one of 'em."

"Walter what?" Todd spat out.

Arrogantly, Herman responded, "Walter F. Tieman, III. Put him in a cell to rot, if you can."

~ * ~

"I have to go now, Mr. Lamont. I'm going to be late for my date. There's nothing else I can do anyway. You need a phone expert now. That's out of my field.

"The server lines are all accounted for except the mystery server and it will be found at the end of that telephone line. The extra server line goes into that telephone junction box right where I showed you, but I don't have the equipment to isolate it from all the phone lines coming out. The phone company can do that for you, probably. What you are looking for is a line coming out that doesn't service a telephone. It can't or the telephone signal would interrupt the server's communication with the main frame."

"Okay, Mark, but tell me. Is this Barry Moran smart enough to have set this system up or did someone else do it?" Lamont asked as they left the clerk's office under the watchful eye of the guard.

"I'm not sure. Barry would like to think he is smart enough, and maybe he is, but I'm not convinced. Though, he would be the guy to have the access necessary to set this up. Could be it was him, but I'm not accusing anyone without proof.

"Just between you and me, though. Barry always was a little too ambitious for me. He does a lot of this computer networking on the side and I don't think it's beyond the realm of possibility that he would try to make an extra buck or two if he got the chance. Still, although he might be smart enough to handle the hardware and software side on this, I really doubt he has the kind of brains it would take to think this scheme up. Someone with a real knowledge of the court system or at least the clerk's office would have to be involved in this set up. You know what I mean?"

Paul nodded and responded, "Just what I was thinking. Thanks, Mark. I'll be in touch."

"Yes, sir. Goodnight."

Twenty-five

Todd's world had come crashing down on him yesterday evening and now he sat staring across his desk at the empty chair that Sam had occupied for as long as he could remember. Sam had been here long before Todd had started; he had been more than a partner. Sam had been a friend, a mentor, a guide through the early days when Todd was just a rookie investigator. Without Sam he wouldn't have developed the skills he had today. Now Sam was gone, by the hand of the very person he had so carefully molded into an investigator.

No, Todd told himself. *Sam was gone by his own hand. By a deed done before he was even a cop himself.* Thinking back across the years, it was hard for Todd to fathom how a man who had done such a horrible thing could himself become an instrument of justice. Just living with a crime such as he had committed would be hard enough, how he could also search out and apprehend men who had done similar things was incomprehensible. It had to be the ultimate in hypocrisy. Sam's whole life had been one continuous act of hypocrisy.

"Sergeant Evans?" came the voice from the doorway and arrested Todd's thoughts. He looked up to see Dan Mosley and Mark Fribley standing just inside the office door.

Mosley continued, "The receptionist said it would be okay to come on back and see you. Are we interrupting you?"

Wrenching his mind back to the present, Todd was struck by the contrast in the two men standing by his door. Dan Mosley was neatly dressed in a nice suit, his large frame was an imposing sight and his mannerisms spoke of comfort with his surroundings. On the other hand, Mark Fribley was tall and skinny. He was dressed in blue jeans and a flannel shirt. His large framed eyeglasses were his prominent feature.

There was another contrast, too. Mark Fribley had brought down Tim Willis, a key TTM executive, single-handed, with his mind alone and Dan Mosley, with all his investigative power, hadn't had the slightest notion of what Willis had been doing.

He wondered what brought these two to his office. It occurred to him that if anyone up at the mill was on opposite sides it should be these two. Mosley had everything to gain by maintaining the *status quo* up there and protecting the mill's key executives. Fribley concerned himself more with what was right, as opposed to what was stable and beneficial to his employment.

"What can I do for you?" Todd asked listlessly.

"We'd like to run something by you. It concerns Mr. Tieman and the fact that you already have him in custody."

Here it comes, Todd decided, *these two were teamed up to perform damage control for Tieman and TTM.* It had to come, he knew. A man like Tieman had a lot of power and it could be wielded from almost anywhere at anytime. Yet it didn't make sense that Fribley would be involved. He had brought Willis down and might be very helpful in clearing up the mess at the circuit clerk's office. *Wonder what happened to that*, he thought, then he turned his thoughts back to the two men standing just inside his office door. "Have a seat."

~ * ~

Phil Stellar sat in front of Paul Lamont's desk fiddling with the papers in his file and speaking rapidly. Charlie sat in another chair and listened. Lamont had invited him to attend this conference with Stellar, who was making a pitch on behalf of Walter Tieman. Charlie listened half-heartedly as Phil continued his rapid-fire monologue, "You've got nothing, Paul, nothing. Who is this clown anyway? I'll tell you who he is. He's a three-time loser of a drunk that's who he is. There isn't a jury in the state that would take his word that the sun will set in the west. On the other hand, you've got Walter F. Tieman, III, whose company makes this county and half the state tick. His company employs more people than all of the employers in Meridian County put together. His word is his bond. Who wouldn't believe him over a three-time felon who is in violation of his probation just being in this county? Paul, we need to nip this thing in the bud, it's already gone too far."

Lamont leaned back in his chair and interjected before Phil could get his breath and start up again, "What about Sam Pinehurst?"

Phil puffed himself up and shot back, "What about him? He hasn't made a peep since he was slammed and I'll wager he doesn't. He's a cop, or was, he knows the ropes. He knows the same thing I know. This degenerate's word isn't worth two cents. All Sam Pinehurst has to do is ride this one out. Besides, even if he did talk, he can't finger an innocent man and Walter is innocent. He's got a list of alibis longer than this Trenton's rap sheet. Walter is never going to take a fall for this trumped up murder charge."

Lamont leaned further back in his chair, propped his feet up on the corner of his desk and said calmly, "You may be right, Phil."

Charlie almost fell out of his chair. He couldn't believe he had just heard Lamont say that. He was about to jump into something that really wasn't any of his business when Paul continued, "But how about money laundering? How about wire fraud? How about federal bank fraud?"

Phil looked as if he had been struck by lightning and Charlie leaned forward in his chair so as to catch every word.

"What do you mean?" Phil found his voice and stammered, "What's that got to do with this?"

Lamont dropped his feet from the desk, smiled and leaned forward saying, "Nothing, Phil, absolutely nothing. But it just so happens that yesterday Sergeant Evans of the Meridian County Sheriff's Department had a visit from Dan Mosley and Mark Fribley. You know them. Mosley is head of security up there and Fribley is the computer nerd that brought Willis down.

"Well anyway, it seems that in the process of gathering the evidence on Willis and springing the Preacher, Fribley downloaded some extra data. At the time he didn't realize he had those extra files, or the significance of them, but later he got to looking at them and decided there might be more to them. He went to see Dan Mosley. It seems that he thought he had evidence of a breach of security up at TTM. He thought he had evidence that some outside party had tapped into TTM's network of computers and was playing with the accounting system, writing bogus checks on TTM and some other fictitious companies. Fribley is pretty good at figuring things like that out.

"To make a long story short, Dan Mosley put the thing together right quick. Sharp guy that Mosley, he figured out in no time that the breach wasn't from the outside, but the inside and it wasn't a breach at all. Tieman and a few of the key executives up there and at other TTM facilities had created their own little bonus plan at the expense of the stockholders. They had a system of invoicing expenses to other companies and when the checks were sent they went to PO boxes and other addresses around the state. All fictitious, just like the companies. The checks were run through accounts set up for these fictitious companies using false employer identification tax numbers and then dispersed back to the boys at TTM, in the form of consulting fees.

"The real rub came in when we discovered that none of this income to the fictitious companies was reported. Only one of the executives out of all who were paid consulting fees reported the income. Did I mention income tax evasion?" Paul said, with another smile, as Phil wilted in his chair. "That's not the whole story, but I gather you get the drift, Phil. Remember your history, Phil? Al Capone never did a day for his mob activities. He did all his time for tax evasion. They couldn't prove his mob activities, but income tax evasion was just as good, even better. That's federal time, Phil, big stuff."

Leaning even further forward, Lamont asked in a placating tone, "That about cover what you wanted to talk about, Phil?"

Stellar didn't respond. He was as flat as a football that had been left out in the cold for too long. He just gathered up his file, stuffed it in his briefcase and left the office. His fine job on the hill was over. If

Tieman was done, along with most of the other executives, then so was he. No one would believe he hadn't had some inkling of what was going on. He wouldn't be charged, but he wouldn't be rehired either. The Board of Directors, after they had elected a new chairman, would make short work of Phil Stellar.

After the door closed, Paul looked at Charlie, winked and said, "I enjoyed that. Phil Stellar, with his obnoxious attitude, has been asking for that for years."

Charlie nodded and said, "Maybe so, but I'd rather have not seen it. I gave up chopping people off at the knees long ago. I prefer to let them fall by their own hand, not mine."

The reproach was gentle, but the point struck home and Paul was a big enough man to admit it, "You're right, Charlie. I guess I shouldn't have enjoyed that quite so much. He was on his way down anyway. I needn't have rubbed his face in it so hard."

Changing the subject, Charlie now asked, "You really think Tieman will skate on the murder?"

Contemplating before he responded, he answered, "Yes. I mean he won't go down for murder, but he's already given us what we need to solve the case. When Evans brought this money laundering to my attention, I sent him in to interrogate Tieman and sound him out for a deal on the murder. Tieman told him all about the fire in return for not being prosecuted. Of course, Evans didn't tell him we had him locked up three ways to Sunday with tax evasion and money laundering. Just like Capone, he won't serve a day for murder, but he'll die in prison, serving his time on tax evasion and money laundering convictions. I've already talked to the feds and they are waiting with bated breath to get hold of this one."

"What did he tell you about the fire?" Charlie asked earnestly.

"It was just like old man Trenton told it. Pinehurst, Trenton, Tieman and three others. Two of whom are dead and another who is not long to be free, but I can't name him yet. They went up there with the premeditated intent to kill those people. No one came around to investigate until the trail was so cold it was no use. It's sad, but that's the way the system worked down here in the south at the time, and for a good many years after the fire. Too many years, I'm sorry to admit.

It's different now, but it won't bring back those people. Neither will catching their murderers. But at least we can say we did it. Better late than never."

Charlie asked, "Merriman, he wasn't there?"

"Nope. It was just like Trenton told it."

"Then where did Merriman come in?" Charlie was puzzled.

"He was the bookkeeper for Tieman. On the side that is. He kept track of all bonus payments, invoice by invoice. Tieman wanted a record just in case someone got out of line. He planned to use it as a lever to shape them up."

"Then the payments that Evans tracked weren't really made to his uncle like he thought, that money came from somewhere else?"

"No, it came from Merriman. That was before the bonus plan started. That's why Merriman was trusted by Tieman to keep the books on the plan. He had been Tieman's bag man for Evan's uncle."

Charlie's mouth dropped open now and he said, "Tieman paid the money. Why?"

"Guilty conscience. Evans told me you had a hunch about that quite a while ago. Anyway, Tommy Trenton said one man looked back before leaving. The one driving the 1962 Mustang. Deep down in his gut, Tommy sensed it was Tieman who was there and who had looked back, but he didn't have enough to make it certain. It was the car that stuck with Tommy. Tieman has a 1962 Mustang convertible and several other classic cars. Apparently he found out that Todd's parents and brother had been killed and felt sorry for him. It seems incomprehensible that a guy who helped burn a hundred people could feel compassion for the one survivor who survived only because he had a bout with the flu at the right time.

"I suppose that if Todd had burned up with the rest of them we would never have solved this one. Todd kept picking at this case like a sore on the palm of his hand. He was the one that made it possible for the Preacher to stay in the area. Without his occasional acts of charity toward the Preacher, he might have left years ago. The Preacher told him as much the other day.

"Todd kept picking at the Merriman suicide, too. That's what eventually broke the money laundering case against Tieman and gave us his testimony. That green ledger book Merriman kept was the key. It helped Todd Evans put everything together, once he had all the pieces."

"So Merriman's death was a suicide?"

"What makes you think it wasn't?"

"Just that Evans kept digging into it and the fact that two of the six that burned the church are dead. Coincidence?"

Nodding adamantly, Lamont affirmed. "Yes, Evans and I discussed that and we did some checking on those deaths. It's all on the up and up. The other was killed in an automobile accident over in Missouri. I talked to the Missouri state patrol myself. At first it looked like there might have been some tampering with his brakes, but it turned out to be a manufacturer's defect. His name was Gene Petrowski and he was the Deputy Circuit Clerk for Meridian County. This case had some real reach to it.

"Funny, at first we suspected Petrowski was killed because he was on to something at the circuit clerk's office regarding the bond scheme your client alluded to, but he wasn't. Old man Trenton was sure he was murdered because of his involvement in the fire. He thought Tieman was trying to eliminate all those involved. That's part of the reason he finally talked to Evans. He was starting to worry that Tieman would send someone to kill him.

"Ironically, Petrowski wasn't murdered by anyone, he was just the victim of a manufacturer's defect and poor traffic control. He was on to something though. Mark Fribley discovered it by accident, just like the bonus scheme at TTM. He sorted it out for us and just yesterday the telephone company isolated the mystery phone line.

"As it turned out, another TTM employee had hooked up an extra computer unit to the circuit clerk's main frame when he was installing the system and was using that unauthorized terminal to alter records. A lot of people had egg on their faces when we found that out. The judges and clerks had gotten in to the habit of believing the computer over the paperwork. Something they should never have done, and I don't think they will again."

Charlie now said, "TTM really took a hit these last few days."

"More than that. It took just six hours of 'stake out' on a little apartment uptown to get the real culprit behind the bond scam. Asher Adams, manager of the Meridian County Credit Bureau thought it up to finance his campaign to defeat the incumbent circuit clerk. Now isn't that novel? Until Fribley picked up on it, Adams had a foolproof scheme. He not only had a way to fund his campaign, but at the same time he was making the current circuit clerk look like an incompetent fool."

"And what of Merriman?" Charlie asked.

"Suicide, plain and simple. Just like Evans first reported."

"That's not what I meant. Suicide is never plain and simple," Charlie observed. "Why?"

"I guess he knew about too many of Tieman's little dirty secrets and he just couldn't live with that knowledge any longer."

"Live with what? You said Merriman had nothing to do with the church burning."

"Not directly, but he was Tieman's bag man and he figured out why the money was being paid to Todd's uncle. Merriman had the ability to clear the case, but he kept his mouth shut. After too many years of living with what he knew, and with what Tieman had done, he gave it up. He couldn't turn Tieman in. Tieman had too much on him about the bonus plan. Plus, Tieman had always treated Merriman very well; there were some loyalty issues there, too. In the end though, Merriman couldn't handle it anymore. People get rid of their guilt in lots of different ways. Some go to church, some blame others and some take their own lives. Merriman took the latter course.

"It all fits. It always did, but Evans didn't have all the pieces until the Preacher broke the church fire case. Once he had all the pieces, it didn't take him long to put the puzzle together. Good man, that Evans. The talk is that he's going to be made chief deputy. I've already called the sheriff and put in my vote of confidence."

Chuckling without real humor, Lamont observed, "Imagine old Tieman's thoughts when he realized that the little black kid he sent to college was the one who brought him down? Ironic isn't it? I mean, how men work against themselves without ever knowing it. What luck."

Charlie shrugged and said, "You call it what you want, Lamont. I call it justice, it has a way of prevailing. Justice isn't always what I think it should be, nor even what I'd call fair, but it's justice just the same."

Paul thought about that for a while and finally conceded, "Okay, sure. I see what you mean. I've not seen a lot of what I would consider real justice. Something close sometimes, but not too often. This one came pretty close."

Charlie responded, "And speaking of justice, Paul. How about a little for the Preacher? He's done you a good turn in this community. Not only helping to solve the church burning, but he put you on to the circuit clerk scheme. I think he deserves better than the state pen or even the county slam. All he ever wanted to do was spread the Word of God. Where's the crime in that? Just because he chose to do it on a street corner at a time when the mayor was trying to make it look like he was keeping campaign promises. How many people who voted for that mayor, or you for that matter, would agree with slamming the Preacher?"

Paul nodded in agreement and said, "Point well taken. I'm up for election soon and I don't need that kind of publicity. I know a little about you, Charlie Chambers, and I know that if I push this case, you are going to make a federal case out of it, no pun intended. Federal cases bring media attention and I don't need that kind of media attention. Besides, you're right about the Preacher, he isn't hurting anyone and he has done this community a good turn. A lot of old wounds have been reopened by his revelations, but I think that's good. Those old wounds were festering and needed some air to heal. But, will you talk to him about staying off the streets? For a while anyway?"

Shaking his head in the negative, Charlie responded, "Wouldn't do me any good. He's dead set on preaching in the streets. He says it's his calling and I can't disagree with him. Unless he gets a call to do something else, which isn't likely, he will stay out on those streets. I do have him inside the homeless shelter for the most part now, but I'm not sure that will last."

Paul said in surrender, "Okay. No matter. I'll dismiss all the charges in the morning. I'll catch it from Ferrell, but it won't be the first time. He knows as well as I do that he can't stop me from dismissing cases I don't want to prosecute, and if he tries, I'll just lose track of them," Paul ended with a chuckle.

"I think Ferrell is more bark than bite," Charlie said.

Paul laughed at that and said, "For a guy who spent the night in jail at Ferrell's hand you are awfully charitable."

Charlie shrugged and continued, "It's just that I size him up as a pretty square shooter. Tough, but fair. In my experience that's a pretty good combination in a judge." Rising now, Charlie said just before he turned for the door, "Just for the record, I wanted Ferrell to put me in jail."

"Why?"

"Like I told Barclay, so that he would think about my case before he pulled the trigger. The fact that he didn't rule when he was mad at me proves my point. Tough, but fair. Of course my opinion of him might change when he does finally rule on my case. The fact that he hasn't yet is a good sign. I got him to thinking."

Shaking his head in dismay as he rose from his chair, Paul said, "I'm dismissing the charges against the Preacher today, forget tomorrow. I want no part of an opponent who would purposely get himself slammed just to further his client's cause."

"So long, Paul Lamont," Charlie said, as he reached the door.

Paul stuck his hand out and said, "Stay out of trouble, Charlie Chambers, but in case you don't, let me know if I can help."

"You bet."

~ * ~

Jeannie Rosmund was flabbergasted at the news of her opponent, Asher Adams, having been the head of the scheme to bilk the county out of all that money. She was also pleased to think that she didn't have a contested election campaign to run. The other party wasn't likely to try and mount a serious write-in candidate, so she could pretty well coast this election. Still, she would have to make her appearances. The ballots were already printed and her opponent's name would still appear on the ballot. She still needed to get a majority just to make it a clean win, but it would be easy with no one campaigning against her. Plus, clearing up this computer mess would make her look even better, even though she didn't do it, her office looked better.

That made her turn her thoughts back to who she was going to get to replace Gene. She thought she knew now. Tess had shown herself to be heads above the others during the investigation by the attorney general and the comptroller. With a little broadening of her knowledge base, she could easily be the second in command in the clerk's office. With that decided, Jeannie called Tess into her office.

"Tess, I need a chief deputy clerk to replace Gene Petrowski and I think you could do it."

Tess was thunderstruck, but finally stammered out a response, "Me. You sure? I mean... I know the bookkeeping, but not the other things. Not like you do."

"Like I do?"

"Yes, ma'am. Among the employees, the word's out on you. There's nothing you can't figure out on the computers and you have a natural ability to organize the office. Everyone agrees. I couldn't do that."

Jeannie was shocked. That was not the word from the employees that she had expected, but she had to admit Tess was right. She had been running this office since Gene had died. It just never occurred to her before that she was doing it. She was just going day by day, hour by hour, handling one crisis after another and focusing all her energy on finding a replacement for Gene. Now that she thought about it, she guessed that was what running an office was all about.

"Okay, Tess, but I need a chief deputy just the same. I'll show you what you need to know. If necessary, we'll work after hours, okay?"

"Yes, ma'am, but not too late. I think I might have a date once in a while," Tess said with a blush.

"Not that auditor?"

"Yes, ma'am," Tess said with her blush deepening.

Jeannie smiled and said, "Good for you, Tess. And please call me Jeannie."

~ * ~

Everything had fallen into place for Charlie, more had been accomplished in Georgia than he had ever imagined. He had come to argue for a man's right to display a lighted cross and wound up uncovering the key to a thirty-five year old murder. He had also found his second love and it was high time he declared himself. After all, he would be leaving for Illinois very soon now and one thing remained yet to be done.

As Charlie approached the gate at Carol's, there was no one at the guard shack and the gates were standing wide open. He saw two police cars and an ambulance up by the house. His heart stopped and he had a sinking feeling in his stomach. *Carol!* He warned her about Dan Chase, and if Dan Chase had done anything to injure her, Charlie wouldn't rest until he saw justice done. And he would never forgive himself for letting it happen again to someone he loved.

Charlie jammed his foot on to the accelerator and shot up the drive to the main house. The car screeched to a stop just as the ambulance and two police cars pulled away and went around the circle toward the gate. Charlie bailed out of his car and ran up the steps to the front door. He knocked furiously, but no one came. Beside himself with fear, he twisted the knob and rushed inside, running directly into Carol. She looked okay, a little shaken, but okay.

"Carol!" Charlie exclaimed and took her into his arms. "You okay? I was so scared when I saw those police cars and that ambulance. I was sure Chase had gone off the deep end. What happened? Did he try to hurt you?"

Hugging him fiercely, Carol explained, "I'm fine. It wasn't about me, I'm okay, honest."

Letting her go, Charlie held her away from him by her arms and asked, "You don't look okay, you look shook up to me. Are you sure you're okay? I'd not be able to go on if something had happened to you, I couldn't bear losing another woman I loved."

Carol caught that last word and that was the only one she was interested in hearing. Then she responded, "I love you, too, Charles."

They looked deeply into each other's eyes and spontaneously moved toward each other. Their lips met with more passion than either knew existed. Breaking the kiss, they held each other firmly for several minutes and finally, Carol said, "Come in and I'll tell you all about it."

Once inside, she beckoned Charlie to sit beside her on the couch, an offer he was pleased to accept. He wrapped his right arm around her, pulling her close. Carol rested her head on his chest and began, "The police came to arrest Dan, they said they had a warrant issued by Judge Ferrell, the charge was murder and conspiracy to commit murder. Apparently he was one of the men who burned the church on Burning Chapel Hill. He tried to run, pulled a gun out and the police shot him. I think he'll live, but they say he was shot at least twice. I knew he had a mean streak, but I never dreamed it ran so deep. You warned me, but I didn't listen. He was dangerous and I'm lucky he was arrested before I pushed him too far. There's no telling what he might have done. It makes me shudder to think of it," she ended and nestled deeper against Charlie.

Charlie now said, "Herman Trenton said he had two names and I never thought to find out who the other one was after Walter Tieman."

"Herman Trenton? Tieman? What's it all about, Charles?"

"Tommy Trenton, he's the Preacher, turns out he witnessed his father Herman help burn that church thirty-five years ago, kept it bottled up inside of him for all those years. I was representing him and as it turned out, I was able to convince him to tell all. I didn't realize what all he had to tell though. Another of the men who was with his father was Walter Tieman, III."

Carol raised her head up off of Charlie's chest and asked in disbelief, "No, that Walter Tieman? TTM?"

"The same. Apparently the other name Herman had was Dan Chase. Now, if Lamont is any good, he'll use Tieman against Chase and vice versa. By the end of the day he'll have one or both of them locked tight, probably Chase, because he already has Tieman on other charges. And I'll bet he gets Tieman to turn Chase, in exchange for a reduction, albeit a small reduction, in sentence."

Seemingly, out of the blue, Carol asked, "Charles, what is moral turpitude?"

"Huh, oh, that's a fancy phrase for good morals, why?"

"Well, I was reading the management contract I have with Dan last night, for other reasons, and I came across a paragraph that said the contract would be terminated, in my favor, if Dan were convicted of a crime against moral turpitude, and I didn't understand what it meant. Is murder against moral turpitude?"

"You bet; it's number one. That means, if Dan is convicted, and he almost assuredly will be, then you are off the hook, you can get a new manager."

"How about you?"

"Me, what?"

"How about you being my manager?"

"No, honey, I'm no entertainment manager. You get yourself a real one. I'll look over the contract before you sign, but I'll bet a thousand good managers will be lining up at your doorstep as soon as the word it out."

"But, if you did it, you could be with me all the time. We wouldn't have to be separated."

"I've been thinking about that. You know, it just so happens that a young man by the name of Mark Fribley, who works up at TTM and who helped Tommy and a lot of others lately, has a brother who is a starving civil rights lawyer in Illinois. I got in touch with him through Mark and offered him a position with my Fund. In fact, he is going to be doing the lion's share of the work. All I'm going to do is point him in the right direction occasionally. That means I'll be free to be a certain country singer's number one fan, and I intend to follow that certain singer, whom I love very much, everywhere she goes until she gets tired of seeing me."

After giving Charlie a deep kiss, Carol said, "Just so long as I'm that country singer, its fine with me. I'm not going to get tired of you, so you might as well get set for the long haul."

"Does that mean you'll marry me, then?"

"Does it! Yes! Yes! Yes!" Carol exclaimed and hugged Charlie around the neck so tight he thought the blood circulation to his brain was going to be cut off, and he didn't even mind it.

"Okay, but I'm warning you, I do not want any of your money and I do not want anyone thinking I am marrying you for your money. So the first thing we do is go see a lawyer and have him, or her, draw up a prenuptial agreement."

"That isn't necessary, Charles, I have plenty of money for the both of us, forever."

"Sorry, I insist," he said with firmness, and Carol saw no reason to argue. It didn't matter to her, all she wanted was him.

"I'm leaving tomorrow for Illinois, " Charlie said. When Carol started to protest, he added, "I have to, there are some things to clean up. I have to get Frank Fribley settled in and I have to arrange a few things so that I can follow you around the country. I intend to be in Nashville when you cut that record, and everywhere else from then on, with rare exceptions. I ignored the last woman I loved, but I won't make that mistake again. I won't ignore you."

"I'll make you live up to that promise," Carol said impishly.

"Good and so we go see Steve Barclay in the morning, first thing. He'll fix up that prenuptial agreement and then as soon as you find the time, and the arrangements are made, we can be married."

"Ummm, I like," Carol purred from her position against his chest.

~ * ~

Steve Barclay had just finished explaining the procedure for preparation of a prenuptial agreement to Carol. Charlie already knew. "Oh, Charlie, I just remembered, John Bullock called this morning and left a message. He said that ARDC thing was off; the complainant was Dan Chase and the case kind of fell through after he was arrested. Then Steve turned to Carol and said, "Okay, Miss Harmon."

"Please call me Carol."

"Oh, okay, Carol, now I'll need a complete list of all your assets so that we can make full disclosure to Charlie, that's part of the deal. Also, Charlie, I'll need a complete list of your assets."

"I can give you that now, pretty much," Charlie responded.

"Okay, certificates of deposit?" Steve asked.

"None."

"Savings accounts?"

"No, not really."

"Cars?"

"I always rent."

"House?"

"Rent."

"Jewelry?"

"Timex watch," Charlie stated flatly.

"Uh huh, so what do you have to declare to Carol?"

"Well, uh, I do have an investment account. You see, after my wife and daughter were killed, I sued the car manufacturer on behalf of myself and all others. It was a huge class action and it settled out of court. It was a big settlement, one of the biggest in the nation. Each plaintiff, including me, received five point four million dollars, and in addition I received my fees for prosecuting the case. Those fees came to another two point two million dollars. I have not spent a dime of it, either the settlement or the fee. I put it in an investment account and it's been growing steadily. All I do is pay the taxes on the income from it. I've never touched a dime of it. I don't feel right about it. It's like I got paid to ignore my family, to isolate myself from them, it can't give me my family back and so I don't want it in place of my family. That's about it, I don't have anything else."

Steve was struck dumb and so was Carol. Charlie had never let on that he had more than two nickels to rub together at one time, and now it turned out he was a multi-millionaire.

Charlie now put in, "Although lately, I've kind of changed my mind about that money. I think I'm going to start spending some of it on Carol, and being with Carol, following her around and the like. I won't let her support me, so I have to use my own money and it's okay, because now instead of replacing my family it will be helping me to preserve my family and maybe someday I'll have another daughter or son."

Smiling, Carol squeezed his hand and responded, "I'd like that, maybe both."

~ * ~

The airport hadn't changed much and for some reason Charlie had expected it to. It seemed as though it had been years since he had been at this airport, instead of just weeks. Weeks it may have been, he thought, but in those weeks he had traveled over many years, with a lot of people. Years that some said would have been better left in the past, but he knew that was wrong. He had some personal experience with bad years, and they were much better off out in the open than left in the dark recesses of the mind.

He had checked his baggage through to St. Louis, but had yet to clear security.

The little knot of people stood just outside the security screening area. Charlie, with his arm firmly around Carol's waist stood facing the semi-circle they made as he waited for his flight to be called.

"Patty, you take care of this clown, you hear?" Charlie said lightly. "Keep him off the streets. I can't be flying down here every time the mayor decides to go on a crime-fighting rampage. I've got a country singer to keep track of now."

Smiling broadly and encircling Tommy's arm with hers, she responded, "No problem. He's moving in with me. I'll be able to keep a close watch on him from now on. We've been on our own too long. It's time we had each other to take care of the small things life throws at us," she ended lightly.

Tommy spoke up now, "You don't have to worry about me anyway, Mr. Chambers. The people at the shelter put me in touch with the Baptist Bible Foundation. They've arranged for me to get my G.E.D. and then study at the Bible College over in Augusta. In a year, I'll be able to fill in when there's a need in a local church. If I stick with it I'll be a full-fledged preacher in a few years."

Charlie responded excitedly, "That's great, Tommy, just great! But don't forget, you already are a preacher, you always have been. You could be a lot better and you will be. Your unique life experiences will be invaluable in your sermons. Especially in the inner city mission field. You need anything you just let me know. Okay?"

"Yes, sir."

Charlie narrowed his eyes and now asked Tommy, "Have you been to see your father?"

After a moment of silence Tommy admitted, "No."

"You go see him, Tommy. Today. You aren't the preacher I think you are or can be, if you don't. If you can't forgive your own father, then how can you teach others to forgive?"